CAFÉ NEVO

CAFÉ NEVO

BARBARA ROGAN

ATHENEUM

NEW YORK

1987

The quotation on page 10 is from:
   "Maggie's Farm" by Bob Dylan.
© 1965 Warner Bros. Inc.
All rights reserved. Used by permission.

Library of Congress Cataloging-in-Publication Data
Rogan, Barbara.
   Café Nevo.
   I. Title.
PS3568.O377C3   1987   813'.54   86-26608
ISBN 0-689-11840-6

Copyright © 1987 by Barbara Rogan
All rights reserved
Published simultaneously in Canada by Collier Macmillan Canada, Inc.
Composition by Maryland Linotype Composition Company,
Baltimore, Maryland
Manufactured by Fairfield Graphics, Fairfield, Pennsylvania
Designed by Cathryn S. Aison

FIRST EDITION

This book and its author owe much to the generosity of Haim Baer, who suggested the café's name.

DEDICATED WITH LOVE
TO MY PARENTS.

CAFÉ NEVO

Chapter One

EMMANUEL Yehoshua Sternholz, son of Rebecca and Samuel Sternholz, father of Jacob, R.I.P., and grandfather of innumerable unborn Sternholzes, was a waiter. He served in a Dizengoff café called Nevo, and lived alone in a two-room apartment on the top floor of the same building. He was seventy-three years old. Except for an occasional touch of rheumatism and a chronic sleep problem, Emmanuel Yehoshua Sternholz was in the pink of health. This was surprising, considering where he had spent his youth.

Nevo consisted of one cavernous room which opened wide as the yawning mouth of a toothless old man, and spilled its tables out all the way to the curb, checking the flow of pedestrian traffic, as if the aforementioned old man had insolently stuck out his tongue. Inside, ancient, dusty signs, advertising brand-name liquor unavailable upon request, and photographs of former Nevo habitués, all of them distinguished for their utter insignificance—for Sternholz would have considered it unforgivably crass to hang pictures of the café's famous patrons—decorated the walls. A long bar ran along the south side of the room, and the gents' was out back, in the courtyard. There was no facility for ladies, nor did Emmanuel Yehoshua Sternholz encourage ladies to frequent his establishment.

He could not keep them out, of course, although he tried his best. He gave them the royal treatment, which was enough to discourage most from ever returning. What was the royal treatment? First, he cleaned their chairs for them. He kept a special rag for that purpose and for cleaning the stove. Then he never served their drinks without inspecting their glasses minutely, in their presence. If he saw even the slightest speck, and that was inevitable, with his half-blind busboy, he pulled out his handkerchief, spat genteelly into it, and wiped the vessel clean. Emmanuel Yehoshua Sternholz was a clean man, and his spit as pure as anyone's, but how were they to know that? If despite the royal treatment some ladies persisted in coming, Sternholz eventually grew reconciled and even, after many years, greeted them civilly.

For he was not a misogynist. Far from it; Sternholz was a man who had loved, loved deeply and more than once. Age had not lessened his appreciation of feminine beauty, though it had eroded his susceptibility to it. No, if Emmanuel Yehoshua Sternholz deplored the patronage of women, he was not moved by personal bias. He simply felt he had enough *tsuris* without them. He was cursed with an obstreperous, argumentative lot of customers, and it was all he could do to keep a reasonable semblance of peace in the café, without adding sexual fire to gunpowder. If asked, or even unasked, Sternholz would assert that mixed café sitting was the root of half the divorces in Israel, and that was true whether a man sat with his mistress or his wife. If the former, it was possible, even likely, that his wife would hear of it and make both of them unhappy; if the latter, his friends would give him no peace.

How many times had Sternholz heard it? "Poor Yoram, his wife has him on a leash."

Look at Peter Caspi, sitting there with his arm around that little starlet half his age. He always had to show off, absolutely nothing subtle in the choices, either; and what did he expect Vered to do about it, just sit and wait till the cows come home? The worst of it was that now *she'd* shown up too, hovering some tables behind her husband like a cross between a good Oriental wife and the avenging Shadow. It would not do. Emmanuel Yehoshua Sternholz, never a man to shirk his duty, went right up to her and said: "Vered, it won't do."

"Hello, Sternholz. I'd like a brandy and soda, please."

Sternholz sat at the table and showed her his palms. "What's the point?" he said. "What's the matter, you don't have enough trouble, you have to go out and look for it?"

She'd been an awkward girl but had grown into her looks. She had a graceful carriage which was thrown away on Caspi, an air of sadness that was all, or almost all, his doing, huge dark eyes, and a frozen mouth. "I don't know what you mean," she lied. "I used to come here a lot."

"Then was then," the waiter said meaningfully. "Now is now."

"What's your problem, Sternholz?"

"My problem is that you are setting a very bad precedent. Look at it from my point of view. What would be if Nevo was overrun by feuding husbands and wives, sitting at separate tables?"

"You'd double your business."

"I'd triple it. Everyone would come to see the show. But that kind of business I need like a hole in the head."

"So throw Caspi out."

"Caspi lives here," Sternholz said. "He's got nowhere else to go. You do. Listen to an old friend. Go home."

"No."

Sternholz compressed his lips. "Look here, Verdele," he said, "you made your bed; right under my nose you made it. So what am I running here, a laundry?"

"A brothel?" she suggested, looking at her husband.

"Vered, you are making my nerves ache."

"Pretend you don't know us," she said.

"I don't know you?" He gave her a dark and wondering look. "Who do I know if I don't know you?" He walked away, shaking his head and muttering, "Pretend I don't know you!"

She watched him go. Mad Muny was up to some nonsense, standing on a chair and haranguing someone. Vered walked unnoticed to the back of the bar, where she poured herself a brandy.

"Dotan! Dotan, you miserable bastard, I'm going to break your neck!"

"Not here, Muny," Sternholz said, touching his arm.

"Get your hands off me! Murder's too good for that bastard. I'd castrate him if he had any balls."

"Get off the table, Muny."

"He's got a nerve, showing his face here. Dotan, get your raggedy ass over here; I want to kick it for you." Rami Dotan waved genially from Caspi's table. "Sternholz, hold my coat!" Muny roared.

"You haven't got a coat, you maniac."

Muny jumped off the table and ran zigzagging through the café. Though he was only five feet two, with a belly like an overinflated beach ball and floppy bum's shoes, he was fast. Sternholz couldn't catch him, and no one else wanted to. Muny leapt onto the table beside Caspi's and dived headlong at Rami Dotan.

The force of the kamikaze attack knocked Rami off his chair and onto his back. Muny landed on top of him. Glass cascaded around them, shattering on contact with the pavement. Scrambling to his knees, Muny raised a shard aloft. "Death to the Philistines!"

Caspi reached over leisurely and relieved him of the shard. "Good show, Muny. Now go sit down, there's a nice boy."

Muny levered himself up, using Rami's head as a fulcrum. "You don't understand, Caspi. You don't know what he did."

"Enlighten me."

"Three fucking months he held on to my manuscript, which happens to be the best work I've ever done. Then he sends it back with a form letter, a goddamn *form* letter! 'Thanks for thinking of us, turkey, but we don't publish shit.' And this after he cheats me out of a million shekels in royalties on the last one."

Caspi clicked his tongue. "Did you do that, Rami?"

Rami stood and brushed glass off his designer jeans. He picked up his pipe and said, "It's broken. Damn you, Muny."

Muny danced on his toes, shadowboxing. "That's nothing. You wait for it, Dotan. Wait for it. One dark night. You wait, and you wonder. Muny never forgets."

Caspi laughed. "The pygmy elephant struts his stuff."

"Shut up, Macho Man. You're riding high now, but I hear things aren't so great in the Caspi eyrie. Look at wifey over there. If that woman isn't starving for it, I've never seen one who was. What's the matter, Caspi? Not enough left to spread it around?"

"Back off," he growled.

Muny tittered. "All worn out, Caspi? Feeling your age? Drying up at the source?" This last was a sly reference to Caspi's literary output, which had been sparse for several years.

Caspi lumbered to his feet. He was a big man, grown

broader in recent years, and he loomed over Muny. The little man looked about nervously for someone to stop the fight. Sternholz stepped out of a sea of avid faces.

"All right," he said sourly, "you've had your fun."

"I exonerate you on grounds of drunkenness," Caspi said softly. "Who can blame you? If I wrote like you, I'd drink, too. But there's no excuse for smelling as foul as you do. Go away, Muny."

A buzz of disappointment rose in the café as Muny turned docilely and returned to his place. Rami examined his pipe. "It's broken," he said again, sadly.

"My God, are you all right?" Caspi's little actress bleated.

Dotan ignored her. "The funny thing is, his manuscript wasn't that bad."

"You're joking," Caspi said. "Muny doesn't write poetry, he excretes it."

"I tell you it was not bad. And we did all right with the last one, too. Not," he added hastily, "that he earned out the ridiculous advance he squeezed out of us."

"Then why not do the new one?"

Rami shuddered piteously. "Never again. God strike me if I ever publish that maniac again. He was in the office *every* day, pestering people, badgering me. He had to supervise everything. Cover, type; he insisted on hardcover and we gave him hardcover. Wanted a picture of himself on the back cover and we did that, too."

"Probably cost you half your sales."

"I don't know, I heard some people bought the book just to throw darts at it."

Caspi's laugh boomed again. Vered glanced at him and away.

"He wanted us to print five thousand. Can you believe it? Five thousand! We finally compromised on two. Then he demands a publication party. Against my better judgment I agreed."

"Was it a good party?" the actress asked wistfully. She was a lover of parties, and regretted every one she missed.

"Terrific, till he showed up. Then he punched out the *Yediot* literary editor and dumped the punch bowl over the Minister of Culture's head." Over their laughter Dotan added gloomily, "He said it was in protest of the cut in theater subsidies."

A voice at his elbow said, "Then why did it take you three months to return his manuscript?" It was Sternholz, kneeling to sweep up the broken glass.

Dotan did not (as one might have expected) reply, "None of your business." He said defensively, "It takes some time till these things reach me."

Sternholz sniffed and moved away.

A hand reached out and caught at his apron, and a slurred voice said, "Get me another."

Sternholz clucked his tongue. "You've had enough, Arik."

"More arak for Arik," the young man chanted. "I'm celebrating. Have one on me."

"What are you celebrating?"

"Freedom! Today I am a free man. No more worries, no more responsibilities—no more job."

"*Oy*," Sternholz sighed. "You quit again."

"Not this time. The bastards fired me."

The waiter went and made two cups of strong coffee, and carried them to the table. "So what now? Back to the kibbutz?"

"Who asked for coffee? I want arak."

"You take what I give you and be grateful for it, boy. Why were you fired?"

"Budget cuts. Last in, first out, they said. But it was political." Arik Eshel was a strapping young man of twenty-nine with the lean, wide-shouldered body that seemed to grow only on kibbutzniks. He had a headful of brown curls, blue eyes, and a cleft chin. Sternholz often saw him promenading on Dizengoff with some woman or another on his arm, but when he came to Nevo he had the respect to come alone.

"Too bad," the old man said. "So now you'll go back to Ein Hashofet. Your father will be glad to have you back."

"No, no, no," Arik said, wagging his finger, and he began to sing, " 'I ain't gonna work on Maggie's farm no more.' "

One thing about kibbutzniks, Sternholz thought: they never could hold their liquor. He left Arik singing to himself, and went back inside.

It was Friday afternoon, and the pavements on Dizengoff were packed with strollers checking out the action in the cafés. Though summer had barely begun, there was enough bare flesh on display to blind a man with worse eyesight than Sternholz. Skirts were high this year, bare midriffs fashionable, and décolleté only reasonable for the climate; and wasn't it a shame, the waiter thought, that men grew old and lost their strength?

Across the street the Sabra was bursting at the seams. With its shocking pink walls and mirrored ceiling, white wrought-iron tables and chairs, and fringed umbrellas, the Sabra looked like a tart's bedroom. It attracted tourists and the young suburban dating crowd, types who could sit all night in Sternholz's sanctum without seeing so much as a glass of water. The Rowal, next door, was also overflowing. The Rowal was the oldest café on Dizengoff, besides Nevo. Modeled after Viennese pastry parlors, the Rowal was no longer the best cake place in town, but it was still the *Yekke* Mecca of Dizengoff. Sternholz called it the chicken coop because it was only women and old men who sat there, gabble gobble all the day.

Only Nevo, of all the Dizengoff cafés, still had empty tables on Friday afternoon. Its front flank was guarded by the overcoat brigade, a row of burnt-out, bleary-eyed, wasted individuals who nodded over chessboards, shivering even in the summer heat. These were the pioneers of yesteryear who fell by the wayside, their stinking but unburied wreckage the hidden cost of the great adventure. To enter Nevo one had to pass through their sad malice; no wonder most people preferred the brighter façades.

Nevo was the oldest and certainly the grungiest of the Dizengoff cafés; in fact it predated the street over which it seedily presided. When Dizengoff was being built, and Tel Aviv was nothing but a miniature white-stoned oasis of a city on the desolate shore north of Jaffa, two enterprising Polish brothers set up a workers' kitchen beside the construction site, to serve the laborers beer, seltzer, and Turkish coffee. The construction ended but the canteen remained, upgraded by the addition of an awning and a hand-painted sign that proclaimed in large red Hebrew letters, CAFÉ NEVO. Though retaining its worker clientele, the café soon began to attract another set, the writers, actors, and artists who by virtue of their socialist ideology styled themselves members of the proletariat, but who in fact constituted the Tel Aviv elite of their day.

The workers had to work, but the artists had nothing better to do than to hang around all day, gossiping, flirting, and arguing. When the brothers realized that not even by starving these customers could they encourage them to turn over faster, they began, grudgingly, to serve food. It wasn't long before they felt the need of additional help. They hired Emmanuel Yehoshua Sternholz, a greenhorn fresh off the boat, for twelve pounds a month.

Years passed, and decades, each with its own war. Nevo weathered them all. The Polish brothers grew rich, but one died childless, the other lost his only son in the war of '56. Emmanuel Yehoshua Sternholz reigned alone, the sole keeper of Nevo. Other cafés sprung up: cafés to the right of them, cafés to the left of them, cafés all around them, strung together by the colorful beads of boutiques, shoe salons, and jewelry stores. Dizengoff grew richer and gaudier and more expensive, but Nevo endured, huddled in on itself, stubbornly filling and defiling the classiest section of Dizengoff pavement with its ragtag collection of gun-metal gray foldaways, its shabby decor and even shabbier clientele.

Not all who penetrated Nevo's front flank attained service, for Emmanuel Yehoshua Sternholz was a jealous and exacting waiter. Traditions had to be upheld, standards maintained. Tourists and gawkers lowered the tone and disturbed the regulars, whose sanctuary Sternholz was sworn to defend. Such callers were ignored until they slunk out ignominiously or, if that failed, were summarily ejected. Nor could a customer on whom Sternholz deigned to wait be secure of getting what he asked for, for the waiter reserved the right to edit all orders. He gave his customers what they needed, not what they wanted.

So it was that when Ilana swirled into the café, parting the ranks of the old men with her scent, Sternholz did not wait for her to order but hurried over with a double shot of his best whiskey (which was not very good).

She accepted it with a smile and said, "How are you, Emmanuel?"

"Don't ask. Muny was acting up again."

"He looks quiet enough now."

"You don't look so great." In fact she looked beautiful, as always; only Sternholz could have seen the weariness in her walk.

"I'm okay," she said without conviction.

Sternholz gave her a sympathetic look. He would have stayed to talk some more, but the animals were clamoring.

Left alone, Ilana looked around the café and caught Vered's eye. The two women nodded and smiled, but did not speak.

A shiny black Mercedes pulled up to the curb, honking, and Pincas Gordon stepped out. Sternholz grimaced. The fat man threaded his way through the café, slapping backs and pounding shoulders on the way, like a politician on the make. In an elegant beige linen suit, with a silk tie thrust casually in a pocket and a white shirt open at the throat, he stuck out like a sore thumb. Both his gold watch and cuff links bore his initials writ large. You'd think (thought Sternholz) that he'd be more discreet about his wealth, considering where it came from.

Pincas paused at Vered's table with a loud snort of delight. "Vered Caspi, darling! One never sees you about these days. What a marvelous surprise." He seized her hand and kissed it. "All alone? May I join you?"

Vered dabbed at the afflicted hand with a napkin. "Yes, I am, and no, you may not."

"My dear," he said reproachfully, "is that any way to treat an old friend?"

She looked at him through dark glasses. "I know what you've been up to," she said. "You disgust me."

"Business is business," Pincas said. "I would never allow *that* to come between friends."

"I would." Vered went back to her newspaper.

Pincas wandered over to a table by the bar and sat down. "Well, well, well," he said, looking at his nearest neighbor, and was about to address her more directly when Sternholz hustled up.

"What do you want?"

"Always the gracious host," Pincas said for the girl to hear.

"You have a complaint, take it up with management. I'm busy. What do you want?"

Pincas ordered a brandy, then, smiling broadly, bent his pudgy face toward the girl at the next table. But Sternholz was back between them before he could make his move. "Don't bother her," the waiter said into his ear.

"Sternholz," the fat man began angrily, but Sternholz held up a peremptory hand.

"Bother her and I'll kick you out of here."

Pincas, who saw nothing comical in this threat from a seventy-three-year-old man, straightened and said, "I'm not in the habit of bothering anyone, you old fool, much less schoolgirls. Why don't you fetch my brandy and keep your nose out of my business?"

"I wouldn't put my nose within ten miles of your stinking business."

The girl at the next table gave no sign of having heard this exchange. She was a splash of sunshine in the gloomy tavern interior. Her hair, the rich auburn of loamy earth, fell in waves down to her shoulders; her green eyes were framed by high taut cheekbones and winged eyebrows. She wore no discernible make-up, save a touch of lipstick that emphasized a luscious lower lip. Every time he looked at her, Sternholz wanted to weep. She was as beautiful as her mother, and Yael Blume had been unquestionably the most beautiful woman he had ever known.

The girl held a sketch pad on her lap and stabbed at it furtively with a soft lead pencil. She sat with her back to the bar, a half-empty cup of coffee on the table before her. With the waiter's jealous eye on her, no one had dared approach her, but that didn't stop them from staring or asking each other, "Who's the new talent?" If she felt the attention, it didn't seem to bother her, or perhaps she was so absorbed by the faces emerging on her pad that she had no notice to spare for their prototypes. Her name was Sarita Blume.

"Welcome to Nevo, the bowels of Tel Aviv. This is our refuge, the bathroom of our souls. Rami Dotan, Khalil Mussara." Caspi did not introduce Dory.

"It's a pleasure. I've admired your work." Rami held out his hand. His English was respectable, his accent execrable.

Khalil touched the proffered hand. He stood, forcing the others to remain on their feet. "You read it in Arabic?" he asked.

"In English. The Oxford edition."

"A poor translation."

"Unfortunately I don't read Arabic."

"Sit down already," said Caspi. "What'll you have? Sternholz!"

The waiter approached.

"Coffee," said Khalil. "Black. Strong."

Caspi added, "Coffee all around."

Sternholz nodded dourly and retired, not before taking a long, hard look at the Arab. Khalil Mussara was a tall, lean man, classically handsome, in his mid-thirties. He wore dark glasses and spoke English with an Oxford accent. When the waiter had gone, there was an awkward silence; then Rami Dotan said: "Caspi has explained the project to you, of course. I only want to add that we at Dotan and Weiner regard this joint Israeli-Palestinian anthology as one of the most important projects we have ever undertaken, and we are prepared to treat it accordingly. It goes without saying that your participation, and that of my good friend Caspi, are essential to the book."

"Indeed," said Caspi sonorously, hand on heart, "if by doing this book we can contribute an iota of understanding, if we can open one single mind to the light of tolerance and mutual respect, then we will all die happy men." He laughed and punched Rami in the shoulder. "Relax, Rami. Khalil is as sold on the project as we are, aren't you, mate?"

Rami's smile faded. Caspi loved to mock him publicly, and he was the last man to stand for it. But Rami, being a publisher, also loved money. Any author who sold 40,000 in hardcover was entitled to his little idiosyncrasies.

"It depends," the Palestinian said. Rami looked at him anxiously. Caspi's smile froze in place.

"Depends on what?" they said together.

"On the contents, on the format, on the question of editorial control."

"What's he talking about?" asked Dory. "Are you doing a book with him?"

"Hush up, little pumpkin," Caspi said, without removing his eyes from Khalil's face.

"The contents," Rami repeated, spreading his hands. "But that is entirely up to the two of you. No politics, of course."

The Palestinian rose abruptly. "Then it is a farce. Goodbye, gentlemen."

Caspi caught his arm. "Just a minute, fellow. Not so fast. Things can be worked out." Though the words could possibly be construed as conciliatory, the tone was most definitely not, being arrogant and harsh. He pointed imperiously to Khalil's chair. The Arab gave him a chilling look, but he sat obediently. "That's better," Caspi said, smiling. He turned to the publisher. "Rami, my friend, you're full of shit."

"I am not. What I meant is that you both will have total freedom within the parameters of the book's definition, which is modern Israeli and Palestinian literature. I'd say those are broad enough areas to give you plenty of scope, without getting political."

Caspi laughed. "Really, man, what would you have us write about, the birds and the bees?"

"That's all you ever write about anyway," heckled Muny from a corner.

Khalil ignored him. Condescendingly, he told Rami Dotan that apolitical Palestinian writing was a contradiction in terms. "In a country where it is a crime to call oneself a Palestinian, to teach our history and display our flag, no writer worthy of the name Palestinian could ignore his people's plight. Any writer whose work does not grapple with our oppression is merely indulging in fantasy. If your intention is to compile a collection of Palestinian fantasies, you have come to the wrong man; and I do not think you will easily find the right one."

Rami whispered in Hebrew to Caspi: "We can do it without him."

"You fool," snapped Caspi, "do you think he doesn't understand Hebrew? If you do it without him, you do it without me."

Rami flushed. Caspi's little pumpkin tossed her head and said, "I know what you can have in it."

All three men turned to her.

"Jokes," she said proudly.

"Jokes?" they said together.

"Sure, jokes. What are you laughing for? I read that in America joke books sell better than anything. And how can any two people get to know each other better than by finding out what makes each other laugh?"

Khalil said stiffly, "*We* find little to laugh at these days."

"Oh, come on," the girl said. "I don't believe you don't have jokes. The Jews were a persecuted minority for thousands of years and it never stopped them laughing."

"Have another cream puff, darling," said Caspi.

Meanwhile Muny, in response to the daily tides that governed his humors, was once again growing rowdy. He peered around the café and focused on Pincas Gordon. "Well," he cried, "if it isn't the old pirate himself, the king of the carpetbaggers, Pincas Lion-of-Judea Gordon in the plentiful flesh."

Pincas, half rising, bowed.

"Dispossessed any widows lately? Bulldozed any orchards? Pulverized any orphanages?"

"We had a good week," Pincas replied, patting his ample stomach. It was never safe to bait Muny. Roaring incoherently, the drunken poet launched himself in Pincas's direction. But Sternholz somehow got in the way. Pinching Muny's arm with amazingly strong fingers, he said, "Once a day is enough. Sit down, or get out." Muny subsided.

Caspi had not failed to notice Pincas Gordon's overtures toward his wife, but what galled him even more was the new Mercedes parked at the curb. "Nice car, Gordon!" he called over.

"Brand-new," Pincas boasted. "Right off the boat. Cost me a mint, I can tell you."

"Good color, too. Fascist black."

"What would you have ordered, Caspi? Pink?"

"I hope you're not implying that I'm gay?" Caspi said in a falsetto. Dory giggled loyally.

"Far be it from me to impugn your cocksmanship. I was referring to your politics."

"You shared them once, or so you pretended."

"But I grew up, Peter Pan."

"You grew out."

"Pretty feeble, Caspi. Is something cramping your style? Someone, maybe?" He waggled a chin in Vered's direction.

"You are," Caspi growled, all the humor suddenly drained out of him. "You've been haunting this place long enough, dead man." The malice in his voice killed all other conversations.

Pincas Gordon's voice quavered indignantly. "I judge my friends by who they are, not what they do, and I expect to be judged in the same way."

Behind the bar, Sternholz snorted.

"You don't have any friends," Caspi stated.

"No friends? I'll show you who has no friends! Waiter! Drinks for the house, on me."

"Pathetic," Caspi commented, and turning away, he resumed his conversation with Khalil. Sternholz prepared drinks for everyone, so he could hit Pincas for the bill, but as he expected, all his customers turned them down. All except one. Sitting so far back in the shadows that he had been overlooked by all save Sternholz and the blindly observant Sarita sat a well-dressed man in his late fifties, early sixties.

Pincas Gordon peered through the gloom to see who had accepted his drink. Then, recognizing the figure, he jumped up and hurried over.

"Minister Brenner, I didn't see you. I wouldn't have thought you'd sit here."

"I've been coming to Nevo," replied the Minister, who wore a knitted yarmulke on his bald pate, "since you were in diapers."

"It's good of you to accept. These characters think they own the joint."

"Don't let it go to your head," the other said shortly.

He would have liked to ask why Pincas came to Nevo, where he was obviously unpopular, but he didn't want to encourage the man. He had accepted the drink on a regrettable impulse of pity for Pincas and dislike of Peter Caspi. The impulse had gone but the fat man showed no sign of following suit. Though Pincas did not quite dare to take a seat uninvited, he planted his back against the wall and settled in for a chat.

It was an unfortunate meeting for the Minister, who had good reason for wishing to avoid association with Pincas Gordon. He looked around for Sternholz, but the waiter was busy making change and didn't notice. As Pincas rambled on about Caspi, Minister Brenner grew increasingly annoyed. Sternholz oughtn't to allow it. In the old days—but before he could complete the thought, Sternholz was there.

"Back!" he ordered Pincas, waving an imaginary whip. "Back, I say!" Pincas balked, but the old man wouldn't have it. "Get back to your seat! Do you think he comes here to get annoyed by you?"

Pincas winked at the Minister and said, "Why do we put up with him?" The Minister stared past him. "Far be it from me," the fat man said unctuously, "to intrude where I'm not wanted." He did not leave Nevo but returned to his own table.

Arik had run out a few minutes earlier, returning with a copy of the *International Herald Tribune*. He pored over the paper, circling help wanted ads with a red pen. Every so often he interrupted his labors to raise his head and stare blearily at Sarita, who was oblivious, still engaged with her drawing. When Sternholz's altercation with Pincas drew his attention to that dark corner, he recognized Brenner and jumped up.

"Hey, you!" he bawled. The Minister raised an eyebrow. Arik waved the newspaper. "See this? You know what I'm doing? I'm getting out of this madhouse for good, and you know whose fault that is? Yours, you bastard; you fired me!"

"I fired you?" the Minister said. "I don't know you from Adam."

"You didn't fire Adam, you old fart; you fired me, Arik Eshel!"

"Arik Eshel? Are you Uri Eshel's son?"

Arik scowled. "I am."

"The one who quit the army over Lebanon?"

"That's right."

Brenner looked at him unsympathetically and declared, "You're a sad disappointment to that fine man."

Arik, who had sloughed his drunkenness with remarkable ease, said, "I doubt my father confides in you. And I don't believe you were uninvolved in my firing. But that doesn't matter. It's not that I object to. All's fair in love and politics, but you shouldn't have closed the center."

"I know nothing about it," the Minister said, and turned his head away.

. . .

A burst of laughter rose from Caspi's table, followed by the writer's booming voice. "No, sir," he said, addressing Khalil, "this is not Mrs. Caspi. This is my darling Dory. Mrs. Caspi is the little frump sitting over there, sulking on her own. Vered, come here!"

Vered didn't stir. Sternholz, bone tired, sat down at an unoccupied table and put his head in his hands.

"Verdele, love of my life, darling spouse, come over here. Someone wishes to meet you. No, don't move, Dory, my poppet. Vered, get your ass over here!"

Vered lit a cigarette and turned over a page of her paper. Khalil gave Caspi an angry look, then walked to Vered's table.

"I'm sorry," he said. "I foolishly thought that girl was his wife and complimented her on her work. An absurd mistake; I apologize for the embarrassment."

"I'm not embarrassed," Vered said.

"I wanted you to know that my friends read your column and respect your work."

Vered removed her dark glasses and looked up at him. "I don't know you."

"I am Khalil Mussara."

She nodded and said, "Thank you." The Arab stood uncertainly for a moment, then turned and walked out of Nevo.

Caspi watched him cross Dizengoff and get into a bright red BMW parked at the curb.

"I don't believe it," he cried, pained to the heart. "I don't believe my fucking eyes. He doesn't own a BMW."

"He does," said Rami.

"Far fucking out," breathed Dory.

"Where does that Arab come off," Caspi asked feelingly, "owning a car like that?"

Dory and Rami exchanged identical, startled glances. Caspi didn't notice. He was staring after the car.

Little Sarita had done enough. The light was fading. She went to Sternholz and, standing timidly by his elbow, asked for her check.

"No charge," he said.

"But I had three coffees."

"It's taken care of."

"By whom?"

The waiter shrugged.

"No, that's impossible. I must pay."

"Look," said Emmanuel Yehoshua Sternholz, getting painfully to his feet, "you sat there all afternoon. You drank your coffee quietly and drew your picture. You didn't do any harm, didn't cause any disruption, didn't start any fights, just sat there and brightened up this miserable place. So why should you pay me? I should pay you. Let's call it even."

Sarita flushed and said with distress, "But if you do that, how can I come back? And I have to come back."

"Next time," Sternholz said, "if it makes you happy, you can pay."

"Well," she said, giving him her hand, *"Shabbat shalom."*

He looked down at the long white fingers, graced by a ring he remembered. Sternholz shook her hand gently.

"Shabbat shalom," he said.

At dawn, Sternholz sat in the armchair by his bedroom window, overlooking the sea. Beside him on a small glass-topped table were a bowl of fruit, a cup of coffee, and an uncapped whiskey bottle. The sea, mantled in royal blue, flecked with white, reflected the rising sun. In the gap between hotels Sternholz saw a narrow silver strand: the city that was built on dunes now had barely a handful of sand to spare its beaches. When he first came, the city at its northern tip was only three streets wide; beyond its eastern edge were sand dunes and orange orchards. The smell of the sea was strong throughout the city and it was a different smell then, wild and briny and sharp. When the wind shifted, the scent of orange blossoms filled the air. Now there was too much exhaust to smell the sea, and the orange groves were long gone. Sternholz had watched the city form and re-form, a seaside city swept by the tide of time. All his life Sternholz had lived in this place, for what came before this place was not life but prelude, a dark prehistory leading to his violent expulsion onto the Tel Aviv shore. He was young with the city and knew it as a time and place of healing grace and light.

Emmanuel Yehoshua Sternholz had had the rare un-biddable fortune of living in the right time and the right place: the gift of timeliness. He had seen the city's decline into greatness, its people's into pettiness, but he regretted nothing. To mourn a city's aging was to curse the wrinkles on one's face: a repudiation of all that had passed, good and bad alike.

Chapter Two

THE calls on Ilana's tape were all from men—not surprising, in view of her vocation—and normally she would not have considered it or given it a thought. Today, however, she was disappointed. She had hoped, as she always did on her birthday, for a call from her mother. Though they had not met or spoken for fifteen years, Ilana knew that Katya had her address and number, because they corresponded by check.

Ilana could not blame her. What mother would rejoice at her only daughter's becoming a whore? Her own father had said it, last time they met, and though she rejected his tone of bitter disapprobation and the implied call to remorse, she did not dispute and never had disputed the definition. Just as extortion on a large enough scale is called manipulation, and gambling speculation, so successful prostitution is honored with finer names. But with the arrogance of great landowners who call themselves farmers, Ilana preferred the common term. She *was* a whore, though no one else would say it. She lived off men without benefit of civil or religious sanction; and if she lived well, that only made her a successful whore.

And she did live well. Her apartment in the King David Towers consisted of six beautifully furnished rooms, replete with Persian rugs, antique mahogany furniture, crystal and china service, and a sunken marble tub large enough for two. When she traveled abroad (as she did constantly, spending more time out of than in the country), she flew or sailed first class and stayed in the finest hotels. Her lovers were successive, never simultaneous, for she believed that any man who met her price deserved exclusivity. They had, in addition to Ilana, two things in common: they were all wealthy, and they were all Jewish.

Ilana was successful at her work. She was beautiful, and if her face was her fortune, it was a fortune so wisely invested as to withstand triple-digit inflation. Her beauty was not skin-deep; it resided in the bones of her face and a natural trick of coloring, legacy of a pair of mismatched parents. She had her Iraqi father's dark olive skin and her German mother's fair hair and gray eyes.

She was fashionable; it was something to appear with Ilana on one's arm. It meant, at the very least, that one could afford her. She conferred a cachet which she believed benefited even the wives of her lovers.

And she was wise. Her exotic crossbred looks were a matter of the merest good fortune, but her shrewd exploitation of that asset was a product of the mind. As every prosperous entrepreneur in the service sector knows, it pays to specialize. Ilana realized that much of her attraction for her Jewish lovers stemmed from her Israeli background. She evoked genetic memories of the hot, fragrant desert, of brilliant light, white stone cities, and robed denizens who cast shadows of knife-edge clarity: these images combined with the subterranean current of guilt and fear that runs in the veins of every diaspora Jew to release tremendous energy,

energy which Ilana harnessed and converted to cash. A simple biological process, a kind of symbiosis. Ilana loved only Jews; and the generosity of her lovers was primed by their knowledge that by contributing (generously) to her support, they were helping the economy of Israel. She had herself incorporated and billed her lovers for public relations services. By rendering their contributions tax-deductible, Ilana was able to elicit quite astonishing sums for services which did not, in the dark, differ greatly from those available for loose change in the back streets of great cities. Her lovers were as large with financial advice as they were with the means to profit by it. Ilana invested wisely; she was a wealthy woman.

Beautiful, wealthy, and in her prime, but not quite happy; and why not? Was it merely the fact that today she was thirty-six years old? But age held no fear for Ilana that her mirror could not allay. She slipped off her dress and went to look.

"Mirror, mirror, on the wall, who is the fairest one of all?"

"You are," said her mirror, "for your age." Ilana knew very well that she did not look like a girl of twenty; she'd lost the innocent grace of youth. But at thirty-six she was handsomer than she had been at twenty, and if her beauty now was sophisticated rather than simple, urban rather than rural, it suited the life she led. In her profession, as in any other, it takes time to reach the top. Ilana was an executive, and looked it. Girls of twenty, no matter how beautiful (she thought of that magnificent young creature at Nevo that afternoon), were not her rivals. They could have nothing to say to the men who sought Ilana as much for her savoir-faire as for her not inconsiderable physical attractions. *They* would be liabilities where *she* was an asset. When she was young and freshly launched on her career, thirty-five had been her outer limit. But she knew better now. She was a young woman still to the men of fifty and sixty who sought her avidly, and with exercise and diet she could retain her market value for many more years.

Why then, if this was so (and it was), did Ilana feel so bad? Something was wrong. She could not eat; she could not smoke; she felt exhausted all the time. Was it an incipient bout of flu? Or could it be the fallout of her recent experience in Frankfurt?

As if on cue, the telephone rang. Ilana visualized her mother, older now and graying, wearied by the long years spent raising five children on a postman's salary and by the time (of which Ilana knew little) that had come before.

But it was a man's voice that said, "Ilana?"

"Hello, David." Her voice automatically assumed the husky pitch reserved for current lovers. "I've missed talking to you. Where are you now?"

"I'm back in the office. Sorry I didn't reach you from Germany, but I did try several times. I was worried about you."

"No need to be, darling. I'm fine. I'm just sorry we missed our time together."

"So am I," he said, and there was a pause. Then he asked hesitantly, "What happened to you?"

She laughed lightly. "God knows; brain fever or flu or something—but whatever it was it's long gone. You were wonderful, David. You were so gentle and kind, afterward. As sorry as I am that we lost the rest of the days, I treasure the memory of that last night."

"Don't say last," he murmured. "I must see you. Will you meet me?"

"Any place but Germany." She laughed.

"No, here, in London. Come next weekend."

"Darling, I'd love to." They discussed flights, then rang off. Ilana ran to the bathroom and retched into the sink.

It must be the flu, she thought, but what flu hangs

about for weeks before stepping forward to declare itself? And what flu made her confront a roomful of perfect strangers on the Theaterplatz and scream "Nazi swine!" into their astonished faces?

It happened right next to their hotel, in one of those irresistible German delicatessens that feature the finest imported foods and wines at impossible prices. David intended to take her out to supper after his day of meetings was done, but Ilana, passing the store on her way back from shopping, decided to surprise him with dinner in their suite. She entered and joined an orderly line of well-dressed customers waiting to be served.

The line moved slowly. To pass the time, Ilana studied the other people in the store. There were two elegant ladies in summer furs, mother and daughter by their age and resemblance. There was a clerkish young man in horn-rims, who read a newspaper as he waited. There was a tall, attractive woman in a business suit who fidgeted impatiently, and a womanish little man with a miniature poodle on a leash. The dog was terminally well behaved and stood in line as if bred to it. Directly behind her stood the only reasonable prospect in the place (even off-duty Ilana saw through the lens of a professional), a tall German in his late forties or early fifties, with thick brown hair graying at the temples, who returned her look with overt interest. Behind him stood two unacquainted women, both middle-aged, one a German matron and the other unmistakably an American tourist. The American wore an oversized Star of David prominently displayed on her chest. Ilana looked at the star, blinked, and turned away.

The service was slow and the wait interminable. Ilana wanted to walk out but something held her back: the desire not to be bested by those insolent clerks, whose purpose, she felt, was to drive her out. She recognized dimly that this could not be, but the recognition did nothing to dispel the anger (and now, insidiously, the anxiety) she felt.

A man came into the store: a big man, a rich man, dressed in a suit like a uniform and owning a palpable air of command, which was bolstered by the harried air of the chauffeur who followed him in. This man strode past the line without a glance and immediately engaged one of the clerks, who was suddenly all eager helpfulness.

The line, as if it were a single organism, murmured, sighed, and fell silent.

Ilana protested—silently. At home she would have gone up to the offender, taken him firmly by the arm, escorted him to his rightful place, and delivered a tongue-lashing to boot. But to do that here she would have to speak; and if she spoke they would hear her accent; and if they heard her accent they might know she was a Jew. Without analyzing the feeling she felt strongly that this was undesirable. Ilana did nothing and, doing nothing, felt worse.

The American woman said shrilly, "What's going on here? Why are they serving that man?" No one answered or looked at her. She stepped out of line, approached the counter, and said, "This man just came in."

The clerk ignored her. The large man gave her a desultory glance, pausing on the Star of David, then turned away with a disdainful expression and resumed his conversation with the clerk. Ilana stood stock-still, hardly breathing, staring at the neck of the man before her.

"Young man, look at me when I talk to you! I *said*, this gentleman just walked in."

The clerk made a shooing motion with his hand, as if to a cat. The American exploded. "How dare you! I want to see the manager! Where is he? Answer me, you!"

There was not a sound in the room. Though all eyes were on the American woman, Ilana felt certain that at any moment they would turn on her. Be still, she prayed. Be still, fool.

The American turned toward the two German women, mother and daughter. "I don't understand this," she said. "I thought *the Germans are supposed to be so orderly, such good citizens*. But I have been all over the *world* and I have never met with such insolence!"

Oh, God, woman, Ilana screamed silently, don't you feel how they hate you? She was terrified; she felt as if at any moment black-booted storm troopers would burst in and seize the woman and herself; and though she recognized the irrationality of her fear, that did nothing to allay it.

Mother and daughter looked at one another; then the elder said, in cultured English, "This man is very important. He is in the Government. He has no time to wait, and we would not wish him to."

"My husband happens to be a very important man," said the American, "but whenever he goes to the store, he waits on line like everybody else."

"No doubt that is suitable for your husband," the elder woman immediately replied, and turned her head away.

Ilana was sickened by her own craven silence but could not resist an exceedingly strong pull toward camouflage. It seemed effective; the man behind her leaned forward and whispered a few words in German, of which Ilana understood only *Ausländer*. She turned to him and said, *"Ich bin ein Ausländer,"* and at once he fell silent and looked away.

The American had renewed her demand for the manager, and both clerks had left off serving and were arguing with her. Though they clearly understood her, they answered only in German. Ilana felt the anger of the waiting customers focus on the foolish woman, who now turned to appeal loudly for their support.

Someone said, *"Juden."* Jews.

She didn't know who said it. It didn't matter. Her fear dissolved in rage. She stepped forth from the line, and so bright was her shining anger that even the American woman ceased talking to stare at her.

"Pigs!" cried Ilana. Her finger swept over the customers on the line and the two clerks. "You haven't changed. You're still the same filthy Nazi scum."

Though she spoke in English it was evident that everyone understood her. Their faces blurred before her, so that all she saw was a single composite expression of shock, fear, and, yes, hatred.

Half a minute of silence, then: "The poor woman's mad," said the German mother. "Call the police." One of the clerks reached for a counter top telephone.

"Drop it!" Ilana screamed, and he did. The big man grunted and walked quickly out of the shop, his chauffeur scurrying behind. The dog began to bark. Its owner snatched it up, clutching it to his chest protectively. The American woman stood frozen with her hand over her mouth.

Ilana split in two. One half of her stood and watched the other rant and rave at a roomful of people, most of whom, she *knew*, were guilty of no more than impatience. That self had no control, no ability to interfere, only a helpless capacity to observe and suffer. Ilana's autonomous voice spewed out a medley of English, Hebrew, and Arabic curses and damnations, poetic in their combination and astonishing in their variety. She spoke fluently for quite a long time before the woman in the business suit took a tentative step forward and said in a sensible tone and passable English, "Try to calm down. Breathe deeply." Sirens sounded in the street, coming closer. The two Ilanas came together with a jolt. Suddenly empowered, she turned and bolted from the shop—

Straight into David's arms.

David took over. He pacified the police and dismissed the two clerks, who had regained their tongues and were demanding an arrest. All the customers had quietly slipped away, except for the American, who fluttered nervously, distressed but helpless, and the German woman in the suit. *She* went up to the officer in charge and said authoritatively, "I believe this woman is Israeli."

"She is," he said.

"Release her. There was some provocation, an unpleasant incident. She had cause to be upset. And we do not know her background. You had better let her go."

David's German was fluent. He told Ilana to wait and approached the officer. "The lady is distressed. The incident is over, and I am going to take her home."

"Is she your wife?" the man asked officiously.

"It doesn't matter who she is. This is who I am. If you need me, I can be reached at the Frankfurterhof." He handed over his card.

"Now just a minute—"

"Officer, I have not yet heard what happened in there. When I do, I may wish to press charges. I suggest you do nothing to exacerbate the situation."

The policeman looked at the card in his hand, then at David's face. He said, "There is no need for charges on any side, sir. You may go. Please take care of the lady. We are sensitive to incidents of this kind; we would not like it to happen again."

"It won't," David said.

"Would you care to tell me what happened?"

"I would if I could, but I can't."

They lay side by side on the king-sized bed in the suite. David had guided her, ashen and stunned, through the lobby and up to their rooms. He undressed her without a word, put her in the bath, left, and came back with two large whiskeys on a salver. "Cheers," he said. Ilana tried to apologize, but he shut her up and began to soap her back and buttocks with good-natured, unpressing lust. After a while she began to cry. David took her out of the bath and led her to the bed and made love to her with a tender passion that astonished them both, having had no precedent in the relationship. Ilana, usually supremely conscious, active, and unmoved during love-making (though skilled at pretending otherwise), allowed herself, in her exhaustion, the sinful luxury of passivity and in the end achieved a long moment of utter forgetfulness. When she came back, she was herself again.

It was then David asked, "Would you care to tell me what happened?"

Ilana's recovery had progressed to the point of worrying about David's reaction. "I would if I could, but I can't," she said almost gaily.

"You must have some idea. All that screaming."

Until that moment it had not occurred to her that he might have seen more of the scene than her exit. "How long were you there?" she asked.

"I saw the last act," he said. "You were magnificent."

She smiled. "Somewhat lacking in motivation, I fear. The last act is all there was."

"That woman said there was provocation, some kind of incident. What happened? Was it—anti-Semitism?" He said the word with the coy thrill of a young boy whispering about sex.

"Someone said, 'Juden,' " she remembered.

He waited. "Is that all?"

"It upset me."

"That was evident."

"I've never liked coming to Germany."

"Neither have I. And Frankfurt is particularly beastly. But still—"

"David, you were magnificent," she interrupted, deliberately changing the subject but meaning it, too. "You saved my life, and I'll never, ever forget it. But, darling, what a scene!" She began to laugh, and he did, too, but not without an edge of alarm in his voice. Hearing it strengthened her resolve. When she said that she was going home, he protested but not too much. Ilana taxied to the airport the next morning.

David didn't call for two weeks. Ilana thought she'd lost him, deservedly. To avoid thinking about what had happened she brooded over the consequences: the very real possibility that she had damaged herself professionally. By involving David in a public scene which might easily have become a scandal, she had violated the strictest canons of her trade. The men she went with were serious men, solid, wealthy businessmen, not playboys who thrived on scandal. If David was harmed and word got about, Ilana could find herself facing a career crisis.

David's belated but loving call, which should have relieved Ilana's anxiety, only exacerbated it by eliminating the cause without eliminating the effects. She knew her body as well as any athlete could, and knew now that it wasn't right. Moreover, the symptoms gave cause to suspect that this particular not-rightness was of a female order.

She waited a few more days, then called her doctor.

Chapter Three

"I AM shocked," said Caspi. "I am appalled. I always believed that for all your manifold faults you retained a modicum of style, if not decency. Suddenly I see that I am married to a stranger."

"Then you are beginning to see the light."

"But no, what am I saying? No stranger would behave as you did. No stranger would deliberately set out to embarrass me in public, making a fool of herself in the process. I don't know how you're going to face the world after this, Vered. Everybody's laughing at you."

"At me?" she asked. "Do you think so?"

"You bitch."

They sat at the kitchen counter, at right angles to one another. Caspi was dressed to go out; Vered wore a kimono over pajamas. They had an oblique way of talking, avoiding names and direct glances. Caspi harangued; Vered analyzed. "Anyway"—she shrugged—"you're exaggerating, as usual. You talk as if I'd stripped naked and strolled down Dizengoff, instead of just sitting for an hour in Nevo."

"On a Friday afternoon, when you knew damn well I'd be there with Dory. That's exactly what you did: stripped naked for all the world to sneer."

"Then it's strange that of the two of us, you're the one who feels humiliated."

Caspi jumped up and threw his cup into the sink. It shattered. At the door he turned back. "If you think you will goad me into giving you a divorce, you're out of your mind. It will never happen." He pulled open the door and stumbled into Jemima. "Damn you, woman, have you been listening at keyholes?"

"No need for that, Caspi. I could hear you down the block. Good morning, Vered."

"Good morning, Mother."

"If I'd known you were coming, Jemima, I'd have left an hour ago. As long as you're here, you might as well give your daughter a few lessons in decorum. She's just made a laughingstock of herself."

"How very trying for you, model of decorum that you are."

"Give little what's-her-name my best regards," Vered called. Caspi slammed the door behind him.

"Coffee, Mother?" Vered said.

"Thank you." Jemima took Caspi's place at the counter, crossing one elegant leg over the other. She wore a crisply tailored pearl-gray linen suit of her own design; her blond hair was gathered in a loose bun at the nape of her neck. While Vered silently cleaned up broken glass, Jemima cast a bleak eye about the room, pausing on the back of Vered's kimono and the proud set of the neck rising above it.

"Where's Daniel?" she asked.

"Playing at a friend's." Vered prepared the percolator, set out the cups.

"I seem to have come at an inconvenient moment."

"It makes no difference."

"Are you wise to antagonize him?"

"No. But it doesn't matter."

"What set him off?"

"I went to Nevo."

"That's all?"

"Yesterday afternoon."

"Friday afternoon. I see. And he was there."

"Oh yes.

"You sat with him?"

Vered placed the percolator on the stove and rather slowly returned to the counter. She spoke with great detachment. "No, that seat was occupied."

"Do you really think you'll win this game?"

"No."

"Then why play it?"

Vered sat beside her mother. Her face was as expressionless as living flesh could be. "I've lost the battle anyway," she said in a tone of perfect finality.

"Vered, I must tell you that I have never cared for your way of looking at me as if I were a census taker. I am your mother."

"I know."

"You don't act like it. Other daughters confide in their mothers. I wouldn't mind your reticence if I knew you talked to someone, a friend, a counselor, but I know you don't. I admire your fortitude but you go too far. The time has come to talk."

"You'd like me to confide in you."

"Yes."

"Open my heart, pour out my troubles, seek solace and advice at your motherly bosom?"

Jemima's "Yes!" was nervous, defiant.

"What for? So you can tell your friends all about it? 'Poor Vered, married to that monster. I warned her, but would she listen? Did you hear about his latest little floozy?' "

Eyes narrowed, Jemima put her hand on her heart and cried, "I wouldn't!"

"You did. All those years after Daddy died, when you called me your ugly duckling and laughed at me with your fancy society friends."

"Oh, Vered, if I was ever so cruel I swear I'm paying for it now. No, don't look at me that way. You were a difficult child, Vered, and hard for me to understand. You still are. Darling, I *am* sorry."

Vered's smile was bright but frigid. "It's all right, Mother. Would you like more coffee?"

"No." Jemima fumbled in her bag for a handkerchief.

"Then I really have to get to work now. I've got a deadline tomorrow, and after this morning I'll have Daniel on my hands all day."

Jemima dabbed delicately at her eyes, to avoid smearing her make-up. She said, "I won't go until I've had my say. When are you going to divorce this Caspi person?"

"I'm not going to."

"Why not?" Jemima said angrily, mockingly. "Do you still love him?"

"Why do you ask? Do you still want him?"

Jemima gasped. "Do you really believe that?"

"No, I suppose not," Vered said without inflection. Jemima, who needed glasses but was too vain to wear them, took a jeweled pair from her purse and set them on her nose. To no avail: the glasses had not been invented that would penetrate Vered's mask.

"You know," she mused, "you've turned into a rather terrifying woman. I wouldn't wonder if Caspi were scared to death of you."

Vered barked a laugh.

"I don't care if you bite my head off, Vered. I want to know: are you still in love with him?"

"I hate him," she said.

Jemima was too pleased with the tone of this answer to reflect that the one emotion did not preclude the other. "Then for God's sake divorce him!" she cried.

"I can't."

"Why not? You surely don't lack grounds." As Jemima leaned toward her, Vered caught a whiff of her fragrance, a green, meadowy scent. "I'm seeing Giora Fliegerman this afternoon."

"Forget it. I already talked to him."

"You did? He didn't tell me that."

"That is surprising."

"Don't be rude. What did he say?"

"He said what all the others said: that I could get a divorce. No problem."

"But that's excellent."

Vered toyed with her cup. "He just wasn't sure I could keep Daniel."

Jemima said angrily, "That's absurd. You must be looking for excuses. Caspi would never contest custody."

"Oh, no?"

"Of course not. What would Caspi do with a three-year-old child?"

"Look after him, he said, as best he could."

Jemima pushed her cup away and stood up. She prowled about the small kitchen like a well-dressed, impeccably groomed panther. Vered lit a cigarette. Her last words, spoken with Caspi's intonation, reverberated in the silent kitchen.

"He's bluffing," Jemima said at last. "He doesn't want the child, and even if he did, no judge would award him custody."

"If Caspi contested custody he'd be more likely than I to win it. All things being equal, the judges and the law favor the father for boys."

"But all things aren't equal. Caspi's got no relationship with the boy. He's a bully, a womanizer, a—"

Vered's cool voice cut in firmly. "I know what Caspi is. Do you know what the Fliegerman creature said?"

"What?"

"He sat down next to me and put his hand on my knee. He was wearing some tacky men's cologne and that ratty toupee. He said, 'Be realistic, Vered. I've known a few women in my day; does that make me an unfit father?'"

"Why, that arrogant little—"

"He's right. They all cheat on their wives; they'd never penalize another man for that."

Jemima shook her head and sighed. "Well," she said after a moment, "I'd call him on it."

"You would, would you?" It was not said admiringly.

"Darling, take my word for it, it's a bluff. Caspi never wanted a child to begin with. He wouldn't know what to do with Daniel if he got him."

"He'd know." Vered lit a cigarette and gave one to her mother. A look passed between the two women: a question, an answer, a judgment? Perhaps something different for each; it was not a look of perfect understanding. Vered said deliberately, "Caspi loves his power over me. With Daniel in his custody there'd be that much more to love."

Jemima slapped the counter top smartly. "That's defeatist thinking. You've got to keep in mind that every problem has at least one possible solution. You're your own worst enemy, Vered; I've been wanting to tell you that for a long time. You analyze instead of acting. Where would I be today if I'd spent my time understanding my problems instead of doing something about them? Beware, my girl. I've known better women than you to grow addicted to their misery. Ask yourself one question: if you're so smart, what are you doing married to that bum?"

Later that afternoon, Jemima sat at the white bamboo and glass desk in her study, unanswered letters strewn before her. She twirled a pen and stared idly out the window at the sea below. Vered, too, was at her desk, which was a sturdy, graceless oak creation, with many drawers and cubbyholes. Daniel was down for his nap, and she had two precious hours to work. There was a blank sheet of paper in the type-writer in front of her. She stared at it as if hypnotized, hands at her side. Both women, mother and daughter, were remembering the same events, though from very different perspectives.

When Caspi first appeared in their lives, there was some regrettable confusion as to where his primary interest lay. Vered was nineteen at the time, Jemima forty and a widow for seven years. Caspi, who had just turned thirty, was being hailed by the critics as the new star on the Israeli literary firmament. When he first came to one of Jemima's salons, produced as a kind of hostess gift by his publisher, Vered was in attendance. A striking but rather awkward sort of girl, not long out of army uniform, with none of her mother's flair or style, Vered regarded these evenings as a kind of penance incurred by her weakness in returning to her mother's house, and thus was not surprised to find herself ignored by the first interesting man she'd met in that house. Instead of noticing the daughter, Caspi wooed the mother with smoldering across-a-crowded-room glances.

Caspi's infamy with women had preceded, perhaps even contributed to, his literary fame. He was known to be arrogant, unprincipled in the means and targets of his seductions, and cruel to the women he used and discarded. This reputation naturally had the effect of inducing otherwise quite sensible women to try to capture Caspi's heart.

The day after her soiree, Jemima went out and bought both of Caspi's books. She read them and wrote a note to Caspi, inviting him to dine next Friday. He came. They dined tête-à-tête but for Vered, whose presence was barely felt. Later they walked through the garden and looked down on the sea. Jasmine and brine mingled in the air. Jemima held Caspi's arm and laughed deep in her throat, while Vered trailed behind, a silent shadow. Jemima gave Vered several looks, but she ignored them and was at last rewarded for her tenacity: behind her mother's back, Caspi plucked a red rose from a bush and presented it to her.

Vered was scarcely to be seen the next week, coming and going without a word of explanation. Jemima wondered about this. Saturday morning after breakfast, she brought one of Caspi's books out to the garden and offered it to her daughter.

"No, thanks," Vered said. "I have a copy. Caspi gave it to me."

"*Caspi* gave it to you! When did you see Caspi?"

"Yesterday, at Nevo." Vered lay on a towel in her bikini; her olive skin tanned deeply. Jemima, in a sundress, sat beside her in a wicker chair. The house was set on a bluff overlooking the sea in Herzliya, a prime piece of property which Jemima had fought long and hard to keep. She said: "Vered, I do not want you hanging around Nevo. A young girl in that place is regarded as nothing but a piece of fresh meat by those hungry dogs."

"They are nothing like that, Mother. They happen to be the most interesting people in the country today, the best artists, actors, and writers around."

"If they were that good they'd be working," Jemima snapped. "Nobody with any serious work to do hangs out in cafés."

"Creative people work in short, intensive bursts," Vered informed her loftily. "They need to escape periodically. That's why so many of them drink."

"I don't like the sound of this." Jemima turned her chair toward her daughter, lowering the rim of her straw hat to block the sun from her eyes. "Have you been seeing Caspi?"

"Just a little," Vered said demurely, but the look she shot her mother from under lowered lids was gleefully defiant.

Jemima leaned back, clasped her hands, and smiled understandingly. "I can understand the attraction, Vered. But I cannot consider Caspi a suitable companion for a young girl."

"Why not? You invited him here to dinner."

"That is different—and it is not for you, young lady, to question your mother. For your information, a person of my age and experience has resources that a girl your age lacks. Caspi is nothing but an amusing acquaintance to me; to you he could be dangerous."

If Jemima knew how she was fueling her daughter's curiosity and resolve she would certainly have desisted, but as she considered her daughter incapable of any serious opposition she took no account of such a possibility. Vered exclaimed, "Caspi hasn't made a pass at me, if that's what you think. And you know what? I'm sorry he hasn't."

Jemima called Caspi and arranged a meeting. He wouldn't come to Herzliya, so she agreed to attend him at Nevo.

"A charming child," Caspi said.

"Child is the operant word. I trust you bear that in mind."

Caspi laughed heartily. "Pedophilia is not among my virtues," he said in an audible whisper. "Let the girl come to me in ten years' time, if she's willing. Then she may interest me. I prefer seasoned women." The smile he gave Jemima was full of meaning, and despite herself, she felt a tingle in the pit of her stomach.

"She said you are a child," Caspi told Vered an hour later.

"Am I?"

"I don't think so." Caspi ran two fingers up her bare arm. "Do you?"

"Of course she's a child," said Sternholz, bustling over. "You could be her father, God forbid."

"Sternholz, go away," Caspi said.

"You want something, little girl? Some milk maybe I should bring you?"

"I'll have a rum and Coke."

"We don't serve mixed drinks."

"Then just the rum."

She got just the Coke.

"Are you a virgin?" Caspi asked when Sternholz had gone away. "I ask purely out of fatherly interest."

"If that is your interest, then it's none of your business."

"So, the little kitten has claws! How very charming. *Garçon!* Beer, and another Coke for the lady."

"I'll *garçon* you," Sternholz muttered, coming over with the drinks. "And shouldn't you be in school, Vered? Does your mother know where you are?"

"No, and no," said Vered.

"There's Dotan. Rami, come here!"

"Hello, Caspi."

"Sit down. This is Vered Niro. Be careful—she scratches."

"Hello, hello."

"I saw you published Oz's latest thing. I read thirty pages and put it down as trash, but Vered finished it and says it has some redeeming value."

"It's doing very well; we're already reprinting."

"Yes, but what's happened to the Oz we all knew and loved? Compare this last one to *My Michael*!"

"*My Michael* sold maybe thirty thousand. I'll be surprised if we don't top that. What's so funny?"

"Vered, don't ever try to talk books with a publisher. All you get back are numbers."

"And royalties," Dotan said.

"Eventually, sometimes."

"Well, Vered," Jemima said at breakfast the next morning, "I hardly see you these days. We have a lot of things to do before school starts. You still haven't registered in the business faculty. And you need clothes. You'll have to come into the place and get fitted up."

"I don't need any clothes."

"You certainly do. Jeans and old work shirts may be all the mode at Nevo, but for the university you need to dress decently. Don't forget that you are my daughter, and your present manner of dressing hardly reflects well on me."

"I'm not taking business, Mother. I've decided to major in literature."

"Literature," Jemima said darkly, "is not a profession. Nor will it prepare you in any way for a responsible position in the firm. I should think you might have learned from my example the folly of a woman's not having a profession. Read books, by all means, but don't let them interfere with your life."

"And I'll minor in journalism. You see, I do care about having a profession. After I graduate, I'll get a job on a paper. I've been meeting people who can help."

"What people? Where?"

"Writers, critics, journalists, all kinds of people. At Nevo."

Jemima rose to her full five feet seven inches. "That was *not* the plan! I have one daughter, and she must succeed me."

"She doesn't want to," Vered said.

"Child, what has got into you? You've never acted like this before."

"I never knew I could."

. . .

"You're encouraging her," Jemima said wrathfully. She stood over Caspi. Sternholz hovered behind, wringing his hands. At the tables around them, people listened openly. "You are deliberately trying to drive a wedge between us."

"You need a wedge between you. It is my privilege to be of service. Do sit down, Jemima. You're embarrassing me. That's better. Now what will you have? *Garçon!*"

Sternholz stepped forward. "You call me that once more, Caspi, and you can find yourself another parking spot. You want something, Jemima?"

"Emmanuel, I have a bone to pick with you. What do you mean by letting Vered hang out here with this riffraff?"

"I don't like it, Jemima, but what could I do? She's a grown woman, and this is a public place."

Jemima glanced around the café at all the occupied chairs angled toward her table. She felt as if she were appearing in a theater-in-the-round. "A very public place," she said.

"You have misinterpreted the entire situation," Caspi informed her and the world at large. "Vered is a treasure, which you, my dear Jemima, do not sufficiently value. Vered's innocence is delectable; I envy you her rebellion. She is a late-blooming rose, and all the sweeter for it."

"She *is* innocent," Jemima said, "and that is what makes your behavior so despicable."

"My behavior, madam, has been impeccable, to her and to you. My attitude toward Vered is that of a kindly father, a role in keeping with the feelings I harbor toward you."

"I am sorry for the day I met you," Jemima said.

As she wove her way out through the tables, Jemima heard one Nevo wit say: "Caspi means to reverse nature.

He's going to wed the younger and bed the elder." A burst of raucous laughter followed her onto the street.

No one ever really understood why Caspi married Vered. The odds were on the mother: she had more to give. There were people who guessed that Caspi's flirtation with Vered was a ploy to force Jemima's hand: take him on herself, or lose her daughter to him. Others said it was merely a joke that went too far. Jemima saw it as a demonic act of destruction. All noted the fact that though impecunious herself, Vered was her mother's sole heir and thus heir to Niro Fashions. Caspi himself gave a thousand reasons, which amounted to none. Most often he claimed that he married Vered because she was a virgin, but that was nonsense, as he'd already dispatched a dozen of those. Vered was amazed to find herself favored over the many women who'd been linked to Caspi in the past. That part of her which fit her mother's conception, sly, awkward, worrisome Vered, could not account for it at all.

But there was another Vered, Vered-seen-through-Caspi's-eyes, and that was a self she would do much to secure. Caspi saw in Vered a canny innocence and the gift of clear sight coupled with the rarer gift of clear expression. He saw a bravery of spirit. He saw a woman unawakened, who stirred under his touch, and he saw himself as both creator and discoverer. The truth was stranger than all the imaginings. Only Sternholz, of all the witnesses to Caspi's strange courtship, had an inkling, and that insight did not cheer him. For the first and only time in his life, Caspi had fallen in love.

Chapter Four

SARITA Blume lived at No. 34 Sheinkin Street in a flat laughingly styled "the penthouse." The apartment was a one-room shack on the flat roof of a three-story building. In the winter, when it rained, the roof flooded and water sluiced over the cement floors. The ceiling leaked, the electrical wiring was dangerously eroded, and there was no water pressure, just the meanest trickle of water from the faucets. The rent, however, was only $100 a month. Sarita deplored the miserliness of the landlord which had brought the apartment to such a state, but for herself, it didn't matter. What mattered were the height, the light, and the place itself.

Sheinkin was the heart of little Tel Aviv, which was the heart of greater Tel Aviv, which was the heart, the brain, the gut of Israel. On Sheinkin you found every type of Israeli all jumbled together: old pensionnaires, who gathered in the bridge club or ran one of the little key-money shops; religious families with dozens of kids; artists and musicians driven out of the north by the prices; refugee kibbutzniks still living in groups; young couples with a baby or two, waiting for a break on the stock market or the national lottery to buy their way up and out. The shops were tiny and graceless and stuffed with merchandise of every imaginable kind for half of what the goods cost anywhere else. You could gut an apartment, reconstruct it, paint it, light it, install new plumbing, furnish, decorate and drape it, stock the pantry with food and the cupboards with clothes and shoes and hats, all without ever going off the street. Alone on her roof, Sarita overlooked the world, and what she saw she painted.

Two months before her first appearance in Nevo, Sarita Blume was sitting where she usually sat and doing what she usually did, painting a scene from Sheinkin Street. From her vantage point on the roof she could see all of Sheinkin spread out below her, from its splendid head, which butted into Rothschild Boulevard, to the bedraggled tail, which wagged into Allenby. It was 10:00 A.M., and the morning sun swept over the stately buildings of Rothschild to illuminate her street. As she sketched blindly, Sarita followed the progress of an old woman, bent almost double, who trundled a two-wheeled shopping cart from grocery to fruit stand to pharmacy to butcher. Two mothers pushed strollers with bags laden from the morning's shopping slung over the handles. When they paused for a traffic light, the old Gruzini flower seller, who (as far as Sarita could tell) lived in a doorway on the corner of Achad Ha'am, left his place to peer at the babies. They laughed at his funny woven cap and grizzly beard, and he handed each one a daisy to hold or eat as they saw fit. The Arab street cleaner was making his stately rounds, trailed by a pack of barking mongrels that pretended not to know him. A tall woman in a fiery red bandana crossed the street and entered Sarita's building.

A few minutes later there was a knock on the door. Sarita laid down her brush and went to see what the woman wanted.

She was close to six feet tall and wore a multitude of

scarves that somehow combined into a blouse, and a long peasant skirt threaded with crimson and gold. Her legs were bare, but on her feet were white anklets and gold high-heeled sandals. This somehow successful profusion of colors and patterns made the woman look like a picture out of the Gypsy's V*ogue*.

"Sarita Blume?" she asked.

"Yes."

"I am Moriah Benveniste," she announced, and seemed confident that the name was enough.

"Come in." Sarita cleared a stack of canvases from her only inside chair and sat herself on the bed. Rings and bracelets jingling, her visitor perched on the edge of the chair. Sarita saw that she was older than she dressed, close to fifty, with jet black braids framing a gaunt, dark, mobile face with a wide mouth. She smiled, and her teeth flashed white.

"I am delighted to meet you. You do not know me, but perhaps you know my gallery, La Benveniste in Jaffa."

"Yes, certainly," said Sarita.

"Actually it's not mine anymore. My husband got it when we divorced, but I expect he'll run it down to nothing within a few months. He never had any taste; *I* was the one who chose the artists and designed the exhibits."

"I saw some. They were excellent."

"Yes," said Moriah Benveniste. "I hated to lose it, but it was either that or a seven-year court battle to get rid of the bastard. Of course it *was* extortion, and lots of my friends advised me to fight him; but I always think that those women who go through hell to keep their property are awful fools, don't you? Children are one thing (fortunately, we didn't have any; I wasn't that much of a fool), but *property*? The one thing I wouldn't give him was his name back. I said to him, 'I *am* La Benveniste, and dumping you doesn't change that.' That's why I'm here."

"I see," said Sarita, who didn't. "Would you like some tea?"

"No, don't bother, dear. So is it a deal?"

"Is what a deal?"

Moriah's laugh was like silver coins clinking. "Didn't I tell you? That's what freedom does for you: rots the brain, like alcohol. I want you to inaugurate my new gallery."

"But I don't show," Sarita said foolishly.

"That's one of the reasons I want you. I've seen some of your work here and there, so *that's* all right. I think you're very good for your age, and very promotable. 'The painter waif of Sheinkin Street': how does that sound?"

"Bad."

"Don't be shy, Sarita Blume. You have to understand that success in this field is ten percent talent and ninety percent P.R. You leave that side of things to me. Now, let's see what you've got."

Without knowing how she came to it, Sarita found herself displaying her canvases one by one to Moriah, who said nothing but looked at them with obvious discernment and at Sarita with growing wonder. When Sarita was done, Moriah selected six from the stack of thirty-odd works and propped them against the wall. Sarita blushed when she saw the selection.

"Where did you get this?" Moriah asked severely.

"From my imagination."

"Horsefeathers. Let me tell you something very few people know. I grew up right here on Sheinkin Street, just a few houses down. I remember this street better than I remember my father (not that he was around much), and I know what I'm seeing."

"I just imagined them."

"Then you have one hell of an imagination." She pointed. "That old kiosk woman, the watermelon cart with the gray horse and the one-eyed driver, that poor old beggar woman—they are all real. I remember them. I remember that restaurant, too, but you don't; they tore it down before you were born. And that beggar died of pneumonia at least thirty years ago; I remember what a scandal it was when they found her body in a doorway. Now, how did you do it? Did you use pictures?"

"Yes," Sarita said quickly. "Old photographs."

"Show me them."

Sarita was silent.

"I heard things about you," Moriah said thoughtfully. "I just never believed them."

"No."

"How old are you?"

"Twenty."

"Very young for such talents. And of course, you have no mother."

Sarita bounded off the bed. "Thank you for the offer, but I'm not interested in exhibiting right now."

"Sit down, child. I promise not to pry. That's better. When I tell you where the gallery is, you'll understand why I need you and you need me."

"Where?" asked Sarita, expecting to hear Jaffa or Dizengoff.

"Across the street, right here on Sheinkin." Moriah smiled triumphantly, and indeed, Sarita's refusal caught in her throat and stayed there. She shook her head in perplexity.

"You must. You are the Sheinkin Street painter."

"I'm not ready."

"You're not perfect, but you are ready. An artist who doesn't exhibit is autistic; he may perfect his technique, but sooner or later he loses the ability to communicate, without which there is no art."

"I understand what you're saying, but I'm afraid."

Moriah laughed scornfully. "Of the critics?"

"No. Of showing those." She indicated the pictures that Moriah had selected.

"You must. They're your best. Listen to me, dearie. I don't know where you got all that detail. I don't buy the old photographs story, but there's no reason why other people shouldn't. At least they can't disprove it, and whatever else they suspect they'll keep it to themselves, for fear of appearing foolish." Staring at the pictures, Moriah struggled with herself and lost. "How on earth did you do it?"

Sarita shrugged.

"Are you psychic?"

"What does that mean?" Sarita fastened her eyes on the ground like a sulky child. "Sometimes I paint what I see, and sometimes I paint what I imagine; that's all."

"That's one hell of an imagination. If we could bottle it and sell it, we'd have it made, kid. We could call it 'Witch's Brew.' "

"I'm not a witch," Sarita said angrily.

"Of course you're not. I was only joking. You're a painter, and a good one at that. Will you accept my offer?"

Sarita looked at her. After a moment she said, "When?"

Six weeks later, the Sheinkin Gallery opened, and with it Sarita Blume's first exhibit.

Sarita came unescorted, dressed in a forest green gown of silk and lace. It was an astonishing dress for Sheinkin Street, which in all the years since its conception had not known an occasion to support it, and no woman less beautiful than Sarita could have carried it off. The dress had been her mother's, who had left her no money but a closetful of magnificent, dramatic clothes, seldom worn but lovingly preserved by the daughter.

The opening also served as a kind of personal debut for Sarita. Her shyness, though habitual, was not inbred, and when the time was right she had no difficulty in discarding it. She invited friends of her parents, some of whom she hadn't seen since the funeral, and they, compelled by guilt and curiosity, attended en masse. They came intending to be pleased, and so they were, as much by the artist as by her work. She looked, they whispered, just like her mother.

The press was tremendous, for in addition to the invited guests, all of Sheinkin Street seemed to have turned out. Among the hundreds who attended was one who looked at the paintings, then at Sarita, and left, quite unnoticed, without a word.

The opening was a great success. Most of the pictures bore little red dots before the end of the evening, and Moriah Benveniste, who had not printed the prices, charged twice as much for the last pictures sold as for the first. Sarita exhibited but would not sell the pictures of old Sheinkin and its inhabitants, for she felt they were not entirely hers to sell. There were viewers who recognized old friends and relations and even themselves as youngsters, but oddly enough they seemed to find nothing strange in this and made no inquiries.

One week after the opening, Moriah called on Sarita at home.

"I've obtained a commission for you," she began with a mysterious smile.

"A commission?"

"For a great deal of money. One thousand dollars, for a single painting."

Sarita gave her a disbelieving look.

"Less my commission, that's eight hundred dollars."

"Your commission," Sarita repeated.

"As your agent. Well, you need an agent, dearie. What do you know about marketing, promotion, pricing, all the business side of art? You don't want to spend your time on that, but you need to make a living."

"But are you an agent?"

"Every dealer is an agent. Trust me, Sarita. Was I wrong about the exhibition? And I did get you this commission."

"But who is it from?"

"From someone," said Moriah, "who wishes to remain anonymous."

"And what am I supposed to paint?"

"Nevo," Moriah said.

"Nevo! The mountain?" The picture presented itself to her: a white stone peak rising from the Moab plateau, fierce and barren under the midday sun. At its summit stands a man alone, pale robes shimmering in the heat, casting a shadow so deep and black it seems to cast him. Motionless, he gazes out at the land which as surely as it has been promised to the people has been denied him. His back is to the observer, his face hidden; all the tragic clash of hope and fate is in the set of his head, the slope of his shoulders, the lines of his dust-hemmed robe.

Moriah's voice recalled her. "Not the mountain," she said, laughing. "The café, on Dizengoff. Nevo."

And yet the picture was slow to fade. She saw it for a moment superimposed on an image of the café, then both were gone, and she was back in her studio, with Moriah studying her quizzically.

"I can't paint Dizengoff," she said.

"Not Dizengoff. Nevo."

"Nevo is on Dizengoff."

"On it, but not of it. Don't you know the café, Sarita?"

"I've passed by it. I know my parents used to sit there."

"Then you know it's a special place, not your standard Dizengoff café. It's loaded with atmosphere."

"Do you sit there?"

"*Me?*" Moriah said scornfully, caught off guard. "I wouldn't be caught dead there." Sarita laughed. "It's not my scene, but so what? Nevo has character. You could do it."

"I don't know that I like the idea of painting someone else's idea. I don't know if it's possible."

Moriah waved a bejeweled hand dismissively. "You think what you do is original? Let me tell you, my dear, that there is nothing in your work that you have not taken from other artists, and don't be offended, it's not only you. All art is derivative; if it weren't, no one would understand it. So what does it matter if the idea for a subject comes from outside you, as long as it's appropriate?

"Besides," she added, "can you afford to turn down eight hundred dollars?"

Sarita said wonderingly, "Who would pay so much?"

"An admirer," said Moriah, and added in response to Sarita's look, "Of your work, my dear, of your work."

"If you don't tell me who it is, I won't do it."

At last Moriah admitted that she did not know. A letter had arrived, with a bank check for $500 payable to Sarita Blume. She produced the letter.

The handwriting was small and spidery, the language unusually formal. "If Miss Sarita Blume will undertake this commission," it read, "I will pay $1,000 for a single painting of Café Nevo on Dizengoff. I would wish the painting to be realistic, faithful to the tone of the café and its constituents. It will, therefore, be necessary for Miss Blume to spend some time in the café before composing her work. The enclosed check is a retainer, to be cashed if she accepts the commission. The remaining sum will be paid upon completion of the painting."

It was signed: "With all good wishes, Yours sincerely, An art lover."

The mystery, the challenge of discovering the art lover, and the money all attracted Sarita; what repelled was the prospect of sitting in that seedy old café for hours and days on end by herself. So she did not, despite Moriah's urging, deposit the check immediately, but went the following Friday to test the waters of Nevo.

By choosing Friday, Sarita meant to try herself. She went early and was in time to get a table inside the café, near the bar, where she could observe without (she hoped) being unduly observed herself. The old chess players goggled, and the waiter looked at her curiously but took her order for coffee with reasonable grace. The café filled up slowly, and people did stare openly; but no one came over. She wondered, once or twice, if the waiter had said something to keep them away but decided he hadn't; why should he?

Because she was too shy to meet the eyes around her, she sketched instead, then studied the sketch closely. There was something there. Those faces, so proprietary, so at home, that they hinted at the existence of a closed and integral society; that precise positioning of chairs in just such a way as to attain maximum exposure while maintaining anchorage to a particular table; the faint indications of an elaborate and formal structure beneath the formless meandering on the surface: Nevo was like some great puzzle whose pieces wandered around of their own accord. When Sarita realized that the point of the picture would be to decipher the puzzle and paint the pieces in their proper places, she knew she had accepted the commission.

Chapter Five

"THEN I quit," Arik said.

"Quit if you must, but not till you cool off."

"You're cool enough for both of us. You know, you surprise me, man. I thought, I come to Seltzer with a problem like this, he's going to help out. He's got the resources. And you do, you bastard. You just don't have the will."

"We don't have the resources, Arik. That's what I've been trying to tell you. Do you know what it costs to run a club like that? Not to mention your salary, which presumably you want paid."

"This party has branches all over the country. You can't plead poverty."

"We're not going to close branches to support your project. Be reasonable. If we put every cent we have into the youth center, it wouldn't be enough, and there'd be nothing left to continue the struggle."

"What struggle?" Arik howled. "The struggle to look yourself in the face every morning? The way you're going it's no wonder you're losing it. You're so in love with the means you've completely lost sight of the end."

"Arik, Arik," Seltzer sighed. "So impetuous, so like your father in his youth, before he sold out to Labor."

"I don't want to talk about my father, and you're in a poor position to talk about selling out."

But Seltzer, warming to the subject, said, "Why don't you talk to *him*? If anyone can raise the money, he can. It would be small change to Labor. Or he could shake down that fat kibbutz of his."

"You hypocrite. What happened to all that crap you've been handing out these past months, about the natural alliance between Sheli and Mitria? All that heart-rending rhetoric about saving their black, Likud-tainted souls and showing them the light? The minute it looks like costing more than talk, you're ready to toss the whole package over to Labor."

David Seltzer was an owlish man of fifty-six. He had a headful of gray curls, beady brown eyes, eloquent hands, and a smoker's cough. He'd been a Hagana comrade of Arik's father, Uri Eshel, and though their political paths had diverged, they'd remained close friends. Arik liked him anyway, or had until today. David Seltzer spread his hands and leaned forward.

"I'm not tossing them away. You've done great things with those kids, Arik, great things. Until you came along, they were nothing but hoodlums; in the course of one year you not only had them organized but had them organizing others. The wonder of it is not that you got fired but that the Ministry took so long about it. Believe it or not, my friend, your firing and the closing of the Jaffa Youth Center are very good signs. It shows they're getting frightened. They're striking out at our alliance."

"What alliance?" Arik hooted. "And who is this 'they' you think you're scaring? Sheli is just a bunch of tired, ineffectual old coots waving red banners they can hardly lift anymore. I've got sorry news for you, buddy: you and your friends couldn't scare a fly. Aw, for God's sake, Seltzer." Arik sat down beside him and took his arm lightly. "I'm not talking altruism here. I know better than that. Saving that center would be the political brainstorm of the century. It would demonstrate once and for all the thing that most people doubt: that Sheli doesn't just talk, it acts, it fights! And with the same stroke you'd win yourselves the loyalty of those kids, who've got more energy in their little fingers than you have in your whole organization."

"You've made a persuasive case, Arik. I wish we had the funds to do it."

In one fluid and furious movement Arik rose and crossed to the door. "Then to hell with you. I've had it with you and your hopeless bunch of crazy dreamers and wishers and wouldn't-it-be-nicers. You can go on playing your games, Seltzer. I've got work to do."

Slamming the door behind him, Arik stepped onto Bograshov Street. I had to do it, he thought. What an asshole hypocrite Seltzer turned out to be. But outside in the cool clear night, Arik felt a heavy fog of bereavement settling in over yet another parting. Then Coby appeared out of nowhere and sidled up to him. He looked up at Arik's face and shrugged knowingly. "I told you."

"Get off my back, Coby."

"What'd he say?"

"He wished us luck."

"Fucking prick!" exploded Coby. "What did I tell you? But no, you had to go running to your *vus-vus* friends, begging for handouts. Don't you have no pride, man? You know something? If they came to us on their knees with a sackful of greenbacks, I'd shove it right up their asses."

"It ain't gonna happen," Arik said, turning up Reines toward Dizengoff with Coby dancing by his side.

Coby was small and fast, taut and mean as barbed wire. At seventeen, when Arik first met him, he was the youngest warlord in his gang's history. Coby had resisted the youth center longer and harder than anyone else. His primary tactic was to heap ridicule on Arik: his illustrious first and last names, his kibbutz background, race, faggot profession (social worker), and general ignorance of the world according to Coby. "Golden boy" he called Arik, who hated the name.

The ragging didn't stop until Arik finally lost his temper and swung at him. Coby swung back, aiming for the face. He blackened one eye and drew blood before Arik flattened him with a combination that came out of nowhere. When Coby came up fighting, Arik kicked the legs out from under him. Then he saved Coby's face by walking away first, saying he'd had enough.

Arik got a professional fighter, a friend of his, to give clinics in the center. Coby couldn't pass it up. Eventually he took Arik under his wing, treating the older man like a slightly impaired younger brother with a woeful lack of street smarts. Of all Arik's kids Coby had taken the news of the center's closing the hardest. He blamed Arik.

As they entered Dizengoff Circle, Coby was still complaining vociferously. "We never should have got involved with those bozos in the first place. That bunch of *vus-vus* politicians: what did they ever do for us? They just wanted to use us. Hey, why don't you say something? What's the matter with you, cat got your tongue?"

"What do you want me to say, I fucked up? Okay, I fucked up. You're right, we never should have joined that coalition. That's what made them close us down. My stupidity."

"Hey, lighten up, man. We'll raise the money. We'll run the goddamn place ourselves with no fucking Welfare Ministry breathing down our necks. We'll hire you ourselves." He thought about that and laughed. "That'll be something. I'll be your boss. 'Hey, Arik honey, make me some coffee.' "

Arik said, "Where are you going to raise that kind of

money? Selling cookies?" Two girls in mini-skirts passed by, giggling arm-in-arm. Arik and Coby paused to look back. With his eyes on one of them Coby said, "We'll raise it." Then he laughed.

Outside Nevo Arik stopped. "I feel like being by myself for a while. I'll catch you later."

"Where're you going?" Coby asked.

"Nowhere," Arik said, and turned into Nevo.

A half dozen old men were hunched over chess sets, and mad Muny drank alone in a corner. Sternholz was perched behind the bar, reading a book. He noticed Arik come in but did not bestir himself except to say, "You again?"

"I thought you liked me, Sternholz."

The waiter snorted.

"Can I have a coffee?"

"You got money?"

"What if I don't? You going to refuse me coffee?"

"No, but I'll send the bill to your—"

"Don't say it!"

A small smile of enjoyment flickered over the old man's whiskery face. When Sternholz brought the coffee over, with an extra cup for himself, Arik noticed that he was all dressed up. Under his great white apron he wore pressed black pants, a fine ivory-toned shirt, shiny black shoes, and, wonder of wonders, a tie. The shoes were a relief to Arik. Lately, Sternholz had taken to wearing his bedroom slippers in the café. On the kibbutz, when old people began appearing unshod for meals, it meant their time was near. Sternholz claimed he was just saving his feet, but Arik didn't like it. One day slippers, the next a cane, then a wheelchair, and finally they tipped you in your grave and tossed dirt in your face. Sternholz shuffling around in mules brought an unwelcome whiff of mortality into the café: for if Nevo had one redeeming quality, it was permanence.

Sternholz spread the wings of his apron and settled stiffly onto a chair.

"So," he said ponderously. "Have you found a job?"

"I'm not even looking. I told you I'm going abroad."

"Yeah, yeah. You got your ticket yet?"

Arik gave him a sour look. "Goddamn, this place is dead, Sternholz."

"Some people have better things to do than sit around cafés all night, wasting money they don't have. Some people have to get up for work in the morning."

"Not your customers." Arik eyed the old man. "What are you all dressed up for?"

Sternholz puffed his cheeks belligerently. "Today happens to be my anniversary."

Although it was common knowledge that Sternholz had lost his wife and child in Germany, he never talked about them, or indeed about his life before Nevo. First Arik blinked and looked away. Then, with an effort, he leaned toward the waiter, opening his mouth to speak, but Sternholz forestalled him.

"Forty-five years in Nevo," he said with dour pride, as a jailer might say, Forty-five years in Sing-Sing. "Forty-five years to the day."

Arik relaxed. "Buck up, old man. Maybe you'll get a remission for good behavior."

"Very funny. Where will you be in forty-five years?"

"I'd hate to know."

"Wandering? Drifting? Blowing around the world like a tumbleweed?" There was an outcry across the room as one of the old chess players checkmated his opponent. The kibitzers murmured approval, and the loser gave way. The board was reset. Sternholz's voice whispered low in Arik's ear. "Look at those poor, homeless men."

Arik's jaw jutted forward, and he cocked his head. It was a mannerism inherited from his father, which he disliked but could not shed. "Lay off," he growled. "I'm in no mood tonight. I just quit Sheli."

"You're getting good at quitting."

"Lay off, I said!"

"First the kibbutz, then the army, now Sheli."

"I thought you didn't like Sheli."

"I didn't say I disliked them, I just said they were losers. That's got nothing to do with it. The point is, you don't quit every time some little thing doesn't go your way."

"I quit the army over Lebanon. That was no little thing."

"You've got great principles, kid," the waiter sneered.

"What is it with you, Sternholz? You were all in favor of my leaving the army."

"It's getting to be a bad habit with you. What are you going to quit next, the human race?"

Arik sighed. "Leave me alone, old man."

"Have it your own way." Sternholz sniffed. "Do what you want. Run away. Join the circus. Desert the ship. Just don't come crying to me, forty-five years from now."

Later, much later, Emmanuel Yehoshua Sternholz rested in his armchair overlooking the sea, and reached down to stroke a dog that wasn't there. Seven years had passed since the dog died, but Sternholz's hand remembered even to flinch. Old Red nipped him half the time. Sternholz had the only bad-tempered Irish setter ever bred, the dog's cantankerous character an argument for the primacy of nurture over nature. Red used to wander the café at will, baring his teeth at some customers, nipping the heels of others, protected from retaliation by the jealous eye of his owner, who would not hesitate to eject anyone suspected of interfering with his dog. Sternholz's better half Muny called him, but Red and Sternholz had the last laugh when Red took a bite out of Muny's ass that kept the poet on his feet for a week. Remembering, Sternholz laughed aloud. Muny had borne no grudges. A few weeks after Red died, he showed up at Nevo with a purebred Dalmatian pup in his pocket, claiming he'd found it. Sternholz was moved but refused the gift. He told Muny it was because he'd never find a dog who'd suit him as well as Red; but later, over whiskey, he admitted to himself the real reason, that he couldn't bear another loss.

The sun was rising. The sea grew softly luminescent. It was Sabbath morn; the city would sleep late. Bird cries filled the air. When Sternholz was young the city was full of terns, sea gulls, and long-legged sandpipers, but they left long ago. Now there were starlings, sparrows, and pigeons, city scavengers.

But Sternholz was not a bird-watcher, just an insomniac. His thoughts returned to the subject that had occupied them all night. If Arik leaves, Sternholz will feel it. Why must he suffer the loss of other people's children? Was it punishment for having lost his own? And how could Uri have been so careless as to let the boy slip away? The way of fathers and sons was a dimly remembered lesson for Sternholz, barely begun before it ended, but still he wondered: how could Uri have lost the boy? No paucity of love there, no matter how rough its expression. It was the life-sustaining tenet of Sternholz's faith that love is absorbed by its object even when the lover, not knowing how little time is given, has stinted on expression.

Perhaps, he thought, they are too much alike. Perhaps if opposites attract, then affinities repel. That would explain why Uri and Arik Eshel, who should by temperament as well as relationship have been the best of friends, could not sit ten minutes in the same room together. For they were very much alike, though not physically; the same hot and restless heart, the same desperate energy informed them. Men whose most vital needs were not food and water but work and opposition, the Eshels took not at all to peace and prosperity; but give them a war, a drought, a plague of malaria, or an uprising in the ranks, and they were content. No wonder Arik can't go home, Sternholz thought, and realized his own mistake in urging it on him. Uri Eshel made that kibbutz. With his bare hands (though not alone) he drained the swamps, cleared the land, built the buildings; and if you asked him why, he'd say he did it for his son. Never mind that it wasn't true, never mind that Uri struggled for the sheer joyous hell of struggling and winning. The point was that Arik was too like him to value anything but what he could do and build himself.

So much Sternholz could understand, and yet he felt that so much love, so truly given, ought not to disappear. Was not love energy, and conservation of energy a natural law? There was a bond; where was it now? Sternholz remembered the brit, remembered Uri Eshel in a clean set of kibbutz work clothes, standing in a young apple orchard under the clear blue sky, his wife beside him and his comrades all around, cradling his first-born tenderly in his arms, bending his massive neck to croon a lullaby. When the mohel cut, and the infant screamed, and the Rabbi spoke the words that brought the man-child into the Covenant, then Uri Eshel wept, and Sternholz, too. Hear O Israel.

Chapter Six

The announcement on the hourly radio newscast that seven more soldiers had died in Lebanon cast a deep pall over Nevo. Only three people, a man and two women whose language and appearance declared them American tourists, continued to converse.

"Where *is* that waiter?"

"He must be deaf."

"Selectively deaf, if you ask me. This is ridiculous. Call him again, Harvey."

"Waiter!"

"Are you addressing me?" Sternholz said, his English as stiff as his back.

"You *are* the waiter, aren't you?"

"I am," he replied loftily.

The man sat between two plump women, who propped him up like matching bookends. "How about some service?"

he demanded, quivering like indignant jelly. "We've been sitting here for half an hour already."

"This is Friday afternoon."

"I know that."

"I'm busy." There was no hint of apology in this observation, which was delivered in a tone of marked disapproval.

"But we were here first," said one woman. "You served those people, and we were here before them." She wore a flowered dress, girlishly styled, of some material that looked like parachute silk. Sternholz ignored her and addressed the man's left eyebrow.

"There's a nice juice bar one block down. You should drink some fresh juice. Excuse me."

Prodded by two elbows, Harvey jumped up into his path. "I want to see the manager."

Caspi and Rami Dotan were sitting at the next table, sniggering as they followed the exchange. Sternholz said with dignity, "The manager is out."

"When will he be in?"

The old man shrugged.

"He ought to be told," the flowered woman said. "The service here is so bad, they're losing good customers."

The other clicked her tongue. "When you think of the millions of hard-earned dollars that have been poured into this country, and then, when you come here, they treat you like dirt!"

For the first time Sternholz looked directly at the women. "You don't like the service here?"

"No, we certainly don't."

"I don't blame you. So go someplace else," the waiter said, and he walked away.

"Well, I *never!*"

"It's disgraceful!"

"I've a good mind to come back here and tell the

owner," Harvey said. He turned to Caspi. "Can you tell me, sir, when the owner usually comes around?"

"I don't believe I've ever seen the owner," Caspi replied. "Have you, Rami?"

"Once, about ten years ago. But he was here for only a few minutes before they came to take him away."

"They're pulling your leg, Harvey. Let's go."

Just then Muny came bustling out. The poet, drunk as usual, had put on an old apron of Sternholz's. He staggered up to the tourists' curb-side table.

"I," said Muny, striking his chest, "am the proprietor of this humble establishment. How may I serve you?"

"If you're the proprietor," the man said, "I'm Peter Pan."

"*Well*," said Muny, simpering, "if you're Peter Pan, I'm Tinker Bell." Throwing himself onto the man's lap, he twined his arms around his neck and gave him a resounding smack on the cheek.

The flowered woman gasped; her friend broke into nervous titters. Caspi and Rami howled. Harvey pushed Muny off his lap and stood up. Face flaming, he glared about him in a manner that, despite all, did not lack dignity. Sternholz appeared as if by magic.

"You should be ashamed," the tourist said. Under stress his voice had taken on the cadences of Yiddish.

Sternholz said urgently: "He's a drunken idiot. I apologize. Sit, please. I'll serve you now."

"Go to hell," the man said, and walked away.

The laughter died as Sternholz glared fiercely about him, like a stern teacher who's returned to find his class in an uproar. "You," he said, pointing at Caspi, "you ought to be ashamed. And Muny, you've had it here. I'm cutting you off."

"Not that, guvner!" Muny clutched the waiter's knees. "Anything but that!"

Sternholz reached down and lifted Muny to his feet with a single gnarled hand. "I mean it. I don't want to see you for a week."

"Come on, Sternholz," Caspi interceded. "You started it."

Sternholz turned on him. "*I* did not humiliate those people. It didn't hurt them to be mad at me. *You* made fools of them."

"He didn't mean any harm, Sternholz," Dory said soothingly.

"It's *Mr.* Sternholz to you, young woman. And don't tell me what Caspi meant. I've known him a damn sight longer than you have, and he's never meant anything but trouble and pain."

"Strong words," Caspi said with an awkward laugh.

Rami put in quickly: "Cool off, Sternholz. Caspi is a great writer, and you should be honored to have his patronage."

"Great writer my ass! Bialik was a great writer. Appelfeld, Amichai, Yehoshua are great writers. Caspi is a pornographer, and not even a great pornographer."

Rami opened his mouth indignantly, but Caspi laid a silencing hand on his arm. "Have you read my work, Emmanuel?"

"Would I say that if I hadn't?"

"And you really believe my novels are pornographic?"

The question was asked seriously. Sternholz sat down at Caspi's table, his great white apron jingling as he did. He leaned forward and spoke softly.

"*Fucking Toward Jerusalem. The Great White Lay.* What kind of titles are those?"

"They sell books."

"Money, money, money. You can't have it both ways, Caspi. You want to write shlock, write shlock. But don't call it art." A bony finger poked at Caspi's chest. "You're talented, Caspi, I'll give you that. You command the language. But what do you command it to do? You can't write out of character, and you know what your character is. It's not enough to be clever, my friend. To be a great writer, you have to first be a *mensch*."

"Bull."

"It's true. You should have been a painter or a musician; then your character wouldn't have shown. Look at Wagner: one of the devil's own, but he wrote music like an angel. Or Picasso—he was a dirty old man, but that never hurt his work; maybe it even helped. But it hurts yours. Writers expose themselves."

Caspi did not answer. He glared at Sternholz, who glared back. Rami Dotan interceded.

"You're full of shit, Sternholz. Peter Caspi outsells Yehoshua and Oz; he sells more than Amichai and Appelfeld put together."

"Shut up, Rami," Caspi said disgustedly.

"You know what I'm saying," the waiter said, nodding.

"Go away, Emmanuel. Go do your job, and leave me to do mine."

Sternholz stood up. "You asked," he said, with surprising gentleness. "You don't want to hear, don't ask."

THREE O'CLOCK

"Emmanuel," said the Minister, "who is that girl sketching over there? Her face is so familiar, but I can't think who she is."

"Sarita Blume," the waiter said shortly.

"Blume. My God, is that Yael Blume's daughter?"

"Yes."

"Good Lord. Ask her to come over here."

"No."

The Minister gave the waiter a quick, diagnostic glance and smiled.

"You again?"

"Good to see you, too, Sternholz." Arik was bright-eyed but unshaven, wearing the same clothes he'd worn the day before, which to one of Sternholz's practical experience meant only one thing. Indeed, he had the air of one freshly arisen; whereas Sternholz had spent a near-sleepless night on his account. The old man had planned a Talk with Arik, a tactful Talk. But his reserves of tact, limited to begin with, were quite unequal to the sight of Arik's bright and chipper face. He therefore said with great irritation, "I don't want you hanging around here like a bum."

"Where do you want me to sit?" Arik inquired cheerfully. "At Rowal or the Sabra?"

"I don't want you to sit anywhere. I want you to get off your ass."

"What has gotten into you, Sternholz? This is getting out of hand. I'm not doing any harm, I'm paying for my drinks, so what's your problem?"

"My problem is, since when is not doing any harm good enough for you?"

"I am just filling in time until I go abroad."

"Still with this going abroad business. What you need, Arik Eshel, is work."

"I told you, I'm not looking for a job."

"I didn't say a job! I said *work*."

Arik looked upward. "God, what did I do to deserve this?"

"You don't want to hear what I think," Sternholz said angrily, "don't come into my home."

"This isn't your home, Sternholz. It's a café."

"It's my home!" the old man insisted. "And I'll tell you something else. This country is *your* home, and if you leave it, you'll never find another." He stomped off, leaving Arik mystified. Why was Sternholz taking on so? What did he care if Arik left? Everyone else was; half the people Arik knew had left or were planning to, and why not? The world was large. A man was not a tree, needing roots to live. A man was free to wander. So thought Arik, but as he did, as he saw himself wandering freely, a pain as sharp as treachery pierced through him and was gone.

Feeling himself observed, Arik leaned toward Sarita. "Did you hear that?" he asked.

She continued to look at, but did not seem to see him. Her face was set in a child-like expression of deep, exclusive concentration, focused not on but through Arik. Then, without acknowledging him in any way, she looked down at her pad and began to sketch.

Watching her profile, Arik surprised in himself an oddly chaste ambition: that she would someday look and *see* him.

FOUR O'CLOCK

"I thought we had an understanding, Vered."

"What about, Caspi?"

"About your coming to Nevo. Don't you realize how pathetic you look, hanging on to my coattails like this?"

"I don't feel pathetic. In fact, I feel pretty good."

"I won't have you coming around here, bothering me!"

"I'm not bothering you, you're bothering me. Why don't you just go back to your friends and sit down quietly?"

"Get out of here, bitch. This is the last warning you get from me."

She laughed up at him.

Caspi turned white. He gripped the back of a chair.

"Why don't you go home where you belong? Make some dinner. Or if that's too much effort, go sit in Stern with your sniveling critic friends. You don't belong here."

"You can't keep me out of Nevo," Vered said. "No one can. Besides, I have an appointment."

Caspi snarled, "Who with?"

"None of your business."

"What's with you two?" Sternholz said, coming between them. "You should behave yourselves here."

"Tell this person to stop harassing me," Vered said.

"You should have told him yourself, ten years ago. Not here, not now, do you understand?" Though Caspi was taller, Sternholz enraged seemed to tower over them both. "We don't do family therapy here. This is not a divorce court or a television studio. *Ach*, you two are making me crazy. Caspi, go sit down."

Caspi obeyed.

Ilana, sitting alone at the next table, made no pretense of not having heard but looked at Vered and said directly, "You're a brave woman."

Vered smiled. Ilana had been one of Caspi's countless lovers; the affair was atypical for both and ended as quickly as it began. Vered knew, but for some reason that she did not understand, she felt no animus toward this one. "Not brave," she said. "Desperate."

Ilana hesitated, then moved her chair closer to Vered's. "Caspi strikes me as the type of man to take his unhappiness out on his family."

"I can take care of myself and the child."

"Of course you can. I'm sorry if I offended you. It's really none of my business."

"You didn't offend me," Vered said. The two women smiled rather shyly at one another. Then Vered went back to her paper, and Ilana turned away.

. . .

"Hey, Coby," said Arik.

"I can't believe you're still hanging out here." The boy danced on his toes. Arik shoved a chair at him.

"You know I quit Sheli," he said.

"Big fucking deal."

"How are the guys?"

"Back on the street. Yossi got his draft notice, but he's not going."

"How not?"

"Easy. The jerk can't read."

"That goddamn idiot, the army's his one chance not to be a bum all his life. What the hell's the matter with you guys, letting him get away with that?"

"Well, what'd you expect?" Coby shrugged Gallically. "If he goes in now he can kiss his ass goodbye. They'll have him in the Lebanese swamp before he knows what day it is."

Arik nodded, his face a misery. Coby drummed the table with his fingertips and cracked his knuckles. "So what's with you?" he demanded uneasily. "You get a job, or what?"

"I'm going abroad."

Coby sneered. "That's rich. Golden boy goes to Europe, or is it America?"

"I don't know."

"Well, that's great, man. Have yourself a sweet vacation, and don't forget to send us a postcard."

"It's not a vacation. I'm breaking out."

The boy looked at him uncertainly. Then he changed the subject. "Hey, I meant what I said about the center. We're going to open it up again. We're going to get the money ourselves."

"How are you going to do that?"

Coby leaned forward. "I'll tell you one thing. We're not selling cookies."

"You're going to get yourselves in trouble."

"What's it to you, anyway? You're jumping ship, right?"

"Right!" Arik shouted. They glared at one another.

Slowly the anger abated. Arik looked away first, half smiling, rubbing his face.

"Hey," Coby said, "you need a shave. In fact, you look like shit, man."

"You better tell me what's up, Coby, so I can figure out what the bail's going to be."

Coby lowered his long lashes. "You'll love it," he said. "It's political."

"What are you talking about?"

"We're going to practice what you *vus-vus* politicians preach: socialism in action."

Arik's mouth twisted. "You're going to rip someone off."

"For the general good."

"Who do you think you are, goddamn Robin Hood?"

"Who's Robin Hood, some *vus-vus* politician?"

"Who's Robin Hood? Jesus Christ, Coby, you ought to try going to school once in a while. And why don't you drop the *vus-vus* shit; it's me you're insulting, you stupid *frank*."

"Jokes aside, man, are you in or out?"

"Are you serious? You really think I'd get involved in some dumb-ass plot that's bound to fail just when I am on the point of getting out of this madhouse?" He lowered his voice. "Who are you hitting?"

"I thought you might have some ideas."

Arik dropped back in his chair. "You really thought I'd do it?"

"Well, it's for a cause, isn't it? Your type are big on causes. When are you leaving?"

"I don't know; soon," Arik said impatiently. "You realize you're going to get caught."

"Not if we plan it right. What we need is a good organizer, a detail man, maybe someone with a military background. Know anybody like that?"

A new black Mercedes pulled up to the curb and

parked, in splendid disregard for the law. Pincas Gordon followed his stomach out into the open air.

"Damn," said Sternholz to himself.

"Hello, Caspi," Pincas said, slapping his shoulder. "How're they hanging?"

"Fuck off."

"Just being friendly." Pincas strolled around the café. If the tourists had still been there, they would have taken him for the owner. He paused beside Sarita. "Hello there, little girl. What a pretty picture." Sarita covered the sketch with her hand, giving him a stricken look. Arik stood and stepped toward Pincas, but the fat man was already moving on.

"Vered, darling! Back so soon, and all by your lonesome?" She turned the page of her paper and went on reading. Pincas looked around, sharing his enjoyment of the rebuff, basking in his unpopularity. He spied the Minister sitting in an ill-lit corner and walked over.

"Good afternoon, Mr. Brenner."

"Mr. Gordon," the Minister said coldly.

"I hoped I'd see you here. I left a few messages, but your secretary must have forgotten to pass them on. You just can't get decent help these days, can you?" He took a seat at the table. "Mind if I join you?"

"Do you know why I come here, Mr. Gordon?"

"Slumming?" Pincas suggested jovially.

"I come here to enjoy some quiet time by myself."

Pincas shook his head sympathetically. "I know just what you mean. It's the same with me. All week long, rush, rush, rush, and then on the weekend the kids are all over me. Friday afternoons are really the only time a man can call his soul his own. You know, in any other café I'd be swamped with people trying to muscle in on my action. Nevo's the only place where you can count on meeting no one of importance." After a moment he added, "Yourself excluded, of course."

"Goodbye, Gordon," said the Minister.

"You're not going already?"

"No; you are."

"Oh, but I haven't said what I wanted to talk to you about." He lowered his voice, effectively silencing all the tables around them. "It's about Keter Shomron."

"There's no such place," the Minister said forbiddingly. His eyes searched for Sternholz, but the waiter was occupied elsewhere. Nevo's other inhabitants had grown suspiciously quiet and were leaning toward his table like plants toward the sun.

"Not yet there's not, but I have information that says there soon will be, as soon as the Ministerial Committee on Settlement pulls its collective thumb out. I am interested in seeing the settlement approved."

"You're way out of line, sir. I'm going to have to ask you to leave." It might seem odd to an outsider that the Minister, who was obviously unhappy with the public conversation, which he knew had already gone so far as to constitute a minor scandal and which would even perhaps find its way into some paper, did not just up and leave. But leaving Nevo under duress was something one simply did not do. Nevo was a place where events and chance meetings broke over one's head like waves. One could duck or jump them, but swimming for shore was not one of the options, not unless one chose to opt out completely.

Pincas winked conspiratorially. "Frankly, I've cornered most of the land there myself, but there are still a few nice lots available, if anyone was interested."

"You're committing a crime."

"Where's the crime in a chat between friends—and colleagues?"

"You're also making a very foolish mistake."

"I'm not worried. Think it over, Minister. Leave word soon." He lowered his voice. "I'm tying up a prime lot next week that's got your name on it if you want it—or rather, your son-in-law's name."

"No one in my family is interested in any dealings with you."

"Any more dealings, you mean. Well, I'm sorry to hear that, I really am. But I do hope we'll see that settlement approved shortly. It would be a great step toward the Judaization of Judea and Samaria."

"How very patriotic of you," said the Minister.

"Who is that pig?" asked Coby.

Arik's face was bleak with rage. He said, "That bastard owns half the West Bank . . . half the fucking Cabinet, too."

Vered had abandoned her paper and was busy scribbling notes.

Sternholz made purposefully for the Minister's table, but as he approached, Pincas stood and tipped an imaginary hat. "Have a nice day," he said, and walked away.

FIVE O'CLOCK

"May I look?" asked the waiter.

Sarita looked up with eyes that took a moment to focus. When they did, she glanced down at the pad on her lap, studied her work with a puzzled air, and then said shyly, "You can if you like," and held the sketch so that only he could see it.

Sternholz looked, blinked, took out a pair of steel-rimmed reading glasses from a shirt pocket, polished them and put them on, looked again, and said, "Good God."

"Who is it?" Sarita whispered.

"Don't you know?"

She pointed to the only woman in the picture. "I know that's my mother."

"That's her. And that's your father on her right."

"And who's this?" She touched the man who sat on her mother's left, leaning toward her and saying something that made her laugh.

Sternholz bent his old head down to hers. "That's Uri Eshel, maybe thirty years ago. You can see the resemblance to his son, over there. Sarita"—he used her name for the first time—"how did you do that?"

She shrugged like a truculent child. Her finger touched the man who hovered behind the trio, his eyes fixed on the woman. "You didn't say who that was."

"That's the waiter," Sternholz said, a trifle glumly.

"He hasn't changed much," Sarita said, studying the picture closely. "I know what he's thinking."

"What?"

She laughed up at him with a touch of her mother's gay wickedness. The suddenly amplified resemblance made his old heart ache. "The waiter is thinking he waited too long," she said.

Rami Dotan, who sat facing the street, suddenly straightened and said, "Look who's coming. I told you you should never have brought him here."

"Khalil," said Caspi, surprised.

"You didn't invite him?"

"Hell, no. We spent the morning fighting over the contents of the anthology. He's a stubborn bastard and a real chauvinist. I'm surprised he would come here; I assumed he went back to Nablus. Maybe he thought of something else to tell me."

Khalil parked his BMW at the curb, and entered the café like a fox prowling in the dark of night, hungry but also wary of larger predators. Head held still, chin high, eyes active. He saw Caspi and nodded. Caspi gestured toward a chair, but Khalil walked the other way, into the inner room of the café. Rami Dotan and Caspi exchanged puzzled glances and turned to watch him. He padded softly up to Vered's table. She looked up, closed her pad, stood, and offered him her hand. "Son of a bitch," Caspi exploded. Khalil kissed Vered's hand, and they sat down together.

"*Oy vey,*" sighed Sternholz.

Chapter Seven

"I KNOW what you're doing."

Vered looked at him.

"I don't mind. But I want you to know that I know."

The assertion created a pocket of intimacy. She said, "Why don't you mind then?"

Khalil showed his teeth, and a fine, even set they were. "I have scores to settle."

"With Caspi?"

"Among others."

Sternholz hobbled over to their table and stood beside Vered. "Enough already," he said to her. "Go home."

"Emmanuel Sternholz, Khalil Mussara," she said.

Automatically the old man stuck out his hand. When Khalil's was in it, he said earnestly, "This isn't nice, what you're doing here."

"Isn't he the waiter?" Khalil asked.

"Of course I'm the waiter; who'd you think I am, Kubla Khan?"

"Bring us some coffee, please," Vered said.

"We're all out," Sternholz said, and stalked off. Khalil stared after him with knowing eyes.

"He doesn't like my coming here," Vered apologized. "It's not you. Sternholz is no racist."

Khalil shrugged. "In this country the only non-racists are fools and hypocrites. If this were Nablus or Hebron and you were an Arab woman sitting with a Jew, do you know what would happen to you?"

"What?"

"You'd die."

"You say that as if you approve."

"Of course. Every morning I pray that education has not distorted my understanding or diluted my blood so that if I ever caught my sister with a Jew I would fail to do the honorable thing."

"How—"

"Barbaric?" Khalil smiled. "You agree with your husband, then. He thinks I am an ape in man's clothing."

"I agree with Caspi about nothing," Vered said. (Khalil's eyes gleamed beneath lowered lashes.) "I object to your regarding your sister's life as your property."

"Your feminism has no application in our world. Men do not free their women before they themselves are free. The Jews stole our homes and our nation. Should we let them cut off our balls as well?"

"Whose balls are you attacking?"

"You chose the place, Mrs. Caspi, and the time."

She was silent.

"Understand me, Vered." Khalil leaned forward and boldly, under the eyes of her husband and all of Nevo, took her hand. "I don't mind playing games, especially with such an attractive and sensual partner. But I know the rules, and I always play to win. By meeting me here and now, you've announced to the world that you're cuckolding your husband with a colleague of his—worse yet, an Arab. I am far from offended; I am delighted to have been chosen. But it would be most dishonorable if, having made the announcement, you were to fail in the consummation."

Without moving, Vered withdrew, hiding behind her sunglasses. Convinced of her own secret cowardice, she feared its discovery by others. But Khalil, an Arab in the Jews' country, knew all the disguises of fear. He pressed his challenge home.

"Right now," he murmured, leaning toward her, "your husband is telling himself you wouldn't dare. Are you going to prove him right?"

"What my husband thinks is no concern of mine."

"No? Then take the first step. Come with me."

"Where?"

"To a place where we can discuss Arab-Israeli relations in private."

"You think I'm afraid?"

He smiled.

"All right," she said. "Let's go." She preceded him, passing Caspi by without a glance. Khalil opened the door of his BMW with a flourish. Vered got in, and they drove away.

"Never mind, darling. It happens to every man sometimes. The important thing is not to worry about it." Dory blew a kiss and walked naked into the bathroom, shutting the door behind her.

"Shit," said Caspi. "Hell and damnation." It was the first time he'd ever failed, and it boded ill; take away his virility, and what was left? Dory's advice-column patter made him feel worse, reduced to the ranks of Everyman.

The fault manifestly lay with Vered. Caspi was on top of Dory, poised for penetration, when suddenly a vision of Vered and Khalil similarly situated flashed before his eyes. He shriveled instantly. As Dory opened her eyes quizzically, he ground himself savagely against her, but it was no good.

Rolling off, he covered himself with a sheet and endured her attempts at commiseration. He knew she would be on the phone before he was out the door. "Oh, Caspi," Caspi groaned, "how the mighty have fallen."

Driving home, he planned his chastisement of Vered. The provocation, the deliberate outrage could not go unremarked, lest she be driven to still greater extremes; but restraint would be the key, moderation the tone of his reproach. His attitude would be that of a rational man coping kindly with an irrational wife, an approach calculated to drive her mad. He would not give her the pleasure of referring to the race of her cohort. Why should he? What was it to him if she chose to sit in Nevo, with an Arab, on a Friday afternoon, when all of his, Caspi's, friends and enemies congregated? And then to leave with the Arab. Waltz past him without a glance, as if he weren't there, and get into that car, which a third-rate pseudo-intellectual A-rab poet had no business owning. No, he decided, the race thing didn't bother him. He ran a light.

Not for a moment did Caspi believe that her betrayal had gone further than display. But if it had, if she really were sleeping with that Arab whelp of a syphilitic dog, he'd slaughter the bitch.

Of course, race aside, one had to allow that Khalil's behavior had been reprehensible. You don't work all morning with a colleague, shoulder to shoulder, then meet his wife in his own café. Among civilized people it couldn't happen. But then Khalil, for all his literary claims and educational pretensions, sprung from primitive stock, one generation removed from peasants who bought and sold their women. In a way, that made his crime the greater. As women were a form of currency in the primitive Arab mentality, it followed that Khalil was an embezzler. As women were chattel, Khalil was a rustler. As women were the ground on which men built their lives, Khalil was a trespasser. Any way you looked at it, the Arab was an outlaw.

Caspi drew up in front of his house, surprised to see that the apartment was dark. He'd expected a penitent little light showing somewhere, most likely in the kitchen, as Vered calibrated her sorrows in cups of coffee. Caspi ran upstairs, threw open the apartment door, and bellowed her name.

There was no reply.

He peeked into the open door of his son's room. The little bed was neatly made, and the tattered monkey that was Daniel's constant companion was gone. The Mickey Mouse clock on the dresser showed ten o'clock.

He entered Vered's study. The empty room mocked him: so dainty, so pretty, so Caspi-free. The divan where she spent most of her nights was neatly covered with the diamond-patterned afghan that Jemima had given her. Her pillow was cool to the touch but bore her scent. He lay on the divan and stared at the prints on the wall and the shelves of books, so prim in their orderliness, as if in reproachful opposition to his own scattered library, which lay in stacks on every flat surface in the rest of the apartment. Her books, carefully arranged by author, looked untouched, though he knew they were not; his own had broken spines, torn or missing jackets, whole sections of text ripped out and used as toilet fodder. (No light reader, Caspi despised writers who couldn't write and envied those who could.)

He got up and looked at her desk. The gray folder which contained her work-in-progress was missing from the desk top. Sometimes she kept it in the top drawer. Caspi reached for the knob, then drew his hand back and lit a cigarette instead, dropping the match onto the floor. She kept her passport in there, too. Caspi had long envisioned himself coming home to an empty house, finding wife, child, and passports gone. In this recurring fantasy, Vered stole *his* passport to hinder pursuit. Caspi had recently locked his passport in his bank deposit box, and would have taken hers, too, but for the fear of putting ideas into her head. He finished his cigarette and stubbed it out on her desk, though an ashtray was at hand. The telephone rang, and he lunged for it. "Yes?"

"Where *are* you? I told Vered I had a party tonight. I'm already late."

"So go," he said. He teased the top drawer open with one finger and rifled through it. The gray folder was there, and beneath it, in a white Peltours envelope, her passport. The pounding in his ears momentarily drowned out Jemima's voice.

"What's your problem?" he said. "Need an escort?"

"Very funny. What do you expect me to do with Daniel, take him along?"

"Daniel's with you?"

Jemima was silent for a moment. "Where's Vered?" she asked quietly.

"Out screwing some A-rab," Caspi drawled.

"I wish she had it in her. It would serve you right."

"Goodbye, Mother."

"Don't hang up! And don't call me that. I'm not your mother, thank God. Would it be too much to expect you to pick up your son?"

"I'll be right over," Caspi said, and hung up. He thought of taking the boy to a hotel somewhere for a night or two, just to give Vered a scare, but decided it was too much trouble.

He returned to his car, and drove down Dizengoff, pausing in front of Nevo. Vered wasn't there. The café was half empty, and Sternholz was sagging against the bar, his head on his hand. Stubborn old bastard, Caspi thought; why didn't he get someone in to help him, beside that useless geriatric busboy of his? Could it be greed? But it was an open secret that Sternholz owned Nevo. Even if his customers were the scum of existence, which they were, himself excluded, their money was as good as anyone's. Perhaps it was another kind of greed. He imagined Sternholz as a vampire, sucking the blood of some customers to infuse others, nourishing himself in the process.

"Old fool," Caspi muttered, pulling away from the curb. What did he know about books? All the critics praised his work. *Yediot* declared him "the master stylist of our generation," and *Ha'aretz* called him "that valiant explorer of the dense underbrush of the Israeli soul." Who was the waiter to judge? Unbidden, a picture arose in his mind of Nevo in its heyday, during Caspi's youth, when the real artists hung out there. Shlonsky, Alterman, Goldman, that maniac Alexander Penn: not one of them that Sternholz hadn't fed.

"That doesn't make him an expert," Caspi argued with himself. Who was Sternholz to say that Caspi's work was trash? To his horror and amazement, Caspi felt tears trickling down his cheeks.

He crossed Ibn Gvirol and drove down Kaplan, leaving the lights of the city behind him. When he hit the coastal highway, he rolled down his windows to let the sea air in.

Jemima threw open the front door and stood with arms akimbo. Her blond hair was upswept, emphasizing the strong bones of her face. She wore a shimmering pale blue caftan of her own design and a choker of luminescent pearls. As he approached, Caspi smelled her scent, a distillation of newly mown grass. "You took your time," she said. "Where's Vered?"

"I told you where Vered is," Caspi said. He entered the salon with its cathedral ceiling and sunken sitting area and looked about. "Where's Daniel?"

"Sleeping, of course. Do you think he keeps your hours?" She crossed to his side and looked up at him. "What kind of foolish joke was that about Vered?"

"No joke, Mother, darling."

Suddenly noticing his reddened eyes, Jemima lowered hers. She sat on a sofa and pointed toward her bedroom. "He's in there."

In her room the surf beat like a heart and the moon shone softly, its glow diffused by white lace curtains. In the center of the large room, on a rattan bed, Daniel lay sleeping. He sprawled on his back, snoring lightly, his monkey nestled beneath his chin. In the moonlight the soft lines of his emerging boy's face regressed into a baby's lineaments. Daniel's hair was soft as down, honey-blond like his mother's. Caspi sat beside him for a moment, just looking. Then he nudged him and, when the child didn't respond, shook him roughly.

Daniel woke with a start. He focused on Caspi and said, "Where's Mommy?"

"Mommy's not here, Daniko. Daddy's going to take you home."

Daniel's eyes filled with tears but as usual he held them back. Caspi didn't know exactly when the boy had stopped crying, only that he had. Vered said it was his doing and he supposed it was, for he used to shout at the child when it sniveled.

"Did you have a good time with Grandma?" Caspi asked as he bundled the boy up.

"Where's Mommy?"

"Mommy's home." He carried the child out to the salon. Jemima came over and kissed him.

"Goodbye, darling."

"Bye-bye, Grandma."

Over the boy's head Jemima said, "Have Vered call me." She touched Caspi's arm, an unusual gesture. Caspi felt the question in the touch, but he shrugged and left.

He placed the boy close beside him in the front seat. As the child's sleepy warmth huddled against his side, Caspi leaned over to lock the door and surreptitiously sniffed

Daniel's hair. It smelled of baby shampoo, milk, and, faintly, Jemima's scent. Daniel looked up and said, "I want Mommy."

Caspi snarled, "Shut up!" and gave the boy a shake. Then he regretted it, but what good did that do? Daniel had already pulled away and buried his head in his monkey's soft side.

Caspi, who loved his son, cursed the day he was conceived. He had tried every stratagem he could think of to prevent conception (save vasectomy, which he believed reduced men's potency). Even after Vered caught on and forced him to desist, he never really believed she would succeed, never believed that an egg of hers and a sperm of his could meet in anything but hand-to-hand combat.

His instinctive aversion to the idea of fatherhood had proved well founded. To have a child meant entering into a state of permanent pillage-and-rape. It meant choosing to live on the cliff-edge of the most intense and untutored love. Loving where one could not afford to hate, loving irrevocably, was a perilous fool's game, and Caspi could never understand who so many men chose willingly to play it.

It was different for women. Formed to nurture, they had defenses men could barely conceive of. Caspi's harshness with his boy was but a poor and makeshift cover for the truth, which was that Daniel had him by the balls. Was it his fault the boy didn't seem to grasp that?

"You know Daddy loves you," Caspi said to the little bowed head. God help him but he could not keep the surliness from his tone. Daniel gave him a boldly dubious stare. Caspi pulled over and stopped the car.

"Daniel, would you like to go look at the sea with me?"

The child nodded, and Caspi carried him down to the water's edge. When he put him down, Daniel began scrabbling at the buttons of his shirt.

"What are you doing?"

He pointed. "I want to swim."

"Not now, Daniko. It's nighttime. Let's just sit here for a while."

Obediently, Daniel dropped cross-legged to the sand. Caspi lumbered down beside him.

"The sand is damp. Come sit on my lap. Look at the stars, Daniko. Do you know the constellations?"

Nestled in his father's arms, Daniel looked at the sky.

"There is Orion, the hunter. Orion loved the goddess Diana, but he died at her hand. Diana didn't mean to kill him, and in her anguish she plucked the living soul from his dying body and flung it heavenward. There he stands, bow drawn, arm flexed, quiver 'round his waist: luminescent but eternally remote." Daniel sighed, and his head fell back against Caspi's chest. Caspi stroked his soft hair and thought that in a world ruled by a jealous god, men never got what they wanted, for in the very moment of attainment the object of their desire was transformed. Certainly this was true of Caspi's women. Vered thought that his philandering was aimed at her, but she took credit where none was due. Caspi sought, truly and industriously, the mystery embodied in women's flesh, but he was questing for the grail. The moment he touched them the mystery was gone.

And it was so with his work. "You see a story," he whispered to Daniel. "You see it shining like a star at the top of a mountain. You labor up the mountainside, sack concealed behind your back because they're cagey buggers and shy: You reach the star and stretch out your hand, you touch it, and for one searing moment you think it's yours—and then it's gone. Shriveled, and in its place a pile of molten ashes, fool's gold. You shovel the muck into your sack because what the hell, you don't want to go back empty-handed, and you trudge down the mountain. At its foot an eager throng awaits you. They raise you to their shoulders and hold up your pathetic loot for all to see and praise. You cry: 'That isn't what I meant. That isn't it at all!' But no one hears, Daniel. No one hears."

They lay on the bed in a dingy hotel room, fully clothed. Khalil stroked her hair. "Don't be afraid," he murmured.

"I'm not afraid," she said, shivering.

He slipped the straps of her summer dress off her shoulders and pressed his lips to the hollow of her throat. "We are closer than cousins. We are brother and sister. Abraham was our father, and our mother is the land, Palestina. You cast us off, but we returned. You cast us off again, and again we return. We will always return. You and I are bound forever. You will never be free of me, nor I of you. I sow my seed in you, my promised land."

Chapter Eight

"WE planted pistachios this year," the father said. "Damn fool idea of Sasha's. From the water each of these trees drinks we could have had a field of avocados, and it'll take five years before we have a crop worth taking to market. Your mother's sick."

Arik stared. "I know. You told me. That's why I came."

"I didn't tell you everything."

"So tell."

Uri Eshel kicked a clod of earth with the toe of his sandal. He was as tall as his son but twice as broad, heavily muscled, with a bushy mustache and a full head of hair, grayer than the last time Arik saw him. He wore khaki shorts, and his trunk-like legs were foliated with wiry white hair.

Father and son left the young pistachio trees behind and crossed through a border of cypresses into the orange orchard. The grove was deserted except for some Arab workers eating lunch under a tree.

Uri picked up a newly pruned branch and stripped the

leaves from it. "I took her to the clinic. We thought it was an intestinal flu, she kept throwing up. Doctor did some tests, did an x-ray and then more tests. A few days later he calls me in. She's sitting there, white as a ghost. 'Your wife's got cancer,' he says." Arik choked back a sound. His father rushed on. "I say where. He says the stomach. Pancreas. Maybe liver. I say, 'Okay, so what do we do to lick this bastard?' He says, 'Nothing.' I say, 'What do you mean, nothing? Are you a doctor or a goddamn undertaker?' He says there's nothing to do except take care of the pain. I tell him he's an incompetent son of a bitch, and your mother starts crying. You ever see her cry?"

"No," said Arik.

"I did, once. When you left the kibbutz."

"What are you saying?"

Uri Eshel shook his head, a confused look in his brown eyes. "I took her to Hadassah. They did all the tests over again, and more. Professor Geller calls me in and says, 'Your wife's got cancer.' I say, 'So cut it out of her.' He says, 'Can't.' I say, 'So what am I supposed to do?' He says, 'Take her home. Take care of her.' I say, 'No, what am I supposed to *do*?' He says, 'Nothing you *can* do.'" Uri Eshel was reliving his rage. His deep voice expanded with it, filling the orchard, bending the trees. He looked down at his large brown hands, calloused and ink-stained both. Twisting the green switch he said fiercely, "She's fifty-six years old, and they're telling me to sit back and let her die."

Arik turned back toward the kibbutz, but Uri caught his arm in an iron grip. "Where are you going?"

"To see her."

"Not yet." Nose to nose they glared at one another. Uri Eshel said, "Let me ask you something, Son. What cause did she have to get so sick?"

"What cause? What kind of question is that? No *cause*. You think it's her fault?"

"Not hers," said Uri.

Arik Eshel laughed in disbelief. "My fault? I did this to my mother? Are you crazy, old man, or evil?"

Again the brown eyes showed confusion, and the deep voice said truculently, "You broke your mother's heart when you left the kibbutz, and mine when you quit the army. If I could I would tear that fucking cancer out of her body with my bare hands—but I can't. The only way I can help is to get you back for her."

"Don't lay this on me, Abba. I did not give my mother cancer."

"I didn't say you did."

"You're thinking it."

"I don't have any alternative," Uri shouted. "Because if you're not the cause, then you're not the cure either— and then what the hell am I supposed to do?"

He climbed the water tower and gazed out over the kibbutz. Beneath him were the dining room and community center, cement buildings built low to the ground, functional but not graceless. Beyond them were clusters of homes, linked by flowering paths. To the left, the swimming pool glistened in the afternoon sun; to the right were the cowsheds, chicken coops, and stable. All around, in every direction and for as far as his eye could see, lay the fields and orchards of the kibbutz, green and fecund, flourishing. A humming sound arose, a blend of machinery, tractors, murmuring men, and lowing cows. When he closed his eyes, the earthsmell wafted up to him, the smell that, more than any other sensation, meant home to him. It was the moist odor of the land in spring, long parched but now sated by the winter rains, drunk with joy, splurging its precious reserves on the profligate lawns and flower gardens of the kibbutz. He felt a thousand miles removed from Tel Aviv, and though sorrow for his mother and pity for his father roiled inside him, they were momentarily subsumed by the sluggish peace that this sight of his home always aroused in him.

It was a strange fact, it was one of those natural puns that fate occasionally indulges in, that many of the high points of Arik's youthful existence had taken place on that tower. It was always his refuge. Whenever parents or peers weighed heavily on him, he would take to the water tower and spend an hour or two aloft, far above his problems.

The tower served another purpose as well: since no one could approach it unseen, it provided the only secure privacy on the kibbutz. Arik had his first girl up there, on a blanket, under the stars.

Eventually he came down. He met a dozen members on the path to his parents' house, who greeted him casually and slowed to talk, but Arik did not pause. He knew them all so painfully well that even if they said no more than "How's it going, Arik?" he could not help hearing their thoughts: why did you quit the army, and drag the kibbutz's name into the scandal? What's the matter between you and Uri? Why don't you come home? Do you know about your mother?

No doubt but that *they* knew. There were no secrets on the kibbutz, and precious little privacy.

Rina was sitting on the porch, dressed in work clothes, when he reached the house. He held back a little from approaching her, as if the cancer were a party to their meeting. She gave him a cool, hard look and said, "You don't look so bad."

He smiled. "Neither do you, Mama."

"Well, what are you waiting for, a written invitation? It's not contagious."

He crossed the porch and bent down, enfolding her in his arms. She hugged him briefly, started to release him, but then tightened her arms, her fingers digging into his back as if they, not she, would not let go.

"Mama," he said, "I've decided to come back."

"What's the matter, you can't find work?"

"It's not that. I want to. It's time."

"Why?"

He hesitated, then said, "This is my home."

Rina tossed her head and sent her hair, long, black, and glossy, tumbling over her shoulders. To the glory of her son and husband, she had never given in to the kibbutz custom of short hair for women. "It's not that simple," she said. "You quit the kibbutz. You'd have to apply for re-admission and be voted on, like any other candidate."

"You think there's a problem?"

"A lot of the members were bothered by the loud way you quit the army. They think you set a bad example for the kids. I know one member who'd vote against you for sure."

"Who?"

"Me."

"Why?" he cried. "I thought you understood why I did it. You said you supported me."

"I did. I still do. That's not the issue."

"Then what is?"

"You don't want to come back," Rina said. "Your father's been getting at you. I knew he would."

Arik didn't know how to lie to her. She'd always seen through him, as she saw through everyone. People in politics called her "Eshel's lie detector," and they feared her. She was tougher than Uri, and she'd never spared her son. If she said she'd vote against him, he knew she would.

He brought over a chair and sat beside her, and though they'd never been a touching family, he took her hand and held it.

"He told me about the cancer. Is that 'getting at me'? It's my right to know, and to do what I want to about it."

"I don't want you here."

"I don't believe you. He told me you cried when I quit."

"So what? I cried when you were born, too; that doesn't mean I didn't want you." She stood, and in the slow movement of her slender body and the reaching of her hand toward the rail, he saw the first sign of her disease. She gazed over the kibbutz, her back to him. "It did hurt when you said you were never coming back to live," she said. "But not because you were wrong. Because you were right."

"You think I don't fit in?" he cried, stung, for there are no more bitter words than these, spoken to a kibbutznik.

Rina beckoned, and he came to stand beside her at the porch's edge. "When your father and I first came to this place, it was nothing but barren earth, so full of rocks you couldn't get a plow to look at it. Now just look at the gardens, the lawns, the fields, the fat animals and fatter children. We have color television in every house, we vacation abroad every year, and every child, like it or not, goes to the university. We're so *comfortable*." She said it with such bitterness that Arik laughed. So, after a moment, did she.

"We Eshels are happier struggling than having. You can't live here, Arik. You need to fight your own battles, carve out your own place from the rock. And what's more, you know it. So don't talk to me about 'coming home.'

"Besides," she said, "you think I want you standing over me, watch in hand, waiting for me to die so you can get on with your own life?"

"Don't say that, Mama. You're not going to die."

"Did I raise a fool for a son?" Rina snapped. "Everybody dies." She waved to some passing friends and went back to her seat on the porch. "Getting sick with cancer has its interesting points," she said. "When people find out, they're either frightened and shrink away, or they embrace you. I've had people I barely know coming up to me and saying that they love me or that they want to thank me for something I once did for them and forgot all about. The kibbutz members wanted to send me to the States when the doctors here said I was inoperable; it would have cost a fortune."

"Who cares what it costs? If there's a chance—"

"There's nothing they can do in America that the doctors here can't do. They're being decent, trying to spare me useless trauma. An operation wouldn't improve my odds with this kind of cancer—so why go through it?"

"How can you be sure?"

"I've taken an interest," she said drily.

He wanted to ask, Mama, what does it feel like? Does it hurt? Are you frightened? But nothing in his kibbutz training or army service had taught him to express such thoughts; besides, there was a part of him that didn't want to know. For if she said yes, it hurts, and yes, I am afraid, then what could he do about it?

"There are two things I want," Rina said, and Arik blurted, "Yes? What, Mama?"

She laughed. "That's the other benefit of cancer. It's like getting a magic gift of wishes. I have only to say, 'I want—' and the whole world jumps to attention. 'Yes, please, tell us, what can we do for you?' "

Arik smiled painfully. He could admire, but not begin to emulate, her cool acceptance of this thing.

"I want you to come see us more often. Spend time with your father. For too long you've been communicating through me; now you've got to learn to talk together." She looked him in the eye. "I want that *badly*."

Remembering their conversation in the orchard, Arik doubted it could be done, but he said, "Yes. And what's the other thing?"

Flushing, she said, "I'm not the interfering type of mother, am I?"

He smiled. "Not even close."

"I wish," she said, looking at her hands, "that you would find yourself a woman. I know you've had plenty of girls, but I wish you would find someone you'd be proud for us to meet. Men are so *helpless* without women."

He thought, he could not help it, of Sarita. It was ridiculous; he'd never even spoken to the girl; for all he knew she was stupid, though somehow he didn't think so. But she came into his mind, and of course his mother saw it. She smiled.

Chapter Nine

SARITA Blume walked into Nevo, empty-handed, and looked around expectantly.

"What are you waiting for, the maître d'?" growled Sternholz, who was very pleased to see her.

"Do you know a man named Simcha Noy? Is he here?"

"Hell, no," the waiter said with a sniff.

"I guess I'm early." Sarita sat at her usual table, beside the bar and under the waiter's protection. Sternholz brought her coffee and sat down opposite her with the groan of a man beginning an unpleasant but necessary job of work.

"So what are you meeting that bum for?"

"He's interviewing me about my work for *Ma'ariv*."

"Noy? He doesn't know art from his *tuches*."

"Why don't you like him?" Sarita asked. Though nervous about the interview, she found talking to Sternholz remarkably comfortable—he was like someone she'd known all her life and didn't need to think about. Sternholz, for his part, treated her with crusty gentleness and watched over her. He had begun to anticipate her visits.

"He's an arrogant pup." The old man humphed. "I like his nerve, setting up dates in my café."

"I did it," Sarita said. "It didn't occur to me that you'd mind. I didn't want a stranger in my home, and Nevo seemed public and sort of *safe* . . . you know."

Absurdly pleased, Sternholz muttered darkly, "Better here than elsewhere."

As he spoke these words, a youngish man with a languid manner, carrying a lizard-skin, initialed briefcase, entered Nevo's inner sanctum. Removing his shades, he looked about and immediately spotted Sarita. Gingerly, as if picking his way through a minefield, he made his way toward her, smiling fulsomely. "You *must* be Sarita Blume," he said.

Looking around at the old men in the room, she agreed, "I must be."

"Simcha Noy," he said. He held onto her hand a few seconds too long, then sat down close to Sternholz, displacing the old man, who rose crankily.

"He's married," Sternholz said dourly.

Noy flicked a look his way. "Bring me a beer," he said. "Maccabi."

"*Please.*"

"Please!" Then he turned to Sarita, a smile brightening his petulant features. "Shall we begin?" He removed a miniature tape recorder from his case and placed it on the table between them. "Tell me," he said, pushing a button, "about your mother."

"My mother?" Sarita flushed. "I thought the article was going to be about my work."

"No, dear. I'm not an art critic. My story is about the woman behind the work. The very beautiful woman." He bowed, without removing his eyes from her face. "Didn't Moriah brief you?"

"No."

"Do you remember your mother?"

"Of course. I was seven when they died."

"What do you remember about her?"

Sarita twisted a lock of chestnut hair around her finger. "Look," she muttered, "I don't really . . ."

"Listen, sweetheart, it's great publicity, and that's what you want, isn't it?"

"No. I mean, I don't want to offend you, Mr. Noy"—"Please, call me Simcha!"—"Simcha, but my personal life is . . . personal."

"Aren't you proud of your mother, Sarita?"

"Of course, I'm proud of both my parents, but—"

"Did you ever see your mother act?"

Sarita stiffened and said carefully, "Twice. I saw her as Mrs. Alving in *Ghosts* and in *The Watchmen.*"

"*The Watchmen*—wasn't that done in the forties? Surely your mother—"

"It was a revival," said Emmanuel Yehoshua Sternholz. He slapped Noy's beer down in front of him, pulled up a chair, and joined them. "Hannah Rovina played in the original, and Yael Blume in the revival. After the premiere there were fistfights outside the theater between Hannah's fans and Yael's. But there was no doubt in my mind who was the better actress."

"Who?" asked Sarita, eagerly.

"Rovina was a great actress, but Yael Blume was sublime. No one could compare to her."

"She was better-looking, that's for sure," said the reporter. "Like mother, like daughter."

" 'Better-looking,' " Sternholz sneered. "With your talent for words, you'll go far in the newspaper business— delivering papers. Yael Blume wasn't 'better-looking'; she was breathtaking, heartbreaking—like Garbo, like, what's-her-name, Hepburn."

"Audrey?" asked the reporter.

"Katharine, you fool. And she had their immense spirit about her, so that when she was present, you felt filled with power and optimism, as if you were breathing richer air. . . . Why, there were so many men in love with Yael Blume—" He stopped to catch his breath, laughing and shaking his head. "They all were. Uri Eshel, young Arik's father, was crazy about her; Muny was her lapdog; Minister Brenner"— he lowered his voice—"wanted to divorce his wife for her, and her without a civil word for him! And there were others who never even had the nerve to speak to her, but who used to hang out here because she sometimes came in."

"And there were some who often spoke to her," Sarita said in her soft voice, "but never spoke their hearts."

When she smiled, Sternholz pulled back, blinking like a surprised turtle. Her smile was so like Yael's that for a moment he seemed to see the mother's face superimposed on the daughter's.

"What was she like?" Sarita asked. "Apart from how she looked—what was she like?"

The waiter's eyes grew hazy with remembrance, and he didn't answer for some time. Then he cleared his throat, hawked once or twice, spit into a handkerchief, and began:

"The first time I laid eyes on Yael was in 1947, after the war but before we kicked the British out. Illegal immigration was at its peak then; practically every night boats came in, to Haifa, Ashdod, Tel Aviv, or the desolate shores of Herzliya, full of refugees from the holding pens of Cyprus. The British knew what was going on, of course. Oh, they tried to stop it, and once in a while they got lucky, intercepted a boat and sent the poor wretches back; but the coastline is long, the captains were experienced, and most of the time the ships got through.

"In fact, so many boats got through that people were beginning to believe that the English were purposely turning a blind eye, but it wasn't true. The British commander of the Tel Aviv region at that time was a mean-hearted spit-

and-polish type with the manners of a lord and the soul of a Nazi—Colonel Andrew Dinnis was his name. This Dinnis was an ambitious man who hated the way the 'Jewish rabble' were making fools of him and his men. He decided to set a trap for the Hagana, especially for the leader of the rescue operation, Yehuda Blume.

"One night word went out through the usual channels (young boys and girls acting as runners, slips of paper inside synagogue prayer books, kiosk message centers, that sort of thing) that a boat would be coming in late at night to Gordon beach. It was risky coming right into the heart of Tel Aviv, but less so on that night than on most others, for it was New Year's Eve, and the British would be celebrating in the barracks. By ten o'clock that night, you couldn't see a single Hagana face on the streets. . . ."

Running blind, the refugee ship entered the shallows of Gordon beach and anchored. Silently, efficiently, a ragged assortment of small crafts—fishing boats, dinghies, rafts, anything that would float and hold weight—was launched from the beach to bring the refugees ashore. They reached the ship and filled up first with children, mothers with babes in arms, and old people. The small armada set out for shore.

Suddenly, the beach was flooded with light! British trucks with searchlights mounted on the roofs lined the street, and tenders pulled up one after the other, discharging dozens of armed British soldiers. Colonel Andrew Dinnis himself stood on top of one of the trucks, dressed in full battle regalia, and spoke through a loudspeaker.

"You in the small craft," he shouted, "come ashore and surrender!"

A terrible cry arose, as if from the sea: an elemental scream of anguish from the throats of those wretched, homeless survivors. It was a sound that would break the heart of anyone with ears to hear. Many of the soldiers faltered and looked to their leader, but he, untouched, stood firm and repeated: "You in the small craft, come in and surrender!

You people on the ship, remain there! My men have orders to shoot the next man or woman who disembarks."

Like lemmings, men and women leapt from the ship into the icy water, heading for shore. Those who couldn't swim were supported by others. Within moments the sea was full of floundering refugees.

"Shoot!" screamed the Colonel.

Some soldiers shot in the air; others pretended not to hear. The small craft milled about in the water, picking up as many non-swimmers as they could hold. A man on board one of the boats shouted through a megaphone. "Plan B!" he cried in Hebrew. "Plan B!"

At once a deafening cacophony of sounds rang out from a dozen hiding places along the shore: whistles, drums, garbage can lids, shofars, and shouts of "Comrades! Comrades!" flew up and spread throughout the city. People in all stages of nightdress began to pour out of the houses along the beach, first singly, then in great streams as the noise and the news spread. Within minutes there were hundreds of men, women, and children massed on the shore, completely overwhelming the few dozen soldiers that the Colonel had deemed necessary to subdue the "Jewish rabble." As each small boat pulled ashore, and each exhausted swimmer crawled onto the beach, aided by people who waded out to meet them, the newcomers were quickly stripped of their sodden rags and dressed in dry clothing that the local Jews kept handy for just such occasions. Refugees fell to the ground, kissing the wet sand and mingling tears with sea water, and all the time the crowd grew larger as more and more Tel Avivans poured onto the beach.

Colonel Dinnis tore at his sparse blond hair and shouted contradictory orders. Soldiers ran about in circles, not daring to unsheathe their weapons or attempt an arrest, and who was there to arrest, anyway? Already it was impossible to tell the refugees from the natives, the Hagana people from the general populace. The Jews formed circles, linked arms, and broke into horas, singing with all their hearts. Some soldiers were pressed into the dance; a few threw down their weapons and joined in.

When all the refugees and their rescuers were onshore (save two, a young brother and sister whose drowned bodies drifted in later, posthumous immigrants to the promised land), the word went out to disperse. Natives and refugees, now indistinguishable, streamed outward into the quiet streets and bright avenues of the city, leaving behind a refuse of drenched rags and bewildered boy-soldiers.

At this point in his narrative, Sternholz was interrupted by raucous calls for service, which had reached a pitch that even he could not ignore. As soon as he had left the table, Simcha Noy turned to Sarita.

"Let's get out of here!"

"Why?" she asked, drawing back.

"Why! Because I didn't come here for a history lecture. The old boy's senile. Come on—I'll buy you a drink somewhere else. Or we could go to your place," he added, with an insinuating look.

"No, thanks."

"Look, if it's because of what Sternholz said before, it just so happens that I'm separated."

She gazed at him opaquely. "I don't care about that. I just want to hear what Mr. Sternholz has to say."

"Could you do it on your own time, then? I have a deadline to make."

"He might not tell me another time," Sarita said. "I have to hear the part about my mother."

Simcha Noy hesitated. It had occurred to him that if Sarita felt guilty about wasting his time, she might be more forthcoming later, in various ways. But as Sternholz bore down upon them, he made up his mind and stood abruptly.

"Au revoir, then," he said, with a malicious gleam. "I'll tell them at *Ma'ariv* that you were uncooperative. They'll kill the story."

"They should do themselves a favor and kill you, you bum," yelled the waiter. "Go on, get out." He resumed his seat with a groan as Noy withdrew. "Did he tell you he's separated?"

"He did."

"He always does that. It would be news to his wife. She thinks they're very happy, poor fool."

Sarita shrugged. "You were telling me about my mother."

The old man wiped his hand across his mouth and resumed without preamble:

"Colonel Dinnis regrouped his forces, called up more from the barracks, and started off in hot pursuit: not of the refugees, he knew he was too late for that, but of Yehuda Blume and his Hagana comrades. Dinnis had never laid eyes on Blume, but he knew his name and had a discription. In those times, there were few Jews over six feet tall. He ordered a cordon around Tel Aviv and sent squads of men to search the cafés and synagogues. . . ."

As soon as Yehuda Blume saw his order to disperse being carried out, he ran to Nevo. It was a cold night, and his clothes were soaking wet. Sternholz sent him up to his own room, above the café, to change.

Just as he came down, dressed in a pair of Sternholz's black trousers and a white shirt, the café was invaded by a squad of British soldiers, headed by Colonel Dinnis himself. Yehuda grabbed an apron and a tray and began to move among the patrons, clearing tables and taking orders.

Dinnis ordered the people to produce identity cards. Sternholz complained so loudly about the intrusion that Dinnis ordered his arrest; but Yehuda Blume caught the officer's eye and tapped his head significantly, and the waiter was released. A check of the customers' cards produced nothing of interest, and the two waiters were overlooked. But as Dinnis turned to lead his men out, his eye was caught by Yehuda's height, and he paused.

Suddenly a young girl of sixteen or seventeen burst into the café, crying loudly and holding a torn dress together under her coat. Sternholz rushed to her side solicitously, while Yehuda Blume ducked behind the bar and poured out a brandy. They got the girl to sit down and sip the drink, but when Colonel Dinnis approached, she began to scream again. He backed off hastily.

"Rape," the girl gasped. "They tried . . . two of them . . . they tore my dress and tried to push me into their car. . . ."

"Who?" demanded Yehuda Blume. The patrons of Nevo crowded 'round, and so did the British; the girl was very beautiful and apparently had not yet recovered sufficiently from her fright to cover herself completely. "Who attacked you? An Arab?"

"No!" she wailed. "Two soldiers." Sternholz translated her reply for Dinnis.

"British soldiers?" roared Dinnis. "Impossible!"

"In a jeep," the girl sobbed. "They chased me into an alley, and they ripped at my clothes, they tore my dress, and one of them . . ." The rest of her words were drowned in a flood of tears.

As the crowd began to murmur dangerously, the soldiers withdrew to defensive positions along the walls of the café. Dinnis said, "If British soldiers attacked you, they will pay dearly. But if you're lying, then by God I promise you'll regret it. Come with me." The girl shrieked, clutching at Sternholz for protection.

"Ach, mein Gott," Sternholz said with deep disgust, "she's a child. Let her go home to her mother."

"Not until she's made a statement."

"Then she'll make it here," Yehuda Blume said firmly. Sternholz translated the girl's description of the two men, which included little more than the fact that they both spoke English and wore uniforms. She had not noticed the number of their jeep. Dinnis noted down the scanty description and ordered his men out. He paused at the door.

"If anyone here has thoughts of retribution, forget them. We'll deal with this matter ourselves. I'll hang any man who lifts a finger against my troops."

In the wake of their departure, the girl demurely fastened her coat. Then she raised her glass exultantly and cried, "*L'chaim.* Long live the Hagana!"

Stunned silence met her words, for the child had fooled not only the British, but also her own people. Even Sternholz, who'd thought himself beyond surprise, gawked stupidly. Yehuda Blume was the first to recover. Laughing heartily, he grabbed the girl and kissed her on both cheeks. Then he tossed his apron on the floor, shook hands with Sternholz, and disappeared into the night.

"That was my mother," Sarita breathed.

"It was," Sternholz said. "In her acting debut."

"What happened then? Did she begin going with my father?"

"She didn't lay eyes on Yehuda Blume for another two years, because shortly after that episode the Hagana sent him abroad. He organized boatloads of refugees and ammunition from the other side and came back only when the war broke out. Yael joined the Hagana and was sent to a kibbutz up north, so I didn't see much of her until after the war, when she moved back to Tel Aviv to take up an acting career.

"And the rest," said Sternholz, pushing back his chair, "is history."

"Thank you," said Sarita, pressing his gnarled hand between her palms. Then, to his astonishment, she ran out of Nevo.

· · ·

Sternholz was busy for the rest of the afternoon and on into the evening. His busboy, Mr. Jacobovitz, was a seventy-eight-year-old man with hemorrhoids, failing eyesight, and advanced arthritis. Since he also had problems with his bowels and his bladder, he spent most of his time in the toilet out back and altogether was of little use to Sternholz. "But what can I do?" the waiter groused to Muny. "I fire him, the old *cocker* will never work again. Besides, watching him hobble around the place makes me feel young again."

"You're killing yourself," the poet replied. "A man your age, look at the hours you work. Noon till one, two in the morning—you've got to be suicidal."

Sternholz laughed. "I got something to save myself for? I'm going to dance at a grandchild's wedding?"

"That's your fault," Muny said. "You could have remarried."

"*Ach*, leave me alone."

Late that night, just before closing, Arik Eshel entered Nevo.

"Sternholz," he said, "have a drink with me."

A sarcastic greeting formed itself on the old man's lips, but he let it go after looking at Arik's face. He brought two whiskeys to the table.

"What's the matter?" he said. "Where've you been? Did you go home?"

"Yes." Arik drained his whiskey and motioned toward Sternholz's. The waiter drank, his face full of dread. "Rina's sick," Arik said.

"Your mother's sick? What with?"

"Cancer."

"*Oy*. Where?"

"Stomach, pancreas, liver."

"*Oy Gottenyu*."

"Sorry," said Arik.

"You're sorry? *He* should be sorry!" He waved a fist at the ceiling, then let it fall. "How's Uri?"

"He wants to *do* something. He's pacing the kibbutz like a caged tiger. He wanted them to operate, but the doctors say they won't inflict needless suffering. They gave him no hope at all, and he doesn't know how to handle that."

"Oh, my poor Uri." A tear formed in the old man's eye.

"He says it's my fault."

"Oh, *mein Gott.*"

"Sternholz? Emmanuel?" A dark shadow approached from the dimness; Muny put a hand under the waiter's arm. "What is it?"

"Go away, I'm all right. Go, my friend."

Muny left, and they were all alone. Sternholz got up to turn off the exterior lights, then returned to the table with two more drinks.

"Your father doesn't know what he's saying," he said. "That's the first thing you got to understand."

"Now that's very reassuring," Arik said. "What's the second?"

Sternholz was saved from replying by the sight of Sarita hurrying toward him, carrying something large wrapped in paper. She did not seem to see Arik at all, but came straight to Sternholz and thrust the package toward him.

"Is it right?" she demanded.

She sat beside Arik without glancing at him. He stared at her; wild-eyed, her hair awry, she was pulsing with energy and looked hot to the touch.

Sternholz unwrapped the package and found a picture inside, a pencil drawing, impressionistic, blurred and yet astonishingly detailed in parts, like a dream or a memory. The scene was Nevo, the year '46, the setting as Sternholz had described it: a young girl sitting in a chair, her clothing in disarray, surrounded by flustered men. In the background some British soldiers cluster around an angry-looking officer.

The girl's hands are raised and clenched in seeming distress, but her face is turned away from the soldiers, toward a tall man in a waiter's apron seen only from the back.

"Did I get it right?" Sarita asked anxiously.

"Perfect," Sternholz replied slowly. "Perfect, right down to her dress."

"I have that dress," Sarita said quickly. "She left it to me."

The waiter's face was angry. "And how did you know what Dinnis looked like? And who was here that night?" His finger stabbed the drawing. "Those are real people; how did you do this, Sarita?"

She gave Sternholz a hurt look and glanced sidelong at Arik. "I don't know," she mumbled.

"Too many secrets are bad for the heart," said Sternholz, who was in a position to know. "You'd better tell."

"I just saw it." She tried a tentative laugh. "You described it so well."

He shook his head.

"Shall I go?" Arik asked.

"Don't move! I'm not through with you. Do you two know each other? Sarita Blume, Arik Eshel. Your father, her mother were friends. Talk to each other, I'm going to the bathroom."

"You're an artist," Arik said, feeling absurdly tongue-tied and young. "I've seen you working here."

She looked him in the face for the first time. "I've seen you."

"May I have a look?"

Reluctantly she handed over the drawing. She was so child-like in manner that he expected naïveté in her work— pretty pieces of fluff, kittens and children with big eyes—and so was unprepared for the combination of immense power and hard-edged skill her drawing revealed. The picture was clear, cold, accurate, and uncanny. Everything Arik thought of to say seemed too personal. In his struggle against an illusory feeling that they already knew each other, he was aided by her utter indifference to him. She looked at him without recognition. Finally he pointed at a figure in the drawing and said, "That looks like Muny, thirty years younger."

"Maybe. I don't know, really."

Her work testified to strength, yet, speaking with her at last, he could not help feeling that he held a small bird in his hand. Though she had a woman's body, and a face he could not help imagining on his pillow, she was still a prodigy: a fierce, obsessive talent burning up a child's mind. He knew now who she was. For the first time since its discovery, his mother's illness left his thoughts; but his sense of impending bereavement acquired the form of pity for this orphaned girl.

Sternholz returned, but remained standing. "You'd better come upstairs, before we have more company."

"I can't," Arik said reluctantly. "I just came by to tell you about Rina. I've got to meet some people."

Sarita shot him a glance of surprised gratitude. He wished she were not so happy to see him go.

"At one in the morning?" Sternholz growled. "Nice friends you got."

"It's Coby and the other kids from the center. I've got to find out what they're up to." Standing, he took Sarita's hand and waited until she looked up at him. "Goodbye, Sarita Blume. I'll be seeing you. So long, Sternholz."

"Let's go up," the waiter said. "Come, it's time we had a talk."

Sarita had never envisioned Sternholz's existence outside Nevo; indeed, since he lived directly above the café, it could be said he had none. She was not surprised by the perfect order and cleanliness of his rooms, which were sparsely but nicely furnished, but she did notice the lack of any personal mementos: no pictures on the dresser or the wall, no remnants of his youth in Germany.

"Sit." Sternholz led her to a chair at the little table beside the window. "What do you want? Whiskey, wine, vodka?"

"Wine, please."

He brought over a chilled bottle of Carmel hock, opened it, and poured two glasses. "*L'chaim,*" he toasted.

"*L'chaim.*" She sipped the wine, avoiding his eye.

"Did you ever think what a funny toast that is for Jews?" Sternholz watched her closely. " 'To life'—when all we've known is death and suffering."

" 'To death' would be an even stranger toast," she said.

"You know, that boy's in love with you. I've never known him at a loss for words with a woman before. I've seen him watching you."

"Who?" she said blankly.

"Arik."

"Oh."

"He's a good boy. A lot of problems, but a good boy." Sarita remained silent.

"You're not interested? Maybe you've got a boyfriend already?"

"No."

"What's the matter, you don't like boys?"

"I don't have room for them," she said.

"His mother's very sick. Cancer, that's what he told me tonight."

"That's sad."

"Losing a mother is a terrible thing. Losing both parents—it's enough to stunt a person's growth."

Sarita set down her glass and met the old man's bleary eyes. "I lied to that reporter," she said. "I saw my mother act three times."

"When was the third?" he asked wearily, knowing what she would say.

"Her last performance."

"So tell me."

"I was seven years old. My parents were going on tour to the northern settlements, and since it was summer vacation, they let me come. Mama was Nora in A Doll's House, and my father was stage-managing the production. The first performance was on Kibbutz Ma'ayan Baruch close to the Syrian border, in a new theater that had never been used before. I could have sat up front, but I preferred to watch from backstage; I couldn't see as well, but I felt more a part of the whole thing. It was terribly exciting, and though I couldn't understand the play, I knew Mama was wonderful. When it was over, I stood just inside the wings, watching her bow again and again. I wanted her to come to me but the audience wouldn't let go of her. I called, 'Mama!' and she blew me a kiss. She was so beautiful, bathed in light, raising up her long white arms, laughing and saying, 'Thank you, thank you,' to the audience. She was hardly my mother at all. . . .

"I remember the light, Mama gleaming white on the dark stage, her hair glowing like a bright halo. Then suddenly the darkness exploded in a blinding red flash. . . .

"And the noise—at first I thought it was the audience roaring, but it grew louder and louder. I covered my ears but I could hear the roof crack open and the timbers of the stage give way, the crash of the chandelier and the screams, the terrible screams. . . . The spotlight never left Mama's face, and though I was knocked off my feet I still saw her face, which was turned toward me, as the stage collapsed beneath her and she fell.

"My father died, too. A lot of people died that night. It was a Syrian missile. They just sat up on their hill and waited till the theater was full. People told me I was lucky I survived." She whispered: "But I didn't—not all of me."

"They told me that, too," Sternholz said, weeping unashamedly. "When I lost my family they said, 'It's a pity about your wife and baby but thank God you escaped.' 'Thank God'—I'd like to thank Him," Sternholz cried fiercely. "He should give me five minutes alone in a room with Him, I'd thank Him good."

"I knew you'd understand," Sarita murmured. "I've never told anyone before . . . but we're alike, you and me."

"Nonsense, child," Sternholz growled in alarm, dashing the tears from his eyes. "I'm an old man; you're a young girl with a lifetime of loving ahead of you."

Sarita's face closed down. "A lifetime of *work*," she corrected. "My poor Mama was cut down in her prime, but she left me to carry on for her, in my own way, as best I can. There's no time for love."

"No time for love!" the old man gasped. "Sarita, child—"

But Sarita stood and snatched up her canvas. "Thank you," she said, avoiding his eye, edging toward the door. "I have to go now. Thank you."

"Sarita, wait!" Sternholz struggled to his feet, but it was too late. She was gone.

Chapter Ten

"CONTRACEPTIVE failure," he said apologetically. "It happens."

A deep flush spread over Ilana's face. She laughed, it seemed in spite of herself, and placed her palm flat against her abdomen, pressing gently. The man smiled a tentative smile. She said, "I'll need an abortion."

"Take some time," he said. "Think about it," he urged.

"There's no need." As she paced the room, she felt a warm glow in her belly, an uproar in her blood, but these found no expression in her clipped voice. "It's out of the question for me to have it. I want you to perform the operation, privately of course. We can do it here, or I can take a room in Assuta Hospital."

"I won't do it immediately." Dr. Steadman leaned far back in his chair and unwrapped a piece of gum. He was a balding redhead of forty-five, with a long, mobile mouth and bright blue eyes behind rimless glasses. He wore an old white shirt, frayed at the cuffs, loosely tucked into a pair of faded jeans. His lab coat was spotless, and his large freckled hands were immaculate. "I'm going to exercise my doctor's prerogative to offer some unsolicited advice, Ilana. God knows we've known each other long enough."

"Rafi," she said, coming to sit down. He held up a hand.

"You are what, thirty-six years old? The clock is ticking. If you ever want to have a child, now is the time, and you do have the means to support it. I'm not trying to usurp your decision, Ilana; I just wouldn't want you to do something you may one day bitterly regret."

"It's no big deal," she said. "Everyone has abortions these days. It's nothing to fuss about."

"It's true, abortions are popular now. That's why some women are having them who shouldn't. The pregnancy wasn't intended, she has other plans, she's going abroad. . . . She never really thinks about it until it's done, and then she thinks too much."

"I've thought about it."

"What's the problem? Is it that you don't want a child? Or is it that you're not married? Are you as conventional as that?"

"It's not convention; it's . . . common sense."

"Common sense?" He raised an eyebrow. "Let me ask you two questions. Can you afford to raise a child by yourself?"

"Yes," she said.

"Do you want a child, ever?"

She tightened her lips, looked down, and did not reply.

"You see," he said, "it's not all that clear-cut."

"I can't have it." She raised her head. "I appreciate your intentions, Rafi, but you're not making this any easier. Since I need an abortion, I naturally prefer to have you perform it. But if you won't, I'll find another doctor who will."

He shrugged, then clasped his hands together. "You

may feel differently knowing rather than suspecting that you're pregnant. If, however, after further consideration you still choose an abortion, I will perform it, provided it takes place within the first trimester."

"I would hardly wait longer than that." Now that she had won, dangerous forces rebelled inside her, clamoring for delay. She cleared her throat and said, "I want to make the appointment now."

"Set up a date with Leah, for no less than two weeks from today. Feel free to change your mind at any time."

Ilana stood and glanced at herself in the mirrored door. "I won't. Two weeks from now is fine. I'm going abroad next week. We can do it when I get back." At the door she looked back at him with an odd tilt of her head. "It is all right to fly?" she asked; then she caught her breath and rushed out into the reception room.

The nurse was taking a history from a new patient. Ilana waited impatiently. A young woman sat in the small waiting room, holding a tiny infant. Ilana was drawn to the baby.

The mother, a child herself in Ilana's eyes, smiled proudly and shifted to show the infant's sleeping face. As she moved, the baby's eyelids flew open, and his eyes, deep dark lakes of solemn blue, met Ilana's. His look was so lucid, so searching, that his incapacity to speak struck her for the first time as pathetic. The creature so clearly longed to communicate. As he held her eyes she felt that not only did he sense the presence of her embryonic passenger, but he advocated its cause, so recently his own, with imperious innocence. Ilana sighed deeply, again touching her belly. "This isn't happening," she said.

"What?" asked the mother.

"Your baby isn't talking to me."

The woman smiled uneasily and hugged the infant tighter. Ilana backed away, and the nurse called out to her.

"Just send the bill," Ilana said. She took a deep breath and glanced into the mirror beside the entrance; then she walked out into the stifling afternoon.

It was a chamsin, the hot wind from the east that periodically sweeps the land. On chamsin days housewives close their windows and lower the shades, but the hot wind gets in anyway, carried like a germ by all who venture forth into its path. The chamsin enters through all apertures: the mouth, the eyes, the nose, penetrating to the heart. So many more family murders are committed during the chamsin that the courts consider it a mitigating circumstance.

Ilana raised her hand to hail a taxi, but lowered it, unable to think of a destination. She dared not return to her empty apartment. As she wandered on foot toward Dizengoff, walking as people must during chamsin, with long, un-hurried strides and lowered eyes, the very effort of wading through the sweltering heat calmed, even cheered her. Pretty soon she found herself outside Nevo. Although Nevo was a place she almost never set out intending to visit, her aimless walks through the city often brought her there; and once she was outside it seemed churlish not to go in. She was thirsty, but wary of Sternholz. The café was fairly crowded, and the waiter would be too busy to pry.

As she sat down, she felt herself enveloped in the loneliness that descends upon patrons of Nevo as they enter its portals and renders them inviolate. Nowhere else could she sit unmolested for as long as she wanted, for Nevo was a place where people came to be alone in the company of others, and this canon, though unspoken, was almost universally observed—except for people like Sternholz and Muny, whose function in Nevo's ecology was to intrude.

Sternholz appeared beside her, nodding dourly. "What do you want?"

"Hello, Emmanuel. I'm awfully thirsty; do you have any fresh juice?"

Sternholz snorted. "This I need? Maybe you want me to go pick the oranges off a tree?"

"If it's not too much trouble."

"Oh, no, no trouble," he muttered, repressing a smile as he hobbled off indignantly.

A few minutes later, he brought a tall glass of orange juice with the pips still floating in it. She drank gratefully, while he hovered, making sure she finished. "You want another?" he then asked, with a martyred look.

"No thanks."

"You look terrible," he said, wagging a finger in her face. "You're not living right. I've been meaning to tell you."

"Not now," she murmured, but this served only to encourage him.

"It's time to settle down. You should get married, have some babies."

"Why are you saying this?"

"If I don't, who will? You're beginning to look tired. It's time for a change."

"But why now?"

He cocked his head, peering at her through bright, knowing eyes.

"Thanks for the juice," Ilana said. Sternholz shrugged and moved away.

Thereafter the city seemed rife with pregnant women. They were all around her, strolling down Dizengoff, sitting in cafés, sunning on the beach in their maternity suits: fertile as the land, Ilana thought, seasonal as the rains. For a short time she was one of them, two hearts beating within her; and in the one that was her own she thanked Rafi Steadman for the enforced delay.

Ilana bore her secret close, telling no one, but it seemed to her at times that one or another of the pregnant women would look at her with uncanny discernment. She prayed for nausea, pain, anything to relieve the physical elation that plagued her: but her body, which never lied, reveled stubbornly in its new fecundity.

The first negative sign of her pregnancy came, perversely, on her first night in London with David. They had been to a West End opening and then the opening party; by the time they returned to her suite in the Savoy it was after one. Ilana left David with a drink and got into the shower. A few minutes later he heard a loud thump and rushed in to find Ilana slumped over the edge of the tub. She stirred as he reached her side, and opened her eyes.

"I'm all right," she said faintly.

"Good God. Here, let me help you." He supported her into the bedroom and laid her on the bed, covering her with a blanket. Then he sat beside her and clasped her hand in both of his.

"I noticed you didn't drink tonight, and you've quit smoking," he said. "Now this. Are you by any chance pregnant?"

Ilana turned her head away, closing her eyes.

"You're not sleeping. Answer me, my dear."

She looked at him. "Yes. I'm sorry. I am. Temporarily."

"It's my baby?"

"Fidelity, as you well know, David, is my stock in trade."

He bit his lips, and his face worked; then he raised his face to the ceiling and burst into laughter.

Ilana, who had expected anything but hilarity, sat up in alarm, clutching the blanket to her chest.

"I'm sorry," he gasped. "It's just . . . I've never had a child."

"You're not going to, by me," she promptly said.

"Don't abort it."

"What else can I possibly do? I'm very sorry you guessed, David. I had no intention of telling you. . . . It's my fault for coming, but this never happened to me before."

"You must take care of yourself."

Ilana faced him squarely. "You don't seem to be hearing me, David. I cannot have a baby."

David walked to the center of the room and stood easily, as if preparing to address a meeting of the board. He was a tall, lean man of about fifty, very dark for an Englishman, but then he was a Jew. He had long fingers and sensitive hands, which he now pressed together in thought.

David Barnardi was an architect and the head of an international firm of architects. His own speciality was the conversion of old churches into residences, a specialty he'd stumbled into by accident when he accepted a commission from an Essex parish to convert an old Anglican church into a residence for the priest.

The tall vaulted ceilings, the vast space and depth of the church inspired him, and he created a house of such eerie beauty that the old priest who was meant to live there could not cope at all and instead took lodgings with an elderly widow. The house was sold for a small fortune, which greatly pleased the parish, and it gained recognition as a paradigm of such conversions, serving as an example to countless aspiring young architects.

If there seems something ironic or even bizarre in the choice by a Jew of this particular field of expertise, it can only be argued that David Barnardi was not much of a Jew. He was far too proud a man ever to deny his religion, but as it was meaningless to him, so was it to others. He observed none of its practices, celebrated none of its holy days, and took secret pride in his ignorance of its tenets. The only positive function his religion served was in providing an unexceptionable excuse to forgo dreary church services on country weekends.

Like many artistic Jews whom Ilana had known, David

possessed a business sense which was as keen as his aesthetic sense. Realizing the potential for a team of architects specializing in unusual, and expensive, conversions, he left the firm that employed him and hired, on commission, two bright young architects whom he knew. One of the two specialized in converting, or sometimes reconverting, multi-unit apartment houses into small mansions, townhouses for the very wealthy. The other designed small, Claridge-type luxury hotels.

With the money earned during their first year of operation, David hired a staff of interior designers to complete the buildings which he and the other architects designed, thus tripling their profits on a project. The next year, he hired three more architects, each of them proficient in a particular field; only this time he hired them on salary. That was twenty years ago. Today, the business which David had started on nothing was worth millions.

David let some moments go by in silence, while he thought. Then he drew a chair over to the bed and sat down. "I have the solution," he said.

"Do you?"

"Marry me, Ilana."

"You're not serious."

"Never more so."

"Would you mind handing me that robe?" When she had donned it, she sat up, hugging her knees. "Darling, that is without a doubt the silliest thing I have ever heard you say."

"No, my dear, it's the perfect solution."

"Have you forgotten that you are already married?"

The smile faded from his face, and his dark eyes grew grave. "We've never talked about my marriage. One doesn't like to . . . I am fond of Lydia, and I wish her well, but our marriage has long been one of convenience, on both sides. We go our own ways. I've stayed married because a man in my position needs a hostess, and Lydia is an excellent one; also because I've never actually found anyone else. I don't know, but I would imagine that Lydia's reasons for remaining with me are similar. We've discussed divorce but never found any compelling reason for going through with it, and the process is *such* a bore that one really doesn't want to unnecessarily. But now I have that reason."

"You want the child."

"I do. Very frankly I do. Lydia never wanted children, and I convinced myself I didn't care. But just now, when you told me that you're carrying my child, I just"—he laughed shortly, turning his face aside—"my heart went through the roof. Suddenly I felt that I'd never wanted anything as much. . . ."

Ilana's voice was noticeably cooler. "You're willing to pay a high price for it, marrying me."

"No," David said slowly, with interest. "No. It's true that I probably never would have thought of it if this hadn't happened, but when the idea did come, it seemed right. Of course, I'm a good deal older than you are, but I think we suit each other rather well. I'm sorry, Ilana, this isn't a very romantic proposal. I suppose I'm not a very passionate sort of man."

"You're a tender, sensitive man and a wonderful lover," Ilana interrupted warmly, and could not help adding to herself that he would make a fine father. It seemed a shame that with all this man had to give, he should have no child to give to. But she rigorously suppressed that thought. "I'm honored, David, but it wouldn't begin to work. You forget what I am"—her voice dropped dramatically—"in the eyes of the world."

"I will not tell you," he said, "that I'm indifferent to what the world thinks, but if its judgment and mine were to differ, I should always rely on mine. I do not think they *would* differ. My dear, you are a woman of character: beautiful, intelligent, charming. . . . I care for you, Ilana, and respect you; I should be proud to marry you and raise our child together."

She was too moved to reply at once. She noticed with something approaching gratitude the absence of any mention of love, for Ilana no more believed in love than a stage magician believes in magic. Her feelings toward David were as his toward her, composed of kindness and respect; under different circumstances these could have been the basis of a good marriage. But, circumstances being what they were, she felt compelled to reason with him.

"Look, darling, you haven't thought this through." She spoke slowly and clearly, as if to a child. *"I've known a lot of men.* I've taken money from them. People know who I am. The papers know me. If David Barnardi were to marry Ilana Maimon, it would be front-page news and boardroom gossip. You would be hurt. Darling, I'm a—"

"Don't say it!" He laid a hand on her lips. "You've said too much already. I don't ever want to hear you talk that way again!"

"But it's true."

"If you think so, then clearly you have not understood your own position. My dear girl, what a prude you are! What unmentionable sin have you committed? You have, by aligning yourself with powerful men, acquired a certain degree of wealth and power; in doing so, you have done no more than any self-made woman has at some point in her career."

"Aligned myself—what a wonderful description!"

"It really doesn't matter in what position. There are many different ways of stroking . . . you at least have always been decent enough to give value for money, if you'll pardon the expression."

Ilana burst into laughter, and after a moment David joined her. Then he joined her in bed. Almost imperceptibly, their talk changed to love-making. It was slow and deep and tender, and in the end Ilana cried out, "Yes, oh, yes!"

Later David asked coyly, "Was that an acceptance?"

She raised her head from his chest to look at him. "No,

it was not! Apart from all the other insurmountable problems, how on earth would you run your business from Israel?"

He looked startled, then amused. "I couldn't possibly. We would have to live here."

"Oh, no," she said. "I couldn't."

"Why not?"

"I can't leave Israel. Not permanently."

"Israel? What has Israel to do with it? We'd keep your apartment, of course; you could visit whenever you wished."

"I couldn't live outside Israel. And I wouldn't raise a child outside." She touched his hand. "Don't tell me it's irrational; I know it."

"This is the first time I've seen this side of you," David said slowly, breathing heavily. It was possible that he was growing angry, certain that he had not expected such opposition. "It's not necessary to live in Israel to remain Jewish, if that's your concern. I don't mind if the child is taught its religion."

"It's not the religion; it's the land," she said. "It's the place. You can't bring that here."

"What difference does the place make?" he cried impatiently.

"All the difference in the world."

He could not understand, and she could not explain. David had been to Israel and found it dusty and provincial, without the charm of Italy or Greece. Jerusalem he acknowledged to be a beautiful city, full of architectural marvels; but its spiritual gravity oppressed him, and he suffered from an unnerving sense that time behaved strangely in the walled city, flickering strobe-like between past and present, too quickly for confirmation but not for perception. Jerusalem was like a seductive woman whom he felt drawn to revisit, but never to live with, for she had the power to negate all that he had made himself. For Tel Aviv he had no use at all.

They resolved nothing that night but continued to talk

all through the weekend. By Sunday David was convinced that she would not marry him. Driving to the airport that evening, he closed the window between them and the chauffeur and said, "Since you persist in rejecting my honorable proposals, I shall try a dishonorable one. Have the child out of wedlock, Ilana, and I will acknowledge my paternity and support you and the boy for so long as you both shall live."

"And if it's a girl?" she teased.

"Don't laugh, Ilana, I'm deadly serious. I beg you not to destroy this child. I may never have another, and neither, my dear, may you."

Ilana took his hand and pressed it to her cheek. With no trace of levity she murmured, "I don't know what to do. I did, but now I don't."

"I know you want this child. A woman who wants to get rid of her baby doesn't quit smoking and drinking. Let me make it possible for you, for both of us. I've thought it all out. I'd change my will, of course, to provide for you both, and acknowledge paternity legally. I can have my solicitor draft something immediately."

"I can support a child without your help. Money is not the issue."

"I agree; what matters to me is that by accepting my support for this child, you're granting me the right to be a part of his life. Or hers—it really doesn't matter. Will you do it, Ilana? Will you have the child?"

The Rolls pulled up at the terminal doors, and the chauffeur jumped out to open the door. Ilana stepped out with alacrity, followed by David. Just inside the sliding doors he waved the porter on ahead and took her arm, stopping her from following. "I want your answer, Ilana."

She faced him, looking up through perfectly made-up, bloodshot eyes. "I can't give you one now."

"Will you promise at least to talk to me before you do anything?"

Unwillingly, she answered, "Yes." He nodded gratefully. Their parting kiss was as solemn as a handshake.

It was only as the plane flew over Greece that the full import of what had happened hit her. David Barnardi had asked her to marry him, and she had refused. The shock of it sent the blood rushing from her head, attracting the attention of a zealous steward. "Are you all right, Miss Maimon?" he asked solicitously. "Can I bring you something?"

"A cup of strong tea, with milk," she said.

"Coming right up, Miss Maimon." He seemed determined to announce her identity to all and sundry; fortunately, few people were flying first class, and those who did were studiously incurious.

Ilana opened a magazine and stared at it unseeingly. He never would have asked me if I hadn't been pregnant, she thought. But what astonished her was his having asked her at all, and not just once, in the excitement of the moment, but repeatedly, over a period of days.

And never, during all that time, did she think about what she was refusing: not only David, who had never seemed as attractive to her as he had these past few days (proving once again a fact she had often noted, that the vulnerability of powerful men was itself a powerful aphrodisiac), but also his money, the wealth she would have shared as his wife. Oh yes, the money: for despite her denials, Ilana was not and had never been indifferent to money. Indeed, she loved it: loved the things and the services it could buy, the respect it engendered, the power it bestowed. Had she not loved money, she would not have accrued so much of it, or continued selling her services dearly when she could well afford to give them away. Instead, she would have channeled her ambitions into more traveled paths and acquired a husband, home, and children.

She had given up these things in favor of a life-style of travel, chauffeur-driven limousines, fine food and wine, glittering parties with powerful people and attentive servants.

And yet, when David had effectively said to her, Have it all, Ilana: a caring husband, a child, and more wealth than you have ever dreamed of acquiring, she'd said, No, thank you.

Why? Here was a courtesan's dream come true, years after she had ceased dreaming it. "I fail to see the problem," he'd said when she pressed home her refusal; rejected, he was at his stuffiest and most English. Of course he failed to see: for he knew nothing about her.

That was no fault of his. Ilana *never* told the truth about her background. She claimed to have been orphaned at a young age; it was the simplest way of dealing with the inevitable inquiries. When she was young, her lovers, always much older than she, had been titillated by the persona of a luscious, Lolita-type girl on her own in the world, unprotected by family; later, too, her lack of encumbrances had been viewed as a virtue. Had she told the truth, she would only have depressed them, and Ilana had not got where she was by depressing her lovers.

The unpalatable truth was that her mother was a concentration camp survivor, and her father had spent three years in an Iraqi jail. Both had undergone torture. Both had dragged their shattered bodies and souls to Israel, where they met, married, and produced five children. Ilana could not know whether their miraculous rehabilitation was a function of the Jewish State or their own natural recuperative powers, but she believed, as they did, that it was the former.

It was not gratitude but a superstitious, magical equation that bound her to the State: as Israel had been her parents' salvation, and thus her doing, leaving it would be her undoing. Also, their experiences (mysteriously conveyed, as they were rarely mentioned) prevented her from ever feeling really safe outside the borders of her own country. It was a fear she kept tightly battened down, but never denied to herself.

If she would not marry David, and it seemed established that for many reasons she would not, that left the matter of her pregnancy unresolved. By increasing her options, he had forced her to recognize her own desire. An unwanted child had better not be born, but one as desperately wanted as this one was by David and, she had unwillingly come to recognize, by herself seemed already possessed of rights.

The fetus, that slumbering life within her which did not yet know itself, was his as well as hers, but she alone was empowered to decide its fate. David could plead, he could even threaten (he had not), but he could not force her to sustain that flickering light.

The choice was hers.

Chapter Eleven

SOMEONE informed. Reports reached Ein Hashofet, and Uri Eshel was dispatched (by his wife) to investigate. He arrived in Nevo late on a Thursday morning, creating a stir in those turgid waters. Even the chess players paused, chessmen in hand, to peer blearily and nod in acknowledgment. Sternholz raised an eyebrow; Mr. Jacobovitz dropped a tray. The Minister, drinking coffee in the back, waved, and Uri Eshel nodded but remained where he was in the middle of the room, peering through the smoky dimness. Arik slowly approached and spoke to his father.

"What are you doing here?"

Uri bared his teeth. Taking Arik's arm, he guided him to a table near the bar, where they sat opposite one another. Sternholz told Mr. Jacobovitz to take over, and cast a threatening eye over his customers. Then, unasked, he brought three beers over to the Eshels' table and sat between them.

"I've been looking for you," the father said, ignoring Sternholz.

"Here I am."

Uri looked about him with distaste. "I heard that you spend most of your time here."

"Where'd you hear that?" Arik glared at Sternholz, who returned a look of injured innocence.

"I also heard that you're looking for work abroad."

There was silence. Arik gazed over his father's shoulder. Seen from Nevo, Dizengoff was a shimmering kaleidoscope of brilliant colors.

"Well? Is it true?"

He met his father's eye with equanimity. "It is true. I'm sorry you heard it from—someone."

"You should have told me yourself."

"I intended to, last time I came home. But as things turned out, it wasn't the time."

Uri nodded curtly.

"Don't worry," Arik said. "I'm not going yet. Not so long as Rina's sick."

Uri Eshel's hands clenched. He looked at them without recognition and thrust them into his pockets. "What the hell does that mean?" he asked softly. "That you'll do us a favor and wait till she drops dead before deserting?"

Arik straightened and froze, ceasing for a moment the incessant, supple movement of his body. They stared at one another for a moment while the last word echoed through Nevo. Pride looked to pride, and Sternholz looked on.

When he could stand it no longer, he poked at Uri's arm. "You should watch your mouth, my friend."

"Don't interfere, Emmanuel."

"Yeah, Sternholz," Arik said, "keep out of it."

"I'm just saying what Rina would have if she were here," Sternholz replied unflappably. "*You* should watch your mouth, and *you*"—he turned to Arik—"better watch your manners."

"No offense, Sternholz, but do you intend to sit here through all of this? Some things are personal, you know."

"You think I got nothing else to do? You think I get a kick out of this?"

"Then why—"

"Don't tell me how to do my job, young Arik!"

Suddenly a portly figure loomed above them, and a voice called out, "Uri, *shalom!*"

Uri rose with a forced smile and shook the proffered hand. "Yosh."

"We miss you, my friend. When are you going to get off that farm of yours and lend us a hand?"

Uri's eye gleamed. "You must feel pretty sure that I won't, to ask me."

Minister Brenner smiled briefly, then grew sober. "I'm sorry about Rina's illness. We all wish her a full and speedy recovery."

"Thanks, I'll tell her."

The Minister nodded a farewell that included Arik and Sternholz, then turned and strutted through Nevo into a waiting limousine.

"Now look here," Uri said, his smile vanishing with the Minister. "Your mother sent me here to talk with you, so by God we'd better do it. Where did you come up with this fool idea of going abroad?"

"There's no point in staying here." Arik shrugged. "This country has had it. We had our chance and we blew it."

"What we? Don't blame yourself, boy; you haven't blown anything, because you haven't *done* anything! Not a goddamn thing, and you're no kid anymore. By the time I was your age"—he paused at a groan from Sternholz, gave him a baleful look, and continued—"I had some accomplishments under my belt. Too goddamn many, if you ask me. We should have left you some swamps to clear, a few borders to secure; taken you out of yourselves a little. As it is you've nothing better to do than sit around contemplating your navel."

"Nothing better to do?" Arik howled. "You're boasting about what you accomplished while the whole damn pack of cards is collapsing around us?"

"You don't like the way they're falling? So pick them up and reshuffle! You're not going to get anything done sitting on your ass in Nevo."

"It's hopeless."

"You are pathetic!" Uri shouted.

"Easy does it," said Sternholz.

Arik groaned in exasperation. When he looked at his father's face, his heart softened, and he reached out a hand, palm up.

"All right, maybe not hopeless, but why should I take it on myself? I've given ten years to the army—I've paid my dues."

"Dues, what dues? What are you talking about, boy?"

"I'm talking about the fact that I am not prepared to devote my life to the service of my country. I'm talking about freedom of choice!"

Uri cast himself back in his chair, gaping at his son's face.

"The country has changed," Arik said more softly. "It's not what you think it is, not anymore. Lebanon—"

"Lebanon is over. We'll be out of there soon. We'll put it behind us."

"Never," Arik said.

"Listen, son. Every country has its stinking mistakes. Lebanon was ours. So we're not perfect."

"Perfect?" Arik laughed. "Lebanon was just a symptom. Lebanon is just the tip of the iceberg. What about the West Bank and Gaza? What about the Palestinians? It's like gangrene: you can cut off the limb, but if the rot's already spread . . ."

"That's a disgusting and unjust analogy," Uri said with

dignity. "But if that's the way you feel, all the more reason to act."

"Where is it written that it's on my head?"

"It just is. We've had our day. Now it's up to you."

"Sorry. Not interested."

Uri shrugged eloquently.

"I've only got one life."

"So what are you wasting it for?" sneered Sternholz.

"There are other places besides Israel."

"Name one," Uri snapped.

"America."

"America!" The father's eyes met Sternholz's. "That degenerate cesspool."

Arik smiled, shaking his head.

"You want America?" Uri said. "Go on, try it. Try living abroad. You'll be back in six months."

"Shut up," hissed Sternholz.

"What makes you so sure?"

"Because you'll find out what I already know: you don't choose your country any more than you choose your parents. You'll see. You'll never breathe freely, never be yourself in a foreign land." He pointed a finger (none too clean, stained with earth, tobacco, and ink) at Arik's face. "Choosing exile isn't freedom; it's self-annihilation. Don't you know anything? I'm beginning to think your mother was right."

"About what?"

Just recalling her words, and the quarrel that had preceded them, sent the blood rushing to Uri's head. His eyes bore traces of wounded astonishment, the look of a lion bearded in his den or a toddler when the world stands firm against his wishes. "She said it was my fault. She said that I was so busy playing soldier, statesman, and super-farmer, I let my only child slip away. She blamed me."

Sternholz sighed and shook his head, but sat on as if in penance.

"Maybe you think I don't understand what you've been

saying. Maybe you think that I don't realize my good fortune in having lived my youth when I did, in a time and place where the efforts of a relatively small group of men and women were enough to tilt the scales. *But I do.* God gave me strength, and the State gave me the opportunity to use it, and for that I am profoundly and humbly grateful." As he spoke, he examined his hands, turning the palms in, then out. They were large brown hands, with little tufts of white hair at the knuckles, lines of sinews like tree roots just under the skin of the earth. Then he threw out his arms in a gesture that encompassed all of Nevo, Dizengoff, Tel Aviv, and beyond. "Do you think *this* is what we wanted?" he demanded. "Do you think *this* is what we meant?"

"Are you saying you failed?"

Uri laughed unhappily. "How can I say that? We got what we fought for, a homeland. But look what it's become: an isolated city-state, plagued by enemies without and within. . . . All we built was the framework, the scaffolding. And I tell you, Son, that if you give it all you've got, if you spend your whole life working, and working well, to shape this country according to your vision, in the end you are going to hand it over to your children and say, 'This isn't it at all. This isn't what we meant. Take it—it needs work.' "

"Then why do it?"

"Because it needs to be done."

"Is that all you can say?"

The father ran his fingers through sheaves of white hair, tugging at the ends. "We're better off now than when we started. What else can a man say for himself? The most you can do is to keep on working, keep on trying, and if you can't hold on to the hope of Zion, hold on to the vision."

They fell silent. Then Uri crossed his thick arms over his chest and muttered truculently, "She said I never talked to you."

Arik shifted uneasily. "True enough," he said.

"But don't you remember all the walks we took, through the orchards and the forests? When I came home from Jerusalem or the army and the two of us would go out hiking? Am I the only one who remembers?"

"I remember," Sternholz murmured, and they stared at him, for how could he? But it was another father he remembered, and another son.

"Don't you?" Uri demanded.

Without answering, Arik looked past his father toward the bright street. His eyes tracked a girl clad in scanty shorts and a tee shirt, but in his mind he sat with his mother in the little house, full of the aroma of cake warm from the oven, waiting for his father's return from Jerusalem. Outside, the shouts of the boys playing ball drifted past on a warm breeze. The clock ticked over Uri's armchair; his mother whittled at a little figurine of wood (she hated knitting but also idleness, and had taken up whittling during her pregnancy with Arik). Uri's arrival was heralded by loud cries from the boys; then more waiting, the clock ticking, for Uri to arrive. He made slow progress crossing the kibbutz, as he paused to talk with the Secretary, chat with friends, shoot a few balls with the kids. Suddenly he was there, filling the doorway, blocking the light with his huge head atop massive shoulders; framed by the setting sun, he cast a tree-like shadow. Rina was swept forward for his kiss. Then Uri approached Arik and shook his hand.

"What are you doing indoors on such a beautiful day?" he boomed. "You should be out playing with your friends." And then, at a prompting look from Rina: "Well, as long as you're here, you might as well come for a walk before dinner. I have some things to discuss with you."

In silence they crossed the breadth of the kibbutz, walking, as men do, in parallel lines that never touched. Arik pretended not to notice the other boys, embarrassed by their envy.

Just beyond the cowsheds they came to the first and oldest orange grove, planted by Uri Eshel and his comrades during Ein Hashofet's first year, when the kibbutz was no more than a jerry-built collection of shacks where the dining room now stood. It was in this gentle orchard, under the soft autumnal sky, the dry, earthy air spiked with a tantalizing hint of the coming rains, that Uri and Rina held Arik's *brit*. Here, Uri knew every tree from its sapling days; and as they walked he sometimes brushed the back of his hand against a trunk, the way Arik had seen housemothers in the children's houses move rapidly from bed to bed, pausing here to touch a sleeping brow, there to adjust a blanket.

Uri Eshel was silent as they crossed the first grove, silent as they entered the next. At first his silence suggested conspiracy, promising matters of import and secrecy to be imparted in certain privacy. Protracted, his speechlessness took on the character of distraction; he did not forget his son but was engrossed in an inner dialogue that excluded him. Arik, with no such interior discourse to occupy him, could only wonder at his father's thoughts. He did not venture to speak first, for what had he to say worthy of his father's attention? There was no common ground. The small affairs of Arik's life—friendships and rivalries, school and work and children's politics—were his mother's province; he would have blushed to speak of such childish things with his father, no matter how much he longed for his advice.

And yet the silence was companionable; despite his disappointment it was something to know that his father felt easy enough with him to drop his social mask and indulge himself in this way. Certainly Arik preferred their quiet walks to the hortatory kind, wherein Uri planted himself in the midst of a grove and lectured, as if Arik and the trees that stood about them in respectful rows were his pupils, and his task were to convey necessary information as clearly and economically as possible. Topics ranged from history to botany to military strategy to politics, and though the material was invariably interesting, Arik's comprehension was hampered by the feeling that he was liable to be tested on it.

They returned to the kibbutz in unbroken silence. As they entered the populated center, Uri's eyes cleared. He turned to Arik and said, with no sense of irony, "Good talking to you, Son," perfectly unaware of the fact that not a word had passed between them in the hour since they had set out.

"All those walks," Uri now mourned, "all those talks. You, my only son. I taught you everything I knew. How could this thing happen?" ("How?" echoed Sternholz.)

"I'm trying to tell you. The things that were possible in your day are no longer possible. A lot of options have been closed off."

"A lot remain," Uri said promptly, in the voice of experience. "And every time you do something, new ones arise. That's what politics is all about; it is a field of constantly changing possibilities." The father's eyes shone with diehard hope. "I've always felt you'd make a good practitioner of the art. I looked forward to seeing what you could do."

Arik's mouth twisted, as if in regret, but he said, "It's you I'm sorry for. You gave it everything you had, and look what you got back."

"A country!" Uri barked. "A homeland! That's your idea of a small return?"

"What *kind* of country?"

"That's for you to determine." Arik did not respond. "Look, I'm not telling you what to do with your life. All I'm saying is, do it where you belong."

Arik was reduced to silence, but not concurrence. He shook his head sadly but firmly.

Uri turned to Sternholz and appealed to him. "Did I leave something out? What more can I say?"

"You could say you love him anyway, whatever he

does," the old man suggested. (Groaning, Arik put his head in his hands.)

"Why the hell would I say a thing like that?"

"Did you *ever* tell him you love him?" Sternholz asked.

"In so many words?" Uri looked and sounded shocked.

"Yes, in so many words. I, love, you. Did you ever say that?"

("Please, Sternholz, you're making me sick."

("Shut up, Arik.) Did you?"

"Hell, no."

"I just wondered," the waiter said mildly.

"Good God, old man, you're worse than Rina." But slowly, Uri turned to his son and asked, "Would that make a difference? Is that what it takes, to make you stay?"

Arik writhed in his seat. "No! What are you listening to that fool for? Leave me alone, both of you. Just leave me alone."

The father passed a hand over his eyes and pushed back his chair. Suddenly, the discreet clamor of Nevo, which had continued unabated during their talk, even rising, with exquisite tact, to cover the noisier altercations, stilled to a gentle buzz. As the three men looked up, Sarita Blume came into Nevo.

Arik leapt to his feet, intercepting her. "Hello, Sarita," he said.

She smiled uncertainly.

Uri Eshel inspected her face, first with dispassionate appreciation, then with closer attention. He shot a questioning glance at Sternholz, who blinked, then looked back at the girl. Pushing back his empty glass, he rose expectantly.

Arik reluctantly performed the introduction. "My father, Uri Eshel. Sarita Blume."

"It's a pleasure," he said, and, despite her reserve, he seemed prepared to stand and chat; but Arik gave him an unmistakable glare, and Sternholz took his arm and drew him away. Arik placed his hands on the girl's shoulders and gently pushed her into a chair. He sat close beside her.

As they walked toward the door, Uri bent his head to Sternholz's. "Yael Blume's daughter?"

"Yes."

"Amazing resemblance. And she and Arik . . . ?" He waggled a hand back and forth.

Sternholz shrugged and looked heavenward. Uri laughed, his sad face brightening. "That'll be something to tell Rina, anyway. Maybe I'll escape with my life."

They walked out to the pavement and shook hands. "Thanks anyway, Emmanuel," Uri said.

Sternholz sat by his window, watching the dappled sea in the early dawn light. Forty-five years ago he had crossed that sea for the first and last time. His body had been washed ashore, emaciated, torn, and bruised; he had arisen, and yet it was but a partial resurrection, a sullied miracle at best, for the reins of his life had been wrested from him, and he never regained control.

Thus Sternholz saw with a dead man's clarity, and understood everything but the motives and consequences of his own behavior. Uri's mute love for his son, and Arik's longing for his father, were transparent to him. But was he right to speak to Uri? Had his interference done any good, or had it merely deepened the rift? He could not tell. He was a man who did not know himself, and believed, moreover, that there was nothing there to know.

For he was the keeper of Nevo, no more, no less. If Nevo was a stage, and all his customers protagonists in their separate dramas, then Sternholz's roles were manifold but uniformly subsidiary. He was the propman, the janitor, the Greek chorus, and the machinist of the deus ex machina; he was everything to others and nothing to himself.

Even his insights came from outside. It was not until Sarita showed him her drawing that he admitted to himself having loved Yael Blume, and it was only when she questioned his silence that he realized, far too late, of course, the possibility of speech.

But Sternholz shied away from even that retroactive taste of freedom, which had no place in his present half-life. The memory of love undeclared and unconsummated was galling to him, as it brought to mind other loves, insufficiently declared, inadequately consummated, and but for the reminding presence of Sarita in Nevo, he would have put it from his mind.

When he crossed that sea (brightening now, struck by the first oblique rays of the sun), he left his past behind. For many years now he had not thought of Greta, or of Jacob. Now, suddenly and for no known reason, long-buried memories were rising from their grave, disturbing his already restless nights. His hand twitched and Sternholz moaned in pain as a small, confiding fist closed around his fingers. "Papa," said his son, "let's go to the park. Bring the ball, Papa." Sternholz wrenched his hand away and covered his ears. "Come on," the little voice piped impatiently. "I'll pick a flower for Mama and one for you. Let's go to the park." Tears streamed from beneath tightly closed lids. "Mein kind, mein kleiner kind," the old man cried.

He opened his eyes, and there before him was the sea, calm, deep, blue. Small boats crossed slowly to and fro over its surface, as fishermen cast their nets. Rising shakily, Sternholz shuffled into the kitchen. He lit the gas ring with a match and placed a blue enamel kettle on the fire. When the kettle whistled, he measured a spoonful of Nescafé into a chipped ceramic cup, added the boiling water, and stirred. He carried the cup back to the window, blew on it, and sipped. That hot and bitter brew was the demarcation of his day and night. Insomniacs cannot avoid their dreams, which will visit them awake if denied access to their sleep; and yet, *like ghosts, they avoid the glare of day. The act of exorcism worked. Even as the hot liquid washed down his gullet, Sternholz felt the room lighten and clear, freeing him to lift his head and look about. Empty. The room was as empty as his life.*

Chapter Twelve

CASPI sat on the toilet, his jeans around his ankles, straining and groaning mightily. He was constipated. In some way not yet clear to him, this, too, was Vered's fault.

After twenty minutes without result, he gave it up and returned to his study. The desk was piled high with books but empty of papers, except for a looseleaf notebook opened to a blank page. Caspi glared at the page for a while, fiddling with a pen. He took a bottle of whiskey from the bottom drawer and poured some into a glass. As he drank, he doodled a series of skulls and crossbones at the top of the page; when that was full, he moved into the left margin. Caspi's mind was blank, he wasn't thinking; but as the skulls grew darker and the crossbones more ominous, anger played across his face. When the margins were all full, the blank white interior of the page mocked up at him. He held his pen, poised to write, but the words wouldn't come. The apartment was too quiet, and the clocks were too loud. "*Damn* the woman," he whispered.

He walked down the hall and into Vered's study. Her desk chair was a delicate-looking concoction of wicker and cloth, unexpectedly comfortable and strong enough to handle even Caspi's bulk without a murmur. He yanked open the passport drawer and checked the white envelope, replacing it carefully when he had done. A half-finished draft of her column lay across the typewriter; Caspi read it, penning in a few corrections and stylistic improvements. It would tell her he had been in there, but she would know that anyway; she always did, even when he had done no more than to lie down on her couch for a moment.

And who had a better right to lie on that divan than he, who had bought it for her on their first anniversary? Scouring the city for the perfect sofa for a left-handed writer who liked to work reclining. Finding at last, hidden in the eaves of a Jaffa antique junk store, an old leather chesterfield, covered with dust, the leather cracked and scratched but restorable, one end curving up to form a padded backrest, the other stretching out long enough—here was his error, witness his naïveté—to sleep on. Too late he learned that couches were anathema in a married home, for, like new weapons systems, they demanded use.

Poor Caspi: little did he know, then, how spitefulness and petty jealousy can lead a woman astray. For the sake of his bride he had broken off half a dozen actual or pending affairs, confining his wenching to married women with reputations to preserve, a far cry in his eyes from the young girls he preferred, but for her sake he did it; and was she grateful? Did she appreciate the sacrifice?

She was not; she did not. Her behavior disappointed him sadly. One day the irate husband of one of his women phoned Vered. Instead of doing the decent thing and blasting the tattletale for impudence, she came to *him*, carping, complaining, and crying, "Was it true? Was it true?"

"Yes, it's true, goddamn it!" he finally exploded. "Did I join a monastery when I married you? Did I become a castrato? You're a charming girl, Vered, but if you really believe all that crap about a man cleaving only to his wife till the end of his days, et cetera, then I've married a fool." He'd blustered on until the matter of his infidelity was lost among the verbiage, and the only remaining issue was whether or not she would ever regain the esteem she had lost in his eyes, through her scene-making and carrying-on.

Caspi sighed, remembering her malleability in the good old days. When had she grown so hard? It must have been a gradual process, though for the life of him he could not recall the stages. (There had been that rather unpleasant little contretemps about the birth control pills—but that thought no sooner presented itself to Caspi than he slapped it down.)

Perhaps, reflected Caspi, it was not entirely Vered's fault. Perhaps there was some natural force at work here. They seem to have got caught up in some kind of marital whirlpool, sucked into a downward spiral. Struggling only increased the rate of descent, but passivity didn't help either and was harder to endure. The more women he pursued, the more Vered rejected him; the more she rejected him, the more frequent and public his outside pursuits. She punished his offenses by withdrawing to her studio, where, though forbidden entry, he gravitated whenever he was alone in the flat. He liked to finger her things, read her letters and drafts; he liked to lay her books on their spines and see where they fell open, to find out what she was reading. Vered hated it. She said he violated her privacy, and she stressed the word "violated."

"What do you want from me?" she demanded, one stormy afternoon. "What are you trying to find out?"

"What makes you tick," he said. "The *womanness* of you. The female soul." Thereafter, whenever he pictured his wife in his mind, he saw her eyes looking at him as they did then: dark, remote, judging eyes that for all their criticism really *saw* him—something Caspi was convinced that no one else did.

"It's spying," she said finally. "I won't have it."

"Fool, you should be flattered I care; instead you accuse me of espionage! I am not spying! It is not information that I seek, but intimacy."

"You have an abundance of intimacy," she'd coldly replied. "Keep out of my room." She put a lock on the door, but he tore it off.

On her desk was a portrait of Daniel, taken when he was two. In it the child gazed at the camera with a serious look in his eyes, which were neither blue like Caspi's nor black like Vered's. They were a speckled green, and they reminded him of someone he could not put a name to. Mother, father, a sibling perhaps; Caspi remembered none of them.

He crossed to the bookshelf and read the titles there. They were Hebrew, English, and French in roughly equal measure, organized by genre rather than language: poetry, essays, political memoirs, and a respectable collection of first novels from which his own was conspicuously absent. Indeed none of his books appeared on her shelves, though he had given her handsome leather-bound copies of each. Perhaps, he thought, the titles were *not* in the best of taste; they had certainly sounded cheap in Sternholz's mouth. But at the time they had seemed right. And Rami had approved. And they sold.

They would not sell forever, however, not without new books to bolster them and keep his name in the public eye. Three years had passed since his last book was published, and during that time Vered's career had blossomed. In addition to her weekly column in *Yediot*—she was the youngest columnist on the paper by eight years—she now edited the literary section. She, who had been "Caspi's wife" for the first seven years of their marriage, had achieved a position of power in his world that rivaled his own. If he didn't start producing soon, he was going to wind up being known as "Caspi's husband"—a fate worse than death.

All of which raised certain questions. Caspi had glimpsed something, a pattern, a structure. He lay on the divan with his sneakers on the lilac afghan to consider. If marriage was a microcosm, might it not be governed by the same physical and economic laws as the macrocosm? Conservation of energy, for example: perhaps marriages possessed a finite quantum of energy, or good fortune, that migrated from partner to partner. Was Vered's success linked casually or causally to his own inactivity? Did her energy level increase as his decreased? Was he, in fact, on a seesaw with Vered?

A pity if it were so, for though the obvious solution in such a case was to dismount, Caspi could no more disengage himself from her than he could cut off his writing hand. Vered was the only creature on earth who really saw, heard, *knew* him. Without her he would be thrown back on himself—that is, truly lost.

Yet Vered, by what Caspi persisted in thinking of as her flirtation, was tampering with the marital ecology, a dangerous tinkering that could lead to cataclysmic upheaval. A lesser man than Caspi might blame himself for the disaster his marriage had become; but Caspi rose above temptation and blamed Vered.

He blamed her unfeeling heart and her petty obsession with his peccadilloes. She had mastered the art of remote proximity; frequently whole days and nights passed by with no more communication on her part than blank stares when they passed in the hall. For Daniel's sake she pretended to talk to him when they met over breakfast, but always with a little smile on her face that seemed to say, I don't really mean this. As soon as Daniel left the room, she fell silent and would not look at him.

He felt the withdrawal of her eyes more than of her

voice. It affected his work and made him feel insubstantial, an invisible man. Oh, she had much to answer for, and wasn't it terrible (thought Caspi) that a man should most desire the very thing that he could never have? Especially when it was in constant view. Caspi felt like Moses on Mount Nevo, overlooking the forbidden Promised Land. Moses held the lease on the land, and Caspi a license to the woman, but neither of them would ever realize his own property.

Caspi was only a man, ungraced by God, silenced by a mysterious affliction, unlike Moses, whose stammer was miraculously circumvented. God had grown stingy in his old age, or weak of limb. Had He but seen fit to cure Caspi's inexplicable silence, releasing that dense cloud of thoughts, images, dreams, phrases, and names which, blocked, exerted such unbearable pressure on his heart, then Caspi could have mimicked His magnanimity by freeing Vered. *Free her first, and see what happens*, said a voice inside his head; but Caspi was nobody's fool. Who dared ask that sacrifice of one who had never, in his remembered life, known a mother's love or a father's embrace?

The Jewish Agency had brought him from Europe at the end of the war, clothed by its charity but bereft of identity. First the Agency sent him to a kibbutz, where he lived for three years until the members, with the serene cruelty of idealists, rejected him. They sent him back to the Agency with a satchelful of clean, pressed clothes and a note (written in English so he could not read it, but he took it to an older boy who translated it for him) calling him incorrigible. Then Caspi was sent to an orphanage outside Holon, where he lived out the rest of his short childhood. He was hungry and he was smart; he got the best education he could under the circumstances, read a lot, and won a scholarship to Tel Aviv University. A self-made man who had never loved anyone until he met Vered.

Moses led his people onward toward the Promised

Land, knowing all the while that he himself would never enter, but Caspi had had none of his advantages. If he could not have Vered, no one would.

Caspi needed a cigarette but found none in Vered's room. He returned to his study. There, sprawled on his desk like a woman with her legs splayed open, lay his notebook. Caspi threw himself into the chair and seized his pen, holding it poised to stab. His mind coughed, sputtered, and went dead.

He tried to squeeze the words out, like toothpaste from a tube, but nothing emerged. Something inside labored fruitlessly to come forth; he had constipation of the brain, a massive inner blockage that exerted unbearable pressure. Caspi, who by now felt very sorry for himself, thought: if only there were surgery for writers, surgeons who could open up his mind and lift those words out whole. If only one could deliver a book the way Athena was delivered, by cranial Cesarean.

Then the telephone rang, and Caspi jumped, banging his knee on the desk.

"Oh, it's you," he growled. "No, it's all right. I've been meaning to call. I'm having second thoughts about the anthology."

Rami Dotan squealed over the wire. With an expression of distaste Caspi moved the receiver further from his ear.

"Shut up," he said. "Don't get hysterical. I haven't made up my mind definitely yet."

"We can't cancel it now," Rami cried. "We've already announced it."

"So worse comes to worst you'll unannounce it."

"Why are you doing this to me?"

"I'm not doing it *to* you, dear boy," said Caspi. "I'm doing it *for* you. I just don't believe that friend Khalil is going to turn out a creditable performance. We don't want to humiliate the cousins, do we?"

"Aha!" said Rami.

"What does 'Aha' mean?"

"I see!"

"What do you see, you moron?"

"I can't let you do it, Caspi."

"Do what?" he roared.

"Make such a tactical error. If you pull out now, you'd just be confirming the rumors."

Caspi took the receiver from his ear and held it away, looking at it. Dotan's high-pitched voice vibrated in the air. After some time Caspi hung up, but continued staring at the phone.

It rang a moment later. He picked it up and said fervently, "You asshole."

"The feeling is mutual, though I deplore your choice of expression. How did you know it was me?"

"I didn't, Jemima," he said wearily. "I'm sorry, that wasn't intended for you. What do you want?"

"Vered, please."

"Is something wrong with Daniel?"

"No, he's fine. He's sleeping. Where's Vered?"

"Sitting at my feet, gazing up adoringly. She says to tell you she can't talk now."

"What a charming sense of humor you have," Jemima said. "Put her on."

"She's out," he said curtly.

"Where?"

Caspi put his hand to his throat, where a tight bubble threatened to burst. He said, "Am I my wife's keeper?"

"You have Arab eyes," he crooned, caressing her face. "Pitch-black wells, deep as sorrow."

"I forgot you were a poet," Vered said.

"I never forget you are a critic. Shall I expect a review of my performance in tomorrow's *Yediot*?"

She giggled. "Not bloody likely."

His eyes grew solemn. "No, you are right. In this room we are only man and woman. We leave our other differences outside that door."

"That's very romantic," she said, a trifle drily; Khalil gave her a sharp look.

"Don't you want to be here with me?" He touched her breast, and she felt his heat through the sheet. Her nipple stiffened, brushing his palm, and he caught his breath.

She said after a pause, "I came to you."

"You did." His hand slid under the sheet and down her body. Vered's breath turned quick and shallow. She closed her eyes.

Sometime later, he paused on the verge of entry, to tease. "Say you want it, Mrs. Caspi," he demanded.

"Don't play games!"

"It's no game. Say you want it."

"God help me, I want it."

"*Allah Akhbar!*" he cried, and thrust home.

But once again he finished quickly and withdrew at once, leaving Vered with no more recourse than a dinner guest whose meal has been inadequate, unequal to her hunger. Khalil kissed her perfunctorily, then sat up and lit two cigarettes. He gave her one.

"Tell me," he murmured, rubbing her shoulder, "is he impotent with you?"

She gasped and pulled the sheet higher.

"I've met a few of his women since we started working together. Isn't it strange that none of them comes close to you, neither in looks nor sensuality?" She looked at him in amazement. "There must be a reason."

"What business is it of yours?"

Khalil showed his teeth. "Anything that concerns you, my love, concerns me."

"How very odd that you should think so, on such short acquaintance."

His grin faltered, then broadened. He bowed his head. "More and more I see that Caspi is a fool. But so, perhaps, are you. I wonder at your loyalty to such a husband."

"Is this loyalty?" She waved her hand around the room, which was hot and sultry despite the open window. Neon flashes from across the street provided sporadic illumination, and the smell of fish wafted in on the breeze. It was a transients' hotel on the Jaffa waterfront, one step above a brothel; one of the few places, he'd explained to her, that a Jewish and Arab couple could take a room together unharassed.

"But you are so reticent," Khalil said. "Don't you trust me?"

Vered looked at him. Stripped of his designer jeans, his corduroy jacket with the professorial patches at the elbows, and his Gucci shoes, clad only in the dusky skin of his race, he seemed more a stranger than ever. His smooth brown body was almost hairless, unlike the hirsute Caspi, whose chest and stomach were so thickly matted with silky brown hair that the skin underneath stayed white even in summer.

She had heard, and her limited sampling tended to confirm, that hairy men make better lovers. Caspi in bed was so different from Caspi out of bed as to suggest a split personality. Out of bed he was cocky, egotistic, and insensitive; in bed he seemed possessed of a genuine desire to please and an uncanny awareness of his partner's feelings. Hence his success with women, including, for too many years, Vered. She could not hate him in bed, so she stopped sleeping with him. Vered had not lain with a man in so long that her body felt dead.

Because no one touched her, except Daniel. Jemima was not a tactile person. Caspi was, but she despised him. She remained a woman only to her son, whose nurturing was the only womanly function she performed. Outside the house, competing in a man's world, she was careful to strip both her work and her relationships of anything that might be construed as femininity, discarding empathy, sympathy, tenderness, and even grace, choosing to display only the bare bone of intellect. Pain especially had to be kept hidden, for while certain vigorous modes of suffering—Caspi's vaunted inner torment was one example—were permissibly male in character, she was not capable of such raucous displays; her anguish was at once too quiet and too deep for expression.

Pity was the other danger. Because Caspi's much publicized philandering left her particularly vulnerable to pity, she could accept none, but invested tremendous energy in creating a persona that repelled, if not the emotion, then at least its expression.

Vered took pride and comfort in her ability to deceive. Even after the most bitter of quarrels, which left Caspi prostrated in his study or sodden in Nevo, she went about her business as usual, with the utmost composure.

So much effort left her drained. She felt empty, desiccated; hardly a woman at all. And because she felt sexless, she was treated that way; if any of the men she worked with had amorous impulses, they kept them strictly to themselves. Until Khalil.

When the Arab turned his dark eyes on her and let them travel down her body before raising them to her face, there wordlessly but openly to proclaim his desire, she was, all unwilling, jolted to the core. Her heart pounded, and her mouth went dry, and a pilot light rekindled in her belly. When their hands touched, his told secrets and asked questions to which hers replied.

But trust him? Trust a stranger? Trust (she was ashamed, but could not help thinking) an Arab? "No," she said.

"Wise woman!" Khalil laughed, not only undaunted but delighted by her reply. "But seriously, what *is* his problem? Why isn't he writing?"

Vered hesitated. "He's not as good as he needs to be to write the kind of book he wants to write. He says he can't get it right."

An odd look crossed Khalil's face, of recognition, almost of sympathy, but he said scornfully, "Is that why he tumbles everything in skirts?"

"No. That's been going on much longer than his writer's block."

"Then why does he do it, with a woman like you at home?"

She shrugged. "It's his problem, not mine. I'm not my husband's keeper."

"Ah! And you don't mind his screwing around. It doesn't bother you at all."

"Does your wife mind?" she countered.

His face darkened; he did not like her mentioning his wife. "She doesn't know. Discretion is not only the better part of valor but also one form of respect I feel I owe my wife. Caspi, on the other hand, flaunts his tarts all over town."

Vered said, "He's a bastard all right," and shuddered deep within her body. She had undressed before this stranger, exposed her breasts, opened her legs: but only now, discussing Caspi with him, did she experience at last the sensual thrill of betrayal.

"He's right about one thing," Khalil said.

"What's that?"

"He's *not* a good enough writer. I've been reading his stuff."

She moved away. "Why?"

"For the introduction I'm writing. Didn't he tell you? I'm writing an introduction to Caspi's section of the anthology, and he's writing one to mine."

"Oh my God."

Khalil chortled. "Wait till you read it."

"Rami Dotan won't publish anything critical of Caspi. Why should he? Caspi's still his meal ticket."

"He has no choice. It's covered in the contract. If he cuts my piece, I can have the edition taken off the market."

"Then he'll drop the anthology."

Khalil's face was gleeful. "If he doesn't publish on time, I have the right to take the whole package to a West Bank publisher."

"I can't believe Rami would sign a contract like that!"

"Caspi made him!" Khalil crowed. "Caspi, the great liberal, patron of the primitive arts, twisted his arm. I can't wait to see his face when he reads my piece; can you, Mrs. Caspi?"

"Why do you keep calling me 'Mrs. Caspi'? You know my name."

"Ah, but I prefer Mrs. Caspi," he said. "It's so much more erotic."

Caspi stood stiffly in the doorway of his study, arms by his side. His bulk filled the narrow space. "Where were you?" he said.

"The same place you always go. Out."

"Don't spar with me. Where were you?"

Vered raised her head defiantly, glancing over his shoulder as she did. The blank white pages of his notebook glimmered in the lamplight. Crumpled balls of paper littered the floor. An impulse of pity raced through her and was gone before she noticed. "It's none of your business. Good night." She turned toward her room.

Caspi's arm shot out. He gripped her shoulder and spun her around. Softly, he said, "Come in. I want to talk to you."

He sat at his desk; she, legs curled beneath her, roosted in the armchair. Caspi stared into the space between them, working his jaw. In the harsh glare of the lamp he appeared, for the first time, his full age and more. He also looked sober, though she'd smelled whiskey on his breath. Vered devoured a cigarette, saying nothing.

"Were you with that Arab?" His loud voice startled both of them.

"What Arab?"

"Is there more than one Arab in your life?"

"No," she said, "only one."

Caspi sucked in his cheeks and chewed on them. After a while, during which all that could be heard was a ticking clock and Vered's mammoth inhalations, he said, "Were you with him?"

"I don't have to account to you."

"Yes, you do. I always tell you."

"Yes, that's the best part for you, isn't it? You really have no right to jealousy, Caspi."

"My wife is shtupping an Arab, and I have no right to jealousy?"

"Why do you keep calling him 'that Arab'?" she asked uneasily. "He has a name."

"His name's not important. His race is."

"I can't believe I'm hearing that from you."

"Face it, baby, if he weren't an Arab, you wouldn't be screwing him. You knew you could never beat me in numbers, so when you saw a chance to even the score qualitatively, you jumped at it."

Vered shuddered. "God, that's disgusting. Caspi, what's come over you?"

"You," he said, "you've come over me. God," he sobbed, hiding his face, "why don't you just get out of my life?"

"Gladly," she said, on her feet, heading for the door.

Caspi jumped up and cut her off at the door. "Sit down!" he roared. She backed into her chair, and Caspi loomed over her, gripping the arms of the chair until his knuckles showed white. He's going to hit me, thought Vered, although he never had. In their quarrels it was always she who flailed out, with all the effect of a sea gull dive-bombing a schooner. His size and strength were so much greater than hers that they had imparted a kind of security: he would not dare.

Caspi looked at her eyes and then down at his hands. He moved away, put the desk between them. "You worked it out," he said, more in sorrow than in anger. "One Arab dick outweighs a thousand Jewish cunts."

"So the great liberal Caspi is a closet racist," Vered taunted wildly. She wished he *had* hit her; at least it would have ended things; she would have had no choice.

Caspi said, "If liberalism means agreeing to share the land, I'm a liberal. But if it means sharing our women, then fuck, yes, I'm a racist, and proud of it."

"This is horrible. I don't have to listen to this." But she sat on, fascinated, her back pressed against the chair.

"You're playing with fire," Caspi said gently. "I'm not the man to sit back and let some primitive wog cuckold me. He's probably laughing up his sleeve all the time he puts it to you. Do you make it in his car?"

"What?"

"Do you? Do you make it in his car? I need to know."

Vered made a disgusted face. "Now you're getting a taste of what I've felt all these years."

"It's not the same thing!" he declared, moving his chair closer to hers. "How do you expect me to swear off women when my wife has sworn off sex? And why should I? Why should I give up my greatest, nay, my only source of pleasure?"

"I thought that was writing," she said, and he gave her a wounded look.

"I adore women. Women in motion, women doing household things: pulling on stockings, lifting a child, glancing into mirrors, reaching for things. Women nursing babies!

"And by God," said Caspi, "I have a talent for them, a

gift of discernment, like less fortunate men have for wine or food. No mere connoisseur, I am a pioneer of women, seeking out beauty in places where other men fear to tread. Why, I married you, didn't I?"

She laughed helplessly. "You bastard."

"And the work I put in," he wailed, encouraged, "doesn't that count for something? What devotion, what sacrifice! Do you think *you* are the only one who suffers for my art? What arrant nonsense, what nauseating banalities, what sentimental sludge I have endured from the mouths of beautiful women! What excruciating boredom, hour after hour of twiddle twaddle for the sake of a relief which is always paltry compared to my expectations! You should pity me, Vered; indeed you should. I am a disappointed man."

"Poor Caspi," she sneered, but he hardly heard her; he was rapt in contemplation of his tormented soul.

"I don't know why it is," he mused. "I don't know where it comes from. Maybe it's hereditary; I wouldn't know. Or perhaps it comes from never having had a mother and so having missed those things that other men had in full measure when they were young."

"Give it a rest, Caspi. Remember, I've seen your orphan act before." As many times as she'd thought these words she'd never said them. Caspi looked genuinely hurt.

"Never mind, then," he said. "The point is, do you really think you are woman enough to compensate for all the other women in the world? Ha! If you were, you could never have stayed out of my bed so long.

"Besides," he said, winding down, reaching for a cigarette, "I need them for my work."

"Your work, yes. You're really touching all the bases tonight, Caspi."

"Cynicism does not become you, Vered. Yes, I need them for my work. How do you expect me to create women if I don't *know* women? Those girls, they are just my research, required reading if you will. *You* were the only one I wrote about. I never betrayed you." His voice trembled with wounded sincerity.

Vered, torn between laughter and tears, remembered nights and nights of lying sleepless and alone, listening for the car door, his foot on the steps, his key in the latch. Remembered him coming in at dawn, whistling and singing off key; dancing into the bedroom, smiling in pleased surprise, and saying, "Vered! Up so early?" Remembered him once coming into the bathroom while she was bathing, perching on the toilet seat, and confiding, as if to his best friend, "I think I'm in love." She had thrown a bar of soap, followed by everything else she could lay her hands on. Caspi had been hurt and offended that she would not rejoice in his good fortune.

She felt the old bitterness slip through her veins like poison. That much of her anger was self-directed took nothing away from the portion directed at Caspi; toward him her wrath was like a mother's love, bottomless.

"You never betrayed me?" she said.

Caspi raised his hand, palm outward. "I swear to God. Those girls had nothing to do with us."

"Then try," she said, "to think of Khalil as having nothing to do with us."

Caspi fell back in his chair, clasping both hands to his heart like a mortally wounded man. To Vered, who knew him well, the theatricality of the gesture was no indication of falseness. In Caspi much that seemed sham was actually a twisted mode of self-revelation—as if Caspi could not deal with emotions on a human scale but had to project them onto a large screen in order to respond. Looking at his shaggy misery, she felt a thrill of pity, which she sternly repressed. She was only doing what had to be done. Caspi staggered to his feet.

"Don't taunt me," he said. "Don't play with me. I'm

giving you fair warning. I've thought it all out and I've nothing to lose. Know, Vered, that I will never divorce you. What I will do, if you continue to see this wog, is to destroy him."

She laughed. Her eyes were watchful. She said, "You're not stupid enough to kill your wife's purported lover."

"He's an Arab. No one would look twice."

"I don't believe you."

"I will do it in a way that makes it look like the work of one of the Jewish terror gangs. A random killing."

"Then why tell me?"

"My dear," he said, with civil astonishment, "I don't *want* to do it. I'm hoping to avoid the necessity."

"You're being ridiculous. You know very well that if you harmed him, I'd go straight to the police."

"You couldn't prove it." Caspi beamed, inviting her to share his delight in his own ingenuity. "I don't mind if people guess, so long as no one can prove it. I'd have an alibi, of course."

"Dory?" she said grimly.

He shrugged. "It would work, Vered. I hope for both our sakes that you believe me."

She stared at him and he returned her gaze. He saw the very moment that disbelief changed to belief. Vered licked her lips and said, "You haven't thought it all out."

"No? What have I overlooked?"

"Picture yourself with a gun, Caspi, aiming it at Khalil. Will you shoot him in the back?"

"No," he said.

"Then you'll have to face him. He's unarmed. He's done nothing to you that you haven't done to dozens of other men. He's defenseless, at your mercy. Can you murder him in cold blood?"

Caspi made a gun of his fist and pointed it at Vered. He cocked his thumb. "Bang," he said, and pulled the trigger.

Chapter Thirteen

JUST outside Afula, the bus's air conditioning broke down, and at once the atmosphere turned close and malodorous. Ilana struggled unsuccessfully with the window beside her seat. Her seatmate, a wizened Yemenite woman of anywhere between fifty and seventy-five, whose black dress exuded an odor of sweat and cumin, reached over and with a flick of her wrists released the latch and raised the heavy glass.

"Thanks," Ilana said.

The woman clicked her tongue. "In your condition," she said reprovingly, "you shouldn't strain yourself." Ilana's hand flew down to her flat abdomen, and the old woman cackled. "Forty years a midwife," she boasted. "No one can fool me. I know before the rabbit does. Visiting someone, dear?" Her eyes glittered with good-natured curiosity.

"My family." Ilana stumbled over the word.

Groaning slightly, the Yemenite bent down to the aisle and extracted a white packet from her voluminous straw bag.

Immediately, as she unwrapped the paper, a strong smell of garlic rose into the air.

"Care for a bite?" Ilana shook her head and swallowed hard, tasting bile. "Got to keep your strength up, dear."

"No, thank you."

The woman nodded sympathetically. "You'll get over that part soon." She bit into the pita and sausage sandwich, then wiped her mouth daintily on her sleeve. Ilana turned to the window.

They had left the coastal plain behind and were traveling through rough terrain. The hills around them were scantily clad in a thin layer of topsoil, through which the bare white rock extruded like a broken bone through skin. Scrawny pines dotted the landscape, and the road twisted upward ahead, glistening with melted tar. It was the hottest day so far. She could have driven up in half the time, in air-conditioned comfort, but for the folly of appearing in a brand-new snow-white Porsche in the village of her childhood. She had dressed carefully for this visit, choosing a simple cotton blouse and an old denim skirt, cinched at the waist by a leather belt that her uncle, the shoemaker, had made for her on her sixteenth birthday.

The belt fit as usual, for she had not yet begun to show. How, then, had the Yemenite known? (Sternholz, that sharp-witted old meddler, had guessed her secret, but that was no mystery; she oughtn't have ordered milk.) The Yemenite's effortless perception worried her. Was it written somewhere? Did it show on her face, in her eyes? And if her condition was so obvious, was not its precariousness equally perceptible? Perhaps the old woman's profession rendered her clairvoyance selective, for though the two weeks prescribed by Rafi Steadman had come and gone, then another week and yet another, Ilana had not decided, but merely postponed.

David called her nearly every night, never pressing the

issue but, skillful negotiator that he was, assuming a positive outcome. He asked her how she felt, discussed his work, made plans for a visit which they both knew without saying was predicated on her continued pregnancy.

Still, she could not make up her mind, or rather could not assert mind over matter, for there was every rational reason in the world to seek an abortion. Having the child would destroy a way of life which Ilana (before) had thought perfect. If she had the child, she would have to raise it herself—giving it up for adoption was unthinkable—and that meant an end to travel and career and the onset of loneliness. She would lose a world to gain this baby, with nothing to replace that which she had lost, for where would she fit in? One can live without friends if one has family and without family if one has friends. But to live and raise a child with neither friends nor family: that was a daunting prospect.

Who would help her? Who would teach her? None of her women friends, ladies of the demimonde, had children. They would think her mad, or wicked, and even the kindest of them would be torn away, finally, by the different style of their lives and that secret envious gnawing that Ilana herself had experienced in proximity to young mothers. Children, it was tacitly understood, were one of the things one renounced, the greatest part of the price one paid. Having a baby at this late stage would strike them as cheating, perhaps even tempting fate. Had they known of David's proposal, and on what irrational grounds she had refused it, they would have cast her off in horror as a kind of Jonah.

To whom, then, could she turn? In desperate hope she set out one sunny morning to visit a nearby park where, driving by, she had often seen groups of young mothers and babies congregating. She managed to approach a couple of women sitting on a bench in the playground, close enough to overhear their conversation. "Poor Dana's teething. She cries all night. I don't know *what* to do." "Try ointment on her gums. It worked for Anati." "Look, there's Nira. Can you believe her big boy's still in diapers!" But the moment they noticed Ilana they fell silent and stared, breaking into excited whispers as she hurriedly strode past, pretending she had a destination. Those women would *never* accept her, save as a curiosity and a subject of gossip. *"Guess who I talked to today, in the park with her little love child?"*

Certainly the men in her life would drop her, terrified of being tagged as the father of her child, and without them, her past, present, and future lovers, whom did she have? Her family, who took her money but wanted nothing to do with her? There was only Sternholz, who nagged her, "Go home."

" 'Go home,' " she mimicked. "Do you know what you remind me of, Emmanuel? Those toy crystal balls that kids used to play fortune-teller with, remember? Ask a question, shake the ball, and read the answer in the little window. Of course, it's always one of the same four answers, no matter what you ask."

"*Nu*, so what are my four answers?" he grumbled.

"Go home, get married, have a baby." She thought a moment, then concluded: "*Sei gesunt.*" Go in health.

Sternholz cackled, slapping the table in his mirth; then, shaking the tears from his runny eyes, he bent his old head down to hers. "They all apply to you," he whispered.

And despite her mockery she listened; for when Sternholz spoke only fools shut their ears. Marry she would not, but the rest of his advice had a cohesive logic she could not deny and an attraction she could scarcely resist. Sternholz spoke to her dreams, her fantasies. He spoke to that part of her that overran her waking and sleeping hours with visions of the sentient fetus growing and moving inside her; of herself, big with child, breasts bursting with milk; of that moment when she would behold her child for the first time, press it to her heart, and kiss its soft cheek. The harsh landscape faded from her sight, and Ilana sat in a rocking chair, in a bright nursery, singing to an infant who sucked at her breast. Its slight, resilient body shifted in her arms, and she smelled its sweet, milky breath as the babe broke off nursing to peer upward at her face.

The familiar beeping tones sounded, introducing the hourly news broadcast. At once the bus quieted. Passengers leaned forward in their seats, and the driver turned up the volume.

"In Lebanon today, the Israeli Defense Force spokesman reported two attacks on Israeli troops. In the area south of Sidon, a platoon on patrol was ambushed from the hills. Two soldiers were wounded, and a third was killed. In the second incident, an IDF jeep ran over a land mine on a routine patrol north of the border. The mine exploded, killing the driver and all three passengers. The names of the casualties have been withheld pending notification of the families. The IDF is searching for the terrorists."

Sighs, clicks, and murmurs from the passengers. "Ai, ai, ai," wailed the Yemenite woman. Tears coursed down the furrows of her cheeks. Ilana took her hand.

"You have children serving there?" she asked.

"They're all my children," the woman wept. "My sweet babes. Ai, ai, ai."

Ilana pressed the hand, then let it go. She never knew when her own brothers were doing their reserve duty in Lebanon and so lived with constant fear.

The nut-brown face then peered into hers, and strong fingers gripped Ilana's arm. "God grant you a daughter," the old woman whispered defiantly. "He should spare you a son; He should spare you the heartache."

"My mother always prayed for boys," Ilana said dreamily. "She said there were worse things in life than a clean death on the battlefield."

"True, true," said the Yemenite, peering at her with frightened, beady eyes.

Embarrassed, Ilana smiled weakly, removed her arm,

and turned back to the window, leaning her forehead against the warm glass. The jolting of the bus aggravated her nausea, which had set in with a passion since her return from London. She wondered how she would stand up to the pain of labor and birth: would she bear it bravely, or would she break down like those women she'd heard of, who filled the labor room with their shrill cries of "Mama, Mama!"? Her own mother had borne her labor pains without a cry or a whimper, but when Ilana was placed in her arms, she sobbed without surcease for three days. Her doctor was astonished. He had been a friend of her family in Germany and had known Katya all her life. "A modern European woman like you," he remonstrated, "should be above such foolish prejudice! I might expect it from your husband, but you!" Too far gone to resent or even notice the racial slur, Katya railed back at him: "What good is a girl? What can she do?" Her Iraqi husband forgot his own disappointment in terror of his wife's, and consoled her in the only way he could. "The next one," he promised, patting her arm awkwardly, "the next one will be a boy."

And though it proved true, that not only the next child but also the three who came after were male, Katya never entirely forgave her first-born. Yitzhak Maimon's preference for sons was shallow, a cultural prejudice that dissipated as he grew to love his daughter. Katya was less easily reconciled. Ilana could not remember a time when she did not know the story of her birth. Sometimes Katya told it as if ironically, hugging her daughter to her side with a bony arm. Other times, in private, she told it in anger, reproachfully. One way or another she told it often. But Ilana was not allowed to blame her mother, who had suffered greatly under the Nazis and would bear the mark of her captivity until the day she died. Ilana was required to understand that Jewish sons were a mother's weapons against the world of Jew-haters, while Jewish daughters were hostages to their hatred; thus sons redeemed their parents' suffering while daughters increased it.

In fifteen years nothing had changed. Inside the Kiryat Ata bus station, old men and women hunkered against the walls, a few pathetic baubles spread out on black cloths before their feet. A hunchback of indeterminate sex pushed a desultory broom across the filthy floor. Ticket clerks drank tea inside their cages, and in the station kiosk, flies buzzed around meat cooking on a rotating shwarma spit.

Outside, shirtless youths lounged on the pavement, smoking, ogling women, talking among themselves. Someone recognized Ilana and shouted her name aloud. A group of boys followed her for several blocks, keeping their distance, until one, more intrepid than the rest, approached and asked if 1,000 shekels were enough. Ilana shoved him out of her way, and his friends jeered.

Her parents lived in a project on the outskirts of town, a thirty-minute walk from the station. As she drew nearer, Ilana found herself walking more and more slowly, until she came to a complete halt just outside their building, which like all the others in the project was decorated with lines of washing. A gaggle of girls younger than Ilana's exile were playing hopscotch in the streets. They stopped to gape at her, for even her simplest clothes could not disguise the fact that Ilana came from another world, and one, the oldest, stepped forward bravely to ask whom she was looking for. Ilana smiled but did not reply.

She climbed the four flights of steps leading up to the apartment. Dimly lit by naked bulbs, the stairwell was not too dim for her to see the grimy hand prints on the peeling walls. Though there was a faint, pervasive smell of urine in the hall, her parents' landing was swept clean, and the door freshly painted. Ilana knocked softly. She heard no footsteps inside; but suddenly the door flew open, and her mother stood before her.

Katya's pale eyes widened; the corners of her mouth tightened. "You!" she breathed.

"May I come in?" Ilana said.

Her mother crossed her arms over her chest and stood pat.

"We *could* talk in the hall." Already doors were cracking open, curious eyes peering out. Grimacing, Katya stepped back. Ilana followed her inside and shut the door behind them. The smell of roasting chicken made her mouth water. "What do you want?" Katya said.

Ilana walked into the salon and saw the same old ugly, functional furniture, somber colors, bare, tiled floors, and drawn draperies she had grown up with. Even Katya's dress was familiar. Like everything she wore, it was high-necked and long-sleeved, to hide not only the tattoo but all the rest of her as well. Her family had been Orthodox, and though she had lost her faith in the camp, Katya retained her modesty.

The immaculate penury of the home and her mother's appearance were what Ilana had expected; she had known that every cent that her mother so grudgingly accepted had gone for her brothers' support and education. The only change in the room was a portrait of Menachem Begin embroidered on velvet which hung over the couch, another of Golda over the table, and a potpourri of photos of her brothers, together and separate, which stood on a side table. Ilana lifted the pictures one by one, examining them closely, saying their names in a small wondering voice, while Katya watched tensely. "They've grown into fine men. I want to know them. Mama, I want an end to it. I want my family back."

Her eyes locked onto her daughter's, Katya picked up the hem of her apron and began to dry her already-dry hands. She breathed deeply through her nose and after a while said without inflection, "What's wrong with you?"

"Does something have to be wrong with me?"

"You never came before."

"You threw me out. You said you never wanted to see me again."

"But I've seen you anyway, haven't I?" Katya retorted savagely. "On magazine covers, in newspapers: 'Playgirl Ilana Maimon.' You might have had the decency to change your name!"

"I didn't want to change my name." Ilana sat on the couch and felt the broken springs sag beneath her.

"Don't get too comfortable," Katya snapped, rubbing the apron over her hands, which now were liver-spotted and —was it possible?—reduced in size. Not only her hands but she herself seemed both smaller and thinner than Ilana remembered. The word "cancer" entered her mind, was examined and dismissed. Her mother's complexion was good and her bearing erect; only her size seemed oddly reduced, as if she'd been washed repeatedly in boiling water.

"How is Papa?"

"Fine."

"And my brothers?"

"Fine."

"And you're fine, too."

"Yes, I'm fine, too. Is this what you came for?"

"Mama—"

"Don't call me that!" A feather stroke of pain brushed over Katya's face.

"I want us to be a family again. Haven't I been punished long enough?"

"You got what you wanted," Katya said. "You can't have everything." Yet Ilana sensed a softening truculence in her tone, a willingness to be overcome, and for the first time she felt hope.

"I'm ready to change my life," she said. This time it was unmistakable: Katya's restless hands stilled, released the apron, and fell to her side, palms opened toward Ilana. She took a short step forward.

Ilana jumped up to meet her. The sudden change of position drained the blood from her head, and she staggered backward, falling into the couch. Katya's eyes widened, then narrowed.

"What's wrong with you?"

"Nothing's wrong." Ilana bent forward, forearms folded protectively across her abdomen.

Katya's eyes followed her arms. "You're pregnant!"

"Mama—"

"You slut!" she screamed. "You filthy slut!"

"Mama, I need you. I need a family."

Katya covered her face with her apron and rocked back and forth on her heels. "Oh, God, the shame. Why did I live, why did I live?" When Ilana arose, more slowly this time, Katya threw out her arms, not to embrace but to ward her off. "Get rid of it," she said, her face pinched and white. "Cast it out."

"Don't say that," Ilana begged.

"Cast out the child of sin, or you, too, shall be destroyed!"

"I *want* the child. I came for your forgiveness, and instead you curse me. Oh, Mama, you would treat your worst enemy with more compassion. Have you no feeling for me at all?"

Katya cried, "It's you who have no feeling for me! No one forced you to become what you are! You, a free Jewish woman, chose to live the life of a whore. You are my punishment, but I'm no fool Christian, to turn the other cheek. Haven't I suffered enough in my life? Oh, no, you wicked Jezebel, you traitor to your race. Get out of my house! I disown you, I spit on you and your bastard. I wish I were rich, I wish I were a millionaire, so that your disinheritance would cost you something you care about."

Ilana stumbled to the door, but turned once more in silent entreaty. Katya shrank back, covering her face. "I thought I had reached the end of my suffering over you, but I was wrong," she said. "You still have the power to torment me. I pray God never to see your face again."

Ilana ran up to the roof and stood close to the edge, looking down. The heat, collected and stored by the tarred surface, burnt her feet through her sandals, but Ilana shivered with cold. By jumping, she thought, she would put an end to three lives: her own, her child's, and her mother's, three generations with a single leap. Though this thought presented itself with cinematic clarity, accompanied by a vision of herself lying crushed on the stones below while neighbors tried to shield her mother from the bloody sight, both the thought and the vision lacked compelling force; she felt no impetus, only curiosity, like someone peering down a well.

Something fluttered inside her, as though the tiny fetus sensed danger and struggled desperately, butting, kicking, and punching with its primitive limbs to make itself felt. Ilana responded with a wave of fierce protectiveness. "Be calm," she crooned, kneeling beside the parapet, "be calm. Nothing will harm us. We are safe here."

The roof had always been her refuge. Especially after fights with Katya, she would escape the crowded apartment (one bedroom, divided by a curtain, she shared with her parents, the other belonged to her four brothers, while the living room was preserved in spotless order and inutility for the entertainment of visitors who never came) for the roof, where she spent hours and days gazing out beyond Kiryat Ata, beyond the industrial wasteland that surrounded it, over the hills to the green slopes of the Carmel, where, in a kind of sustained dream nurtured over years, she imagined herself living, a grown woman, beautiful and skilled in the usages of beauty, powerful, with men at her command and a palatial apartment all her own, staffed with invisible servants who cooked and cleaned for her—although being so very much in demand, between parties and dances and dinners in the finest Haifa restaurants, she made little use of the cook, except for intimate, candle-lit dinners for two.

Her family did not totally disappear in this opulent dream world, but were relegated to their proper places: her brothers confined to the kitchen, her parents, with the respect due their relationship if not their behavior, allowed into her reception rooms when no one else was there.

Twenty years later, as she stood in the same spot overlooking almost the same vista, Ilana was struck by how much of her dream she had achieved. She was as rich as she needed to be. She had traveled further, and in a more luxurious manner, than the child-Ilana had had scope to dream of. And although she had little power of her own, she had access to those who did, and she was an expert borrower and user of others' power. Her only failure lay in preserving her roots; that connection had been severed, her four little brothers grown from children into tall attractive men without her knowing them.

She saw her mother's face again, heard the bitter words, "You got what you wanted." It was true: she had been determined enough and unscrupulous enough at twenty-one to discard her family to attain it. Even now, she could not regret it.

Not for anything would she go back to that tiny, airless apartment, designed, as David would say, by men of little soul for men of little soul, to that press and stink of bodies, the snatched privacy, and the constant noise.

Longing, suddenly, to be safe in her apartment, cocooned in luxury and alone, Ilana decided to find the nearest cab stand and taxi back to Tel Aviv. But as she reached the door leading to the stairwell, it opened, and her father stepped out onto the roof.

He blinked in the strong sunlight, squinting at Ilana, who backed away warily.

"Your mother called me," he said. "The neighbors told me you came up here."

"I was just leaving," she said.

"Yes," he said. "But come for a walk with me first."

He led her to a forest on the outskirts of the village, behind the housing project. When Ilana had played there with her brothers, it was a child-sized forest with trees no higher than a grown-up's head. Now the trees were tall enough and the foliage broad enough to block out the sun. A cool breeze shifted through the trees, and in the shade the temperature dropped ten degrees. By mutual accord they paused to rest just inside the wood, leaning against two trees some feet apart. Staring at the ground, her father said, "Your mother tells me you are with child."

"Yes."

"Is the father Jewish?"

"Yes."

"Are you going to marry him?"

"No."

"Are you going to have the baby?"

She paused. "I want to."

"And keep it?"

"If I have it, of course I'll keep it."

Her father nodded and said, "That is right." Ilana lifted up her head and gazed at him, remembering him as he had been: a stern man, not given to laughter, fair and judicious with his children. She had feared him in those days, feared his untold stories, which must have been too terrible to tell— for if not, why not tell them?—and his temper, which, though well controlled, was fierce. He believed in respect and discipline, and would strap his boys (though not Ilana) for serious infringements. The worst offense of all, for which corporal punishment was mandatory, was rudeness toward their mother. The children learned very young that nothing but absolute respect toward Katya would be tolerated; they were taught to rise when she entered a room and to address her as "ma'am."

She felt none of that fear now. Perhaps all those years of sinning had produced some wisdom after all, or at least an area of clear vision, for now his emotions seemed as legible as any other man's, though his purpose was firmer. She saw that he felt love as well as anger for her, that he was torn in his feelings but not in his determination. She read fatigue in the postman's slump of his shoulders, as if he'd been carrying that bag for too long now ever to straighten up. For no particular reason she remembered the time her brother Hezi brought home a stray. Katya, always indulgent toward the boys, shook her head doubtfully and said, "Ask your father." When Yitzhak came home, all five children were lined up at the door to greet him. He looked pleased, then suspicious; his eyes traveled over the ascending line of his children's heads to meet his wife's. Katya shrugged and nodded toward the kitchen. When Yitzhak saw the rangy yellow Bedouin mutt, a half-breed Canaani, his brows came together fiercely. "Can we keep him?" the children chorused hopefully.

"Keep a dog?" he thundered without raising his voice. "Keep a dog, feed a *dog*, when Jews are starving?"

The children fell back, but need not have bothered; Yitzhak had eyes only for his wife. "Feed a dog?" he asked, reproachfully.

He ordered the children to find another home for it or else give it to the pound the next day. The dog was allowed to stay the night, but Yitzhak absolutely forbade them to feed it. "If you feed it," he said, "it always comes back."

Sadly, the children went to bed, where they fell asleep to the plaintive lullaby of the dog. Very late at night, Ilana awoke to silence. She slipped out of bed and crept past her parents' bed, through the living room, and into the kitchen. Her father stood beside the icebox, watching as the dog lapped up a saucer of milk. He looked up and said sharply, "What are you doing out of bed?"

"I woke up," she whispered. She expected to be sent summarily back to bed, but instead, her father fixed her with a brooding stare, then shook his head and said in a voice that was neither apology nor explanation, but trembled with passion, "I *hate* hunger. Even in a dog."

Now her father shook his head to rid himself of her gaze. "You shouldn't have come here," he said. "You had no right to upset her like that."

"It was a mistake. Quite useless. I see that now."

"Worse than useless. Wrong."

"Wrong" was a word seldom heard in her walk of life. In her father's mouth it clamored like an old church bell.

"*She* was wrong," Ilana said, her voice strident. "*She* was cruel."

The forest was very still. Yitzhak clenched his fists but did not raise them from his side. "Cruel?" he said. "She is charity itself."

"But I came to beg for forgiveness and reconciliation. What charity is it to turn away the prodigal daughter with a curse?"

"You don't understand how she suffered—"

Ilana clicked her tongue impatiently. "Was there ever a day in my life when I didn't know she suffered? And I *do* understand. She suffered, you suffered, everyone suffered— but not everyone lost their humanity. I know you think I'm a terrible sinner, Papa, but at least I'm human, I have feelings! *She* has none for me. She never had."

"She had feelings," Yitzhak said. "You just never understood them."

"She hates me."

"Did you say that to her?"

Unwillingly, she answered, "More or less."

"And she said . . . nothing?"

"What could she say? It's true."

"Her charity lies in silence. Even as you rub salt in her wounds, she protects you."

"From what?"

"From the truth." He added with a terrible coldness: "But now you will hear it."

"No." She stepped back. "I've heard enough."

"You must." He came closer, until face to face she could smell his sorrowful breath. "You deserve to know."

"Let me go. Let's forget I ever came back."

Closer still, he murmured: "How do you think she survived the camp? Didn't you ever ask yourself? She wasn't strong; she had no skills they needed. All she had was a pretty face, as pretty as yours, and a youthful body. How do you think she survived?"

"I don't know."

"You must have wondered."

"No, no," and she pushed him away and stumbled into the forest. As she ran, half blind with tears, she heard his flatfooted, shuffling run crashing through the undergrowth, his harsh breath coming closer. In a short time he passed her and then turned, thrusting himself before her so that she must either stop or crash into him. She stopped. He crossed his arms over his chest and did not touch her.

Lowering her head, she wept. "I'm sorry I came here."

Her father's voice was not without kindness. "You can't undo the things you've done, any more than we can undo the things that were done to us. You made your bed, and now you have to lie in it." He reached out as if to touch her, but his hand fell short. He straightened his back and said, "I brought you here for a purpose. Come."

Powerless to refuse him, she followed. As they walked deeper into the wood, she felt herself diminishing in size and age until she was a little girl again, trailing in Papa's footsteps. She remembered other expeditions to the woods and knew suddenly and with absolute certainty where he was taking her now. Her legs quivered, and she halted.

Yitzhak looked back sternly. "Come."

They emerged into a small copse lit by the filtered rays of the setting sun. In the center of the clearing was a circle of young pines, surrounding a twisted, hardy oak. Her father stepped into the circle and laid his old hands on the bark of the oak. "This was your mother and I." Touching each young pine in turn, he said, "These were planted upon the birth of each of our children. Yehezkel. Joshua. Avram. Eliezer." Then he pointed to a gap in the circle where stood the stump of a tree that must have been cut down young, for it was very slender, overgrown with moss and wildflowers.

"That," he said, "was my only daughter."

Ilana felt pieces of herself break off and disappear, like fragments of an ice floe swept away by an Arctic sea. Her legs could no longer support her body. Dropping to her knees beside the poor aborted stump, she laid her cheek against its blanket of moss. She felt a sense of mourning, of irreparable loss, as if her own child lay buried in this place. For a time she could see nothing but deep inner darkness, illuminated by intermittent flashes of lightning. Though frightened, she knew that she was not alone; a second heart beat inside her, shoring up her own. When she returned to herself, her father's hand was stroking her head.

Chapter Fourteen

FOUR men pulled stockings over their faces and gloves onto their hands. While one hunkered down in the garden beside the house, the others slipped the lock and went inside. Moving silently over the carpeted floor, they checked the house to make sure they were alone (the children were away at camp). Upstairs they walked through the open door of the darkened master bedroom and took up their positions: Yaki by the door, Coby beside the wife's bed, and Arik next to Pincas Gordon. Arik drew a snub-nosed revolver from his pocket and with a shrill and wordless shriek leapt onto Gordon's bed, landing with his knees in the small of the sleeping man's back. At the same time Coby dove onto the wife, pinning her to the mattress.

Pincas Gordon started awake, breathless and with a crushing pain in his back, certain he was experiencing a heart attack until he felt the cold metal kiss of the revolver barrel pressed to his temple and heard his wife cry out. Twisting his head back, he caught a glimpse of Arik's masked face;

then his head was slammed back onto the pillow, his neck pressed down with what felt like an iron bar but proved to be a forearm.

"What do you want?" he gasped.

These words, that tone of abject terror, were shamefully familiar to Arik. Slipping into his army persona as easily as into battle fatigues, he barked, "Get up!"

Gordon stiffened to attention but did not rise; he caught his breath and held it. "Hey, man," Coby called softly. Suddenly Arik realized that he'd spoken in Arabic. Angrily, he repeated the command in Hebrew.

The fat man sagged in relief. "D'you mind if I get dressed?"

"Get your ass out of bed before I cripple you." Without waiting (for in Lebanon the drill had been to carry out the first threat simultaneously with its utterance, so that the subject would not think of doubting the second), Arik jump-kicked the fat man in the side, sending him crashing to the floor.

Gordon used a sturdy oak night table to lever himself up to his knees, then climbed shakily to his feet. He wore a pair of stained blue boxer shorts, overhung by his gross belly. In a voice higher than usual he asked, "What do you want?"

"Open the safe." As Gordon shook his head, Arik pointed a finger at his forehead. "There are two possibilities. The first is that you do it now, quietly, with no trouble. We take what we came for and get out."

"But there *is* no safe in the house. Only in my office." Gordon glanced sideways at his wife.

"The second," Arik continued as if he had not heard, "is that you tell me there is no safe. I don't think your wife would enjoy the consequences—but you never know."

The woman sat up in bed, clutching the sheet to her chest. "It's over there," she said. "Behind the mirror. Open it, take the money and go!"

"You stupid bitch!"

"Maniac! It's only money."

Yaki was already at the mirror, lifting the heavy oak frame from its moorings. Behind it a steel safe with a combination lock was set into the wall. Arik asked the woman for the combination.

"I don't know it," she said.

Coby grabbed an inch of flesh on her upper arm and squeezed. "Then how are we supposed to open it, *darling*?"

"Stop that!" she squealed. "Break into it; you're thieves."

"Open it," Arik told Gordon.

Gordon spat in his face.

It was the second time in Arik's life and the second time that day. That morning he'd attended the funeral of a young soldier from his unit, killed by a sniper's bullet in Lebanon. Half the unit had been given leave to attend the funeral; after services, a few of his men, as he still thought of them, came up to shake hands with their former commander. The rest turned their backs. At the grave site ululating women kept up a high keening. When Arik approached the dead boy's father, the old man spat on his shoes. "Deserter!" he shouted. "Where were you?" Arik walked away, crying.

But not this time. This time he reached out and whipped the gun across Gordon's face. His nose cracked, and blood gushed out over his pale belly in two red streams, like firemen's suspenders. The woman gagged.

"Forget that asshole," Coby said disgustedly. "Wifey here will tell us. What's your name, darling?"

"Liora. But I don't know the combination. I'd tell you if I did."

"If you don't know it, you must have it written down somewhere. Now where could you have hidden it?" Suddenly he twitched off the sheet, revealing a *zaftig* body in a pink satin negligee. The woman crossed her arms over her chest in a hopeless attempt to hide her plump breasts. "Oh, sweet, sweet Liora," cried Coby in delight, "you have plenty of hiding places! This is going to take some serious searching. Hey, man," he called to Yaki, who was ogling the woman, "want to give me a hand?"

"Get away from my wife!"

"Give it to them, Pinny, give them the goddamn combination, *please!*"

"Liora, mon amour!" said Coby.

With an inchoate cry of rage Gordon attacked Arik, grappling for the gun. But Arik was ready; tossing the gun across Liora to Yaki he hammered Gordon with his fists. Out of shape, hampered and shamed by his near-nakedness, the fat man was no match. When Gordon was subdued, Arik turned on Coby and Yaki with eyes so hot his stocking smoldered.

"What the hell's the matter with you," he growled. "What are you, animals?"

They looked up in astonishment.

"Not in front of her husband," Arik raged. "Take her outside."

Whooping, they fell upon the woman and half dragged, half carried her out of the room. Arik followed as far as the doorway, where he could watch both man and wife. He winced sympathetically when Liora screamed, and shrugged apologetically at Gordon.

Gordon's face was bright red with the effort of keeping silent. He moaned through tightly closed lips each time his wife cried out.

Arik was intrigued. His work had taught him that where there is serious resistance there is something to hide. Gordon believed that his wife was being assaulted, and yet he was silent; therefore, either Gordon had a silent-alarm setup and expected help momentarily, or something in the safe was worth more to him than his wife. That *something* was not likely to be money, for the cash in that safe could not be more than a fraction of Gordon's wealth, which was in land and numbered Swiss accounts; whereas if his wife divorced him over this night's piece of work, as well she might, he would lose half his kingdom. Surely a rational man in his position would comply now, then comb the land to find the thieves.

Minutes ticked by. Liora's screams had changed to steady sobbing and the grunts of ecstasy from the men had grown ragged and quizzical. Arik was wondering what to do next when suddenly Gordon's face disintegrated; he threw up his hands with a loud cry and screwed his mouth into a grimace, as if trying to prevent the words that issued forth. "Stop them, stop them, goddamn you. I'm opening the safe!" He hobbled over to the safe with as much dignity as his naked paunch and dimpled thighs would support. At the wall he faced Arik.

"Tell them to leave my wife alone."

"Let's get it open before we break their hearts, shall we?"

Gordon glared but bent over the safe and opened it without further ado. Blocking Arik's view of the gaping safe with his bulk, he demanded: "Call them off *now*."

Smiling, Arik pushed Gordon ahead of him into the living room. Liora sat upon a sofa, dressed in her nightgown, one arm held behind her back by a disinterested Coby. Her breast heaved attractively as she wept into a delicate lace handkerchief. Yaki stood at a window overlooking the garden.

Gordon stared at his wife, disbelief and fury playing across his face. "They didn't hurt you?"

"They *did*," she answered tearfully. "This one twisted my wrist, and the other one stepped on my foot!" As her husband advanced on her, she shrank back into Coby. "What are you looking at me like that for? Would you rather they'd raped me?"

"You'll wish they had, when I get through with you," he muttered. "Jezebel!" Arik spun him into a chair and covered both with the gun, while Coby and Yaki returned to the bedroom.

"My God, there must be fifteen, twenty thousand bucks here," Coby crowed. "We'll be able to—"

"Shut up!" Arik said.

Silence thereafter, broken by the rustle of paper and Gordon's hoarse breath. The land broker sat rigidly at the edge of his seat, his eyes glued to Arik's, his concentration on the bedroom sounds so intense he seemed to be toting his losses.

Liora stared fixedly at her husband, her lips moving silently. Arik thought she was praying until she said aloud, "Ten minutes."

"What?" he asked politely, when Gordon ignored her.

She spoke to her husband. "It took you ten minutes. You thought they were raping me and yet you waited ten minutes before you—"

"Shut up," growled Pincas.

"Why is this happening to us?"

"Why do bad things happen to good people?" Arik put in helpfully. "And you *are* good people, aren't you, Pinny? Contributions to the arts, charity committees, and all that, right? Never mind where you got your money."

"There's something else," Coby called from the bedroom.

Pincas Gordon jumped up. "That's nothing for you," he told Arik earnestly. "They're just personal papers."

"Take them!" Arik ordered, his eyes on Gordon's face.

"No! They're personal. You have no right. . . . They're no good to you." He was on his feet, advancing.

"Stop right there."

"You said if I opened the safe you'd take the money and get out—you promised! Keep to your plan and you just might get away with this. Take those papers and I'll hunt you down and crush you like roaches; I swear to God you won't live to spend the money."

"Comrade Gordon, calm yourself. We'll be gone soon, and then you can beat your wife or call the cops or do whatever you like. Don't worry, *Pinny*, if they really are no use to us, I'll mail your papers back to you myself."

"NO!"

Coby and Yaki walked side by side out of the bedroom, grinning broadly. Coby carried a bulging cloth satchel slung over his shoulder. The moment Arik's eyes flickered toward the satchel, Pincas Gordon took two steps and hurled himself onto the man he had marked as ringleader. They fell with a crash that shook the house. The gun slithered across the floor, but Gordon ignored it. Grabbing the stocking's slack, he yanked it upward to reveal Arik's startled face. Gordon stared, then turned away, covering his eyes. "Oh my God."

"Holy shit," Yaki hissed. "What do we do now?"

"I can't see a thing without my glasses!" Pincas Gordon scampered on all fours toward his wife, clutched her legs, and buried his head in her lap. "I don't know you," he puled. "I didn't see you. Go away. Leave us alone."

"He recognized you," Coby murmured to Arik.

"Tie them and let's go," Arik said. He made no further attempt to hide his face.

The city slumbered audibly, snoring buses rumbling through the streets. Arik sent the money away with Coby but kept back the folder that had been in the safe. A glance at its contents had relieved him of the fear that the police would be called in; any attempt Gordon made to recover the evidence would have to be extra-legal.

Arik dared not return to his apartment until he had stashed the file safely, which could not be done until morning, so for the rest of the night he roamed the cloistered, mysterious alleys of Neve Zedek in a silence broken only by the yowling of cats in heat. At first gleaming he sat on a door stoop and thoroughly and systematically read through the papers in the stolen file. It took an hour, with cross-checking. When he was done, he replaced the documents in the folder and the folder beneath his arm, and resumed walking northward, through the maze of small factories, print shops, outlets, and wholesalers south of Shalom Tower.

In a tiny hole-in-the-wall workers' café he ate an omelette and drank his mud in the company of a dozen work-bound men, printers' helpers and factory hands, who were arguing about Meir Kahane. One, a man with a thick Iraqi accent, said Kahane was the first politician with balls since Golda Meir, at which a burly man in a mesh tee shirt jumped up and said, "That's an insult to Sharon!"—whereupon the Iraqi answered, "No, man, no offense intended. Sharon's got guts, and his heart's in the right place; he's just too tied up in Likud politics. Kahane's the man to get things done."

"He's a fascist," said the proprietress of the café, a granite woman of Sternholzian bent. "He wants to be the Mussolini of the Jews."

"So what if he's a fascist?" said the Iraqi. "Do you want a Jewish state, or Arab, that's the question."

"The question is," Arik put in, "do you want a state that *we* control, or do you want our lives run by Kahane and his goon squads?"

Silence. Everyone stared at the stranger who, though unshaven and dressed in worn jeans and a torn tee shirt, stank of privilege. *He* could not conceivably work in the quarter, though he might be the prodigal son of one of their bosses.

The man who had defended Arik Sharon stood with arms akimbo. "I know what your problem is," the burly man told Arik. "You're pissed because you're not drawing your cut anymore. It's your type—"

Arik leaned forward, hands on the table. "What type is that?"

"The type that lived off the fat of the land while we sweated to feed our families. We were the niggers of this country, till Begin got in. Let me tell you something, boy. You and your kind have had your day." He sent a chair crashing in illustration. "Your type are finished here. We're running this country now, and we're running it our way. And if you don't like it, you can go to America." Arik rose lazily, and the other man took a step forward. They measured one another.

The Iraqi said to his friend, "Cool it. I know this guy."

"You know this pinko Arab-loving creep?"

"Yeah, I know him. He's okay. He was my brother's commander in the army."

He whispered something to the big man, who answered, "I don't give a shit who he is. That just proves my point." He turned to Arik. "What gets you is, you're losing control, you know it, and there ain't a goddamn thing you can do about it." But he sat down, relinquishing the present fight.

When you get right down to it, Arik thought, he's right. Without another word he paid his bill and returned to the street, the folder warm against his skin.

After wandering aimlessly a little longer, he found himself in front of Café Nevo. The door was open, but the tables were not yet set out. Sternholz dozed in a chair beside the bar.

Suddenly feeling his fatigue, Arik went in and poured himself some coffee. He dropped money in the till and sat down next to Sternholz.

He found the old man's snoring restful, companionable. Sternholz sounded like the deep, distant roll of thunder in the mountains or a train, running on a circular track. Wearily Arik thought about hopping aboard, but he knew that if he tried, the old man would be up instantly to repel him, jabbing away with his stoking shovel. It struck him suddenly how fervently Sternholz tried to expel Nevo's patrons, and how rarely he succeeded. He was always telling customers, "Go home, get a job, get out of here." Sometimes they went, but they never stayed away. Whatever changes, growth, or petrification took place in their outside lives, they kept on coming back, as if Nevo were their spawning or their burial ground.

Just then Mr. Jacobovitz, the busboy, stepped off a number five bus and stumbled to his knees on the pavement. A young woman hurried over to help, but the old man, after waving her off irritably, got up, brushed off his suit, and limped over to Nevo. With a glance and a sniff at Sternholz, Mr. Jacobovitz began noisily and laboriously moving chairs and tables out to the pavement, one by one.

A man sat down in one of the pavement tables, facing the street. Arik nudged the waiter. "Sternholz! Hey, Sternholz!"

The waiter stirred. He opened his eyes to Arik's face and groaned. "Go home and shave."

"Good morning to you, too. Look what just sat down."

Sternholz peered outside, squinting against the light. "I don't believe it."

"Could be the harbinger of a whole new clientele."

"He doesn't want service. They won't even drink the water here. It must be the heat."

"No, he's looking for girls."

"Wouldn't surprise me. But not in my café." Muttering to himself, Sternholz hobbled over to the Hassid, who wore a striped caftan and a broad-rimmed fur *shtreimel*. The man's chin hung down almost to his chest, and his black hat was pulled down over that part of his face not covered by a long red beard. "You want something, Rabbi? You want I should call somebody?"

"A little wine," the Hassid said breathily. "I am overcome by the heat; a little wine, my good Jew."

"But, Rabbi, the wine's *trafe* here."

"No matter, my son. The Halachah tells us that when life is at stake, even the laws of *kashrut* must give way."

Sternholz had bent down and was peering into the

Hassid's averted face. Suddenly he grabbed the man's red beard and yanked.

Inside the café, Arik gawked. Had the old man gone mad?

The waiter raised the beard, which had come loose, in one hand; with the other he swept the *shtreimel* off the Hassid's head. His earlocks came away with it. Shorn and dehatted, Muny's bulbous face emerged.

"Bless me," he said, rabbit eyes blinking up at Stern-holz, "for I am saved."

"Muny, you're beyond salvation."

Muny looked hurt. "That's a terrible thing to say."

"Where'd you get those clothes? Did you steal them?"

"My friend, you wrong me." He climbed up onto his chair and, waving his arms, proclaimed: "Yea, I have played the fool, and erred exceedingly; yea, I was one of those who rebel against the light. But hey, it's never too late to repent." He did a soft-shoe shuffle on the table, ending up on one knee. "God has redeemed my soul from the power of the grave. Behold, before you stands a new man, a phoenix risen from the ranks of the secular to soar through the heavens on the breath of our Lord, Blessed-Be-What's-His-Name."

"*Oy, Gott*," said Sternholz, sitting down at Muny's table.

"Arise, my son."

"What?"

"Arise, and fetch me a beer. It's thirsty work, getting saved."

"All right, already, we got the joke. How long are you going to keep this up?"

"It's no joke, Emmanuel." Muny clambered off his chair and pulled it closer to Sternholz. He murmured, "Did you know that if a Jew wants to repent, the religious are obliged by Law to support him? And when I say support, I mean support, *in style*; I'm talking three, four hundred green-backs a month, my dear, free, gratis, for nothing!"

"Nothing?"

"You're supposed to study," he said dismissively. "Hell, I know the Torah backwards and forward; I was reciting it by heart before those little Yeshiva pissers were ever born. It's a hundred percent cinch! Emmanuel, I've got it made!"

Sternholz freed his arm from Muny's clutch and rubbed it testily. "They won't have you."

"They have to, that's the beauty of it! It's the Law."

"They'll change the Law before they'll accept you."

Muny belched and sat back heavily, fanning himself with the fur hat. "You really think so?"

"I just told you, didn't I? They'd burn the synagogues, raze the *cheders*, dissolve the religion rather than let you in. And you've got to admit they got a point."

"Well, if that's the way they feel, who the hell needs them? Emmanuel, these robes are killing me. Get me a beer."

"How about paying your bar bill? It's been a month already; I'm not Bank Leumi here."

Muny snatched up the *shtreimel* and set it on his head lopsided, so that one earlock hung in back like Davy Crockett's raccoon tail and the other lay across his face. Rocking back and forth in his seat, he said in a singsong voice, "But is the reborn man responsible for the debts of his predecessor? The great Rabbi Hillel of blessed memory said . . ."

Sighing, Sternholz went to fetch his beer and to take care of other customers, who'd sprung up like mushrooms.

Arik snagged his sleeve as he passed. "Sternholz, wait a sec."

"What do *you* want?"

"Do you know where that girl lives?"

"What girl?" he growled.

"You know. Sarita." Her name, still unfamiliar, tingled in his mouth. "Sarita Blume."

"What if I do?"

"Please, Sternholz. Don't fool with me. I need it."

The waiter looked him up and down distastefully. "Like *that* you're going to see her?"

"I can't go home."

Emmanuel Yehoshua Sternholz did not ask why. He reached under his apron into his pants pocket and brought out a key on a silver chain. "Go upstairs and take a shower. Shave."

"I don't have time now."

"You want the address?"

"Yes."

"So go wash yourself. Use my razor. Take a clean shirt from the cupboard."

Laughing unwillingly, Arik accepted the key.

"She lives at thirty-four Shinkin Street," Sternholz said. "Leave the key under the mat."

"You don't want to check behind my ears?"

"Somebody should." As Arik turned toward the courtyard staircase, Sternholz caught his sleeve and poked a bony finger at his chest. "Just a minute, *boychik*. In case you don't know: for this girl you show a little respect."

"I know that."

"She's a lady." Jab. "A *lady*."

Chapter Fifteen

THE knocking when it penetrated sounded disheartened, as if it had been going for some time. Sarita hesitated, then stepped back for a critical look at her work. It was just a sketch, the first idea she'd had since accepting the commission to paint Nevo; there was a picture in her mind's eye and she knew that if left alone, she could capture the outline before it disappeared. Sarita shook the cramp out of her right hand and, picking up the brush, would have continued—but the knocking came again, this time accompanied by such a plaintive sigh that she gave in. Laying down her brush, she walked with quick, impatient steps to the door.

It was that man from Nevo—the Eshel son. Arik. "What do you want?" she said.

He sagged against the doorframe. "I thought you were out. I was cursing myself for waiting too long."

"You should have waited longer. I can't see you now."

Alarmed, he looked past her into the room. "But you

are alone," he said. "I'm sorry to intrude, but could I come in for a moment?"

She stepped back watchfully, waving him to the only chair in the room. With his legs splayed and his hands on his knees, he filled the room. Sarita skirted him, turning the easel toward the balcony as she passed it, and sat stiffly at the foot of her narrow bed.

"I need help," Arik said.

She looked him over critically. His face was clean-shaven, but his eyes were bloodshot; and the shirt he wore was obviously not his, being tight in the shoulders and short at the wrist. Sarita felt an impulse to shove him back outside, before he could explain himself; but her mother's eyes were on her back and so she said, rather grimly, "What can I do?"

"Keep something for me." He reached under his shirt and produced the brown folder.

"What is it?"

"You don't want to know."

"If I didn't want to know," she said tartly, "I wouldn't have asked. I won't keep it if you don't tell."

Arik shrugged. "They're papers that document some land deals between Pincas Gordon and Minister Brenner."

She was silent for a moment, considering. "West Bank land?"

He nodded, impressed.

"What are you going to do?"

But that very problem, which had loomed so large during the long night, had been supplanted by a greater. Arik had loved before, but those had been passing affairs of choice, not of compulsion. He had never been *obsessed*. He had never been seriously rebuffed. He feared that both experiences were about to come upon him linked, in the person of this strange female, this grown-up Lolita who wrenched his heart even as she fired every erotic trigger in his body. She wore a man's long-tailed cotton shirt belted over snug blue jeans. The cotton shirt appeared to be her smock, for it was daubed with paint. Her figure, wide-shouldered and slender-hipped as a boy, was elegant; her bearing, forbiddingly reserved. He had observed within seconds of entering the room that she wore no bra.

To restore his faltering composure, he looked about the room, which was neat and bright with bare floors and undraped windows. Dozens of paintings, their backs to the room, were stacked against the walls. One alone hung: above Sarita's bed was an oil portrait of the beautiful Yael Blume, standing in a flood of light alone on a dark and empty stage. She seemed to be gazing straight at him with a mother's suspicious scrutiny, a look not unknown to Arik, though rather bizarre under the circumstances.

The resemblance of mother and daughter was at once striking and uncanny, for when he compared the two, he saw that feature by feature there was little basis for it. Sarita's mouth was wider and more generous than Yael's Cupid's bow, and their noses were quite different. Sarita's skin was darker than her mother's, her hair a deeper shade of burnished copper. Though Yael in the painting was not more than six or eight years older than Sarita was now, her face was marked with lines of character and humor that were lacking, or latent, in Sarita. Only the cool green intelligent eyes and the fierce eyebrows were the same.

He had been staring from one to the other. Sarita stirred restlessly under his scrutiny. "What are you going to do?" she repeated.

"What would you do?"

"You're asking me?"

"Why not? You came up with the right question, maybe you'll come up with the right answer."

Sarita laughed grimly. "I'd expose them both. I'd throw them to the press. *Yediot, HaAretz, Ma'ariv, Davar*—I know some people from *Davar*, down the street. I could talk to them if you want."

"It's a possibility," Arik said. "I'm not sure it's the best way."

"What is?"

"I haven't decided yet. That's why I wanted to leave the papers here for a few days."

He paused hopefully, but Sarita only said: "I hope no one saw you come in here."

"I was careful. No one saw me, and no one will connect us. Only Sternholz knows I was coming here."

"Sternholz!"

"He gave me your address. Not that he approved, you understand. Sternholz thinks I'm a bum."

"No, he doesn't. He likes you." She stood abruptly. "Would you like some coffee?"

He followed her into the tiny kitchen. Although he carefully avoided touching her, and she ignored him, he had the sense of being enclosed in a small room with a trapped bird. In his state, this seemed encouraging.

With her back to him she asked, "What are the alternatives?"

"Blackmail," Arik said. The cups rattled in her hands. "The nice kind," he added. "Political, not monetary."

"I see." Sarita sounded relieved. She carried both cups back to the bed-sitting room, waiting until Arik had resumed his seat before handing him one. She sat as before, on the corner of her bed farthest from him.

"Were you in the army?" Arik asked.

"Of course. I'm a reserve officer in Nachal. Why?"

"It shows in the way you bypass trivialities and go for the heart of the matter."

Sarita shrugged. "If you mean trivialities like, how did you get these papers—I want to know that, too. I just hadn't come to it."

"It's not in your best interest to know."

"I'll look out for my best interest."

"And so will I," Arik said more vehemently than he had intended. She gave him a smoldering glance.

"You asked for help; I'm giving it. Let's leave it at that, okay?"

"Okay," he said agreeably.

"So. Where *did* you get this stuff?"

"I stole it."

"Who from?"

"Pincas Gordon."

She gasped. At first he thought it was shock, but later he realized it was envy. "You robbed Pincas Gordon?"

"Yes, I did."

"Was anyone hurt?"

"Just some bruised feelings."

"So you're a thief and a blackmailer," Sarita remarked.

"Potential blackmailer."

"And actual thief."

"Yes. Does this change your feelings for me, Sarita?"

"What feelings were those?" she asked sternly, but the corners of her mouth curved irrepressibly upward. Arik leaned back, well pleased.

"You know, that's the first time I've seen you smile. You should do it more often."

"I'm surprised that in your situation you've got time to flirt."

"I'm not flirting. I mean every word I say to you."

"Cut it out." She was blushing as if he'd made a crude pass. Quite suddenly it dawned on Arik that Sarita was not as insensible of him as he had believed, that there was something promising in the very fervor of her resistance. She avoided his enlightened eye.

"Could we stick to the business at hand?" she said.

"Certainly."

"Why did you do it?"

"Because I was angry," Arik told her. "Because while my men were being shot at and killed in Lebanon, that bastard was profiteering in the West Bank. Once when I was home on funeral leave, I stopped by Nevo to see Sternholz. Gordon comes up to me, dressed in a suit, and grabs my hand, pumps it, and says, 'Good work, my boy, keep up the good work.' 'What's with you?' I say to him—this was in the beginning of the war, when everyone was called up. 'Deferred for essential business, old son,' he says, winking, 'but I'm doing my bit anyway. What you're doing to them in Lebanon, I'm doing to them in Judea.' "

Sarita made a retching noise in her throat; Arik nodded and boldly crossed the room to sit beside her on the bed.

"I wouldn't have done it to anyone else, but in Gordon's case," he said, "I enjoyed it."

"Was he home when you broke in?"

"Yes."

"And his wife?" Sarita asked. "He *is* married?"

A shadow passed over Arik's face. He looked away from her. The wife was the single irritant in that otherwise pleasing memory. Terrorizing women was not his idea of manly behavior, even if the woman was one who lived high off the spoils of her husband's carpetbagging. Toward Gordon himself he felt no regret. The man was a leech; he got off easier than he deserved.

"His wife?" Sarita prodded gently. She had turned toward him.

"She was there. No one harmed her."

She stared at his face, his downcast eyes no barrier. "But you frightened her," she said, with the certainty of one who had been there, and at that moment Arik saw how like his mother she was. Women of relentless discernment, though Sarita's gift was encased in gentleness and Rina's in boldness, and Sarita expressed hers through a medium while Rina favored direct action, political manipulation.

Arik looked into Sarita's emerald eyes and confessed: "We did frighten her."

Then for the first time Sarita touched him. She laid her slender hand on his brown forearm and let it rest there while she seemed to study the contrast in texture and color. Inhaling sharply, Arik turned toward her; Sarita's hand flew off his arm and to her mouth. "Don't," she said, and backed away. Arik put his hands on his thighs and tried to smile.

In a clear, bright voice Sarita said, "What makes you think that Gordon's going to tie you into this thing?"

"Only that he saw my face," Arik replied diffidently.

"That was careless of you." Suddenly her eyes widened. "I hope you don't imagine you can hide here."

"Of course not. I'm leaving town for a day or two. I need to talk to some people."

"Won't you want to show them the papers?"

"I've made copies. It's the originals I want to leave with you, for safekeeping."

"I suppose you're going to your father," Sarita said.

"Not necessarily."

"*I* would. No offense, but who knows more about black-mail than a politician?"

"Good point," Arik said, suppressing a smile because she was so serious.

"All right. I'll keep the papers for you. Good luck," she said briskly, holding out her hand. Arik brought it to his lips and kissed it.

"Do I have to leave now?"

Blushing, she drew back her hand. "What do you mean?"

"Since I'm here, I wondered if you might show me your paintings."

She looked at him as if he'd surpassed her wildest imaginings.

"I know you've exhibited them," he said beguilingly. "Couldn't I have a private showing?"

Sarita picked at a loose thread in the Indian cotton bedspread, raveling the cloth. "I have work to do," she muttered.

"Maybe next time. When I come back."

"When you come back," she said, her voice faintly questioning.

Arik reached over and took her hand, resting his on her knee. She felt a line of fire leading from her knee directly to her groin, and she made her face a blank.

"You never asked, 'Why me?' " he said. "That was your only mistake. It means you already know."

"Don't get the wrong idea," she said. "I'm happy to help in such a worthy cause, and maybe I did enjoy talking to you; but I'm not looking for anything more . . . personal. We could be friends."

"Whatever you say." Arik smiled. His thumb made little circles in her palm that radiated in waves to the pit of her stomach.

"It's nothing against you," Sarita said weakly; "it's just that I've got no time or energy to waste on"—but then he silenced her with his lips. At first she was stiff in his embrace, though not resistant: more as if she were steeling herself for an injection. But slowly she melted, her body softening against his, her lips parting.

A moment later she broke away and hung her head and would not look at him. Arik stood up with a little groan. "Don't be afraid," he said. "I'm going. But I'll be back. I'm telling you now, so you can start getting used to the idea. I want you, Sarita, and when I get out of this mess, I'm coming for you."

His rubber-soled shoes made no sound, but the stairs creaked as he ran downstairs. Sarita picked up the folder gingerly; it was still warm from his body. She looked through it briefly, then hid it under her mattress.

She went back to the easel and turned it around, knowing as she did that it was no good: the sketch told her where she'd been, not where she was going. She'd lost her destination. Knowing that visions, like dreams, return sooner if not pursued, she gathered up the used cups and carried them into the kitchen. Next to painting, warm water running over her hands was the most comforting feeling in the world, and Sarita was in need of comfort. Arik Eshel, she thought, was an impudent, conceited, presumptuous person. If he thought he could force his way into her well-ordered life, he greatly overestimated his powers and underestimated hers.

He did have a certain charm about him, she conceded, drying her hands. His countenance spoke well of him; his body was at ease with itself. She could have painted him, leaning back in that chair, looking perfectly at home when he should have been, anyone else would have been, dreadfully embarrassed. He had a masculinity that did not question itself, a wolvine grace; her painter's eye saw nothing wrong with him, and much that was right, but her mind was set against him. Coming into the bedroom, Sarita met her mother's eye. Yael seemed to be laughing at her.

"It's not funny," she said indignantly.

She often talked to the portrait, and it to her—not in words (she was not mad) but in looks. Her mother's eyes followed her about wherever she went, and though Sarita herself had created the effect, it was out of her control.

It was strange, she thought, how you could make something up out of whole cloth, and all the while you were making it, it was yours; but as soon as you were done, it separated itself from you and claimed autonomy—like Pinocchio, running away from Gepetto.

Now her mother's eyes were twinkling.

"Don't give me that look," Sarita said. "I only did what I had to. In fact, I did what you did, Mama, that time in Nevo. You never even thought about it, did you? You were passing Nevo, you saw what was happening, and without stopping to think, you plunged right in. You were brave, Mama."

The sun passed over the roof of the house, and the light softened; so, too, Yael's eyes.

"I know you think you got your reward," Sarita said. "A husband and child came out of what you did that night, though you never planned it.

"But it's not that way for me. You had just your own life to live, your own work to do. I have mine, and yours, and Daddy's. You were cheated of life, and life was cheated of you, and whose job is it to make up for that if not mine? I don't have room for a man in my life. I don't have time."

Sarita ended the argument in the only way she could, by leaving the room. Leaning on the roof's parapet, she watched the busy street below, filled with women shopping for their families. Sarita knew that she was right. She was a woman apart, cut off from the general course of women's lives. She had a special purpose, which had sustained her through times of unbearable sorrow and would continue to sustain her for as long as she kept up her side. If she were susceptible to men, Arik might have been a contender; if she were seducible, he might have been dangerous. It was her good fortune to be neither.

Chapter Sixteen

CASPI was holding court in the center of Nevo, where his remarks, ostensibly addressed to his companions, could be heard by all.

"I went through half a dozen translators," he was saying, "and fired them all. I felt sure they were not doing justice to his work, yet I found it odd that all of the samples had a common failing, which was lack of cohesion. The poems contained some beautiful images, juxtaposed in a manner that made no sense at all. I knew the poems must have some sort of center—after all, the man is the leading poet of his benighted generation—but for some reason the translators were missing it. So I decided to have a go, at the expense of my own work."

Appreciative murmurs came from his audience, Rami Dotan and two girls. Caspi held out his hands to ward off their praise.

"It was the least I could do," he said modestly. "My whole conception in doing this anthology is to try to put forward and support struggling Arab writers. It would be criminal to burden them with poor translations on top of all their other natural disadvantages."

"Their natural disadvantages?" said Sternholz, serving a round of beer. Caspi ignored him.

"I took the first poem to hand," he continued. "My Arabic is rusty, but I knew as soon as I read it that something was wrong. Not only was the imagery old and tired, phoenixes rising from ashes and that sort of thing, but the poem totally lacked coherence. It simply made no sense. It *sounded* as if it meant something, the title—'Rebirth'—promised something, and yet the poem itself was like a baby's babble. Every so often a few meaningful words would emerge from the midst of nonsense. It was ironic: I set out to be a midwife and ended up participating in a miscarriage."

The girls giggled. Rami Dotan murmured warningly, "Enough said, Caspi."

"What's your problem?" he growled.

"We still have a book to do together. Don't forget you have an interest in that."

"A great interest," said Caspi. His eyes gleamed. "Money being the least of it."

"For you, maybe," the publisher muttered.

"I have been writing my introduction," Caspi announced. "We owe these people the respect of telling the truth about their work. I hope I have done so kindly. After all, it is hardly their fault. They are a people without a land; little wonder their poetry lacks grounding. As the Arabs lack cohesion, so, too, their thoughts and writing. You will find that in my essay I have leavened honesty with compassion and a generosity which, I'm sorry to say, is sorely needed."

Rami said nothing but stared down at the table with an embarrassed expression. The two girls exchanged a look. Then Muny barreled over and shook his finger under Caspi's nose.

"You should be ashamed," he scolded. "That's nothing

but racist slander dressed up as literary criticism. I never thought you'd stoop so low, Caspi, even if your wife *is* screwing Khalil."

Caspi turned white beneath his tan. He stood, towering over Muny; he clenched his fists. The café was dead silent. Muny held his ground.

"I'm glad it was you," Caspi said in a carrying whisper. "If it was anyone else, anyone in his right mind, I'd have had to kill him." He grabbed Muny by the forearms and effortlessly raised him onto his toes, shaking him and spitting into his face as he shouted, "My wife doesn't sleep with Arab filth!"

At that very moment Vered was looking at the watch which was all she wore, lying naked on top of an un-rumpled bed. She was thinking about Daniel, whom she had dropped at Jemima's, wondering what she would give him for supper, since there was no food in the house; and she was worrying over the subject for an unstarted column that was due in two days. Her lover sat hunched over a table with his back to her, typing in rapid bursts punctuated by bouts of giggles.

They had not yet made love. When she first arrived, Khalil had risen from the table, embraced her excitedly, and asked her to strip for him. As she did so, blushing, he pressed himself against her and ran his hands up and down her body, as if he meant to have her on the spot, against the wall. "Beautiful, beautiful," he murmured, leading her by the hand to the bed. But when she lay down, he looked once more, sighed, and returned to his typewriter.

At first she was astonished, then embarrassed, but as Khalil continued working, seeming to have forgotten her presence, she forgot his. Her mind drifted away on a tide of things forgotten and postponed.

She was tired. She had so much work to do, and never,

since taking this putative lover, enough time to do it in. Daniel needed new shoes, and his booster shot was overdue. She felt guilty at leaving him so often with Jemima; her mother loved the child dearly but was overworked herself and too nervous to deal with a three-year-old. Caspi was no help, almost never home, and when he was, shut up in his study, pounding away at his typewriter.

She took some pleasure, strange under the circumstances, in Caspi's having once again begun to write, and some pride in being the cause, though it was hate, not love, that had loosened his tongue. He was writing his introduction to Khalil's half of the anthology, as Khalil (she surmised by his glee) was to Caspi's. It seemed that everyone but she had time to write; and with that in mind she glanced at her watch, and a surge of irritation swept her to her feet.

At the sound, Khalil whipped around. "Where are you going?" he said, more sharply than he'd intended.

She stared at him.

"Just a few more moments and I'll be done." He flashed an ingratiating smile. "I count on your generosity as a fellow writer."

"I find it easier to be generous with my body than with my time. I suddenly realized that I don't have enough of it to spend listening to you write when I should be working myself. I count on your understanding as a fellow writer," she said as she dressed.

"You're angry with me."

"Not at all; only maybe next time we could meet in a library, so we could both get something done."

Crowing, Khalil crossed the room swiftly to stand before her.

"I love it when you show your vixen teeth, my delightful Mrs. Caspi." His hands went to her dress; hers rose to deflect them.

"Did it give you a thrill," she asked, "to write about Caspi while his wife lay there naked?"

"Of course it did." He laughed, and putting his arms around her, he tumbled her to the bed with a force that straddled the line between lust and coercion. Vered pushed him away, averting her face. The struggle was silent and lasted two or three minutes. Then, with a curse, Khalil let go.

Vered smoothed her dress, glanced in the mirror, and left without a word.

His enemy's turf was the worst possible place for a confrontation, but Khalil was too angry to be wise.

Vered Caspi would not be back. That bird had flown, and it was no comfort to know that his own stupidity had done it; indeed, that knowledge only aggravated his anger. His wrathful eyes parted the hordes of Jews out for their Sabbath stroll; more than one soldier touched his weapon as Khalil passed, and he, who usually passed unchallenged, was stopped no less than three times by police and civil guards, forced to submit to the indignity of having his identity card checked and his business questioned. These coals of humiliation fueled the fire that was burning bright by the time he reached Nevo, but Khalil, having grown up in occupied territory, was incapable of showing his true face to the oppressor. He stepped into Nevo and looked distastefully about the crowded room, with the manner of an English don entering a den of undergraduates.

The old waiter hobbled over purposefully, clawing at Khalil's arm. "Go away," he muttered, "Caspi's here."

"What's that to me?" said Khalil.

Rami Dotan spotted him and wailed. "Oh, my God. Caspi, be cool," he pleaded as the Arab approached their table. A murmur of anticipation, like the hum in a theater when the lights go down, swept through the café. Khalil ignored Caspi and addressed the publisher.

"I thought I'd find you here. I was in town on"—he paused, smilingly seeking the right word—"personal business and thought I'd bring you this." He tossed a slim manuscript onto the table before Rami.

Caspi snatched it up. He read the first page; then, slowly, his eyes rose to meet Khalil's.

Khalil smiled.

Caspi read another page. Then he ripped the manuscript in half.

Rami cradled his head in his arms. The two girls slipped away.

"The truth is never easy to take," Khalil said sympathetically. "Don't worry, Dotan. I have plenty of copies."

Rami pulled himself together with a visible effort. "If we could just discuss this calmly, I know we could work it out. Sit down, Khalil."

"Don't sit down," growled Caspi, "and if you value your jackal hide, you'd better get the hell out of here."

"That's enough from you, big mouth," said Sternholz, coming quickly to Caspi's side. "No use making a bad thing worse. As for you," he told Khalil, "you get while the going's good. Now. Go. Goodbye. *Salaam Aleichem.*"

"The hell I will," said Khalil.

"I mean it. I'll have no fighting in my café. Caspi, you shut your mouth. And you, Mr. Big Shot Poet, get out."

Khalil sneered at the old man. "You want me out? Throw me out."

Puffing his cheeks out furiously, Emmanuel Yehoshua Sternholz bore down on the interloper. He was blocked by Caspi's rising bulk.

"We don't talk that way to Mr. Sternholz," Caspi said with gentle menace. "I know life is crude where you come from, my little baboon friend, but when you visit Nevo you must act like a man."

"Stop it, stop it," moaned Rami Dotan. He took a calculator from his pocket and set to figuring frantically.

"I wouldn't give advice about manhood, in your position," Khalil said. "From what I hear you're not much of an expert."

"You're dead meat," Caspi roared. "You're history."

Khalil laughed scornfully. "Scratch a liberal and find a racist. You're proving that every word I wrote about you is true."

"It's not your race I'm insulting. It's you, and your syphilitic bitch mother, and your ass-licking father, and your whore sisters and their whore sons, and—"

Khalil swung at him. Caspi ducked. Rami, dancing ineffectually in the background, caught the blow squarely on the jaw. He crashed to the floor, where he lay still for several moments before scampering away on hands and knees.

Nevo's patrons scrambled for safety and a view.

Caspi lunged for Khalil, but the younger man skipped out of the way. Seizing a chair, he wielded it like a lion tamer while he taunted Caspi. "You call me animal names because you envy my virility. You pathetic old cuckold!"

Charging, Caspi wrenched the chair out of his grip and tossed it aside. They closed on one another in a flurry of fists, elbows, and knees.

Women screamed. A crowd gathered outside, but no one tried to intervene. Someone spoke of the police; but the only phone was behind the bar, and Sternholz made no move toward it but stood morosely with his arms folded, watching fatalistically. The fight was silent and vicious, as each man tried to inflict maximum damage in minimum time. For some time they traded blows, but Caspi had fifty pounds on Khalil, which he used to advantage. Though the Arab was wiry and surprisingly strong for a pen-pusher, Caspi had him pinned to the ground and was beating his head against the floor when three men finally stepped in and pulled him off.

"I'm going to get you, you lying Arab bastard prick," Caspi bawled as they hustled him toward the back. "I'm going to destroy you. You're a lousy poet!" he screamed as they shoved him out the door.

Chapter Seventeen

THERE is no more intimate meeting place than a gynecologist's waiting room, for the range of reasons for being there is so limited, and those reasons so very personal. Dr. Steadman's specialty, fertility and its various effects, further narrowed the range of possibilities and increased their sensitivity.

Fertility is a tricky commodity for a doctor to deal in. Most women wish they had either more or less of it, and it was a matter of continual distress to Dr. Steadman that half his patients seemed desperate to abort what the other half so desperately sought to conceive. The doctor had a Sabra's fine disdain for the law. When he agreed with a patient's decision to abort, he obliged without submitting her to the indignity of appearing before the requisite abortion committee of three. But when he disagreed, and especially when he sensed she had been pressured into a decision, he adamantly refused to perform even legal abortions, citing no reason but his own peace of mind.

Despite his habitual bluntness, Dr. Steadman respected his patients' privacy by spacing appointments so that only one woman at a time would have to wait. But today an emergency had backed up his schedule. Ilana Maimon had been waiting for forty minutes when the outer door opened and Vered Caspi walked in.

Both women were surprised. Vered, the first to recover, said hello; Ilana smiled in return. After some hesitation, Vered took a seat two places away from Ilana. They smiled at one another again; then Ilana looked down at her magazine, and Vered opened a book.

No sound came from the doctor's office, and the nurse was nowhere to be seen. Several minutes passed in uncomfortable silence. The two women had a degree of acquaintance which called for casual conversation, but under the circumstances they were shy. Finally Ilana cast her magazine aside. "I didn't know you use Rafi Steadman," she said lightly. "He's a good man."

"As men go," Vered said morosely, closing her book but leaving her finger in place. "I like him. He delivered my first baby."

"And now you've come about your second," Ilana said without thinking. Vered flushed, and Ilana hissed in self-contempt. "I'm sorry," she said, to pass it off. "I have babies on the brain."

"Do you?" Vered said thoughtfully. Their eyes caught and held. Suddenly, with the sixth sense that pregnancy bestows in such matters, each discerned the other's secret.

The door to the doctor's office opened, and the nurse stepped out with a harried air.

"Dr. Steadman is sorry, but he's got to go to the hospital," she said. "Would you ladies like to reschedule?"

They did, then walked out together and stood on the pavement, reluctant to part.

Ilana said nervously, "Would you like some coffee?"

"Yes, I would," said Vered.

On Dizengoff Circle they both paused to gaze at a very pregnant woman sunning herself on a bench by the fountain, and again their eyes rose to meet in mutual understanding. Ilana laughed under her breath, and they continued in unspoken agreement along Dizengoff until they came to Café Nevo. Vered glanced inside and, seeing that Caspi was absent, led Ilana to a table in the back, far from the chess players. Sternholz gawked when they came in together; when they sat down, his jaw sagged. He attended them with unusual precipitance.

"Cappuccino," said Ilana, adding to Vered: "I've always found cappuccino to be the most consoling drink in the world."

"Then I'll have one, too," Vered said.

"Cappuccino," sighed Sternholz, and hobbled off.

"Silly old man," Ilana said fondly. "Why doesn't he get some help in here?"

"He says the owner won't let him."

"I wonder why he keeps up the pretense. He knows that everyone knows that he's the owner."

Sternholz lingered for several moments after serving the drinks, but as they did not speak, he gave up and stalked away, puffing his cheeks indignantly as if he had been thwarted in the performance of some natural duty or function.

Then their heads came together, and Ilana murmured bravely, "You, too?"

"Yes," Vered said.

"You're sure?"

She nodded. "Are you?"

"Oh, yes. For almost two months now."

"Two months!" Vered said wonderingly. "Then you're having it."

"No . . . yes . . . I don't know." Ilana laughed a little shrilly. "I still don't know. It's crazy. You are, I suppose?"

"I don't know either." Their hands met across the table and for a moment they were almost like lovers, lost in a world of their own.

Sternholz could not fathom it. What had Vered Caspi to do with Ilana Maimon, or Ilana with Vered? They were birds of a very different feather, Ilana a peacock, Vered a hawk; all they had in common was beauty, but their types of beauty were exclusionary. No one man (Sternholz did not count himself in that category) would see it in both.

Though perhaps there *was* some resemblance in character, he thought. Vered was a loner, and so, despite her professional gregariousness, was Ilana. It was, perhaps, not the friendship itself which was so strange, but the fact that it had come about outside his auspices, for where else could those disparate lives touch?

Muny approached the bar and burped beerily into Sternholz's face. "What's the story with those two?" he asked.

"Mind your own business," Sternholz growled. "Stay away from them."

"Maybe Ilana's giving Vered some pointers," said Muny with a nasty laugh.

"That's some dirty mouth you got there."

"Is that any way to talk to a customer?" Muny whined.

The two women were oblivious to the curious stares and comments they attracted. No one actually intruded, and engrossed in a conversation that seemed to have had no beginning and promised to have no end, they paid no heed to the ebb and flow of the café around them.

It was not an altogether pleasant feeling, this uninvited, unbridled intimacy, but it was powerful. Vered was frightened by its suddenness; in general her life, which had been as placidly bitter as a poisoned well, was now moving with dizzying speed—her affair no sooner started than ended and on its heels this pregnancy, this biological booby trap into which she had fallen. As for Ilana, though she had heard numerous (male) confessions, she'd never made one of her own to man or woman, never opened her heart to another living soul. The sensation was something like riding a roller coaster, rising to dizzying heights, then plummeting with stomach-jolting speed.

Once begun, they could not stop talking, but held each other's hand for courage.

"But why shouldn't you have it?" Ilana whispered. "You're married."

"To Caspi," Vered said darkly.

"He doesn't want it?"

"He doesn't know! But no, he wouldn't much care for the idea."

Ilana maintained a delicate silence. Like everyone in Nevo, she knew about Vered's affair with the Arab Khalil; Caspi had ensured that with his grandstanding. Though inexperienced in friendships with women, Ilana knew the general limits of intimacy far too well to trespass here.

"It's not his," Vered murmured, to her own intense surprise. "It was someone whom I don't see anymore. Someone . . . unreliable."

Ilana thought it served Caspi right; the trouble was, serving Caspi right could cost a woman dearly. She knew his type, much better than she knew him. But what she said, bluntly, was, "It's your baby now. Do you want it?"

"Do I want it? I didn't, but that doesn't seem to help. It's in me. I've carried a child; this is very real to me. I didn't want it, but can I kill it?"

"Can you?"

Vered laughed harshly. "What choice do I have? The poor thing has no chance. Caspi would murder me."

"Then leave him! Walk out right now. You're not his prisoner."

"It's not that easy."

"Not that easy? Do you hear yourself, woman? First you say the man is going to kill you; then you say it's not *easy* to leave him? How much easier could it get?"

"He would fight me for Daniel. And I've given him just the ammunition he needs to win." Suddenly Vered hid her eyes behind her hand. "I know Caspi will kill me if I try to have this baby, and then what would become of Daniel?"

Ilana did not answer. She reached across the table to press Vered's shoulder, her face tense with thought.

Vered regained her composure and looked levelly, with a touch of defiance, across the table at Ilana.

Hesitantly Ilana asked, "Would you leave the country?"

"To go where, do what?"

"Work. Live."

Vered laughed incredulously. "I'm an Israeli political columnist and a Hebrew book reviewer. Neither profession is particularly viable outside."

"I could help you find a good job, if you wanted. I have friends in industry and communications . . . but perhaps you wouldn't want to leave."

Vered thought about it for a few seconds. "I wouldn't," she said. "Not that way. It's not hopeless. I'll find another way. I'd rather have the abortion than take my son into exile."

"Exile," squealed Muny. "I distinctly heard her say exile. Whose exile? What is she talking about, Sternholz?" The little man could not contain himself but jerked in his seat like a marionette. "Look at them, crying into their cups, holding hands like a couple of dykes. What's going on?"

"Pipe down," Sternholz muttered. "I can't hear a thing over your heavy breathing."

· · ·

"I don't know," Ilana was saying. "My head tells me one thing, my heart another. I dial Rafi's office to schedule an abortion and catch myself doodling names on the telephone pad."

They shared a painful laugh.

"But why not, if you want it? You're a free woman," Vered said enviously.

"Oh, yes. Free as a bird."

"And not poor."

"Not in money."

Vered looked at her but did not speak.

"It wouldn't be fair to the child."

"As opposed to abortion," said Vered.

Sarita looked but did not see. She drew as if her eyes fed directly into her fingers. On her sketch pad the forms of two women were taking shape. Leaning together, looking intently into each other's eyes, one talking and the other listening, they did not notice the little beggar standing silently beside their table, palm outstretched. He—she?—was a barefoot little urchin of four or five, dressed in a short gown of coarse cotton like those worn by peasant children in Egypt. But where were its people? Where did the child spring from, and why wasn't Mr. Sternholz doing something? Sarita looked up from her pad and saw the waiter standing unconcernedly by the bar. She glanced over at Vered and Ilana. The child was gone.

"I'm not fit to be a mother," Ilana said. "I don't know the first thing about babies."

"Were you an only child?"

Ilana hesitated. "I have four younger brothers, but my

mother never let me touch them." She paused, frowning. Vered waited in sympathetic silence. "Would you believe," Ilana said with a laugh, "that I actually went back home, when I found out. . . ."

"What happened?"

"They threw me out on my ass. I can't blame them," she added quickly. "They have their own problems."

Vered thought of Jemima and how she would suffer if Vered had the baby. Or tried to.

"It was sad," Ilana said after a while. "I'd imagined it for years: the prodigal daughter returns, bearing gifts. . . . Stupid fantasy." She dabbed at her eyes furtively with a lace handkerchief.

"Thomas Wolfe was right. You can't go home again."

"Have you tried?"

"Once. I left Caspi and went home to my mother."

Ilana raised her head and stared. "You mean you left him and went *back*?"

"I was weak," said Vered. "I was incredibly stupid. I thought the world consisted of my mother and Caspi, and if I couldn't live with one, I had to live with the other. Living in my mother's house made me feel like a child again, and act like one, too, I'm afraid. Caspi said he needed me, and I thought I needed him." She laughed, shaking her head. "I was such a patsy. The wonder is not that I went back to him; it's that I ever had the guts to walk out."

"Why did you?"

"I had no choice." Remembering, Vered felt her chest fill with liquid rage, her heart beat like subterranean thunder. The wretched memory, fetid with betrayal, had long lain dormant in her body, like a spot of cancer, quiescent but threatening, or a killer virus biding its time. She knew it was there but practiced avoidance, on the principle that tampering makes things work. But Ilana's clear gray eyes bore down on her with magnetic force.

"He promised me a child," Vered murmured, staring

stonily past Ilana's shoulder. "We tried for a year, but nothing happened. I got very depressed, but, for the first time since our marriage, Caspi was wonderful: he comforted me, coddled me, brought me coffee in bed. The one thing he absolutely refused to do was to see a doctor with me, so finally I went by myself."

"To Steadman?"

Vered nodded. Her face was pale. "All it took was one blood test. I was sitting in his office when he came in with the results. He was smiling, but he seemed angry. 'What's the verdict?' I asked him.

"He leaned back in his chair and folded his arms. 'Generally,' he said, 'when women want to get pregnant, they quit taking the pill.' "

"Oh, my God," Ilana breathed.

Vered nodded wildly. "In the coffee," she cried, as if *that* were the ultimate betrayal. She rummaged blindly through her bag, then accepted a slightly damp handkerchief from Ilana. "You see what an ass I was, going back to a bastard like that? This whole thing is my fault; I really and truly made my bed."

Ilana clicked her tongue impatiently. "That is the dumbest proverb. It's not even true; if you had to lie in every bed you made, chambermaids would never finish working."

Pincas Gordon stopped by Nevo as he had several times a day since the robbery. He looked around, then walked up to Sternholz and Muny at the bar.

"Seen Arik?" he greeted Sternholz.

"I would tell you if I did?"

"What do you want him for?" asked Muny.

The Prince of Judea smiled unpleasantly. "I have a job offer for him. Seen him around, Muny?"

"What's it worth to you?"

"A whiskey?"

"Make it a double."

Pincas nodded, and Muny served himself. He drained the glass, wiped his mouth on his sleeve, and belched.

"Arik who?" he said.

Sternholz guffawed.

Looking around to see who else had noticed Muny's little joke, Pincas espied Vered and Ilana. "What's with those two?"

"They're an item," Muny said. "They're doing it."

"No kidding!"

"Idiot," Sternholz said, jabbing Muny with a swizzle stick. "You should wash your mouth out with soap."

"Vered's looking fetching these days, isn't she? Almost womanly." Pincas leered distractedly. "Ever since she let the gates down for that—"

"Why don't you try hitting on her, Gordon?" Muny cut in. "See what happens."

"I just might do that, when I get a moment." Pincas Gordon sighed and turned to the waiter. "Where is he, Sternholz? Where's the punk hiding out?"

But Sternholz did not seem to hear. He was staring at Vered with a grave new look in his eye.

"I'm afraid to go through it alone," Ilana said.

"Every woman does that. No matter who's with you, you're alone with the pain."

"You didn't take any painkiller?" Ilana asked eagerly. She had been longing for just this sort of conversation, but the only person she could talk to was Rafi Steadman, and what did he know? *He'd* never had a baby.

"No, nothing. The pain is endurable, and it's good to feel it happening."

"But didn't it help to have your husband with you?"

Vered was startled into laughter. "You don't think Caspi would stay with me? He threw me into a nurse's arms and bolted. I didn't see him for three days."

"Bastard," Ilana said with feeling.

Vered shrugged to show that Caspi was irrelevant. "When the baby comes out and you touch him and hold him next to your heart, and he *looks into your eyes,* that moment —oh, God, Ilana, it's worth a lifetime of labor."

Ilana sat still for a moment, a wistful look on her face. Then she shook herself. "It's not just the giving birth alone part that frightens me. It's what comes after, raising the child alone. I have no family or friends to help."

"No friends?"

"None who've raised children."

Shyly, Vered said, "I would help you."

"You?"

"I mean, if you needed advice, or someone to talk to . . . or someone to hold your hand during labor."

"You would do that for me?"

Vered smiled. "What are friends for?"

"I don't know, but I've heard they're for helping each other." Suddenly Ilana was shaking with excitement. She reached across the table and grasped Vered's hand. "We could do that," she said. "We could help each other have these babies."

Vered's reply was lost when a great white heron swooped down upon their table.

"Vered Caspi," said Sternholz in a sepulchral voice, "I want a word with you."

Chapter Eighteen

WHEN Uri Eshel dealt with matters of state, party, or kibbutz—in other words, when he was most himself—he exuded an air of determination, acuity, and confidence bordering on arrogance. But when he met with his son, a sort of diffusion of personality occurred: his thoughts wandered, memories surfaced, old wounds and guilt appeared on his face, and a general aura of self-doubt surrounded him.

If the Eshels had produced other children, Arik would have made a perfectly suitable black sheep, but as an only child he seemed to Uri woefully deficient. Looking at his son was like glancing into a mirror and seeing a reflection that was subtly, disturbingly wrong. Was the mirror distorted, or was it his self-perception? When Arik quit the army and there was all that fuss—reporters swarming over the kibbutz, buttonholing members, whose loyalty lay in praising Arik to the cameras while savaging him in kibbutz meetings—then Uri had suffered and suffered deeply. Arik could not hate that war any more than he, who had watched it approach, fought against it, and lost the last great battle of his career; but there were things you did and things you didn't do, and deserting your post during wartime was one of the things you did not do.

Rina urged him to talk to Arik, to hear his explanation, and for the sake of peace he agreed. Arik came twice to speak with him, but each time it ended badly, with raised voices and slammed doors. So great were Uri's anger and vicarious shame that he could not spend five minutes in a room with Arik without losing his temper, but so great was his love that he could not bear to lose his only son. Thus he did what he had to do: he found a justification he could live with. All wars, but particularly this one, had two fronts, the military and the political. Arik had not dropped out; he had merely transferred from one front to another. Uri's theory seemed confirmed when Arik took the job in the Welfare Ministry and immediately began organizing the local youths. He was disappointed when Arik joined Sheli instead of Labor, but it was a warm kind of disappointment: choosing the radical over the practical program was a mistake, but the right mistake for a young man to make.

Thus, after a proper period of penance and hard work, Arik was invited home to the kibbutz for a weekend. At Sabbath dinner in the communal dining room, Arik Eshel sat at the first table between his mother and his father, facing the kibbutz members, who thereby understood that a reconciliation had taken place.

But despite this outward reconciliation, the rift remained in their hearts, so that when on infrequent occasions they found themselves alone together, without Rina's buffering presence, they soon grew mute with embarrassment and pain. Of the two, Uri suffered more from this state of affairs, for he was of an age to look back, Arik to look forward.

Late one night, Arik arrived at Ein Hashofet, knocked softly on his parents' door, and let himself in. Uri, for whom midnight awakenings portended war or disaster, pulled on his pants in a panic and ran into the living room. Hurrying forward to meet him, Arik thrust a bundle of papers into his hands. "Read these, please," he said.

Half an hour later they all sat in the living room, Rina lying on the sofa wrapped in an afghan, holding Arik's hand. As Uri reread the photocopied documents, his usual air of befuddlement brought on by Arik's presence gave way to his sharp-eyed political mien, and when he finished reading, he looked at Arik and in a voice free of any paternal sentiment ordered him to approach. Arik obeyed instantly, slipping his hand from his mother's and crossing the room in three strides. He straddled a chair across the dining room table, facing his father with his back to Rina.

And though this was the very thing she had prayed for in her private foxhole, Rina's mouth filled with bitter gall as the thought came from somewhere outside her that she would be better off dead, for the dead are remembered, while the dying are shunned. Her son had deserted her.

Such thoughts came and went with increasing frequency as her disease progressed and she began to see that it was her death, not the world's, that was approaching. Every time life showed signs of planning to continue after her demise, a jealous wrath arose in her—and then subsided, without residue of guilt or shame. She regarded these rages as symptoms of her disease, as foreign to her as the cancer that was ravaging her body.

"These are photocopies," said Uri. "Do you have the originals?"

"They're in safekeeping with a friend."

"Is he reliable?"

"She is."

Rina looked up sharply but said nothing.

"Where did you get them?" Uri demanded.

"They're dynamite, aren't they?"

"You know they are. Answer the question."

"You don't want to know."

"The hell I don't."

"I stole them."

No sound from Rina; Uri's face was thoughtful, wary. "How did you know the papers existed and where to look for them?"

"I didn't. It was chance."

"I see. Am I to understand, then, that you have taken up larceny as your latest career and that in the course of business you stumbled across this?"

"Not quite. It was a one-shot deal. You could say," Arik said daringly, "we chose our victim well."

"We?"

"I."

Uri grunted. "Who was it, Pincas Gordon?"

"Yes."

"May I see the papers?" Rina's clear voice called from the sofa. Arik carried them over. "Did you take anything else?" she asked her son.

"Money," he answered, not looking at her.

There was a pause; then Rina said, "How much?"

"About twenty thousand."

"Dollars?"

He nodded, and walked back to the table. He forced himself to meet his father's eyes, expecting anger and bitter disappointment but to his surprise finding a neutral, speculative look instead.

"You blew it," Uri said softly. "You're a thief. You can't do a goddamn thing with that." He nodded toward the file, which Rina was skimming at high speed.

"I didn't take it for myself—"

"It doesn't matter a good goddamn why you took it."

"The money is intact. I thought of returning it."

"Don't even think it!" snapped Rina. Both men spun

toward her. "It was bad enough your stooping to robbery, but it would be *unforgivable* for you to return a cent to that bloody tapeworm Gordon."

Uri's eyes sought hers. "What choice does he have? If he doesn't give back the money, he can't make use of the documents."

"Send him a receipt," she said.

Arik and Uri stared at her, then turned toward one another.

"She's right," Uri said at length, in a wondering tone. "What thief sends his victim a receipt?" He leaned forward and slapped Arik's shoulder. "Give the money to Peace Now and send the shmuck the receipt. He'll choke on it!"

"He knows I took it," Arik said, and Uri broke off in mid-laugh. Again he sought Rina's eyes, and they spoke wordlessly, as a lifetime of political collaboration had taught them to, with eyes and eyebrows and little shrugs and nods. Finally Rina said, "You're right, it doesn't matter."

"Why not?" demanded Arik, who as a child had always resented these silent, over-his-head colloquies.

She said patiently, "Because as soon as you approached Brenner, he would know who the thief was, anyway. As it is, they're probably *more* nervous, knowing it's you. Which is not to say that you weren't deplorably careless."

Rina levered herself slowly to her feet, using the sofa's armrest. As the afghan fell away, Arik noticed that she had lost weight, quite a bit of weight, since he saw her last.

"The person you gave the originals to," she said, "was it Sarita Blume?"

Arik laughed shortly. "Your information is as impeccable as ever, Mother."

It was not her information but her intuition, which increased even as her power to act on the resultant insights waned. Rina saw into his heart; nor did he deny her intuition, but returned her gaze levelly. Lit with mournful love, her eyes shone upon her son; and for the first time since her illness was diagnosed she experienced a lightening of spirit: a joy free of resentment and a great rush of that bewildered, atheistic gratitude that knows not where to turn. She would never see him a father, nor would she know her grandchildren: those were unconsolable regrets. But she had lived to see her golden boy reach full manhood, and might yet meet his wife, and those were no small compensations.

"Bring her to me," Rina cried softly. "Bring her soon."

"As soon as I get out of this mess," Arik said. She sputtered with laughter.

"This 'mess' will be with you for the rest of your life. I can't wait that long." She went over and kissed him lingeringly on the forehead, as she had when he was small. She smelled to him of medicine and something else, something sweet, organic, and corrupt. "I'm tired. I'm going back to bed. Work it out between you." She crossed to the bedroom and disappeared inside, leaving the door ajar.

As they listened to the weary creaking of the bedsprings, Uri's face tightened, and he grimaced and put his hand on his gut. After a moment he straightened, and he turned sharply to Arik.

"So much for Gordon," he said, and with the air of one who knows the answer and is only testing asked, "What's your next move?"

"I'd thought of going to the press," Arik replied, with the same air.

Uri clicked his tongue impatiently. "A waste. All you'd get would be a mini-sensation, a few headlines, questions asked in Knesset: 'Is it true, Minister, that you have been speculating in West Bank land while serving on the Ministerial Settlement Committee?' 'No, sir, it is not. Next question.' The P.M. can't afford to rock the coalition boat. He sets up a committee to appoint a committee to determine the appropriate forum to investigate the allegations. Eventually the scandal dies of old age."

"That's what I figured," Arik said.

"You see"—Uri leaned forward to make his point—"in this case your bark is stronger than your bite. Brenner will be more put off by the prospect of scandal than he would be harmed by it. If you defuse the money situation, you can approach him and set your own terms. He'll bitch and cry, but he'll meet them. He's a prudent man."

"What do I ask for?"

Uri hissed, his eyes flashing contempt. "Is there nothing you want?"

"I got into this because of the Jaffa center. I want it reopened."

"That's peanuts! How often do you get a Minister by the balls? Make use of it, man!" It was not the father's voice, but the general's, and Arik did not fail to notice that for the first time his father had addressed him not as boy but as man.

"I want a lot of things," he said defensively. "It's like suddenly being granted three wishes: what the hell do you choose?"

"Good health," quipped Rina from the bedroom, and laughed alone.

"Play your cards right," Uri said, "and you'll get a lot more than three wishes. For one thing this could launch your political career."

"The truth is, I know exactly what to ask for," Arik said. "It's just that I'm not sure I want to play the game."

There was silence in the living room, a listening silence from the bedroom. Arik heard the ticking of the clock that used to measure his father's coming; now it seemed to mark another approach. He looked at Uri and for the first time saw him not as his father but as a man, an old man: his lion's mane gray and rumpled; his broad neck, wide as the head it supported, creased and wrinkled; loose skin dangling in folds beneath his throat. The hair on his arms was also gray, and there were dark spots on his hands that Arik had never noticed before. But the arms were as firmly muscled, the tensed sinews as clearly etched, as ever he remembered.

"Why not?" Uri asked at last, through clenched teeth.

"I don't have the faith. I don't believe that if we work hard, it will all come out okay."

"Thank God," Uri muttered.

"Sometimes it seems like we've lost before we even begin."

"That's true. If you've grasped that on your own, there's hope for you yet.

Arik gaped. "What kind of doubletalk is that?"

"That's politics. The name of the game is you never get what you want. The art is in losing profitably." Arik made a disbelieving sound. Uri reached across to grasp his arm. "You say you don't want to play the game; but I'm telling you that it's the only game in town, and what's more, it's a game you can never win. You can't lose, either, except by default. Look." He took a pad and pen from the telephone table and drew two points connected by a line. The line he labeled "C," the dots "A" and "B." "A is what you've got," he said. "B is what you dream. C is a constant. Nudge reality toward the dream, and the dream recedes. Move away from the dream and it follows, diminishing as it comes. Men can never reach their goals; all they can do is shove reality in the right direction."

"I can't believe you really feel that way. That's pure defeatism, the politics of despair."

"No, no," said Uri, waving a stubby finger in Arik's face. "Quitting is the politics of despair. Doing nothing, giving up. Consider Herzl: he did more than any man to establish the State, yet not only did he die without seeing it, but he lived *knowing* he would never see it. Because of his perseverance, it happened. It came to pass."

In his father's glowing face Arik saw the past, what was and could have been, not what would be. "Times have changed," he said, "the country has changed, to an extent you don't perceive here. Kahane is growing stronger; Arik Sharon is a national hero. Fascism is on the rise."

"So what?"

"The country is moving away from everything I believe in and value, heading in the exact opposite direction."

"So? What's your conclusion?" Uri paused for an answer that did not come. "That it's every man for himself now? Maybe you intend to make personal use of those documents? They're worth a fortune."

Arik glared at him angrily, not deigning to answer. After a moment Uri nodded slowly, a slight, inappropriate smile on his lips.

"All right then," he murmured.

"All right what? I know what you're thinking. 'Ask not what your country can do for you,' and all that jazz."

"I believe that," Uri said quickly.

"So do I, goddamn it!" Arik bawled; then he raised his eyes to the ceiling and laughed. "Why do I feel like I'm standing on the edge of a precipice and everyone is yelling, 'Jump!'?"

"You don't get to choose your time." Uri pulled his chair closer and reached across the table. "Your duty is to retard the progress of the right until the pendulum swings back."

"Will it swing back?"

"It always does," he said. On bad nights Uri lulled himself to sleep by counting the scars on his body, which were many and various. Now, in his son's face, he saw one he himself had been spared: the scar of fighting in a foreign war. They studied one another intently, like strangers assigned to the same tank crew.

"When you quit the army," Uri said, with obvious effort, "I consoled myself with the thought that you were doing it to get closer to the source, to get into politics. You would have been welcome in the party. I know they approached you."

"Because I was your son."

"You are what you are, regardless of whose son you are."

"Are you suggesting that I turn the file over to your comrades?"

"You could do worse things with it."

"Like what?" Arik said scornfully.

"Like nothing."

"Nothing isn't exactly what I had in mind. Perhaps," he said with a wily look, "I should hand it over to you. You'd know just how to use it. Who knows more about blackmail than a politician?"

Uri crossed his arms over his chest and sat upright, staring through hooded eyes at the young man, who returned his gaze unflinchingly. After some moments he said, "You're tempting me. Fair enough; I tried you, too. People do, when they have to get to know each other quickly. But let's not waste any more time on it." He leaned back, tilting his chair perilously.

"When you were thirteen," he said, "we had the first bar mitzvah ever on the kibbutz. Neither Rina nor I gave a damn about the religion, but I couldn't offend my religious colleagues. It turned into a big deal: to avoid any appearance of partiality, we had to have both Chief Rabbis officiate jointly. When the day came, you went up to the improvised *bima* and read your Torah section. The Rabbis spoke in turn, and then I blessed you. 'Today you are a man,' I said, but I didn't see you as a man. I never did, until today.

"You were my wayward shadow. Everything you did reflected on me. But now, suddenly, I see a man who has stumbled into a position of extraordinary power, and I wonder what he will do with it. And because I'm not quite sure what he'll do, I take a long, hard look at him. At you. And I see what you are."

"What do you see?"

"I see a man who knows the score, even if he doesn't like it. You know damn well that you have the means to influence Brenner, and through him his party, the fulcrum of the coalition. And you know that since you can, you must.

"Maybe I don't know you well; in fact"—Uri laughed—"I feel like I never knew you at all, until you stood before me as a stranger. And yet something in me knows your heart. Listen, Arik. I don't give a damn that you stole that file. Your mother does, but I don't. I only care how you use it. Politics is the business of life," he said, raising a finger, as if he were back in the orchard, lecturing the biddable trees. "A man is not a man if he's not engaged."

A smile tugged at the corner of Arik's mouth, struggling to break loose. "Are you finished?" he asked.

"Yeah I'm finished," Uri growled, noticing his upraised finger and lowering it.

"Sure?"

"I said all I have to say."

"That's too bad. I was hoping for your comments on a little list I drew up." He produced a sheet of paper from his shirt pocket.

"Give me that!" Uri snatched the paper, which was covered with close handwriting. He scanned it quickly, then reread it, and finally looked up, his face split by a huge grin.

"Any comments?" Arik asked blandly.

"This is audacious."

"I thought you'd like it. Will he go for it, do you think?"

"Not all of it. Maybe not even most. But some." Beaming, Uri leaned over to catch Arik's neck in the crook of his arm. "You had this up your sleeve all the time. You came here knowing just what you were going to do. Oh, man, you had me going." He mimicked Arik's voice. " 'What should

I ask for?' 'I don't know if I want to play the game.' I should have known." Sitting back, he laughed heartily.

They heard a disembodied cackle. "You should have," Rina gloated from the bedroom. "He's *your* son."

Both Arik and Uri jumped. They'd forgotten she was in there.

Chapter Nineteen

INSPIRATION was an overrated commodity, thought Sarita, who had never tried working without it. The muse's signal, being remote, was often distorted and always incomplete; and between the static-marred vision and its realization lay an impassable jungle, through which the painter must hack her way. The labor was grueling, and made more so by the heat, which by mid-July had grown quite unbearable. She could no longer paint on the roof, for the tar had melted into hot sludge, and her little room was like a broiler lit by the sun. More and more Sarita took to working in Nevo, under the watchful eye of Sternholz.

But she had another reason, even more compelling than the heat, for working in Nevo. The vision that had come to her just before Arik's intrusion left with him but returned later. When she tried to capture it on paper, the composition flowed freely and fluently. After two hours of intense effort she turned away from the easel, yawned, stretched, rubbed her eyes, went into the bathroom, and splashed water on her face—then went to look at the draft. The painting quivered with motion. People were twisting in their seats, standing, conversing, playing chess, laughing with heads thrown back, arguing with balled fists, pointing, shoving, and shouting; but they all had one thing in common, and that was their face-lessness. They had heads, but no features, distinguishing or otherwise.

This gave the draft an eerie, Magritte-like surrealism that was far from Sarita's intent; it implied a sameness and interchangeability that directly contradicted her experience of Nevo. Of course, Nevo's patrons were all or nearly all Jews, but that similarity served only to set off their essential differences. The ingathering of the interbred exiles had brought the whole world together under one roof, as it were, and that grand disparity was well represented in the real Café Nevo, of which hers was but a woefully inadequate representation.

The relationships, composition, and flow were all right. The observing eye followed the action in an inward spiral, coming to rest in the center of the painting on its only identifiable figure: Emmanuel Yehoshua Sternholz, who seemed larger than life in his great white apron. But what was Nevo without its faces?

Sarita took up her brush and closed her senses to the world, willing her mind to go blank and her fingers to take over. She called on her muse, but as usual there was no reply (muses being notoriously hard to reach, far more often out than in). Her hand remained still, her subjects' faces stubbornly obscure.

Thrown back on reason, she decided that since the problem was one neither of conception nor of understanding, it must be one of information. The faces remained blank because she lacked the necessary information to fill them in. Garbage in, garbage out: too little data were reaching her muse, and she had only herself to blame.

She had huddled in Nevo like a little mouse, scared to

death that someone would speak to her, not daring to look at people lest they look back. While the café surged and seethed around her, she clung to her little boat, all adrift. Those blank canvas faces reproached her timidity, a slothful habit and one that had long outlived its usefulness.

She began going daily to Nevo, varying her times and sitting at different tables for different perspectives. The regulars knew her now and signaled their acceptance, each in his own way. The old chess players acknowledged her comings and goings by a slight raising of their bent heads, Muny paid court with an exaggerated but by no means unfelt deference, and Caspi (who had much on his mind) had at last rewarded her unrelenting blindness with resigned indifference. The regular women, Vered Caspi and Ilana Maimon among them, smiled and said hello, while the transient women, mostly groupies attached to Caspi's crowd, continued generation after short generation to stare at her suspiciously.

People *did* look at her, and Sarita learned she could look back without blushing and even answer with composure when addressed. She began to feel at home in Nevo. The old waiter watched but no longer hovered; in sketch after sketch his craggy face stared out at her with crusty approval.

As she surrendered to the rhythm of the café, Sarita acquired the twin Nevo knacks of selective eavesdropping and brazen staring. By focusing her attention on one table, she found that she could eliminate almost all interference; and as she looked and listened, she also drew. Between what she overheard and what her sketches later told her, Sarita penetrated a score of secrets.

She was the first, after Sternholz, to guess what Vered and Ilana had in common, a guess confirmed by a second look at her sketch of the two together. The presence of the unseen child was explicit enough to arouse suspicion in others, and Sarita had a few moments' compunction about using that scene in her final picture; but her callousness in the service of her art was that of the true practitioner and far outweighed her discretion. The scene fit, it was true, it was intrinsic; therefore she would use it.

Sarita's blooming was noted by Sternholz, who attributed it to other factors, one in particular.

One slow afternoon, he lowered himself ponderously into a chair and gave a preparatory cough. Sarita turned toward him with a smile.

"You should pardon the intrusion," the waiter said, with that elaborate sarcasm that served him as courtliness, "but all these pictures you've been making, are they for posterity or are you planning to show them?"

"They're just studies," she said, closing her pad.

"Studies for what?"

"For a painting of Nevo."

"And when do we get to see this masterpiece?"

"I don't know. I'm not doing it for myself. It was commissioned."

"Commissioned!" scoffed the waiter. "Who would want a picture of this dump?"

Sarita smiled. "Someone who is attached to it, maybe. Or someone who wanted to help. Or both."

The old man harrumphed and changed the subject. "How's young Arik doing?"

"Who?" she said, chipping with a fingernail at the cracked linoleum table top.

"I haven't seen him for a while," he said slyly.

"That's too bad."

"No, it's good. It's about time he got off his bum. What's he up to, and why is Pincas Gordon looking for him?"

"How should I know?"

Sternholz linked his hands behind his head and leaned

back. "Only that the last time I saw him, he asked for your address," he said innocently.

Sarita chewed the inside of her lip, not answering. After a moment she began flipping rapidly through her sketch pad. When she found the drawing she was looking for, she held it so that only he could see.

Sternholz sucked in his breath. He brought his chair down with a thump and leaned closer, his eyes darting from one side of the sketch to the other, as if he were reading rather than scanning a picture. Sarita watched him anxiously, though not without amusement. When Sternholz finally looked up, his face was white, with vivid red patches on his cheeks.

"How do you do it?" he whispered.

"It just happens. Not on purpose. I look at one thing and draw another."

Sternholz pushed away the hand that held the drawing. "It's a heavy burden," he muttered.

"It's no burden at all." She shrugged. "I don't care how I do it. It's not important. I thought you could tell me if I got it right."

The drawing, which lay open on her lap, showed Nevo on a wet winter day. Though the café, whose furnishings have not been changed in thirty years, looks the same, the people in the drawing are dressed in an old-fashioned style. At a center table sits a youthful Yael Blume, surrounded by young men and girls. Across the room, the waiter Sternholz leans against the bar, his great white apron dangling limply from his shoulders, like melted wings. Believing himself unobserved, he gazes with unguarded longing across a sea of heads toward the beacon of Yael's fair, unconscious countenance. Neither she nor anyone else in Nevo regards the waiter.

"What I particularly wondered"—Sarita broke into his reverie—"was whether she knew how you felt about her."

"What was to know?" muttered Sternholz, not looking at her. "Everyone loved her."

"But were you a suitor? Did you try?"

The old man scrunched up his lips. "It would have been stupid to try. I'd only have embarrassed her; she'd have stayed away, and I'd have lost her. Besides—damn it, girl, it's none of your business. You're not your mother, no matter what you think." He cranked himself upright and loomed threateningly over her. "You should mind your own p's and q's and not muddle about with what did or didn't happen before you were born. Your mother is dead, rest her soul. You're alive: and what are you planning to do about that?"

"I plan to work," she said. It sounded hollow to her own ears.

"Work," sneered Sternholz, "that's very nice. I'm all for work. What else? Don't give me that wide-eyed look; I'm talking turkey here. What are you going to do about Arik? That's what I want to know."

"I hardly even know him."

"Know, shmow. Do you like him?"

"Yeah," she muttered, "I like him."

"So?"

"So what?"

"This is like pulling teeth," Sternholz complained heavenward. He pulled his chair up close and leaned forward confidentially. "So, what are you going to do about it? You think boys like Arik grow on trees? I've watched him grow up, I know that boy like my own—" He started to say "son" but, remembering that he'd hardly known his son, substituted, "like my own hand. He's bright, he's hard-working, and he comes from a fine family. What more do you want?"

"You sound like a *shadchan*."

"So?" he snapped. "Someone has to do it." Smoothing his ruffled apron, he added more calmly, "Even for a beautiful girl like you Arik is a good match. He's got a great future, *if* he marries wisely, like his father did."

"I'm not ready," she said; Sternholz snorted rudely.

"If you were any more ready, you'd burst your britches," he blurted, then blushed and mumbled an apology. "But you're a grown woman now; it's high time you started living your life."

"Is it?" she asked doubtfully.

"Yes," insisted Sternholz. "And Nevo is no place to live it, commission or no commission."

Suddenly her face lit up with that teasing smile that so reminded Sternholz of Yael. "I can't help that," she said. "I took the money."

"The money doesn't matter," the old man said, waving his hands in agitation.

She laughed. "Ah, but it might to whoever paid it."

"I wouldn't know. You mark what I say, Sarita Blume. Nevo is a good place to visit but a bad place to put down roots. What *you* need, little Miss Head-in-the-Clouds, is grounding." He turned his back on her deliberately and surveyed his domain. The natives were restless and clamoring for service. As he walked toward the bar, Sarita's voice followed him.

"I wondered"—it teased—"how you happened to know my address."

Sternholz pretended not to hear.

So he never even tried, thought Sarita, following his indignant back. Would it have mattered if he had? Was he always so odd and cranky, or had he become like that after Yael was gone? Was there ever a time when Sternholz might have had a chance?

Somehow she doubted it. The waiter was so much a fixture of Nevo that she could not conceive of his ever having been (or being) otherwise. Sternholz was that which remains the same, whereas Yehuda Blume and Uri Eshel and the other young men whom Yael had met in Nevo must have seemed fatally dashing, with their male friendships, gallantries, secret meetings, midnight forays, and skirmishes.

It had, perhaps, been a little wicked to show him the drawing, not least because it portrayed him as an old man, obviously a refugee, whereas Yael was young, vibrant, and native-born. In fact, he could not have been more than twelve or fifteen years older than Yael, yet for some reason, all of her sketches, regardless of their time frame, showed Sternholz as his current crotchety and faintly decrepit self.

She had not, however, meant to startle him, but only to change the subject and satisfy her curiosity at the same time. Sarita took her strange ability so much for granted that she sometimes forgot how unsettling it was to others. She judged her own work by its inner integrity: the rightness of the composition; the flow of color and form. Though she was a painter of people, her people mattered primarily for their relationship to the whole, not as individuals. She had heard that there were correlations between her imagined people and real ones of an earlier time; this claim was made too frequently for her to dispute the correlation, but she could and did disregard it. When pressed, she would declare that like most artists, she drew on her imagination; what fed her imagination was beyond knowing and therefore uninteresting. Further pursuit of the subject would meet with sullen dismissal.

Even she was startled, though, by the frequency with which Yael cropped up in her studies of Nevo. Her method of blind sketching certainly contributed to the phenomenon. Free of the constant check and correction provided by the critical eye, Sarita's hands seemed plugged into her imagination, or whatever faculty it was that informed her work. While she drew, she looked only at her subject, never at the pad; and sometimes she was jolted at the end to look down and discover that she had grafted Yael's head onto someone else's body.

Sarita was not a superstitious girl (though some might say she had reason to be); she did not believe in spirits, or automatic writing, or automatic drawing for that matter. She did not, therefore, conclude from this odd manifestation that Café Nevo was haunted by Yael; indeed, she drew no conclusions, preferring not to question, not to know. For if she harbored any superstition at all, it was the fear that if she understood the phenomenon, it would cease to exist, and Sarita was too dogged in pursuit of her craft to welcome such impoverishment.

She decided—and it was a measure of her as yet unrealized but dawning emancipation that *she* made the decision—that since Yael was so insistent on being in the picture, she would put her in, center stage, as befit a star; let people say what they would, when the painting was seen. (They would say, of course, that she was fey; but they wouldn't say it to her face, and that was all she cared about.)

The odd thing, even by her liberal standards of oddity, was that by admitting one ghost, she seemed to have opened the door to a host of others. Strange faces began appearing in her sketch pad; some she didn't know at all, others she recognized as younger versions of Nevo's current clientele. A few of the old chess players cropped up as younger men, and in one sketch she made, an old chess player was pitted against himself, thirty years younger; by their faces the younger man was winning, and cocky about it. A young Muny turned up here and there, and Arik's father appeared as his contemporary. Sternholz himself remained ageless and unchanging.

The silver sea beckons, the moon lights the way, and soft sea breezes carry the scent of distant forests, green beyond imagining, in a land where water flows like sorrow. That land Emmanuel Yehoshua Sternholz has forsworn, and faith-

fully kept his vow: never, since his homecoming, has he left the borders of Israel. He has kept even his thoughts from straying.

Memories buried by the force of disaster are like petrified wood, perfectly preserved in form, albeit changed in substance. The sea beckons; the old man is weary but cannot sleep. Seductive sirens sing to him, their rippling voices carried on the breeze. Sternholz closes his eyes; he surrenders.

The memory comes clothed in a young man's senses. Sternholz smells the majestic scent of living pine and feels the moist earth slip through his fingers as he crouches by a stream. He tastes water: clear, running brook water, a lovely taste and a great wetness to his parched mouth. (Slouched in his armchair, the old man runs his tongue over his lips.) He hears—oh, treacherous memory: like a broken projector it rattles on, unstoppable—he hears a volley of shots; screams and moans; a second round of scattered gunshot; then silence.

He was far away, a kilometer or more. It was not possible for him to distinguish voices. Yet he heard then and hears now the voice of his small son, screaming, "Papa! Papa!"

Weeping, the old man covers his ears.

He has not thought of that night since he reached the shores of Palestine. Though he retained the bare knowledge that his wife and son were rounded up and shot, he had succeeded in forgetting that he heard them die.

Amnesia is bliss, for what is memory but a comet with a tail of guilt? Sternholz ought to have been home when the Nazis came; instead, he was out searching for work. Not that he could have saved them; but at least they would not have died alone. A man who lets his wife and baby die alone has no right to exist, and Sternholz, an educated man, a former schoolteacher, knew that in a deterministic universe, that which has no right to existence cannot exist. If it was a matter of pure chance that he had survived, then to all intents and purposes he was dead, buried in the same mass grave in the forest where Greta and Jacob lay.

Being dead has its disadvantages, sleeplessness chief among them, but it is peaceful. Things happen around Sternholz, not to him; he is the unmoved mover, a material ghost. No wonder so many ghosts are poltergeists; with opportunities for mischief so plentiful and tempting, the wonder is that any refrain. In his public life Sternholz sees himself as a deus ex machina—not a deviser, but a device. His personal life barely exists; he is just marking time, serving out a life sentence without parole.

Lately, however, Sternholz has noticed some cracks in his prison walls. That sly girl, Sarita, with her insinuations like constant drops of water chiseling through rock: what was her interest in unsettling the dead, himself included? What was it to her, how he felt and how he acted toward Yael Blume? Must he account to that little slip of a girl?

Yael Blume was dead, like everyone else he had ever loved; she was dead nearly twenty years. What spell had Sarita cast on him to reopen that old wound? And what right had she to reproach him with inaction, she who was no less ghost-ridden than he? How could she mistake him for a man capable of acting on his feelings?

"We're alike, you and I," she'd said to him, in this very room. He denied it then and denies it now. "Live your own life," he told her; who would dare say that to him, who has none? Yael is dead; Greta and Jacob are dead; and so is he.

But dead men don't love, he thinks suddenly. Dead men don't cry. He wipes his eyes with his sleeve and shuffles to the bathroom. Dead men don't piss, either, he thinks as he relieves himself. A peculiar sound escapes his throat: Sternholz is laughing.

His window faces west; he cannot see the dawning of

the sun, but he feels it nonetheless. The silver sea turns a steely, opaque gray, the moon loses its sway, and the wind shifts, coming from over the land. Sternholz drinks his morning coffee and smacks his lips. He has been drinking coffee all night, but this cup is different. The long night is almost over.

Chapter Twenty

IN his heart, Caspi knew himself for a family man. He saw himself surrounded by children young and old, half a dozen kids all looking up to him, whispering outside his study door, shushing each other, vying to bring him bottles of beer and cups of coffee while he works. He saw them all together at table, himself at the head and Vered at the foot, as he carves a joint of meat and passes down the serving plate. He saw Vered walking with him in the garden (which they don't have) like Beauty with the Beast, and when they quarreled, he saw his eldest son lead his mother aside and say to her, "Come on, Mom, you know how Dad is. You know he loves us." He saw Vered smile fondly and hug the boy and say, "Yes, I know." In this context she could forgive his little peccadilloes, knowing that nothing could cleave the rock of such a family.

Over the years Caspi had nurtured this fantasy in secret, giving names to the children, inventing escapades for them, binding their wounds, solving their little crises. And this was odd because when Vered wanted children, then he, Caspi, had resisted with all the strength and guile at his command. Somehow he had conceived the notion that children drain the creative juices of men, while stimulating those of women; every child borne, he declared, is a book unwritten.

As Caspi's creativity waned, his fantasy solidified, becoming more real for him than the angry woman and frightened little boy who were his true family. His fantasy children were far more unruly than Daniel, who would not dream of troubling his father for a glass of water or help in tying shoes. Sometimes these naughty children went so far as to tug on his arm while he was writing and to whisper in his ear while he was trying to concentrate, destroying his train of thought. They seemed determined to prove the very antithesis of Caspi's theorem by demonstrating (or ensuring) that every unborn child was a book unwritten.

Caspi had a mental morgue for unwritten books, like the back room of an abortion clinic where the poor rejected "products of conception" lie awaiting burial. His lost masterpieces, he called them, his miscarriages. Every time a book broke away from him before it was viable, achieving independence at the cost of life, Caspi felt a sharp *ting* inside him; he wept and raged, but the process was irreversible.

He mourned these books as a mother mourns a stillborn child: he gave them titles; he held them in his heart. His sorrow was cumulative and invasive: after so many fruitless attempts he could not sit down to start a book without a foreboding of failure. In his youth Caspi had worked joyfully, with unflagging endurance and unquestioning confidence, but somewhere along the line he had sinned and been expelled from Eden. Henceforth, like Adam, he would toil for what had once come effortlessly; like Eve, he would give birth in pain and suffering. And though he had worked conscientiously these past three years, sitting at his desk for hours each day even if he produced nothing more than a doodle or a dirty limerick, Caspi had had no success. Everything he touched turned to ash.

That is why when he finished his introduction to Khalil's section of the anthology—a mere twenty pages of polished vituperation, a bauble in comparison with the tomes that used to pour out of his typewriter—Caspi was ecstatic. He threw the pages up in the air and let them shower down on his head and shoulders; he kissed his image in the small mirror on the wall and said, "Good morning, Sleeping Beauty"; he opened his study door and bellowed, "Vered!"

There was no reply. His voice echoed down the hall. Daniel was at nursery school; Caspi had no idea where Vered was. Since she moved into her study, they met only in passing.

His muscles ached from sitting so long. He went out into the hall. Vered's door was open. She looked up from her desk and said, "Come in."

Caspi looked behind him, then cocked his head and pointed at himself questioningly.

"Come in, I said."

The room, having no closet, was strewn with clothing. He shoved aside a pile of dresses and sat on the sofa, crossing his legs. Since Vered no longer shared his bed, and bristled whenever he came within three feet of her, Caspi had been reduced to divining her activities and mood by omen and augury. Bags under her eyes? She was losing sleep over him. Snappishness at the breakfast table? She'd been talking to Jemima. A queasy look about the mouth? Remorse and guilt. Her craving for solitude, the mysterious silences that emanated from her room, so unlike the familiar sounds of her working (pen scratching on paper, the sigh of the settee and the creak of the chair as she migrated restlessly between them): these betokened secrecy and strong emotion, rigorously contained. Was she plotting his demise? Did she know something he didn't know? Or was her distraction related to his miraculously regained concentration? Caspi remembered his theory that he and Vered were on a seesaw. Here was evidence for it.

Today Vered wore an apple green cotton smock that he had given her before they married. It had been a favorite until she grew too large with Daniel; then she put it away, and he hadn't seen it since. For one elated moment Caspi imagined that its resurrection signaled a desire to return to the time of courtship, but Vered's stern face killed that train of thought and suggested another, more ominous interpretation: she had forgotten the giver.

Vered turned her chair to face him and sat bolt upright, hands folded in her lap. "I want a divorce," she said.

Caspi began to whistle. He picked up a book from the night table and thumbed through it, then settled back to read.

"Look at me."

His eyes rose; he smiled. "What, darling?"

"I want a divorce. I'm leaving you."

"If you must, you must," he said genially. "Just give me a few days' notice, so I can make arrangements for the boy."

"I'm taking him with me."

"Over my dead body," said Caspi, smiling no longer.

"That would be my first choice, but in any case I'm leaving and taking my son with me."

"I can't let you do that," he said quietly, looking across at her. "You knew when you married me that I was an orphan. You don't give an orphan a family, then take it away."

"You threw it away. I'm just picking up the pieces."

He stood and lumbered toward the door, where he looked at her without aggression but with steadfast determination. "You want to sleep in here," he said, "fine, sleep in here. I don't understand why *I'm* being punished for *your* infidelity, but hey"—he placed an expansive hand on his heart —"I don't claim to be the perfect husband.

"There's no scarcity of cunts," he said. "I don't need yours.

"But don't even think about leaving," he said. "I couldn't allow that, Vered. You push that far and somebody's bound to get hurt."

Shaking, less with fear than with anger, Vered stood in the doorway and shouted down the hall: "If you mean Khalil, it won't work. I don't care about him."

Caspi stopped and looked at her. "I mean anyone who tries to take my son away."

"If you gave a damn about Daniel, you wouldn't try to take him away from me."

Caspi came toward her slowly, with nothing in particular on his face. Vered felt like a trapped animal watching the trapper's approach. In a clear, cold voice she said, "I'll never let you have him."

"I'm not a monster. I'm his father. I love the little bastard."

"You never wanted him. You tried everything to keep me from getting pregnant."

"Not everything, evidently," said Caspi, with a flash of his old humor. Vered hissed at him. "Maybe I didn't want a kid," he said, "but now that he's here I'm keeping him. He's my family."

"If you love him, then let him go. He needs me."

"I need you," Caspi whispered, and reached for her. Recoiling, with a cry of disgust, Vered slammed the door in his face.

Caspi had attached an 8 x 10 photograph of Khalil Mussara, which he had filched from the offices of Dotan and Weiner, to a corkboard in his study. The poseur was wearing tweeds, smoking a pipe. "This is all your fault," he said to it, weighing the darts in his hand. He selected one and threw it; it sliced through Khalil's left eye.

"You brought this on yourself," he said, placing a second in his right temple.

"You can't write," he sneered, skewering the Arab's throat.

He had seen Vered's fear and it shamed him. In fact, Caspi blamed her far less than he blamed Khalil, whose dismissal as Vered's lover did nothing to assuage his wrath. As his marriage deteriorated, his anger grew and attached itself, naturally, to the interloper. Politically, Caspi understood the Arab's tactic—understood it all the better for having used it himself on occasion. It was a form of sexual terrorism, and like all terrorism, it struck at the strong through the weak. Vered's seduction had nothing to do with *her*; it was addressed to Caspi, like a letter bomb intended to blow up in his face. And so it had.

Caspi was not a religious man. He did not believe in God, but he did believe in Biblical-style vengeance: an eye for an eye, a tooth for a tooth. It was his only form of observance, the essence of his faith. If Khalil went unpunished, the sin was on Caspi's head.

But he would go about it in his own way, in his own time. If private vengeance was sweet, public vengeance was sweeter still. The hatchet job he'd done on Khalil's work in the introduction was just one level of a multi-tiered plan.

He'd thought with no particular repugnance of murdering Khalil. He wouldn't be the first Arab Caspi had killed. Of course, that had been during war, but wasn't he at war with Khalil? He could have killed him that day in Nevo and gotten away with it, or as near as made no difference. Witnesses would have sworn that the fight was provoked by the Arab, *and* Caspi had been drinking. The judge would have slapped his wrist and sent him home.

Killing him now, in cold blood, would cost much more while offering but a paltry return. Khalil Mussara was, most undeservedly, a prominent West Bank figure; Peter Caspi, an internationally known Israeli writer. The murder of one by the other would not pass unnoticed by the press. Though Arab lives weren't generally worth much in Israeli courts, in this case the judge would have to make an example of Caspi.

Besides, death was too light a punishment. Caspi had no truck with an afterlife. He'd seen enough men die to know that when a person dies, he's dead and that's it; no consciousness survives. The Arab would suffer for a few moments before the end; and what did that amount to, compared to the weeks and months of torment he'd inflicted on Caspi?

Khalil deserved the torments of Job, but Caspi didn't have God's stomach. He might have settled for a simple assassination—were it not for his fear of losing Vered and Daniel.

According to Jewish and Israeli law, women cannot divorce their husbands on any grounds without their consent. Since no force in heaven or on earth could make Caspi consent, he ought to have felt safe. But Khalil's invasion of his home had overthrown Caspi's hard-won security; he felt like an invaded country, spread-eagled before an advancing, rampant army.

All his adult life Caspi had championed the underdog. "I'm a Palestinian," he declared at every opportunity, to the confusion of his audience, and though this statement was generally interpreted as an expression of sympathy for the underdog, what it really meant was that since Caspi didn't know who he was, he might as well be an Arab as a Jew.

Khalil had done him the service of exploding this delusion. When the conflict came home, when his bedroom became the battlefield, Caspi knew exactly where he stood. If a man doesn't fight for his family, he's not a man. If you love him, let him go, Vered had said, but what bosh! What an absurd demand, meaningless and cruel. Vered ought to know better. Half an orphan herself (the better half), did she not possess half an orphan's wisdom? In the courtyard of the

orphanage the children had chanted: eeny, meeny, miny, mo;
if you love her, don't let go.

"The first time I laid eyes on you, drunk in Nevo, you
demanded that the Jaffa Youth Center be reopened. Today
you want that *plus* an appointment to a senior government
position which does not even exist but is to be created ex-
pressly for you. This suggests to me," Minister Brenner said,
bridging his hands and resting his chin on them, "a touch of
megalomania."

"I see your point," Arik said cheerfully.

"Why on earth should I help you?"

"You're not obliged to. I didn't ask you to. I came to
interview you for an article I'm writing, and in the course of
conversation you asked about my plans. That's all."

"Not quite all," said the Minister. Both men avoided
glancing at the small stack of photocopied documents that
dominated the desk between them.

After a silence the Minister said, "You are trying to
blackmail me." His face and voice were expressionless; he
might have been talking about the weather.

"God forbid," said Arik. "I am confident that you'll
come out smelling like a rose from any possible investigation."

"Your father put you up to this," Brenner said.

"No."

"No; on second thought, he would have advised you
better. What you ask is impossible."

"I have asked for nothing. I have made a few sugges-
tions, none of which is inconsistent with your party's policy."

There was a knock on the door. The Minister's secretary peeked in. "Sir, your two o'clock is here."

Arik rose at once, reaching for the pile of papers.

"Sit down," Brenner growled. "Postpone it," he told
the secretary, who withdrew.

Arik resumed his seat. Though his posture remained

respectfully erect, he somehow gave the impression of having his feet up on the desk. Brenner's expression when Arik stood up had been that of a souk merchant pursuing an escaping customer: capitulation.

"Who has seen these?" Brenner asked, poking distastefully at the papers with a pudgy manicured finger.

"No one but myself," Arik said. Brenner's eyes tore into him, disbelieving.

"And what would become of this article of yours should you find more pressing matters to pursue?"

"I would have to put it aside," Arik said regretfully.

"And the originals of these documents. . . ?"

"Will remain in my safekeeping."

"Unacceptable!" snapped the Minister, shaking his head so forcefully that the knitted skullcap slipped off his bald pate. He caught it in midair and replaced it. "The papers must be returned to their owner, who, I understand, is considering pressing charges. Apparently a considerable sum of money was stolen. I might be able to persuade him to hold off, if all his property was returned intact. In view of your mother's state of health—"

"Leave my mother out of this."

The Minister's eyes gleamed maliciously behind his thick glasses. "Poor Rina. What would it do to her to see her only son charged as a common thief?"

Arik said with effortful calm, "Rumor has it that Pincas Gordon had a considerable quantity of foreign currency. I don't have to remind you, sir, of the penalties for illegal possession of foreign currency. Rumor also has it that he donated some money to Peace Now. I doubt that, under the circumstances, Gordon will press charges against anyone."

"I believe he will follow my recommendations, whatever they may be," Brenner said. They regarded one another thoughtfully.

He's a clever man, Uri said, the night they talked till dawn. He's also a proud man. He will be angry. Let him have his anger. Let it wash over you. Don't fight him. And *don't* discuss politics. When his anger subsides, explain the advantages. He'll listen then.

Arik did not know if that time had come. Behind his calm exterior the Minister still looked furious, as if any moment now his hand would dart out to the buzzer on his desk, and men would swarm into the room, drag Arik out, and shoot him in the courtyard. If he had the power, Arik thought, he'd do it.

"I think, Mr. Eshel," said the Minister after some thought, "that you leave me no choice but to send you to the devil. Publish and be damned." But this was said in a probing voice, and Arik heard it and was heartened.

He said, "Regardless of what happens to me, Minister, I hope you'll consider establishing the commission we discussed. Since questions have arisen, and will no doubt continue to arise, about the provenance of many of these land transactions, would it not be to your Ministry's benefit to have some impartial body overseeing these transactions? Wouldn't that take the heat off, as it were?"

Brenner is a world expert in cover-your-ass, Uri had told him in their all-night session. Talk to him in those terms, and he will respond. Arik saw it happening before his eyes. The Minister's face changed. His thoughts turned inward. He had the look of a man who has accepted a disaster and is now contemplating damage control.

"Is your appointment as head of this 'impartial body' an integral part of this *proposal*?" he asked brusquely.

"It would be to your advantage," Arik said carefully.

"There are a thousand men more qualified than you."

"By appointing someone known to have no sympathy for speculators, you would demonstrate your impartiality and further distance yourself from any hint of . . . irregularities."

"My integrity has never been questioned," the Minister put in angrily.

Arik smiled.

The Minister picked up a pencil and examined it in detail, turning it this way and that. "What you seem to be asking for," he said, "is carte blanche authority to allow or disallow all land purchases in Judea and Samaria."

"Only land purchases by Israelis."

"That is a position of tremendous power, which is properly invested in elected, not appointed, officials."

"This overseeing committee would not usurp your power, Minister. It would draw from it."

"But to what end?" Brenner said quickly. He pointed the pencil at Arik's face. "To what end, Eshel?"

"To the end that no more Palestinians will be forced or tricked into selling their land; that no more developments will be built on stolen land; that no more facts will be created on the ground. I would ensure," he added deliberately, "that there are no further conflicts of interest, no land speculation by people with inside information."

The Minister glared.

"That can't continue," Arik said softly. "It's finished."

"For the Arabs you're doing this?" Brenner burst out. "For the goddamn *Arabushim*? Have you forgotten that your precious Ein Hashofet was built on what was previously Arab land?"

"Not for the Arabs. For my country," Arik said with obvious embarrassment, "and myself."

"Mostly for yourself," the Minister sneered. "You're more like Uri than I thought. Fighting for the underdog was his shtick. Made a damn good living at it, too."

"I've heard a lot of assessments of my father's career," said Arik. "That was by far the most offensive."

"I know him better than most," the old man said drily. "Like father, like son. But tell me, young Eshel, what would you do with your power, should it please me to grant it?"

"I would review the applications that came in."

"And?"

"I would interview the buyers and the sellers. I would visit the sites. I would institute title searches."

"These things take time," the Minister said. It was a phrase he used so often, it slid off his tongue like oil.

"Precisely."

"It's a dangerous position, for a man of your moral caliber. Temptations abound."

Arik smiled through his teeth. "I put up with your talk of blackmail and robbery, but I draw the line at bribery."

Brenner gave him a sharp look. "So it's power, not money. You dream of glory. You want to make yourself into a one-man stumbling block on the road to Jewish settlement. That's like putting a stop sign in the path of a herd of stampeding elephants." He laughed.

"I like a challenge," Arik said blandly.

"But seriously, boy, what do you hope to gain? What do you hope to accomplish? At most you'd be delaying the inevitable."

With immense enjoyment, Arik stuck his hands in his pockets and drawled, "Mr. Minister, suh, I am just holding the pass, waiting for reinforcements."

Brenner scowled. "I hear your father talking."

"We have pockets of agreement," Arik said.

"So it seems, and yet I wonder." Brenner emerged from behind his desk, motioning Arik to remain seated. He sat beside Arik and leaned forward with an avuncular smile. "You cut short a promising army career on a matter of principle. You then took a social working job far below the level of opportunity open to you. These are the acts of a man of quite fanatic conscience. And yet you come into my office, blustering and threatening—"

"I'm not—"

"You attempt blackmail, you commit a robbery—and I understand that Mrs. Gordon was deeply upset by her treatment at the hands of the thieves." Arik shifted involuntarily; the Minister registered the movement and continued sorrowfully: "These things are out of character; what is more, among men of honor and good will, they are unnecessary." He took a cigar from his jacket pocket and offered one to Arik, who shook his head without speaking. The Minister lit his and puffed, with a sigh of gratification.

"Had you come to me as the son of an old, respected colleague, then regardless of party affiliation I would have gone out of my way to make room for you. You will forgive the immodesty if I point out that with my support, you could have gone far." He waited. Arik said nothing.

"You still can. It's not too late. We would attribute this unpalatable incident to distress over your mother's illness and start with a clean slate. But I cannot allow myself to be moved by threats. I'm sure you understand that," said the Minister.

"Restore what you have taken to its rightful owner, and then come to me. Then it will be possible to discuss a position . . . of power."

Against his father's advice, which had been emphatic on the subject of relinquishing the documents, Arik said, "Will you return what *you* have taken, to its rightful owner?"

Brenner's face flooded with color. His eyes fixed on Arik. It was not a look of love.

"If you are referring to these"—the Minister waved disdainfully at the papers—"they have nothing to do with me. They are forgeries. But even if I were in a position to do so," he said, "I would never lend a hand to those who would return liberated Judean land to Arab ownership."

Arik reached out for the stack. Brenner caught his wrist in an iron grip and lifted it away. "In the interest of harmony," he purred, "I am willing to take the first step. Call it a demonstration of good will." Smiling unctuously, he lifted the receiver of the desk phone.

"Bianco? I want the Jaffa Youth Center reopened. Take care of it, will you? Right away." He hung up without waiting for a reply.

"It's as easy as that," the Minister said, with the smile of a man too long in politics. An inch of ash detached itself from his cigar and fell onto the Persian carpet. He ground it underfoot.

"One phone call. And my orders will be carried out, I assure you.

"That's power, my boy. Oh, you've got a fine poker face, but I can see that you covet it. And you can have it, too, but not this way. Not by trying your strength against mine. I am a powerful man, and in the exercise of my power I can destroy, as well as create. With all due respect to your expert coach, you are out of your league. A man in your position needs friends, not enemies.

"I have proven my good faith," the Minister said reasonably. "Will you now prove yours?"

Arik shook his head in wonderment. "Minister Brenner, that was very impressive and most persuasive. Your generosity is staggering. I hope you won't think I'm being ungrateful by refusing to profit by your advice, sir, but I think I'll sleep better at night knowing the documents are in my possession."

"You go to hell," said the Minister, in a voice as cold as ice.

"Is that your answer?"

"It is my prayer. I haven't given you my answer."

"I have to hand in my article by Wednesday, the day after tomorrow."

"Whatever the outcome may seem to be," the Minister said, "you will live to regret what you've done today."

"Wednesday morning," said Arik. "You've got my number."

. . .

What Caspi hated most about Khalil Mussara, besides his having screwed Vered, was his BMW. It was not envy that prompted his hatred, but indignation on behalf of the suffering Palestinian masses. The fact that he himself drove a six-year-old Fiat had nothing to do with it.

Thus it was with a warm sense of political righteousness that Caspi placed the explosives in Khalil's car. He'd considered placing it under the house, which stood on pillars, but was deterred by the thought of the children. Not, he told himself, because Khalil deserved clemency—had he not tried to destroy Caspi's family?—but because the children were innocent. Vered was wrong: he was not a racist.

Acquiring the material, once he decided what he needed, had not been a problem; if one knew the right people and had the right currency, it was easily arranged. Khalil lived in a house on the outskirts of Nablus. It was not a large house, hardly bigger than the detached garage that stood beside it. Caspi thought with deep satisfaction that whatever money Khalil had must have gone into the luxury car, which was not even large enough to hold his entire family.

After attaching the bomb to the car, and setting it to go off in ten minutes, Caspi hid behind a stand of olive trees in the middle of a deep field across from Khalil's house. His own car was parked on the far side of the field.

At that hour there was a definite chill in the air, but Caspi, clad in jeans and a black sweatshirt, did not feel it. He was a veteran of three wars, four counting the Sinai war of attrition, which was in some ways the nastiest; he knew that feeling of lightheadedness that precedes combat and recognized the feeling now. Events that were now totally out of his control had been set into motion. He felt the peacefulness of being a pawn.

A loud explosion rent the air. The windows of the garage shattered, and debris rained down from the roof. Lights went on in the house. A moment later the front door burst open and Khalil ran out, wearing only a pair of pants.

As he caught sight of the collapsing garage, his steps faltered; he stopped and stared, holding his head. A woman appeared beside him, a passel of children visible behind her. Khalil said, "Call the fire department. Stay inside," and herded them back into the house. He walked down the porch steps and stood in the yard, peering out into the black night.

"Caspi!" he screamed.

Caspi watched through infrared binoculars. He could see Khalil's face perfectly. He had no difficulty hearing him, either.

"Come out here, you fucking coward," Khalil hollered. "Show your face, you fucking kike—get it out here. Show yourself, you motherfucking bastard, you chickenshit Nazi swine." The garage had caught fire, and Khalil was silhouetted by the flames, a perfect target, had Caspi chosen to kill him. But Caspi wouldn't have killed him for the world. The Arab was sobbing. He punched the unresisting air furiously, his body palsied with frustration.

"I know you're out there," he shouted through his tears. "I know you're watching. You coward, Caspi—come out and fight like a man!" He danced on his toes. "I'm not armed. What are you afraid of? Come out!"

Hearing sirens, Caspi turned away reluctantly and sprinted for his car. Khalil heard his heavy footsteps and plunged into the field. Khalil was faster, but Caspi knew where he was going and reached his car without being seen. Not that it mattered; he was sure Khalil would identify him anyway. Over the revving engine he heard Khalil's last despairing cry.

"I'll kill you for this, Caspi. I'll kill you."

Driving home, Caspi was suddenly struck by fear, not for himself but for Vered and especially Daniel. Was Khalil canny enough to strike at his heart's blood? He imagined a bomb going off in his home, Daniel lying torn and bloody—

and Caspi got to shaking so badly that he had to pull over and stop. How could he have overlooked the danger? His action so far had succeeded beyond his wildest hopes—might not the inevitable reaction exceed his wildest fears?

He had reckoned on Khalil's fury but, despite the evidence, had persisted in regarding the man as impotent; this led him to overlook his own vulnerability. A serious error, and one that needed to be rectified, Caspi decided. He had brought a clean gun with him, in case of emergency, but even as he put his car into gear he realized that it was too late. The police would be there already; the Shin Beth and the press would soon follow. It was too late now to do anything but carry out his original plan.

But when he thought of Khalil's stricken face, mourning his car as if it were a child, Caspi's panic subsided. A soothing contempt stole over him. Khalil had the will but not the intelligence to pinpoint Caspi's Achilles' heel. That Caspi truly loved Daniel, would kill for him, would die for him, was a secret known only to himself; no one else believed he gave a fig for his family. In his eagerness to tear out Caspi's heart, Khalil would certainly assume that it beat in Caspi's body.

Chapter Twenty-One

"DAVID'S coming," Ilana said.

"David? Your . . . ?"

She nodded.

"Oh, Ilana. Does that mean you've decided to go ahead with it?"

"Decided?" Ilana said, laughing. "By default, perhaps. I kept postponing and postponing a decision, and last night, I know it's impossible, but last night I could swear I felt it move.

"After that," she said, "I couldn't possibly . . . Even if I just imagined it, I couldn't. So you see, I'm stuck." She didn't look stuck, though. She looked triumphant, like a child who's just pinned the tail squarely on the donkey's rump.

Vered said, "I'm so happy for you," and her smile momentarily eased the lines of tension etched on her face. "It's the right thing," she said.

Ilana was observant, but needn't have been, for even a blind woman (or a sighted man) could have seen the trouble on Vered's face. She leaned forward. "Is there any way I can help you? There must be. Tell me how."

Vered's eyes filled with grateful tears, which she blinked back. She shook her head.

"Have you decided what to do?"

Vered laughed helplessly. Even if she wanted to explain, it was impossible. The problem of her pregnancy had been utterly subsumed by another more urgent problem: Caspi. In her desperation she had this week consulted those organizations designed to help women like herself, who were trapped by the state's archaic divorce laws. But their legalistic remedies took no account of Caspi's devastating anger, and their tactics relied on attrition, which would take more time than Vered thought she had.

They all asked if Caspi ever beat her. She told the truth: he never had. They advised her to remain in the home and try to get him to move out. She laughed. One young woman had looked very grave then and suggested a shelter for battered women. "But I'm not a battered wife," Vered had retorted indignantly.

"Not physically," the young woman gently replied, "but brutality takes other forms as well. Your husband sounds like a dangerous man."

Vered knew the shelters. The women who ran them were all friends or acquaintances of hers. Appearing as a supplicant on their doorsteps would be an unbearable humiliation, fatal to her pride; the scandal when it got abroad, and the pity of her colleagues, would be insupportable.

She was afraid of Caspi. She was also afraid *for* him if she left. He would go to the devil. She oughtn't to care, but she did. It was a no-win situation, a classic double bind that left her paralyzed.

.　.　.

Emmanuel Yehoshua Sternholz sat shamelessly nearby, pretending to nap, with a newspaper spread over his face to protect him from importunate customers and flies. Nevo on this hot Tuesday afternoon was full of the latter pests but almost free of the former. Mr. Jacobovitz dozed upright on a bar stool. An overhead fan drowned out most of the women's conversation. Sternholz inched closer.

Vered, that inveterate smoker, had not lit one cigarette since she came in. Sternholz was almost confirmed in his diagnosis, despite the fool's denial when he confronted her with it. It was enough to drive a poor waiter mad. How in God's name was he supposed to get people out of trouble if they didn't confide in him? Those who should didn't, and those who shouldn't did. He wasn't a magician; though, by the look of her, he suspected it would take a magician, or at least a sympathetic doctor, to get Vered out of the mess she was in.

"I have a plan," Ilana said.

"Yes?" Vered said politely.

"You need to get away for a while, to sit and think quietly without interruption." Ilana chose her words carefully. Caspi had not yet been mentioned between them. She did not know what Vered knew or suspected about the bombing, but there were lines on her face that had not been there two weeks ago. "Take Daniel, and both of you come stay with me," Ilana said.

Vered looked at her in amazement. "You have no idea what you're suggesting."

"I think I do. Vered, my building has twenty-four-hour security. *No one* can get in, without our permission."

Vered closed her eyes. Turgidly, as if half asleep, she said, "I thought of going to my mother."

"But you haven't gone."

"No."

"Have you told her?"

"No."

"Why not?"

"It would just hurt her without helping me."

"But she must see that something is wrong."

Vered raised her face. Two red patches glowed on her cheeks. "Jemima and I don't talk very much," she said.

Ilana thought of her own mother and sighed. Then she said, "I know Jemima. She's obviously a very strong-willed woman, but I found her sympathetic." Vered snorted. "I suspect that she might be more helpful than you think. But as far as staying with her . . . I know Jemima's house. It's a lovely home, but I would feel terribly exposed, up there alone on the cliff." As Vered looked at her in perplexity, she added briskly, "I think you would feel better in my place. There's plenty of room. You could stay until you decided what to do, or—Vered, are you listening to me?"

Vered said vaguely, "It sounds a little far-fetched."

"You haven't even heard half of it. After our last meeting, I had an idea, a fantasy, really, about the two of us deciding to have our babies and going through with it together, helping each other." Ilana paused. Vered was silent. "I guess you think it's a dumb idea," she mumbled.

"It's a lovely idea," Vered said in a gentle, sad voice, as if she knew it would never happen.

"Why not?" Ilana stared insistently into her eyes. "You've got to make some decisions. You can't seem to do it at home. My suggestion is a perfectly good, practical first step."

Vered did not speak for five minutes. Then she said, "What about David?"

"He's coming for just a few days. A week from Wednesday he'll be gone. You could move in then."

Just then, loud voices from the pavement heralded the entrance of Caspi and his entourage.

Sternholz hustled over, waving his white apron like a farmer's wife shooing hens. "Get out, get out," he shouted, "I told you I don't want you here."

Caspi was at the vanguard of his little band of merry men and women. One arm was around the waist of his current flame, an American girl named Judy, who had been kind enough to supply his alibi for the night of the bombing; the other he slung around Sternholz's shoulders, to the old man's evident disgust. "Sternholz, old friend, you are too harsh. Even if I had played that little trick on the *Arabush, which I did not*"—he winked broadly—"the punishment does not fit the crime. Am I to be exiled forever from the one vale of peace in my otherwise turbulent existence? Cannot a man, hounded by the police day and night, persecuted by the press, find a moment's refuge in his own café?"

As he spoke he bore forward, drawing the others in his wake, until he reached his usual table, front and center. He noticed Vered sitting with Ilana and blew a kiss.

"You're a bum," said the waiter. "I don't want you here." He snatched away the chair that Caspi was about to sit on, but Caspi took another.

"You do me wrong," he cried, hand on heart. "You have tried, convicted, and sentenced me to exile for a crime with which I have not even been charged. Is that fair, I ask you?" He appealed to the café at large. "What possible reason could I have for wishing Khalil harm?"

"Everyone knows you did it," Sternholz said angrily.

"Everyone does me too much credit. Unhappily, I am innocent." Caspi smirked. "Pure as a virgin, innocent as my sainted wife."

"Let's go," Ilana murmured, but Vered sat on, still and heavy as stone.

"I'm actually sorry for the poor bugger," said Caspi. "The guy's got this inflated image; but he can't write worth shit and he knows it. All he's got is his fancy car, and then one fine night someone comes along and blows that to smithereens. I tell you I really pity the poor bastard; in fact," he said, "I felt so sorry for him that at great trouble and expense I personally went out and bought him a present."

"A present," tittered his sycophantic chorus. "Generous Caspi, what did you get him?"

"A donkey," he said triumphantly, "and I sent a note with it. 'Dear Khalil, So sorry to hear of your most recent disappointment. Please accept this small gift as an accurate token of my esteem. I hope that it will enable you to return to the roots which nourish your work. Yours in brotherhood, Peter Caspi.' "

The silence that followed was broken only by the senseless giggling of Caspi's girl, whose Hebrew was rudimentary. Two of Caspi's satellites, a man and a girl, broke orbit and spun away to a table far from Caspi's. Others turned away in shame. Sternholz sucked in his breath, saddened to the marrow of his bones; he was beyond indignation.

Ilana took her friend's arm and led her out of Nevo.

A man sitting in the outer lobby of the King David Towers jumped to his feet as Ilana entered. The well-built young man in blue overalls was no one she knew, so Ilana smiled politely and walked by. As the doorman opened the inner door for her, he murmured, "That fellow's been waiting for you."

She looked again. The man stepped forward. "Don't you know me, Ilana?"

She knew the voice, though it had deepened; it took her a moment longer to recognize his face. "Oh my God," she cried, "Hezi!" She reached up to embrace her brother.

He sat upright on a love seat, knees together and elbows in, as if afraid of breaking something. When Ilana came in from the kitchen carrying a tray, he leapt up to take it from her. "You shouldn't be carrying that," he scolded.

Ilana sank into a chair. "You know."

"I stopped by the house the day after you were there. Papa told me." He twisted the cap off a beer and started to put it to his lips, then changed his mind and poured it into a glass.

"That was a month ago."

He centered the glass on a coaster and looked up to meet her waiting eyes. "When you left home, Mama made us promise never to see you again. It wasn't hard to keep my promise. Mama never stopped grieving, and I never forgave you."

"Mama knew what she was doing, wanting sons," Ilana muttered.

"You broke her heart."

"Her heart was broken before I came along. But if that's the way you feel, why did you come?"

"Because of what he told me. About the baby, and about the money, too."

"What money?"

"The money you kept sending, even though no one ever acknowledged it or thanked you. The money that put Josh and Avi through college and got me started in my business. Ilana," he said urgently, "we didn't know. If anything, we thought that Mama must have accepted German reparation money, but no one liked to ask. If we'd known it was you, we'd either have refused the money or come to thank you,

I'm not sure which, but we wouldn't have taken it and kept away. I felt sick thinking what you must have thought of us all these years."

"I knew she wouldn't tell you. I was glad she accepted the money. It was no hardship for me, and it gave me at least the illusion of being still a part of your lives." Ilana could not stop staring at his hands. When they were children, they used to press their palms together, to see whose hands were biggest. Hers still were when she left. Now one of his was large enough to encompass both of hers.

"Tell me about yourself, Hezi. What work do you do?"

"I'm a carpenter," he said. "I've got my own shop in Haifa, and three workers. I do okay. Nothing like this, though." He looked about in awe.

"What did you expect, a pink bordello?" She laughed when he blushed. "Are you married?"

"Yeah, two kids." He handed her his wallet, open to the photo section. As she bent her head over the pictures, Hezi smiled at the golden head. A forgotten image of the past arose: he saw Ilana bent over a book, reading *Treasure Island* to the boys. They were so dark, and she so fair, they called her their Snow White.

She was still beautiful, but it was a different, uprooted beauty; she was a lily floating in a pond instead of the hardy wildflower she had been. Ilana looked permeated in money; she looked as if she had never been poor.

"They're beautiful children. What are their names?"

"Maya and Dror. They're twins, a real pair of rascals. Ruti, my wife, does a great job with them, but you know, children need a father, too."

Her voice hardened, and he knew her again. "You're not suggesting that I give my baby up?"

"No, God, no. Why should you?" Hezi tugged at his hair, which was thick and curly like their father's. "I'm making a mess of this," he said. "Papa told me that you're not planning to get married. Since the kid won't have a father around, I thought that maybe the next best thing would be an uncle."

"Hezi," she said after a moment, "my baby will have a father, even though I don't intend to marry him. I hope that doesn't mean he can't have an uncle, too."

"I'll be an uncle if you'll be an aunt," he said. "Ruti is dying to meet my glamorous sister. She wants you to come to dinner Sabbath eve. Will you?"

"I'd love to."

Hezi reached out and shyly touched her hair with a calloused finger. "Snow White," he said.

Ilana leaned forward, wrapped her arms around his neck and pressed her cheek to his. He smelled of sweat and sawdust.

Thank you, Papa, she thought.

Chapter Twenty-Two

DANIEL was going through a rebellious phase. Vered worried that his crankiness and hair-trigger aggression sprung from the tension at home, but their pediatrician blamed it on his age. Three and a half, she told Vered, was the adolescence of infancy; the baby stands on the threshold of childhood, and a painful transition it is. Vered's desire to believe this was bolstered by the observation that as much as she and Caspi strove to protect the boy from their troubles, he protected himself more effectively. Whenever both his parents were home, Daniel would either coerce Vered into playing with him in his room or else run giddily, prattling like a baby, from one parent to the other. He never acted spontaneously with Caspi but, with a slyness that troubled her, did all the things expected of a child: sat on Caspi's knee, pulled his beard, kissed him good night. Outright rebellion he saved for his mother. At least three times a day he told her, "I hate you!," following this with a frenzied leap into her arms, where he clung like a monkey.

This morning he had insisted on dressing himself and got hopelessly tangled up in his shirt. Vered's attempts to release him met with shrieks of rage. Finally she left him to it.

Within minutes he was on the floor, kicking his heels and screaming for her. Vered rushed into his room. The shirt was wound around him like a straitjacket, pinning his arms to his body. She ran over to help, but Daniel screamed and kicked at her.

Just then Vered caught sight of her face in the mirror above Daniel's bed. Her mother's face overlaid her own reflection, revealing a similarity less of feature than of expression. Jemima, Vered realized, had often looked at her with just that blend of pain and frustration, never more so than on the day Vered announced her intention of marrying Caspi. I have done things to my mother, she thought, that I pray God Daniel never does to me. She imagined having a child like her young self and shuddered. Daniel resembled her too much, with his slyness and reserve, so different from Caspi's habitual acting out of every stray impulse, but as a child she had been even worse than Daniel, hoarding secrets the way other children hoarded candy and treating her mother like a foreign spy.

This sudden attack of empathy knocked the breath out of Vered. She had always known that Jemima the mother was lacking in ways that Jemima the businesswoman was not, but now she said aloud in wonder, "I was a rotten kid." Daniel was so shocked, he stopped screaming in mid-shriek and sat up.

She bribed him with a lollypop and planted him in front of the television. Then she called her mother.

They sat on Jemima's patio overlooking the sea, while Daniel puttered about on the beach below, safely out of earshot. He was, not surprisingly, given his situation, the kind of child who likes to eavesdrop on adult conversations.

Ever since Vered had accused her of coveting Caspi, an accusation that had taken days to sink in fully, Jemima had been most uncharacteristically afraid of opening her mouth. As a consequence, she remained in the dark while rumors flew like bats around her head. When Vered called and asked if she was free, she said yes, then hung up and canceled her hairdresser and luncheon date.

Vered sipped her lemonade. Staring out to sea, she said, "I'm pregnant."

"*Mazel tov*. Who's the happy father?"

"Not Caspi."

"Thank God," said Jemima, before considering the alternative.

Vered looked at her in amazement. After some moments she said, "I don't know what to do."

"What are your options?"

"Abortion's one, of course."

"Do you want an abortion?"

"It's the logical choice."

"Do you *want* an abortion?"

"No," she admitted. "Strangely enough, I don't."

"Then don't have one," Jemima said calmly.

The conversation was not going along the lines Vered had anticipated and rehearsed. Jemima seemed so business-like: interested, certainly, and not unconcerned, but unmoved by her concern.

"Does Caspi know?" Jemima asked abruptly.

"No."

"Are you sure? If he did, it would explain—"

"What he did to Khalil?"

Jemima nodded, clamping her lips together. Years of dealing with Vered had taught her to approach sensitive matters the way Alice negotiated the looking-glass garden: by moving away from her destination.

"The other day," said Vered, "in Nevo, he read a letter he wrote to Khalil. The most vile, racist, stupid letter . . . And he sent him a donkey."

"Caspi is a pig," Jemima observed. Always was, she added to herself.

"The letter was even more malicious than the bomb. It was meant to humiliate Khalil *as an Arab.* Caspi always had a temper, but this is something else. He's turned into a racist."

"Has he admitted to planting the bomb?"

"He doesn't trust me. But he knows that I know."

Though gratified by this unexpected flow of confidence, Jemima was wary of responding too eagerly. A single wrong word could dam it. She wanted so badly to ask, "Why are you still with him?" that she dared not speak at all.

Vered took pity on her mother. "I won't go on living with him. That's not an option anymore."

Jemima closed her eyes in silent thanksgiving. "If you've made up your mind," she said carefully, "why delay?"

Vered did not answer.

"Do you still buy his bluff about the boy?"

"It's not a bluff," she said almost dreamily. "He'd sooner die than give him up."

"Then what are you going to do?"

She shrugged.

"And what will he do when he finds out about the baby, if you do go through with it?"

Again Vered sighed and made no answer.

Her vagary troubled Jemima; so, too, the quality of her silences. Vered had never been a communicative child, but she had always, no matter how obliquely or misguidedly, been a fighter. Her silence now, however, seemed not of thought but of exhaustion, and there was nothing combative in this miserable woman who sat slumped in her chair as if she hadn't a bone in her body. Jemima guessed that Vered feared Caspi, but could not see why this fear should leave her so paralyzed that two weeks after Caspi's terrorist outburst she was still sharing his home, if not his bed.

That Vered still cared for Caspi never even occurred to her; nor did her daughter think to enlighten her. Though Vered had come fully intending to speak frankly, she could not break the habit of a lifetime in a single day. She still feared her mother's scorn, which would surely be hers in full measure if she admitted to pitying Caspi. And why not? She despised herself. She was living not even in the past but in a world of could-have-beens, of dreams beyond redemption.

Jemima said in a brisk voice, "Where do you intend to go?," assuming without question that Caspi would not leave.

"I don't know. I thought," Vered said tentatively, "of coming to you."

Daniel had found a friend, a little girl. They were digging a hole together. When it was deep enough, the girl got inside, and Daniel started burying her. Like father, like son, thought Jemima. After some moments she said, "Where else did you think of going?"

"Are you saying I'm not welcome here?"

"I said nothing of the kind. You and Daniel are always welcome in my home, and you know it. I doubt, however, that it's the ideal solution. You tried it once, remember."

"I was young and stupid," Vered said quickly, "and I realize now how much pain I must have caused you. I know myself better now. I would never go back to him."

"I should bloody well hope not," Jemima blurted.

"I've thought of renting an apartment, but if I do have the baby, I'd have to hire a full-time baby-sitter, and that plus the rent—"

"But, darling, you must know I'd help. You and Daniel are my only family; could you really believe I'd hoard my money while you were in need?"

Vered began to say reflexively that she wanted no help but stopped. What she wanted was no longer the issue.

"There's another possibility," she said. "Ilana Maimon has invited me to move in with her, at least for the time being and maybe for a longer period." Then, having secured Ilana's permission, she told her mother about Ilana's pregnancy. To Vered's surprise, Jemima seemed taken by the idea.

"I've always liked that girl. She's one smart cookie, and she's got guts. Does she plan to go on, ah, working?"

"No," said Vered with a hint of anger.

"It would be practical," Jemima mused. "You could hire one woman to help with all three children . . . but does she really have room?"

"She says she does. Mother, do you really like this idea?"

"Why, what's wrong with it? She seems an intelligent woman, and the two of you obviously get along."

"We do, though we're very different types. You know what people will say, though."

"What?" asked Jemima, who knew perfectly well.

Vered blushed. "That we're lesbians."

"So what? People will say anything. Is she?"

"No!"

"So who cares what the fools say?"

"Then you think I ought to do it?"

"Did I say that?" Jemima said sharply. "I've given you no advice."

"But I want you to. What should I do?"

"Don't you lay that on me," Jemima said in sudden wrath. "Don't put that responsibility on me. You've got a decision to make, and for once in your life you're going to make it without reference to either me or Caspi." Vered reached out for her, but Jemima pulled away. "No. You must decide what's right for yourself, and then do it. If you want, you are welcome to come here. You can go to Ilana or rent your own place. You can have an abortion or a baby. You can even, God help you, stay with Caspi. The one thing you cannot do, Vered, is drift."

Vered said with difficulty, "I feel some responsibility for what Caspi has done."

"Really? Did you help him plant that bomb?"

"Mother! If I hadn't had the affair, or if I'd chosen anyone but an Arab colleague and rival of his—"

"Very naughty of you. But do you deserve a life sentence? Does Daniel?"

"What about Caspi? Do you know what my leaving will do to him?"

Jemima clucked impatiently. "Daniel is your responsibility, not Caspi."

"Even so, he's in bad shape."

"Yes he is. And so are you. Are you going to let him drag you down with him?"

Vered shook her head with resolution, which soon gave way to another fear. "I'm afraid he'll come after me."

"Of course he will. So what? At this point there are risks in any course you take. I may not be the most perceptive mother, Vered, but I do know that it's not your nature to be ruled by fear."

"It's not—but I'm so confused. I go back and forth in my mind, day in, day out. I can't decide."

"Darling," said Jemima, "I believe that people make very few real decisions in a lifetime, maybe only one or two. The rest of our ostensible choices are actually dictated by timing and circumstance. When your father died and left me with this house mortgaged to the hilt and a failing business, I had to make one of those rare, critical decisions. Friends advised me to sell the business for whatever I could get, before it went under. Instead, I chose to take over and run it myself. It worked out, but it might easily not have. Still, I made the decision, I took the responsibility. I didn't run to my mother, asking her what to do.

"Now it's your turn. No one can decide for you, and time won't resolve this problem. Delaying can only make matters worse, for you and for Daniel."

Vered looked at her hopelessly. Tears collected in the corners of her eyes and slipped down her cheeks, but she seemed unaware that she was crying.

"Vered," said her mother, "all I can tell you is that the answer is in your heart. Listen to it."

Chapter Twenty-Three

THE painting was almost done. Sarita stood back to admire her work.

For a while she had been so bombarded by importunate faces appearing out of nowhere in her sketch pad that it seemed as if the quick would be squeezed out by the dead. Each session of painting had been like a game of musical chairs: when the music stopped, who would still have a place? Some of the figures in her Café Nevo had been painted over so many times that they stood out in relief. In the end, however, the living had asserted their rights, though their domination was not complete; here and there some former dénizens of Nevo, living or dead, clung stubbornly to favorite seats.

Among these was her mother. Yael Blume as she ultimately evolved on the canvas was not the youngster of Sarita's early sketches but was close to her age at the time of her death, perhaps even a little older. She sat between her husband and Uri Eshel, who appeared no older than Arik.

The three friends had raised their glasses high in a toast. Yael, smiling from the heart, was looking over her shoulder, out of the picture and directly into the eyes of the beholder: in this case, Sarita.

"Who are you toasting, Mother?" asked Sarita, but there was no reply. Ever since Yael had fought her way into the Nevo painting, her voice in Sarita's mind had faded, receding into a distance, as if, having found her place, she had grown thoughtless of her daughter. Sarita turned to look at the portrait above her bed, but there, too, Yael's eyes were opaque and unresponsive.

There came a knock on the door. Sarita wiped her hands on her smock, threw a cover over the painting, and opened the door. Arik Eshel strode into the room.

"Hello, Sarita," he said; then he gathered her into his arms and kissed her.

She struggled free. "How dare you!"

"I missed you."

"You think you can just walk in and out of my life, appear and disappear like a Cheshire cat?"

"I'm sorry I was gone so long," he said soberly. "I had work that had to be done."

"You needn't apologize. You owe me no explanations. What do I care what you've been doing?"

"I saw Brenner."

He sat on her bed, patting it invitingly. Gingerly, keeping her distance, Sarita sat beside him. "What happened?"

He told her what he had demanded and what the Minister had said.

"You're mad," she breathed.

"It worked," he said.

"It didn't! Brenner agreed?"

"He agreed to establish a committee to oversee land sales. He agreed to install me as the head. We're still arguing over the other members. And he wants it to be strictly advisory."

"That's no good."

"No," Arik said contentedly. "There are some major battles ahead."

"He must hate your guts."

"He said to me, 'Eshel, you're going to regret the day you pulled this stunt.'"

"I wouldn't laugh. That's one hell of an enemy."

Arik smiled beatifically.

"And what," Sarita added irritably, "is that dumb grin doing on your face? Anyone would think you're pleased the man hates you."

"I am. It's the best feeling I've had since I quit the army."

Sarita gave him a thoughtful look. "So you're going into politics. Following in your father's footsteps."

"Would that bother you?"

"Would it matter?" she countered, and immediately regretted it. Arik seized her hand.

"Of course it would," he said. "You're going to be my partner."

Sarita shot a panic-stricken look at the portrait behind her, but Yael's eyes were blank reflective pools of paint that told her nothing. She listened but heard only silence. Arik squeezed her hand with gentle insistence, forcing her eyes back to him. "You know that, don't you?" he said.

Now Sarita was frightened, but she was also excited and, like any young woman, curious to test her strength. "What if I said I don't like politics?"

Arik laughed. "Do you like Brenner and Gordon divvying up the West Bank?"

Her lip curled. "No."

"Would you stop them if you could?"

Without hesitation she said, "Yes."

"There you are then. I'm just doing what I have to do."
How many times had he heard his father say those words to
his mother, who when she heard them would laugh, sometimes in despair, and roll back her eyes? Rina always argued,
and Uri always listened meekly and then went out and did
just exactly what he wanted to do. And she supported him.
Whatever she said in private, in public she supported him
and savaged his enemies. Rina was half Uri's strength; without her he would be Samson shorn. Arik's recent battles had
loosened the tight knot that had settled in his throat since
he learned of Rina's illness, but suddenly, in Sarita's room,
Arik remembered that which he had never for a moment
forgotten. He closed his eyes.

Sarita's fingers tightened on his; her warm breath
brushed his face as she turned toward him. "How is your
mother?" she said.

He let go her hand and put his arms around her.
Sarita remained very still. Slowly he tightened his arms, drawing her near. He put his head on her shoulder and Sarita
closed her arms around him, awkwardly patting his back.

"I'm sorry," she whispered, but Arik had succumbed
to hormonal amnesia and was no longer thinking of his
mother. He pressed his face into Sarita's neck, which smelled
faintly of turpentine; in his state, and forever after, it seemed
the most seductive of perfumes. He kissed her throat. Sarita
trembled and thrust him away.

"What are you afraid of?" he asked.

"I'm not afraid."

He waited. His hands still played over her back and
shoulders; he touched her beautiful hair.

"I can't do this," Sarita said.

"Why not? You're allowed."

"It's not right for me."

"Why, have you taken vows?" he teased.

She said indignantly, "I have other things on my mind."

With his hand flat against the warm flesh of her back,

Arik could feel her heart beat. "Sarita," he said gently, "you keep saying no, and I keep feeling yes."

In a low voice she said, "I hardly know you."

"You know I'm in love with you. You know I want you. Don't you like me a little, Sarita?"

"A little," she said, and Arik exhaled a great, noisy, joyous breath and reached for her again. "I was so afraid of coming back from Jerusalem and finding you married or gone," he murmured.

"You were only gone two weeks."

"It felt like months."

This time Sarita did not pull away. She stayed in his arms, but it took an act of will, like a child being brave for the dentist; Arik felt it, and after a few minutes he forced himself to release her. He kissed her brow and pushed the hair back from her face with a touch that bespoke gratified surprise. "Let's go out," he said.

"Where to?" she asked, surprised, perhaps a little disappointed.

"Anywhere. Nevo. Let's go and see Sternholz." He thrilled at the idea of entering Nevo with Sarita on his arm. Seeing the old man's eyes would be almost worth the pangs of delayed gratification.

Sarita smiled. "Mr. Sternholz says I spend too much time there. He said not to come around so much."

"You should be flattered. Sternholz only insults the people he loves," said Arik.

"David," said Ilana, "this is my dear friend Emmanuel Sternholz. Emmanuel, David Barnardi."

"How d'you do," said David, rising to shake the waiter's outstretched hand. Though he found the Israeli tendency to obviate even the most basic social boundaries mildly distressing, David, a traveled man and tactful, believed in doing as the Romans did.

As they shook hands, Sternholz turned to Ilana. "This is the one?" he muttered, sotto voce.

"Behave yourself," she warned silkily.

Sternholz cast a critical glance about his domain, which was growing crowded as the Sabbath closed in. Caspi had established himself with his new entourage, which was not quite his old entourage, at a central table. On the pavement, just behind the front rank of chess players, Arik and Sarita sat close together. Mr. Jacobovitz was polishing glasses behind the bar, a never-ending task since as he finished wiping each glass, he put it at the end of the line of glasses to be wiped. Muny had preempted one of Sternholz's aprons and was serving drinks. Punctilious in his dishonesty, he pocketed exactly half the take. Satisfied, Sternholz pulled up a chair and sat ponderously between Ilana and her lover.

He looked the Englishman over with no approving eye, from his school tie down to the tips of his Gucci shoes.

David suffered this scrutiny as he had that of El Al's security agents—in dignified silence. Conscious of Ilana's amusement, he was determined to betray surprise at nothing this eccentric person might do or say. It may be said to his credit that David did not actually mind the waiter's having joined them; it just had never happened to him before.

"So you're the one," Sternholz finally said.

"I beg your pardon?"

"It's not my pardon you should be begging."

"Emmanuel," Ilana murmured, in a tone of indulgent censure.

"What are your intentions?" he demanded.

"To visit Jerusalem, of course, and perhaps a few days at the Dead Sea; nothing more ambitious in the way of sightseeing," David said.

The old man clicked his tongue rudely. "About Ilana, you fool."

"Emmanuel!" Nothing playful in Ilana's tone now. "How dare you speak to my guest that way?"

"If I don't, who will?"

"Were you ever a schoolmaster, Mr. Sternholz?" David said. "I ask because you remind me very much of an old master of mine. The Grand Inquisitor, we called him. Respectfully, of course."

Sternholz quelled a tremor in his lower lip that might, unattended, have developed into a smile. "I *was* a schoolteacher once," he said grandly, "but I gave it up for a higher calling. You, I believe, are a Jew."

"Does that matter?"

"Does that matter?" mimicked Sternholz. Turning to Ilana, he tapped his temple.

She scowled at him. "If you weren't," she told David, "he'd be charming. Emmanuel saves his rudeness for his own people."

For the first time in his life, David felt proud to be a Jew, a strangely placed pride indeed, if being a Jew meant being scourged by this frightful old man.

Sternholz and Ilana maintained injured silences. David, disinclined to end the odd colloquy, said, "This is quite an establishment you run, Mr. Sternholz."

"Establishment? Asylum, more like it." He cackled, though his face retained its dour set.

"I wondered about the name. Does 'Nevo' mean anything in Hebrew?"

"It's a Biblical name," the old man said shortly.

"Biblical. Are you a religious man, Mr. Sternholz?"

"God forbid."

Ilana said, "Nevo is the mountain somewhere in Moab where Moses stood to survey the Promised Land, knowing that he would never be allowed to enter."

David glanced around the room. Impatient faces everywhere were focused on Sternholz, who did not notice or, if he did, paid no attention. "It's an odd name for a café located inside Israel," he ventured. "I mean, you've already arrived, haven't you?"

A momentary silence fell over the café, the sort of silence commonly ascribed to angels passing overheard; then a wave of laughter arose, starting from Caspi's table and spreading from the depths of Nevo to its gleaming Dizengoff shore. The toothless old men, the young lovers, Muny, and the senile busboy all roared together. Ilana's face, too, dissolved in mirth, though she pressed David's hand penitently. Even Sternholz permitted himself a dry titter.

The Englishman's dignity was sorely tried; at first he found himself, as always when he visited this country, infuriated by the rudeness. But the old man's bleary eyes were almost friendly now, and David felt that this mass amusement was not altogether at his expense, but at their own as well.

"Did you ever wonder," Sternholz said, when the laughter had subsided, "why Israeli Jews still pray each Pesach, 'Next year in Jerusalem'?"

"I didn't know they did," said David.

"Think about it," said Sternholz, laying a finger against his nose.

"I suppose it means that though the State of Israel has been established, Zion has not yet been redeemed."

"So, you are not entirely a fool." Understanding this, correctly, as high praise, David felt absurdly pleased. Sternholz lowered his voice, in the manner of one adult speaking to another in the presence of children. "In a sense, you see, Israel *is* Nevo: it is a vantage point onto the unattainable."

The waiter winked and lumbered painfully to his feet. Bemused and somewhat short of breath, David leaned back in his chair. It crossed his mind that he must be suffering jet lag, for it was highly unlikely that this old waiter could have afflicted him with such disorientation. The old man had a shtick, that's all, a routine for the tourists.

But as Sternholz walked away, supremely indifferent to the cries for service that rose from all quarters, his apron swaying like a greatcoat, David saw clearly the great dignity of the man, which enveloped him like a blue flame. Unbidden, there came to him an image of Sternholz as a general, striding through a fieldful of wounded.

Arik and Sarita had ordered espressos, but a beaming Sternholz had served champagne, or the closest Nevo ran to it, and then tiptoed off.

"Sarita," said Arik, "come to the kibbutz with me."

"What?"

"I have to go up tomorrow. I'm meeting Brenner again next week, and I've got to see my father first."

"But what's that got to do with me?"

"I want to be with you." He took her hand and looked intently at her.

She felt the champagne rise to her head. "I couldn't," she said hastily. "I'd feel like such an outsider."

"Please come. My mother's asked to meet you, and she can't get out."

"Asked to meet me? Why should she? She doesn't even know me."

"Somehow," Arik said airily, "she's got it into her head that you and I are going to marry."

"What nonsense!" Sarita exclaimed sharply.

"So go already," said Sternholz, sidling up. "A boy wants you to meet his mother, you don't say no. Besides, Rina could use the *nachas*. So be a good girl. Go."

As the old man bustled away, Arik turned to Sarita and saw acceptance trembling on her lips. Suddenly he spied Coby strutting purposefully toward him. He waved him off, but the boy, ignoring Sarita, dropped into a chair at their table.

"Hey, man, where the fuck you been? I've been looking all over for you."

"Watch your language, punk."

Coby goggled, then turned to Sarita with a ready leer. She smiled at him. "Sorry, lady," he said surprisingly, with a little bob of his head. Then, to Arik: "Did you know they reopened the center?"

"Yeah, I know."

"Yeah, so when are you coming back to work? They've got some geek in there now, man."

"I'm not, Coby. But I'll try to get you someone decent."

Coby's face shut down. "Yeah, right. Golden boy's got better things to do with his time than waste it on a pack of street rats."

"Hey, man, I thought we were past that."

"Right. So. When are you splitting?"

"What?"

"Jumping ship, asshole. Going abroad, okay?"

At first Arik wondered where he'd come up with such a stupid idea. Then he remembered. Sarita's unguarded face betrayed a disappointment tragically shot with resignation, a look that cut him to the heart. "I'm not going anywhere," he told her fiercely. "It was a long time ago, and a bad idea to begin with."

Vered and Jemima came strolling up Dizengoff with Daniel in tow. When she spotted Caspi, Vered stopped. Jemima put a hand on her sleeve and whispered urgently. Vered listened, then shook her head.

"Stay with Grandma," she told Daniel, and placed his hand in her mother's. She entered the café.

"Oy Gottenyu," sighed Sternholz to Muny. "Trouble."

"That's Vered Caspi," Ilana said excitedly to David. "The friend I told you about. I want you to meet her. Vered!"

Vered waved but continued on toward Caspi. He looked up with a startled face, and his arm dropped off the shoulder of the girl beside him.

Caspi's eyes were bloodshot, his hair and beard unkempt. He looked with trepidation at his wife.

"This is an unexpected pleasure," he said. "Ladies and gentlemen, meet my wife."

Vered glanced disdainfully at the circle of new friends, most of whom would not have had a word from Caspi a few weeks ago, and whose current acceptance proved the proposition that beggars can't be choosers.

"I'd like to speak with you privately," she said.

They moved to a table deep in the bowels of Nevo. Like an ant scenting a picnic, Muny sidled up; but Caspi tossed some stale coffee at him and the little man scurried away.

"I thought it only fair to tell you," Vered said. "We're leaving today."

"Yeah, yeah," said Caspi.

"I didn't want you to come back unexpectedly to an empty house."

"Darlin', we've been through this. You know I won't stand for it."

"There's food in the fridge," she said; "eat it or throw it out, don't let it rot. I'm leaving you the car. There are some unpaid bills on the kitchen pegboard. I've taken half the money from our accounts."

"Forget it, baby. I won't have it. I lost one family; that's enough for a lifetime. I'd sooner—"

"Caspi," she said, "I'm pregnant."

His mouth fell open; he stared stupidly and began to breathe stertorously. Then two things happened simultaneously. Daniel recognized his father and, slipping his hand from Jemima's, ran dodging through the café toward him. And a long white Peugeot with rental plates and tinted glass pulled up in front of Nevo.

Caspi opened his arms. "Daniko! Come to Daddy!"

"Daniel, no! Go back to Grandma," called Vered.

"I knew it, I knew it," muttered Sternholz. He began hobbling purposefully toward the Caspis.

The passenger door of the Peugeot opened, and a man stepped out. His face was wrapped in a keffiyeh. The man pulled back his arm and hurtled something. A silvery bird soared leisurely over the heads of Nevo's inhabitants.

Arik leaped onto Sarita, wrestled her to the pavement, and lay on top of her.

The chess players scattered like sparrows.

Ilana screamed, her hands flying down to her belly. She dove under the table. One arm snaked up, grabbed David's, and pulled him down.

Muny ran toward the Peugeot, brandishing a beer bottle. The car sped down Dizengoff.

Caspi jumped up when he saw the silver bird flying toward him. He grabbed Vered's arm with one hand, Daniel's with the other, and with all his strength he hurled them aside. They crashed into the wall and fell heavily to the floor. Vered wrapped her body around Daniel's.

Sternholz froze.

The silver bird landed at Caspi's feet, sputtering and hissing. He picked it up, screaming, "Clear the back!" Caspi pivoted toward the open back door of Nevo, ten feet behind him. The way was clear. He swung his arm back to throw. The grenade exploded.

The poet Rachel wrote that at the hour of his death each man stands upon Nevo. Emmanuel Yehoshua Sternholz thinks of this as he climbs the mountain. Though he never entered Moab in his life, he recognizes the rich shades of amber, gold, and sienna in the blue-veined rock. The air is as clear as crystal. It is not yet dawn, and dark at the foot of the mountain; but as he ascends, light gathers around him. The climb, though steep, is effortless. Sternholz cannot put a foot wrong; he clambers like an ibex, limbs bathed in agility.

As he rises, the air thickens, growing viscous and golden. On the higher reaches of Nevo it is almost liquid, but Sternholz breathes the strange element with ease. The lightness of his body delights him; he lifts up his apron and does a little jig upon the mountainside.

He is alone on the mountain but others have gone before: here and there along the wayside he sees discarded shoes, sloughed outer clothing, a worn teddy bear. The path snakes upward. He cannot see what lies ahead but pushes forward with all the yearning of his heart. Out of the perfect silence comes a child's laugh. He knows that laugh, though half a century has passed since he heard it last. Sternholz hurries forward, upward.

The light is intense, but rather than blinding, it clarifies. Sternholz has never seen so immediately; it is as if a filter has been lifted from the world. He rounds a bend and comes in view of the summit. Two figures stand on the mountaintop; they face him; they are waiting for him. A woman and a small boy. Sternholz starts to run.

Another bend, and they are lost to sight; another, and they reappear, closer, more luminous. The woman sees him. She waves and lifts the child for him to see. The boy laughs and raises his arms aloft.

Sternholz is on the last leg of the climb. He can almost touch them now. Greta is smiling with all her heart. Jacob reaches toward him.

He cannot move.

He presses forward against an invisible barrier. He stretches out an arm and encounters an impassable nothing.

He begins to slip backward.

"Greta," he cries. "Jacob! God, no," he sobs. Though he struggles fiercely, the downward tug is irresistible.

Greta's face is suffused with sorrow now. She touches her heart. Her lips form a single word: "Soon." She throws a kiss. Jacob is still, clinging to his mother.

Sternholz is swept backward into a vortex. As he descends, his limbs grow heavy and his breath rattles inside his chest. Darkness and pain overtake him. The sweet liquid air of Mount Nevo is gone, and in its place comes something rank.

"He's back," says a voice.

A bristly mouth fastens itself to his, and a blast of fetid air fills his mouth. Sternholz gags and turns his head aside. He opens his eyes. Muny's mottled face is inches away.

"Oh, God," cries Muny, "I thought we lost you."

Sternholz closes his eyes. A tear trickles down his cheek.

Chapter Twenty-Four

DYING changes a lot in a man's life. Sternholz resurrected was a different man from what he had been, though the differences were subtle and not easily seen. Strangely enough, although he'd enjoyed his short death and resisted his revival, he was in no hurry to return to that state. It seemed to him that he had lived all his life in fear and a kind of retroactive foreboding and that now (miraculously, considering whose rancid breath had saved him) he had been afforded a chance to live out its final stage in a state of joyous anticipation and secret serenity.

When he was dead, nothing mattered, but after his revival Sternholz was troubled by his lack of forethought. If Café Nevo died with him, what would become of his poor old derelict chess players? He could not bear the thought of them cast out into the cold, cruel worlds of Café Rowal and the Sabra, where they would be bilked for every lousy cup of coffee and plagued for tips by insolent young waiters.

He was not foolish enough to believe that Nevo could

endure forever, for in the Promised Land the only constants are change and disappointment. Nor did he consider Nevo a suitable candidate for permanence, even if such an unnatural state were presumed to exist. Nevo was by nature a way station, never a destination; but it was his duty to make Nevo as permanent a way station as could be contrived.

And so to that end Sternholz, while still in the hospital, drew up his last will and testament. The stewardship of Café Nevo he assigned to Muny, who, though manifestly undeserving, was the only person he knew foolish enough to take it on. Since (he wrote) Muny would pilfer anyway, he was not to be paid a salary, but allowed to keep what he took, which would not exceed his needs; the rest would be paid into a fund for the preservation of Nevo, not as a landmark but as a living café. Mr. Jacobovitz was given tenure for life and a pension if and when he should retire, and Sternholz bequeathed the rest of his estate, including his apartment, to Sarita Blume, because she had no parents to take care of her, and he no child to care for.

When the document was ready, Sternholz signed it, put it aside, and forgot about it. He had other matters to attend to. Through Muny he directed the repair of the café, which, though damaged by the blast, was yet structurally sound. The café remained open during the work, most of which was carried out by Nevo customers. Sternholz criticized his doctors and lectured them on proper medical procedures; he interviewed the police, under the pretext of being interviewed by them, and evinced an odd satisfaction in their failure to arrest a culprit; and he received visitors, resuming his interrupted direction of their lives.

One of the first and most frequent of these was Ilana Maimon.

Ilana had been wounded by shrapnel, but only superficially: the cuts on her arms and face were shallow enough to require only cleaning. However, because of her pregnancy, she was hospitalized for several days' observation.

On the second day, a nurse carried in a large potted plant wrapped in foil. "A man brought this for you," she said. "I told him he could come in, but he didn't want to."

"What man?" Ilana asked.

The nurse shrugged. "He wouldn't give his name. An old guy, with an Iraqi accent."

Ilana took a couple of deep breaths. "What did he say?"

"He just asked how you were and asked me to bring this in. A secret admirer maybe?"

"Take the paper off, please."

Beneath the foil was a young pine tree. The nurse detached a card from the slender trunk and brought it to Ilana.

"Care for this young one," the card read. "Feed it, nurture it, and when it is strong enough, plant it with the others in the forest." There was no signature.

The next day Ilana was released. She sent a roomful of flowers to the children's ward, but the pine sapling she took home.

"Nu?" demanded Sternholz, when she appeared in his hospital room. He stared pointedly at her midriff.

"It's all right," Ilana said. "No harm done."

"Thank God," the old man sighed.

"How do you feel, Emmanuel?"

"How should I feel? A man gets killed, he doesn't feel like dancing. And besides, I can still taste Muny's breath. Feh!"

"He saved your life, Emmanuel. While everyone was standing around screaming and crying, he dove right on top of you and started pumping."

"And broke my rib, the old fool. Where's that Englishman of yours?"

"David had to go back to London."

Sternholz sniffed.

"He stayed until he knew I was all right," she said defensively.

"And I thought he was a *mensch*."

"He is."

Sternholz curled his lip. "What line of business is he in?"

She looked a little startled. "David's an architect."

"So? We don't build houses here?"

"He's rather a grand architect," she said gently. "He heads his own firm. David specializes in converting old churches into gentlemen's residences."

"Churches we got. Gentlemen . . ." He waggled a hand from side to side. "Fine work for a Jewish boy."

"He's not much of a Jew, really."

"He's not much of a man," Sternholz sneered, "but he's as much a Jew as anyone. What does it take? A Jewish mother."

At last Ilana took offense. "It's none of your business, you rude old man, but I'll tell you anyway. David asked me to come with him. He wants to marry me."

Sternholz nodded thoughtfully. After a moment he said, "And you refused."

"Yes." She shut her lips firmly.

"You prefer to raise the child on your own?"

"I prefer to live here. I don't know why I tell you these things. Besides, I'm not all alone. I have family," she said. Such a simple word, yet it tasted like champagne. "And a friend."

"Vered Caspi?"

Ilana nodded.

"She's in a delicate condition." He gave her a sharp look. "Isn't she?"

"Ask her."

"Where is she? I have something to say to her," he said fretfully, sounding, for once, like the old man he was. "Tell her to come."

"I will when I see her."

"Is she all right?"

"She wasn't hurt," Ilana said carefully. She had assumed that Sternholz knew what had happened that day. If he didn't, she wasn't about to tell him.

But Sternholz asked no more questions. A few moments later he closed his eyes and instantly sank into sleep. One thing dying had done for him was to cure his insomnia.

Ilana did pass on the summons, but Vered stayed away from the hospital. Sternholz sent additional messages, through Muny and anyone else whose services he could commandeer, but these, too, were ignored.

A week after Sternholz was sent home with strict orders to stay in bed, he was sitting in his armchair at the window overlooking the sea when he heard high-heeled shoes coming up the wooden stairs. There was a brisk knock, the door to his apartment opened, and Vered Caspi stepped over the threshold, stopping just inside the room.

"Go ahead and say it," she demanded, arms akimbo.

"Say what?"

" 'I told you so.' 'It's all your fault.' Whatever this message is you've got for me. Go on, get it out of your system."

Sternholz drew his bathrobe shut. Without his apron he seemed half his former size, a fallen angel. He said, "Sit with me, *maidele*."

She leaned against the door. "Just get it over with, will you?"

"Come in and shut that door," he growled, and, with a sigh she closed the door and sat opposite him on a folding chair from the café.

Sternholz studied her in silence. She had always been what people called "fashionably thin," and Sternholz called "skinny"; but now she was as gaunt as a starving street urchin. There were dark smudges under her eyes. She wore no make-up, and her hands moved restlessly.

"You look like hell," he said.

"Thank you."

"Is the baby alive?"

"Alive and kicking," she said after a pause. No point denying it any longer. She had just come from Rafi Steadman's office. He had taken one look at her and offered her an abortion, which she refused, having carried the child long enough to feel a fierce protectiveness toward it. What had happened was not the baby's fault, and she was damned if she would add it to the roster of victims.

Sternholz nodded. "How's Daniel?"

"Okay," she said. "He cracked his collarbone, but it's already healed. He's fine."

"So is Caspi."

Vered looked shaken. "What are you talking about? Don't you know?"

"More than you think. I've been there."

She'd heard of people turning gray overnight, but not senile. Perhaps it was the shock. Gently she said, "Sternholz, Caspi died."

"I know that," he replied peevishly. "So did I."

"No, I mean really died. Permanently. We buried him."

"Caspi is happy," said the old man.

"Oh, Sternholz."

"Don't 'Oh, Sternholz' me, *maidele*. I know what I know and I know where I've been. Caspi is with people who love him. He's with his family. You can take that or leave it, but if you've got a drop of good sense, you'll take it."

Vered laughed fearfully. "Sternholz, have you gotten religion in your old age?"

Astonishingly, the old man blushed. "Not the kind you mean. But something happened when I died."

"You keep saying that. But you didn't die. You just stopped breathing for a moment, that's all."

"My heart stopped, too. I *was* dead. And I came back."

"Full of revelations," she mocked.

"Just a few," he said calmly.

"All right. Tell me what happened."

"I don't want to talk about that. I want to talk about you."

"What's there to talk about? I was Caspi's wife; now I'm his widow. Maybe you're right about him being happy," she said bitterly. "He got what he wanted."

"What's that?"

"Me. Forever and ever." Her mouth twisted. She covered it with both hands. Sternholz tried to stand but the old ticker gave a warning pang. He sank back, breathless.

"Verdele," he said when he could, "listen to me. Peter Caspi died in the best way he could, saving his wife and child. With all my heart I envy him his death. It was the making of him."

"His death was the making of him? You're mad, Sternholz." She started to laugh, then hiccuped, sobbed, and laughed again. "He always said I would leave over his dead body. He was right."

Sternholz scowled. "You're not going to get hysterical on me, are you?" and he gave her a look that cowed her into calmness. "Caspi died a liberating death. His last act was to thrust you away. He freed you; you mustn't refuse that gift."

"And I thought you of all people would dare speak the truth to my face."

"What is the truth?"

"That I am responsible. I got Caspi killed." She spoke with great tragic consciousness. Unforgivably, Sternholz sniggered.

"That's *funny*?" she said incredulously.

"It's silly. You're taking credit where none is due."

"What the hell do you mean?"

"*If* the grenade was meant specifically for him, which is far from certain, by the way, don't you think maybe Caspi brought it on himself?"

A gleam of hope showed in her eye, fading quickly. "You know what my last words to him were? 'Caspi, I'm pregnant.' Of course, he knew it wasn't his." She crossed her arms and leaned back triumphantly.

"You said the words; then came the explosion. B follows A; therefore, A caused B. Very logical thinking. I'm glad to see that all your education hasn't gone to waste."

Vered found herself laughing. "You old fool. You know what I mean."

"I know you're a mixed-up child who ought to listen to her elders and betters. I'm sure Jemima's saying what I say. If Caspi was murdered, you didn't do it. Khalil Mussara did, with a big assist from the victim."

"No, no, no."

"Ah, you don't like that." He bared his teeth. "Caspi and the Arab were like two dogs, fighting over a bush to pee on. Is it the bush's fault if they tear each other to shreds?"

"How dare you make such a comparison!"

"Why? Is it harder to admit that you were used than to take all the blame on yourself?"

Sternholz was so adept at being cruel to be kind that sometimes even he doubted his good intentions.

Vered moaned, "Leave me alone, old man," but she remained seated, head bowed.

"How did you feel when it happened? A little relief mixed in with the horror? 'The King is dead; long live the Queen'?"

"Shut up!" She covered her ears.

"Is that why you're starving yourself? Vered Caspi is human: shame, shame."

"Stop it!" she screamed. Sternholz gave her a diagnostic look, then changed the subject.

"The boy is really all right?"

Her hands came down; her head rose. After a moment she nodded.

"Does he talk about it?"

"He says, 'Daddy saved us. Daddy was a hero.' He's proud. I don't think he misses him particularly."

Sternholz thought about his own son, who had died at the hands of soulless enemies whose malice the child could not begin to comprehend: Jacob had cried out for his father, whom he believed invincible, but his father had come too late. Sternholz would have given all the subsequent years of his life for the chance to do what Caspi had done. The man was blessed beyond imagining, almost beyond bearing.

Sternholz turned his head aside, rubbing his eyes surreptitiously. "He did die well, God bless him," he said gruffly to Vered. "He lived like a pig but he died like a lion. Who would have guessed that Caspi had it in him?"

"*I* knew he had it in him," Vered said, and for a moment her voice and eyes were fiercely proud. Caspi was still her man, and if by his preemptive act of self-sacrifice he had defeated her bid for freedom, he had also proved her right. He had shown a sign of the greatness she had never ceased to believe was in him, buried deep, and in so doing silenced those who believed she had wasted her life on a worthless man. Though she failed, she had attempted something manifestly worthy. "He did a noble thing," she said.

"Noble?" Sternholz cackled. "Let's not get carried away here. Let's not forget who we're dealing with. Caspi had a thousand chances of making you and Daniel happy. Did he ever take one? So he made a nice gesture in the end —that doesn't erase the slate."

As she listened, Vered thought of the myriad insults to her pride that the old man had witnessed, for Caspi had always brought his women to Nevo. People die, she thought, but humiliation doesn't. Her heart hardened; she said, "Caspi did it to entrap me. And he succeeded. He saved the life of my child, and if Daniel had died because of my stupidity, my *sin*—"

"Your weakness," Sternholz corrected pedantically. "Your error."

"—I would not have survived him. I promise you I would not have. So Caspi saved both our lives. I owe him something I can never repay, and I *know* what he would have claimed in payment. I'm honor bound—can you understand that, Sternholz?"

"This is foolishness," Sternholz cried, casting his eyes upward. "This is utter nonsense."

"Why? Because nothing is owed to the dead? Just moments ago you were arguing for some kind of survival after death."

"But not of debts," he said quickly. "Not of accounts to be settled." The words reverberated strangely in his head.

Vered looked at him, willing to believe but not quite able. "I'll never be rid of him now," she said. In her voice was a discernible plea for contradiction.

"He acted without thinking," the old man answered sternly. "He acted through love. No one ever said that Caspi couldn't love, but he surpassed himself at that moment. You've no right to take that from him."

"I wish to God I could believe that."

"Believe it, child," he said. "Come here."

Vered slipped out of her seat and stepped forward, but her legs would not support her; she fell to her knees before him. Sternholz leaned forward, pressing her head to his chest and wrapping his strong arms around her. "Just mourn for him," he whispered. "Poor fool: I know you loved him." Vered began to sob. Her thin body shuddered convulsively. The old man tightened his hold and rocked her back and forth, back and forth, crooning a German lullaby.

Three weeks after he died, Emmanuel Yehoshua Sternholz donned his white apron and descended to Nevo. His doctor had forbidden it, but what do doctors know? Sternholz was a man of manifold responsibilities. When his time came again, he wanted to go out with his apron on.

He said he meant to slip in without fanfare, as if he'd never been away, but if that is really what he wanted, would he have told Muny? Who knew better than Sternholz that telling Muny anything was like announcing it on the evening news?

Precisely at noon, Sternholz descended the rickety steps leading from his apartment to the back door of the café. When he appeared in the doorway, a great mass of people arose, cheering and crying out his name as if he were Moses descending from Mount Sinai. Sternholz flapped his apron to clear a path to the bar, where Muny awaited him. The little man fell to his knees, covering his eyes as one stricken by the presence of the Lord. "Hail to Sternholz, who has arisen from the dead!" he cried.

"Get up, you idiot," growled the waiter, shoving him aside. From his sanctuary behind the counter Sternholz began to distinguish faces. Ilana in smart maternity clothes, arm-in-arm with Vered Caspi; Sarita, Arik and Uri Eshel, and Rina in a wheelchair; the old chess players in their nattiest rags; Mr. Jacobovitz, wide-awake for once and smiling toothlessly; even Minister Brenner had turned up, like a bad penny.

"All right, all right," Sternholz shouted irritably over the din, "don't you people have any work to do? Drinks on the house." Another cheer arose, this one from the ranks of the chess players.

One by one, customers stepped up to shake his hand or embrace him. Sternholz set his mouth in a disdainful grimace, but his eyes sparkled like a bar mitzvah boy's.

When Uri Eshel began to wheel Rina toward him, Sternholz hurried forward to greet them. Despite the heat, Rina was wrapped in a woolen shawl.

"*Nu?*" he said to her, squatting creakily beside her chair, and indicating Arik and Sarita with his eyes. The two stood nearby, side by side, fingertips touching.

Rina nodded and squeezed his hand. Sternholz sighed from joy and planted a kiss on her head. "So. We'll dance at their wedding, you and I."

"In spirit, anyway," Rina replied, without a mote of bitterness.

Then Arik came to him while Sarita hung back, and he said, "You finally get your wish, old man. I won't be coming around much anymore. I've got a job in Jerusalem."

"*Nu, mazel tov.* Sold out, have you?" growled Sternholz.

Arik grinned. "Wait and see."

The old man grunted, like a workman who's finished a job, then turned his beady eyes on Sarita. Though she was as always effortlessly lovely, she no longer reminded him of Yael; he could see hardly a trace of that former resemblance. Either her face had changed over the past few months or his vision had improved; or was it simply that Sarita was her own woman now? She returned his look with one as steadfast, perceptive, and engaged as his own.

"You didn't come," he said, getting to the heart of the matter.

Sarita stepped forward into the light. "I called the hospital. I made sure you were all right."

"But you didn't come."

"No. I was angry with you," she said simply.

"I let you down?"

"You almost got killed." Her lower lip jutted out like an angry child's.

"But you've forgiven me," Sternholz said, frowning at Arik to keep him quiet.

"Yes. But if you'd died, I wouldn't have."

"Someday I'll die. Everybody does."

"But not like that. And not in front of me," she said,

very seriously. Sternholz nodded, and Sarita relaxed and smiled at him. "I finished your painting," she said.

"Good." (It never occurred to Sternholz to deny that it was his. That little stratagem had eroded into nothingness.)

"Do you want it now, or later?"

"Now," said the waiter, who had waited long enough.

Sarita fetched the painting, covered with brown wrapping paper, from a corner. Sternholz stood it on top of a table, leaning against the bar. He stepped back. Sarita unwrapped the canvas and came to stand beside him. Everyone else lined up behind them in a semicircle four people deep. There was silence in Nevo.

The painting was actually two paintings, one superimposed on the other. Drawn from the perspective of someone standing behind the bar, Café Nevo was reproduced realistically, down to its cracked linoleum tables, dusty photos mounted on the walls, dirt-colored walls, and peeling ceiling; and so too Nevo's people, living and dead. There were cries of pleasure from the crowd as, one after another, people recognized themselves and old friends.

In a detail almost identical to the sketch Sarita had done, Vered and Ilana shared a table. Hands clasped, heads bent in conversation, they seemed oblivious to the importunate child who, not content to beg, had drawn a chair up to their table and was clambering aboard. Muny, dressed in his floppy bum's shoes and old army jacket, sat just behind Ilana, leaning toward her at a perilous angle, cupping his ear. Behind and to one side of Vered, Peter Caspi stood alone, gazing at his wife with uncharacteristic tranquility.

A young Uri Eshel sat between Yael and Yehuda Blume. Their glasses were raised in celebration, and the men had their arms around one another's shoulders. Yael met the viewer's eyes, as she had the painter's, with a smile of benediction.

All about the café's perimeter were the tattered chess players, like a decrepit palace guard. At the very center of the painting stood Emmanuel Yehoshua Sternholz, tall and white, his apron wrapped around him like a *tallith*, his face stern and his gaze turned outward. It was at this point that the inner picture broke through the outer, for Sternholz seemed to tower above the heads of his customers. He did not float above them like a Chagallian angel but stood with his feet planted firmly on unseen ground. Sternholz's elevation provided a secondary perspective on the painting, all of whose characters could now be seen to occupy different levels, as if the café were not built on flat land but set upon a mountain.

The vision of the mythical Mount Nevo that had visited Sarita when she first received the commission had endured to inform the portrait. In this underlying, half-seen painting, Sternholz the waiter stood at the summit of Mount Nevo; and beyond the periphery of Café Nevo's low-life praetorian guard, at the top of the painting, one could dimly see not Dizengoff but a vast, shining expanse of golden land, the Promised Land; and everyone who gazed upon the painting felt the promise, its pathos and its hope, as if it were made to him.

Thus the present mingled with the past, reality with vision, and the painting said, as a thousand words could not, that the one was forever immanent in the other.

Tears came to Sternholz's eyes, but they were tears of joy, not sorrow. It seemed to him suddenly that he was blessed, that an angel watched over him, that there was meaning and purpose and a cohesion in life. But then his old skepticism asserted itself, and he thought, It's the painting that makes me feel this way; it's art, not truth. But clear-sighted Sarita tugged at his arm and said firmly, "I only paint what I see," and Sternholz remembered Greta's face and Jacob's, and their expressions of joy untrammeled by any need for forgiveness; and in that moment of grace he perceived the universe as mysterious and hard but ultimately benign. He felt a great movement of charity, a loosening of bonds, the exultation of a prisoner set free, if only for a day. "God bless the child," he said, and taking Sarita's face into his hoary old hands, he kissed her brow.

A native New Yorker, BARBARA ROGAN graduated from St. John's College in Santa Fe and moved to Israel, where she founded a literary agency and became active in Israeli politics. Her first novel, *Changing States*, was published in 1981 to strong critical acclaim. In 1984 Ms. Rogan returned to New York City, where she resides with her husband and son.